SECRET
OF THE
KIAH

Kathleen Garnsey

Paperback-Press
an imprint of A & S Publishing
A & S Holmes, Inc.

ISBN-10: 1-945669-33-0
ISBN-13: 978-1-945669-33-0

DEDICATION

I dedicate this book to my son Brent Garnsey, who has made me so very proud and is a real-life hero.

ACKNOWLEDGMENTS

I would like to thank every member of Ozarks Romance Authors (ORA) from the time I joined in 1988 to today. This group taught me so much, and the friends I made there are irreplaceable.

PROLOGUE

"Tie him between those two trees," Damek said. "He will pay for his refusal."

Rydor held his head high and prepared himself for his father's wrath. If he died on his sixteenth annual-cycle, so be it, but he would never kill an old man to secure his rite of passage into adulthood. It may be their custom to kill the helpless to make room for the virile, but he would not be a part of the senseless Voltran ritual.

Two warriors grabbed him, one on each side. They tied one end of the rough rope around his wrist and secured the other ends around the trees. The ropes were pulled so tight he thought his arms would separate from his body. He bit his lower lip to stifle a scream. Tighter, inch by inch, the men pulled until blood seeped from beneath the bindings and slowly trickled down his arms.

"You are no longer my son!" Damek Celon raised the whip in his hand and unleashed it across Rydor's chest. "You disgrace me, your ruler, and your people. You're not fit to be a Voltran warrior!"

Rydor lost count of how many times the whip made contact with his chest, but he held his head high and faced his accusers with honor. The sticky warmth of warm blood oozed from his wounds. It was not the pain that would remain in his memory, it was the satisfied look on his father's face. His chest burned as welt after welt swelled then bled, but it was his soul that cried betrayal.

A hand grasped his hair and jerked his head back. The razor sharp blade of a cutter rested against his forehead, and he knew it was his younger brother's turn to inflict punishment. He felt the painful pull while the irritating hacking sound of Turic's cutter ripped through his hair. Out the corner of his eye he watched long, dark strands fall to the dirt.

While the tribe witnessed his humiliation, he fell into an abyss of emptiness. Rydor had always known he was not his father's favored son. Now he had no father, no brother, and no home. Rydor held his breath as long as he could while every warrior in the tribe inflicted whatever punishment they deemed appropriate.

Some whipped his back; others used their cutters to slice his arms, legs, and feet. He refused to buckle under their cruelty, cry out in pain, or wretch at the metallic taste of his own blood.

Fingers of darkness clutched his heart. His mind and body knew only death would release him. Rydor Celon, first born son of ruler Damek Celon, a disgrace to his people, would pass into the depths of the damned, and not one tear would be shed—not for a coward.

"Enough! He's not to die in the presence of warriors. Cut him down. Take him to Spirit Mountain and leave him for the Semitas to feast upon, and may the souls of the damned claim him." Damek turned his back to the bloody sight. "Come Turic, you're the only son I have now. We will celebrate according to custom when we rid ourselves of a coward."

Turic smiled at his father. "As it should be. We only have room for warriors."

"Even though you're an annual-cycle younger, at fifteen, you're twice the man Rydor could ever be. His conscience would never permit him to become a warrior. He was weak." Damek slapped Turic on the back. "You will serve me proud in the future. Our time is near."

"For what?"

"To control every inch of Zanthus. But first you must begin your training, for it is you who will fight in the Ultimate Battle as prescribed by the Gods."

CHAPTER ONE

Planet Zanthus
Annual-cycle 2232

"Shayla, please, listen to me." Ruler Nuri put both hands on his desk. "It is written. It's your duty."

She shook her head. "You are the leader of the Zared Tribe and far more qualified than I to choose the warrior fit to become Kiah Master."

Nuri shook his head. "It was preordained by our forefathers that only the first born offspring of the highest ruling council member can decide who will represent their tribe in the Ultimate Battle. They must either fight, or choose a warrior as their surrogate. And that is you, my beloved daughter."

"Because I am a woman, I cannot fight. The elders won't even allow me to rule as my heritage dictates when the time comes, so why would they trust me to choose the man who is to be our salvation?"

"Because it has been dictated by our ancestors." Nuri ran his fingers through his hair. "And the Gods. You cannot deny our laws."

"I cannot." The words stuck in her throat. Shayla was sworn to obey the elders and the word of her father. Yet something inside her said no Zared warrior would be capable of wielding the power of the Kiah.

"At noon every eligible male in our tribe will assemble in the main courtyard for your inspection." Nuri stood and walked to his daughter. He placed his hands on her shoulders. "This will be your greatest service to our people."

Shayla swallowed hard. The overwhelming importance of her choice induced a fear she'd never known. If she made the wrong decision it would be the last service her people would need. Failure meant a fate worse than death as every man, woman and child would become slaves to the victor. "I will do my duty."

Nuri smiled. "That's all I ask."

***

High noon arrived and one virile male after another grasped the Kiah rod in his hands, closed his eyes, and willed power into the black crystal length. None changed its color, none made it sing, none made it move. None!

Supposedly, according to the forefathers and their rules, only the first born male of a family possessed the powers necessary to wield the Kiah. She wished they had given some clue as to what function the rod served, and what qualities she needed to look for in a Kiah Master.

The call this sun-cycle was only first born sons, yet not one had been successful. Finally, the last man stepped up on the podium in front of her and took the rod from her outstretched hands. He repeated the words, "I am Kiah Master. I am worthy."

Shayla held her breath while she studied the warrior named Eaton Merrick, the man her father had planned to announce as her future life-mate. Thank the Gods, the Voltrans' challenge put a stop to every sun-cycle concerns because she was not ready to take that step. Dark blond hair rested on the wide shoulders of Eaton's gray uniform, his green eyes fixed on her. He cared about her, he'd told her so, but her feelings for him were no different than for any other friend. She did not desire him in any way, and the thought of sharing his bed was not a pleasant one. She couldn't imagine having his child, or spending the rest of her life with him. Eaton was no different than the rest of the men her father considered. They all wanted the position afforded them by marriage to the ruler's daughter. He was very handsome, well built, but she was not attracted to him in the life-mating way.

Eaton struggled with the Kiah, gripping it tighter and tighter. As she predicted, he elicited not a sound, not a glow, nothing. Since the Kiah had never been used, no one knew exactly what to expect, but the sound of silence became more deafening than the roar of a raging storm. Shayla took the rod from the embarrassed warrior who then joined his failed comrades. She inhaled deeply and contemplated the meaning of her next words. This could sound like a death sentence to everyone in attendance, and even those who were not here.

"I, Shayla D'Par, first born of Ruler Nuri of the Zared Tribe, shall continue my quest to find a Kiah Master to defend us in the Ultimate Battle."

The crowd clapped and roared, but she heard the unmistakable sound of disappointment in their voices. So far she had failed them. She had rejected every Zared Warrior as unworthy. Every member of the tribe knew the Kiah had mystical powers, yet no Zared man had been able to ignite the magic of the crystal. They were doomed if she did not find a Kiah Master in time.

She turned slowly, entered the palace and walked silently to her room. The search for a Kiah Master would take her from her home in Terita to the Badlands, the only place left to search since every man here had been tested. Only criminals and men who had no tribe loyalty lived there. Not a promising place to find a worthy warrior, but she had no other choices. She could not ask a Quelan, they were looking for their own Master, and a Voltran was out of the question. The Voltrans were the enemy to both the Zared and Quelan Tribes.

The journey ahead would be fraught with danger and laced with disappointment. If she failed to find this unknown warrior she could never return to her people, her father...her home.

***

Rydor paced the confines of his cave. His senses seemed unbalanced in a manner he had never experienced before. He glanced at Una, but the Semita lay calm, her claws curled, her big eyes half-closed, her breathing slow. How could the mountain cat remain so placid when he felt the tides of change coursing rapidly through his veins?

It was an unsettling feeling, a foreign sensation he could not describe, but he had no one to describe it to even if he could. He'd lived alone on Spirit Mountain since he was left for dead sixteen annual-cycles ago. His only companion was Una, the Semita who saved his life. Of course there were frequent visits by Olin, the mysterious wizard who appeared at will and left even quicker. Where was Olin when he needed him?

Olin had taught him to commune with nature, listen to the animals, and to respect the voices in his head that seemed to know more than he did. He said those voices were his guides and teachers, but at the moment they were silent. He felt as alone as he had that fateful moon-cycle, strung between two trees, his very life force being beaten from his body.

"Rydor, my boy, you're upset."

He spun around to find the familiar white translucent cloud that turned to a solid form before his eyes. Olin's aged body and gray hair materialized into the torchlight of the cave. His deep purple robe blew in a breeze that settled with the haze. "I was wondering when you'd show up."

"I had to, I heard you screaming my name. What has caused that troubled look on your face?"

"I can't explain it, there are no words." Rydor poured a glass of wine for his mentor and handed it to him.

"May I touch your mind?"

"It's the only way you'll understand." Rydor felt a faint tickle in his head as the only man he trusted read his thoughts and feelings. It was like the most delicate feather of the smallest bird, floating on air then gently fluttering to the ground.

Olin nodded. "I knew you'd feel it. The time has come to begin your training." He took the wine from Rydor's outstretched hand. "Sit, my boy. This could take some time."

"Your voice sounds grave. Have I done something?" He took a seat on the bench across from Olin at the table he crafted long ago.

"It's not you, Rydor, it's the Voltran Tribe. Your father, Ruler Damek Celon, has initiated the Ultimate Battle sequence, and nothing can stop it. The vault in the temple has been opened and the Kiah rods have been distributed, one to each of the three tribes."

"I have no father. How dare you speak his name! Nothing that man does concerns me. I belong to no tribe."

"Easy, Rydor. I know how you feel, and I've respected that all these annual-cycles." Olin held out his hand and a goblet of wine appeared. "But you cannot escape your destiny."

"Destiny? Have you gone mad?"

Olin took a sip of his wine and stared at Rydor. "You will be a part of the Ultimate Battle whether you like it or not. Some things cannot be changed."

"I will not fight. I'm a coward, remember?"

"Your bravery is unmatched on this planet, Rydor."

"You mean untested, don't you?" He watched the wizened old man smile. "And so it will remain."

"Since Una and I found you near death, have we ever let you down, or asked anything of you?"

"No. But I ask nothing. I expect nothing."

"I know, and you're about the most stubborn pupil I've worked with in the last two-hundred annual-cycles."

"How old are you?" He watched Olin chuckle, his long gray beard bouncing up and down. Olin claimed to be as old as time, and Rydor was beginning to believe him.

Olin set his goblet in front of him on the table. "Rydor, this is serious. You are going to have a visitor who will seek what only you can give."

"Is this more of your esoteric mumbling?" Rydor picked up his goblet that sat in front of him and downed the rest of his wine. He set the empty goblet on the table.

"It may seem enigmatic to you, but the very existence of this planet lies in your hands."

It was Rydor's turn to laugh. "You've lost your mind, Olin. I'm the outcast, the coward. I couldn't even save myself let alone an entire planet!"

"You're no coward, and you'll have the chance to prove it—to yourself and all of Zanthus."

"I have no desire to prove anything."

Olin shook his head. "You are a stubborn one." He held out his cup. "May I have more wine?"

Rydor poured more purple liquid into the cup. Olin's hand shook, but the twinkle in his lavender eyes held the joy of a child and wisdom of the ages. "Tell me more of my destiny."

"It's not for me to tell, it's for you to discover."

"Must you always speak without saying anything?"

"Patience, my boy. All will make itself known when the time is right. Now, if you'll excuse me, I need to rest."

Olin turned into a puff of smoke that disappeared instantly. Rydor smiled. He was fond of Olin. Actually, he loved the old man deeply. Olin was more of a father to him than the man who... He refused to think about the people he once called family. They were cruel and inhuman. He needed no one. No visitors, no friends, no family. He was more than happy on his mountain living alone.

* * *

Shayla climbed the weathered wooden steps to the primitive inn while her guards secured the solorair cruiser and carried in the luggage. She had no idea what she would find here, but it was past time to stop for the moon-cycle. They had been on the road three sun-cycles and learned nothing to lead her to a capable warrior. The only thing the desolate desert provided was a vast array of creatures she would rather not think about.

Rumor held there were several wanderers who might suit her purpose, but she had yet to find them. Rumor also said the men were loners and only made their presence known when they wanted to be found. She hated all the false leads and gossip she'd been fed. She swallowed her fear, gathered her courage and entered the Blackheart Inn.

She approached the barkeep and took a seat on the tall stool. "I'd like a fruit cooler, please." The man behind the bar looked rough. He had a shaggy beard, dirty, shoulder-length brown hair, wore clothes that were dirty and smelled of liquor.

The barkeep laughed. "Don't have none of them fancy drinks. Only ale and wine. Which will it be?"

"Wine then." She silently groaned, but wine did actually sound like a better option, especially in the mood she currently festered deep inside.

"Traveling alone, Missy?"

"No." Shayla met his gaze and took a deep breath. "I'm looking for a warrior."

He laughed. "All women are looking for a warrior."

"I'm looking for one with special abilities." She took a sip, not surprised to find the drink laced with alcohol.

"Will I do?"

She quickly pulled her arm back when the obnoxious, laughing man reached for her hand. It would not serve her purpose to anger him, so she choked back a few choice words and forced a smile. Out the corner of her eye, she saw her guards step inside with the luggage which renewed her confidence. "And what special abilities do you possess?" Shayla already guessed his answer.

"I'm good with the ladies, if you know what I mean." He licked his lips. "Give me a try. You won't be disappointed."

Shayla swallowed hard. "I'm not seeking a companion for my bed. I'm looking for..."

"You don't fool me, Missy. I know exactly what a woman like you wants."

Arden, her personal guard, rushed to her side. He grabbed the man by the collar and lifted him halfway over the bar. She wanted to laugh at the look of fearful surprise on the wimpy man's face, but she knew better.

"Don't ever talk to the lady like that again. Now tell her what she wants to know, or you'll have me to deal with. What shall it be?"

"I...I...I'll be glad to help the little lady. Just put me down."

Arden released the scraggly barkeep. He straightened his filthy clothes and groaned. Shayla was glad her father insisted on sending two guards along, even though she had protested against the idea. "Tell me about the mercenary warriors that live in the hills."

"There's three of 'em, and they ain't too friendly."

"I'm not looking to make friends."

"Suit yourself, Missy, but don't say I didn't warn ya."

Shayla took another sip of her drink. "Just tell me where to find them."

"Take the road east, the one that leads into the hills. You won't have to look for 'em, they'll find you."

"Thank you. Now, I'd like two rooms for the moon-cycle."

The barkeep mumbled his price, which was highway robbery considering the shabby accommodations. She paid him since these were the *only* rooms within a hundred megators, then took the keys from his shaky hand and headed for the stairs at the back of the dimly lit room.

Every patron stared as they walked through the crowd. They were out of their element in the Badlands. These people were outcasts from each of the three tribes, and it was obvious why most of them had left, or were thrown out. She ignored their crude whistles and rude comments. Not one other woman in the entire building. It was only for one moon-cycle, she reminded herself as she climbed the rickety steps.

CHAPTER TWO

It was no wonder the frontier wilderness had been dubbed the Badlands. How did the inhabitants live without the comforts afforded in each of the three main cities? No power, no fine buildings, no decent bathing facilities, and no form of communications.

The early morning sun warmed the inside of the cruiser as it skimmed the foreboding, rocky surface. Even the desolate scenery was a welcome relief from the primitive, dingy room where she'd spent the moon-cycle. The dinner she'd ordered had been even worse. Small Badlands' towns were all the same.

The journey seemed endless. Megator by megator the craft skimmed the red rocky surface toward the forbidden hills of the Badlands, a place no civilized tribesman would enter. The climate was too hot beneath the sun and too cold under the moon. It was a place suited only for reptiles and outlaws, both of which flourished in abundance. She had not trusted the slimy barkeep, yet she was compelled to follow his suggestion. Anything to find a Kiah Master.

Apprehension of the unknown spread through her. Arden and Rance were seasoned warriors and had warned her they sensed a trap. She had to admit, this lead seemed shaky at best. The guards straightened in their seats which caused her pulse to quicken.

"Princess D'Par." Arden pointed through the windshield. "There they are."

"Slow down and stop a good distance away. I don't want them to think we're a threat."

"As you wish."

The craft pulled to a stop and the engine shut down. Both warriors got out and Arden opened the winged door for her. She exited the cruiser and walked away from the vehicle, her guard's right behind her. Her fingers tightly gripped the leather case that held the Kiah rod, and she hoped the three ominous men she approached did not see her shaky grip.

"That's far enough!" one of the men called. "State your business."

"I represent the Zared Tribe. I'm looking for a Kiah Master." The three men closed in and stopped a few feet from them.

"We've heard of your quest. How much does the job pay?"

Shayla could not believe they were concerned about credits when the well-being of the entire planet was at stake. "Before we discuss compensation, I must know if any of you are worthy."

"We are superior warriors," the silver-haired man replied.

"Will you take the test?" Shayla opened the leather case and removed the black crystal rod and held it toward him. He took it from her and grasped it firmly with both hands. "You know the words?" She watched him nod and silently prayed he was not the man she sought.

"I am Kiah Master, I am worthy."

Relief spread through her when nothing happened, but the poor man had the most shocked look on his face. It was obvious he felt he would be the chosen one.

"Give it to me."

The second man grabbed it from his friend and held it in his hands. He said the words and stared in disbelief as he too failed to elicit a response in the crystal. Disappointed, he handed it to the last man who tried with all his might to will magic into the black rod, but again, nothing. He raised the smooth, round crystal length over his head and threw it to the ground.

Shayla gasped in horror as the Kiah rod struck a rock. She bent to pick it up, horrified to find it broken in half. With a piece in each hand, angry tears welled in her eyes. "How could you!"

"We do whatever we like! And if you don't get out of our hills, we'll do the same to you and those two sissy guards of yours."

"You're animals!" The words had no sooner left her lips when the three men charged. One man grabbed Arden, one attacked Rance, but the silver-haired one tackled her to the ground. He pinned her shoulders against the gravel and pressed his mouth to hers. The rancid odor of sweat and dirty skin assailed her senses. Her stomach tightened and bile rose in her throat as he straddled her. She dropped both pieces of the Kiah and beat against his chest with her fists.

The animal ripped down the top of her tunic and began to slobber on her skin. Her mind screamed for help but not a sound escaped her lips. She was trapped. She tried to poke his eyes, but he threw his head back and laughed in her face, his foul breath sickening her even more.

She could see nothing except his blackened teeth and disgusting grin. She managed to pull her knee up, making swift, hard contact with his groin. He bellowed obscenities, but his hold never wavered. She'd die before she let him violate her. When he reached for the band of her pants, she lifted her head and bit his arm, the taste of his blood making her sick stomach wretch.

He raised his fist. She closed her eyes, prepared for the worst. Instead she heard a mournful grunt and felt his weight lift. Her eyes flew open and relief flooded her when Arden and Rance pulled him away, quickly rendering him unconscious.

"Are you all right, Princess?" Arden asked, gasping for breath.

"I will be as soon as we get out of here."

Shayla grabbed the broken rod, shoved it into the case and jumped into the back of the cruiser while Arden and Rance got in the front, the quiet hum of the engine music to her ears. She pulled a bag from behind the seat, found a clean tunic and quickly changed, brushing small rocks and gravel from her skin.

Arden turned toward Shayla. "Are you sure you're all right?"

"I'm fine. I can't thank you enough for saving my life."

"It's our pleasure, Princess." He smiled. "Where to?"

Her mind was a blur. She picked up the map from the seat next to her and studied it. "Where indeed? I wish I knew. From the looks of it, North is the only direction we haven't tried, so head that way. We'll get rooms when we get to Dartron. It can't be any worse than where we've been."

"Let's hope for the best," Rance said, turning north.

She sighed, wondering if she'd ever see her father or home again.

CHAPTER THREE

Rydor stared at the vast wilderness that surrounded him. He had always loved Spirit Mountain. From the moment he took refuge in the beautiful mountains, peace had been with him. Now he had the unmistakable feeling it would soon be invaded. No man had ever breached Olin's protective spells, yet the premonition was real.

Una growled and crouched in an attack position. He smiled. She was after dinner, and he felt sorry for her unsuspecting prey. The lone call of a Perdair circling gracefully overhead drew his gaze. Talons silhouetted against the evening sky hung long and sharp, a reminder of a past encounter he'd once had with one of the large, dangerous birds.

Even the serenity of his mountain could not dispel the feeling deep within him that something was inexplicably wrong. There were times his animal instincts served him well, and times like these they simply tormented him. The danger was real, like a thick black cloud, but he could make no sense of why. He shrugged and tried to release the agonizing thoughts into the wind, to be forgotten forever.

In a flash, Una sprang from the rock below him and pounced on a Maletice. Fur flew in every direction while the large rodent struggled to his death. Semitas loved Maletice, and he was glad they did, because he hated the nasty scavengers.

"Rydor?"

He turned to face a puff of smoke that materialized into Olin. "And to what do I owe this visit?"

"Just wanted to check and see if you were ready for your visitor."

"I've never had a visitor, except for you, and I don't plan to have one now."

"My, my. Being a little testy, don't you think?" Olin chuckled. "Be that as it may, you'd better get ready. A good host is always prepared."

"I'm not a good host, nor do I need to be. I have no one to impress, remember?"

"You have no faith. We need to work on that." Olin stepped closer. "Have you been doing the breathing exercises I prescribed?"

"And the physical tests you want me to conquer." Rydor studied the small man before him and wondered just what he was up to. Olin had a reason for everything, and Rydor knew better than to question his insight.

"Good. I also want you to work on your meditations. You must learn to transcend physical reality and float in the fourth dimension."

"Sounds dangerous, floating in the unknown."

"We only fear that which we don't understand. But of course you know that."

"You have taught me well." Rydor looked Olin in the eye. "Why exactly do I want to float in the fourth dimension?"

"Trust me, you want to. It will prove very productive for you. Now, get to work, you don't have much time."

"Time for what?"

"Patience." Olin laughed. "Don't forget to work on your patience too. You're going to need a lot soon."

"Say what you mean for once." Olin turned into a puff of smoke before his eyes and he heard him whisper, "I said what I meant!" His form faded from view.

He had never known Olin to be so secretive. It was his manner to be reticent, but he was acting strange, even for a wizard. Then again, how could he judge anyone's behavior? He had not seen anyone other than Olin in sixteen annual-cycles.

There were times he longed for a woman's soft flesh against his. Someone to hold during long, cold moon-cycles, someone to love. Love. What did he know about love? There was a girl his age he liked and became close to before he was beaten to near-death. Granted, it was a case of young love, but it was nice, very nice.

All he knew about love was that it was a painful emotion he never wanted to experience again. He had made one exception; Olin, but the man was indestructible, and his principles were higher than any mortal man could ever hope to attain.

Life on Spirit Mountain was solitary, but good. He was content to have nature as his home, and Una by his side. She may not be as comforting as a woman, but he only had to allow her to hunt to please her. The mountain cat was faithful and protective, and that was all a man could expect.

***

Dartron was another primitive wilderness town with little to offer a traveler, but the Snaketor Inn was slightly better than the Blackheart. The people seemed a bit cleaner, but no friendlier, except for the leers and jeers of men who passed her table. Shayla had to keep Arden and Rance from fighting twice, and they had not even been served dinner yet.

Arden shifted nervously in his chair and stared at her as if she would break. He was overly attentive, a good trait for a personal guard, but she was beginning to feel smothered after ten sun-cycles of nonstop attention. She longed for her room in the palace, a hot bath in her large, sunken marbleous tub, and to share a good dinner with her father.

Her mind returned to the broken Kiah rod. How could she tell her people she had failed to protect it? Even if she found a Kiah Master, how could he wield the power with the rod in two pieces? She wanted to hide from the world and cry for sun-cycles, but reality would not permit such behavior.

"Princess? Did you hear me?"

"I'm sorry, what did you say?" Arden did not seem surprised she had not paid attention to him. She knew they had been away too long when her guards knew her this well.

"What is the plan for tomorrow?"

Rance cleared his throat. "Arden, it's not for us to question."

"It's all right. You both have a right to know." She studied their worried faces. They were handsome warriors, and she wished with all her heart one of them had proven worthy. "There is no plan."

An attractive young woman, dressed in a very short, low-cut green shift, brought their dinner. Shayla suppressed a smile when the waitress ran her hands over Arden's shoulders. She could swear she saw him blush.

She took a bite of the stew and wrinkled her nose. It was not what she was used to, but she had eaten worse. A second server strode over to Rance and wiggled her way onto his lap. There was no mistake about the look on his face. He liked it way too much.

"May I have a word with you?"

Shayla turned toward the voice behind her and saw an old man with gray hair that hung way past his shoulders and a long gray beard. He wore a funny purple hat and matching floor-length robe, but he appeared harmless. "Sure."

"Please, join me at my table."

She picked up her stew and her wine and followed him to the back corner and took a seat at the small, round table. He sat across from her and she couldn't help staring. For a man his age, he had few wrinkles, despite all the gray hair on his face and head. His velvet hat was full, fluffy, and sagged in all the right places. For some reason she felt at ease and instinctively knew she could trust the man.

"What is it you wanted?"

"I know you are a seeker, and I'd like to help."

"What is it that I'm seeking?" she asked, wondering what he could possibly know of her quest.

"A Kiah Master, of course," he said with a smile.

"And where might I find him?"

"On Spirit Mountain. But you must go alone."

"It's too dangerous without my guards. We've encountered trouble and I was attacked. Without them I wouldn't be here speaking to you."

"Trust me, you will be safe. Travel by Esroth and take enough food for three sun-cycles. You will also need warm clothes for the frigid moon-cycles."

"More wine, Missy?"

Shayla turned toward the waitress with glass in hand. When her gaze returned to the old man her jaw dropped. He was gone! She looked at the server. "Did you see the old man leave?"

"I didn't see anyone, Missy. I thought you moved to get away from them." She nodded her head toward the two warriors with women on their laps.

"You had to see him, he was sitting right there." Shayla pointed to the empty chair in the corner and looked up at the waitress.

"Maybe I shouldn't have given you more wine. Seems you've had enough."

The waitress laughed at her as if she had lost her mind. She returned to her original table and took a deep breath. "Arden, Rance, dismiss your friends, we need to talk."

They promptly obeyed. Shayla cleared her throat and tried to decide what she could tell them that they would believe.

"Sorry, those two women—they just..."

"That doesn't matter. I've learned where there may be a Kiah Master."

"Let's go, right now," Rance said.

"No. I will go alone in the morning."

Arden bristled. "That's not possible. I swore an oath to your father to stay with you at all costs. You know how dangerous this mission has become."

"This is different. If you go with me, I will never find him."

"That's ridiculous. What difference could our presence make?"

"The old man insisted I go alone, and I believe him."

"No. Absolutely not." Arden glanced around the room. "What old man?"

"He's gone now."

"I agree." Rance shook his head. "We will not let you go by yourself."

"You have no choice. My orders must be obeyed. You know that."

"We're under orders from Ruler Nuri."

"He's not in command here, I am. And neither of you will follow. Arden, I want you to secure an Esroth for me to ride, a comfortable saddle and saddlebags. Rance, you are to purchase enough food for three sun-cycles, also some warm clothes and a fur coat." Shayla eyed her guards. "I remind you, the supplies are only for me. You two will remain here until I return."

Arden leaned forward. "And what if you don't return?"

"Then take the cruiser home and report to my Father." She reached into her pocket and handed them cash. In a town like Dartron, credit vouchers held little value. Shayla stood. "I want this taken care of as soon as possible. I leave at dawn."

CHAPTER FOUR

Shayla stepped outside the Snake-Eye Inn in the predawn darkness and found an Esroth tied to the porch rail. She approached the large, brown animal slowly and wondered where Arden and Rance were. They had not answered the door when she knocked, but it was early. No doubt they had spent the moon-cycle with the two wenches who could not keep their hands off them. They were probably exhausted and still sleeping.

The mysterious old man had been specific about going alone. She could not shake the feeling her guards would follow her. They were the best guards the Zared tribe had to offer and were devoted to their duty, as well as their ruler. She could only hope to make her escape and lose them on the trail. Too much depended on finding a Kiah Master and time was her enemy. She could not fail.

She patted the animal's sleek, long neck. "Good boy." She slipped the Kiah Rod and her personal belongings into the saddlebags and tried to remember the last time she had ridden. It had been many annual-cycles ago, but she always loved the freedom she found on the back of the sure-footed animals, running through fields, the wind on her face and blowing through her hair. However, this was not a pleasure ride.

She untied the Esroth, slipped the reigns over his head and placed her left foot in the stirrup. She hopped three times then swung her right leg up high enough to clear the saddle. Instead of finding herself on smooth leather, she landed on the rough, rocky ground. She stood, dusted off the seat of her pants and glanced around. Thank the Gods no one witnessed her disgrace. Getting on the tall beasts had always been a problem. Rather than admit she was too short to mount gracefully, she just insisted they were too tall—and they were!

Shayla led the Esroth to stand still in front of the inn's wooden stairs. She stood on the second step, hopped once and successfully mounted. With a gentle nudge the animal trotted off down the dirt road. Arden and Rance picked a fine cooperative mount and a comfortable saddle. Usually a rider had to work to earn the trust of an Esroth, but once the bonding took place they were devoted.

After a graceful canter out of town, Shayla slowed to a walk and stopped behind a large boulder and waited. She reached in front of her and smoothed the fine hair of the animal's neck. She needed to gently reassure the Esroth they belonged together. She surveyed the area. If her hunch was right, Rance and Arden should be here before her Esroth caught his breath. They could no more disobey her father's orders than she could. The distant sound of thundering hooves verified her suspicions.

Two riders flew past her at a dead run and she laughed to herself. There was no sense trying to hide from them. They were excellent trackers and would not stop until they found her. She decided to simply saunter in their direction to teach them a lesson. It did not take them long to backtrack. She heard their furious ranting long before they were close enough to reprimand. Worry and anger sparked in their determined eyes while they drew to a stop in front of her.

"Don't ever do that again!"

Arden yelled at her, and that was something he had never done before. "Do what? You're the ones who are disobeying orders."

"We're here, and we're not leaving." Rance sat back on his saddle.

Arden straightened. "Do you know you're headed for Spirit Mountain?" He shook his head. "No man who has ever gone up there has come back."

"I don't care what fables surround that mountain, I'm going."

"It's not folklore, Princess, it's fact. There is an evil force. It's not safe."

"And who told you about this folklore? Could it have been those two buxom waitresses who took your fancy?"

Arden and Rance blushed, a rare sight for a warrior. "I'll take my chances."

"We're going with you. It's our duty," Arden said.

"Time's wasting, let's go." She spurred her mount into a gallop and headed for the tall, tree covered mountain in the distance. The early morning sun peaked a hill to the west and spread its orange glow over the rocks and boulders of the flat, desolate valley.

An eerie feeling began to form in the pit of her stomach and grew with each megator they traveled. There was a ghostly fog surrounding the base of Spirit Mountain that took on a supernatural glow as the sun's rays struggled to penetrate its density.

The words of the old, disappearing man at the inn still rang in her ears. He had looked so kind and understanding, but she had also seen a twinkle of mischief in his eyes. Was she going to Spirit Mountain simply out of desperation, or because she trusted the man who seemed to possess a wisdom she could not identify?

Shayla's hand instinctively reached back to check the Kiah Rod. Her fingers touched the leather case, but she did not feel reassured. Even if that old man was right and she found a Kiah Master, what could he do with a broken crystal rod? It seemed hopeless, but it was too late to turn back. Her people relied on her, and she refused to succumb. Her people would never accept the demands of the Voltran Tribe should they be the victor. That was an outcome she would give her life to avoid.

"Princess!" Arden called.

She pulled her Esroth to a halt, Rance and Arden taking their places next to her. "What is it?"

"Look." Arden pointed behind them. "We're being followed. Ride on ahead as fast as you can, we'll deal with whoever that is and catch up to you later."

"But..."

"Go Princess, you'll be safer on the mountain than you will be here." Arden reached over and swatted Shayla's Esroth on the hindquarters.

The hooves of her mount pounded the ground as he broke into a run. When she glanced back, she saw three riders approaching her guards and prayed for Arden and Rance's safety. She knew as Zared warriors they were sworn to give their lives to save hers, but the thought struck terror in her heart. Her father's expectant face when he said good-bye flashed through her mind. Failure was not an option.

She urged the Esroth faster toward the fog ahead, desperate to reach the protection it afforded. The moment she entered the mist, her lungs began to burn. The cloud reached for her with icy tendrils. The odor was sweet, yet not suitable to breathe. She buried her nose deep into the high collar of her fur parka and rode on, praying the fog would lift.

Time seemed suspended as she forced her way through the noxious haze. Even the sure-footed Esroth began to stumble, unable to see where his next step would take him. No wonder rumor held no man ever came out alive, they probably never even set foot on the mountain.

Mournful cries sliced through the smoky nebula. It sounded as if thousands of voices called to her, all expressing agony and pain. Was it a trick of some kind to scare the fainthearted? She hated to admit she found it effective. The Esroth tried to turn tail and run, but she held the reins steady and kicked his flanks.

Her mount snorted and tried to clear his nostrils of the sickly-sweet fumes that burned with each breath. The scared animal began to shake, a sure sign he was about to bolt. She dismounted, grabbed the reins and led her groaning mount deeper into the never-ending fog. When would it cease? There was no trail—no way out.

Large rocks and tall trees became visible only when she bumped into them. How could any fog be so thick? It felt as if nothing existed and she had fallen into another realm of existence. The animal protested and tried to pull her back. He threw his head and stomped the ground. She rubbed his neck.

"It's okay, boy. We're almost through. Come on, baby, come on." She pulled the reins and forged up the steep incline. Thank the Gods she was going up a slope or she would have no sense of direction at all. But if she did not find fresh air soon she would surely die. Breathing through the parka helped, but her lungs felt as if they might explode from the pressure of the heavy mist that held a steadfast death-grip on her.

Ahead she spotted a white glow. What it was did not matter. She concentrated on the light and trudged forward, determined not to let the swirling mist consume her. The gossamer glow was like a presence, another entity, and she thought she heard a voice say, "You're almost free, don't stop."

Several more steps put the fog behind her, and she fell to her knees in a large, grassy meadow that stretched long and green before her. The reins slipped from her hand when the Esroth pulled. She could no longer hold on, all her energy was gone and so was the Esroth. She could not chase the animal. Then the majestic Esroth dropped to the ground and rolled in the luxurious greenery and a smile crossed her face.

Shayla laid on her back and took long, cleansing breaths. The bright sun in the cloudless yellow-tinged sky warmed her face and she glanced back at the fog that hung like a tall gray wall. Whoever guided her through had her eternal thanks. Spirit Mountain was indeed a mystery, and she was only at the base. What secrets would unfold? How many more perils awaited?

Fresh air and the warmth of the orange sun revived her. She sat up and surveyed the countryside. Wild flowers grew in clumps throughout the tall grass, creating a colorful quilt of deep purples and reds. The Esroth lay close by, his long legs furled beneath him while he leisurely chewed bits of sweet grass without a care in the world. It always amazed her how quickly animals adapted. She wished she could do the same.

"Come on, boy, time to go." The hairy, four-legged beast rose and shook his body several times, dumping the contents of the saddlebags.

As she picked her clothes from the ground and stuffed them into the leather pouches, she stared at the one last item lying in the grass—the Kiah Rod. Carefully she picked it up and studied the black case. Was she wasting her time looking for a Kiah Master now that the crystal had been broken?

"Continue. Have faith."

Shayla spun in a circle. Where had that voice come from? She was not losing her mind, she heard a man's voice, yet she was alone in the pasture, except for her Esroth and a flock of birds that landed in a nearby tree. It sounded like the same voice she heard in the fog. Probably one of the spirits rumored to inhabit the mountain.

She shook her head, placed the case securely in the saddlebag and led her Esroth to a large rock. Thank the Gods for a short, flat boulder from which to mount the tall animal. She nudged him into a trot and headed up the slight incline toward a steeper slope.

CHAPTER FIVE

Rydor stared at Olin seated across from him at the small table, his shadow dancing in the torchlight on the stone walls of the cave he called home. "Answer me, Olin. Who could possibly breech the protective spells you've placed around the mountain?"

"Someone very special."

"That's all you're going to tell me?"

Olin chuckled and leaned back in his chair. "What more can I say? You refuse to listen."

"I've been listening, but you haven't been making sense, talking about scriptures from the Gods, and things that don't concern me."

"Aah, but you're wrong. These matters do concern you, that's the part you refuse to hear."

"I will not swear allegiance to any tribe, and I refuse to fight."

"It's a battle, not a fight." Olin smiled. "Are you ready to listen?"

"Battle, fight, what's the difference?"

"You fight with your body, but you battle with your mind. There is a world of difference."

Rydor stood and began to pace. Apprehension crawled across his skin and sank into his bones, a sensation he did not like. "I feel..." He stopped himself, not sure whether he should confirm Olin's predictions, yet he knew it was inevitable.

"Feel what, my boy?"

He stared out the opening of the cave and watched the late afternoon storm clouds turn dark and threatening. "Someone is on my mountain."

"Good, good. Now we're making progress. Can you visualize this person?"

He closed his eyes and took several long, deep breaths, clearing his mind, concentrating on the presence he had sensed for the last two and a half sun-cycles. Whoever it was seemed too far away to get a clear picture, but then he had only practiced with animals, never a person. It was easier to picture animals since their intentions were clear, and he was more familiar with their vibrations.

"Tell me what you see," Olin coaxed.

"I see an Esroth with a light-haired rider, but I can't make out the face. Whoever it is seems small, not much of a warrior."

"So you don't see this person as a threat?"

"No. I could defend myself with little effort should the occasion arise."

"Are you admitting you would fight?"

Rydor turned abruptly. "I said defend." He walked back into the inner chamber and returned to his seat at the table. He rested his forearms on the wood and refused to look at Olin when he joined him. "I've seen what fighting does to men, and I know how cruel they can be." He pulled open the front laces of his leather tunic. "Aren't these scars proof enough?"

"The scars on your body, Rydor, are not the problem. It's the scars on your soul you must heal."

"Some things are best forgotten and never spoken of again."

"How can you mend old hatreds if you refuse to speak of the terrible wrong that has been done to you? Surely you want to leave one sun-cycle, make your mark in the world, find a life-mate, have children."

He shook his head. "Those things mean nothing to me. I will live and die on this mountain, and the world will be better for it."

"Next you're going to tell me you should have perished sixteen annual-cycles ago when you were left for dead."

"It would have been easier."

Olin smiled. "But you've never taken the easy way out, have you?"

"Nor will I."

"Then it's settled." Olin stood. "That's what I've been waiting to hear."

"What? Nothing has been settled." Rydor banged his fist on the table. "What do you mean, Olin?"

"You told me all I need to know."

In a flash Olin turned to a puff of smoke and disappeared before his eyes, a sight he was used to, but it never ceased to amaze him how the wizard did his tricks. But the old man frustrated him when he left before a conversation had ended.

A loud clap of thunder pulled him back to the opening of the cave where he watched bright flashes of lightning. The sheer, two megator drop from the entrance to the valley below was an awesome sight, and he had wondered more than once how long it would take him to fall to his death should he take the wrong step.

Rydor had been left at the foot of the mountain by his tribe to die a painful death. Why had he been spared? What purpose could he possibly serve living alone his entire life. When he perished not another living soul would know he ever he existed.

All three tribes of Zanthus talked about the Gods, but he did not believe in them. It was not the Gods who saved him, it was Una and Olin. He turned to gaze at the golden-haired cat who stared with dark intent eyes, as if she sensed his gloomy mood.

"Come, Una. We have hunting to do." The silly cat turned her head away from him. "You will not melt in the rain, but you will surely starve." He headed toward the back of the cave to use the hidden passageway that led to a small, tree lined meadow just below the summit.

Una ran past him, leaping over rocks, suddenly anxious for the hunt. Rydor picked up his bow and cutter from their concealed resting-place by the exit. The moment he stepped into the rain he stopped dead in his tracks. Danger. A cry for help echoed in his mind. Was it his own thoughts, or had he heard someone?

With caution he headed down the mountain and followed his hunter's instincts. Olin warned he would have a visitor. He told Olin he had seen a figure on an Esroth, yet he was not anxious to meet a stranger, or share his home with another man. Even for one moon-cycle. The call for help grew louder, but the voice he heard in his mind sounded soft, almost feminine. Whoever called to him was desperate, and he was the only person who could offer assistance.

***

Shayla led the Esroth up the steep, rocky slope, barely able to keep her footing in the pouring rain. May the Gods help her. Then she remembered what the warriors had told her once after returning from a dangerous mission in the mountains. She patted the wet animal while she inched her way across the slick mud to stand behind him. With one hand she firmly grasped the long, wiry-haired tail then swatted his rump with the other.

The Esroth trudged upward and dragged her along behind. It was certainly easier than trying to lead the animal with his hooves on the heels of her boots. Four legs were way better in this terrain than two. She stumbled over fallen limbs and slippery, moss covered rocks. Was there any human life to be found on Spirit Mountain?

Thunder roared, and a bolt of lightning cracked through a tree that once stood tall in front of them, but now lay smoking on the ground. The Esroth panicked. "Easy, boy!" Her words had no effect. The large animal bolted and lunged up the hill out of sight, leaving her face down in the mud and pinups needles.

She opened her mouth to scream, but her words were silenced by the rain that fell so hard all she managed was a watery gurgle. How she wished Rance and Arden were here. All she could do was pray they were safe. She searched for anything to hang onto so she could gain her footing and make her way up the mountain. Thoughts of a heroic rescue disappeared from her mind. She was alone, the way the strange old man instructed, and she feared she might die on this God-forsaken mountain—cold, wet and very alone.

If she had four legs like the Esroth, she might make it up the slope. Instead she slipped back faster than she could forge ahead. She grabbed the base of a small tree and held on for dear life when water gushed toward her from above. She looked up only to find an endless, impossible climb ahead of her. Cold, stinging raindrops pelted her face with increased intensity while she slid farther down the slope, barely maintaining her grip on the end of the young tree.

The first sun-cycle on Spirit Mountain had brought gale force winds that knocked her to the ground. Last sun-cycle swarms of insects threatened to consume her. Her skin still itched from their painful stings and bites. She glanced behind her toward the rising creek and sharp rocks below. If she lost her grip, she would certainly fall to her death.

The temperature dropped several more degrees and her body shivered violently. Where was the top? She could not hold on much longer. The young sapling began to uproot in the saturated earth. More icy torrents flowed toward her and washed the ground from beneath her feet. The small tree could take no more and her weight pulled it from the saturated earth. She careened down the cliff, her hand frozen around the uprooted bark. She screamed at the top of her lungs, but there was no one to hear her desperate cry.

She closed her eyes and prayed while she bounced over rocks and fallen trees and slipped farther into the clutches of nature. The gorge below came toward her fast and furious. She was not sure which was worse, the fear of failure or the physical pain of her own death.

***

Rydor ran toward the scream that echoed in the crevasse he knew all too well. Many animals had fallen to their death in that very place, unable to escape. He was forced to slow his pace when he approached the loose shale cliff. Even Una would not bound carelessly on this ground.

He eased to the edge and peered down and his heart pounded heavily in his chest when he saw a small body sprawled face down in a stream that grew swifter by the moment. If he did not hurry, the body would be swept away toward the falls and disappear for all time. "Una, go," he commanded.

The cat was careful while she agilely hurried down the steep, rain-washed mountainside. Rydor followed, but he could not match Una's pace. He half-slid, half-walked while he made his way toward his faithful companion. Una pulled the body from the water, the parka firmly between her teeth. She swished her tail which was her way of telling him the prey was still alive. Una stood guard, her foot on the body while he made his way toward the uninvited visitor.

He made it to Una, knelt and rolled the body over. His jaw dropped at the sight of a woman. He had seen long blond hair in his vision, but he was not prepared for a woman, especially one this beautiful. His fingers found the artery on the side of her neck. Her pulse was strong. He let out the breath he'd been holding. She would live.

Una bent and licked her face. Rydor pried a small tree from her hand then pulled her to a sitting position. She coughed and retched water. It was a wonder she had not drowned. Her eyes fluttered open and focused on the cat. He heard her startled gasp before she fell unconscious. Seeing Una would be a shock since the giant mountain cats were known as killers. He had the same reaction long ago.

Rydor brushed leaves and gravel from her face. Even through the mud her delicate, flawless features were far too pale. He cupped her cheek in the palm of his hand. The simple act caused his heart to race. He had not touched another human in over sixteen annual-cycles, which had to be the cause of his reaction, yet it did not explain the odd warmth that spread through his body.

If the woman was to survive, she needed immediate shelter and warm blankets. The torrential rain had turned the creek into a rapidly rising torrent. He picked the small woman up and cradled her in his arms.

The feel of her body against his stirred something inside him, something he believed long dead. He ignored the odd sensation and headed toward the cave. Olin should have warned him his visitor was a woman. He would not have believed Olin if he said a woman would venture up a dangerous mountain and pass through three protective spells to find him. The real question only she could answer—why?

The megators home never seemed longer. He had to carry her over his shoulder part of the way because of the rough terrain. He suspected her whimpers were from bruised or broken ribs. She fell quite a distance judging from the hole in the slope where the tree had once been. If he had not stepped in the indentation and lost his balance he might never have noticed.

He felt her shiver and shake against him. It was cold, slightly below freezing now. Soon there would be ice. He had to get her home before she froze to death. The terrain finally leveled out so he was able to pick up his pace. Una was always faster than he was, but she would stop and look back. Why a Semita would be worried about a woman he did not know, but she was very concerned. Of course, Una was no ordinary Semita.

The cave was just around the corner and he could not get there soon enough. He entered through the back way and hurried to lay her on his pallet. Her body shook constantly. He had to undress her quickly to keep her alive, so he untied the laces that held the parka closed then pulled her arms free. When he tossed the soggy fur garment on the floor it began to form a large puddle. Her clothes were just as wet. He reached for her tunic, but hesitated. Now his hands shook and it was not from the cold.

Her top was molded to her body and the unmistakable swell of her breasts caught his eye. He should not stare, but he had not seen a woman since he was a boy. Memories and reality were entirely different matters.

Una lay beside the bed and swished her tail. He patted his cat on the head. "Yes, she's alive. Very much alive." He could swear the animal smiled. When he turned back to the woman he could not take his eyes off the rise and fall of her chest. It was impossible to ignore her hardened nipples which were all too visible under the wet fabric. He took a deep breath, grabbed the bottom of her tunic and pulled it up over her head. Beads of water clung to her rosy nipples and glistened in the flickering torchlight. The urge to feel the softness of her skin made his fingertips burn.

She was so beautiful, so perfect, so tempting. His masculinity reacted and he took a step back. He had no right to look at her, and even less right to touch her. He opened a wooden box and removed a cloth to dry her. A slight moan escaped her lips when he spread the soft fabric over her ice-cold skin and patted, careful not to touch the fullness of her breasts. An unfamiliar warmth spread through his body. A man could only handle so much temptation before he lost control. He recalled being with one girl in his youth, but he felt nothing this intense.

This woman stirred potent, threatening lust. It was common knowledge that Voltran warriors had stronger mating urges than other men on the planet, but he never expected an instant response so intense it rocked his very core. But he had to finish this quickly so she could get warm. He removed her boots, socks, then made quick work of her pants. She now lay before him in only a skimpy pair of underpants of some type he had never seen.

Her pinkish-white skin indicated she did not spend much time in the sun. Who was this mysterious beauty that lay on his pallet? He dried off her legs and decided to leave on whatever that last garment was called. He pulled the heavy fur cover up then reached under to remove the towel, not trusting himself to look at her nakedness again.

Rydor needed to regain his sanity. He smiled when Una jumped up on the foot of the bed and curled up, making herself quite at home. "Being a bit possessive, aren't you?" He laughed at her half-growl half-purr. "Guard her well, she looks fragile. What are we going to do with her, girl?" He wished the mountain cat could answer, because he certainly had no idea what to do with a beautiful woman in his bed, alone on a mountain. He knew what he wanted to do with her, but that was out of the question. Rydor Celon may have been branded a coward, but he had ethics and high moral principles. He would never take advantage of any woman.

He picked up her wet clothes, carried them to the main chamber and hung them on the tree rack which had never held garments that small.

"And the fun begins."

Rydor turned at the sound of Olin's voice and sent him a scowl while he followed the wizard back to his sleeping alcove. "Fun? I believe you have a twisted mind, Olin."

"This beautiful creature arrives and your humor deserts you?" Olin chuckled.

"This is no laughing matter. I cannot keep a woman here!"

"You can, and you will. She is the visitor I warned you about, and she has come to seek your services."

"Services? There is only one thing I could do for her, and I'm quite sure she hasn't come for that reason. Now tell me, wise man, why is she here?"

"I think that is for her to say." Olin stopped by the pallet and touched her forehead.

There were times Olin could be most infuriating, and this was one of those times. "She has a fever."

"She'll be fine." Olin smiled as he stepped back. "She's in good hands."

He suddenly questioned Olin's judgment. "She needs a healer to quell the fever."

"You are all she needs."

"Indeed." He stared at the sleeping woman and wondered if she would feel the same when she woke. How had she braved the forces of Spirit Mountain when she was so small and unarmed? Vicious beasts roamed freely, the terrain was rugged, and Olin's spells had never been breached before.

"Rydor," Olin began, "you must promise to seriously consider her request."

"Explain why I should."

"You have an old score to settle, and she is here to provide the opportunity to prove yourself." Olin stepped to Rydor's side and laid his hand on his student's shoulder. "All I ask is that you follow your heart and open your mind. Contemplate her words carefully before making a decision that affects far more than you could ever imagine. Can you do that?"

"If it is your wish."

"It is. Have faith in yourself and in her."

Rydor stared into the depths of the wizard's violet eyes. Olin had asked nothing of him since they met, and he owed him more than he could ever repay. "I will do as you request."

"You're a good man, Rydor. I knew I could count on you."

"I have only agreed to listen."

"Aah, but you also agreed to follow your heart, and that is a far greater promise."

The wizard waved his arm and disappeared into a puff of smoke. As usual, Olin left him much to contemplate. Olin's words always held a deeper meaning than their simplistic indication. Why was Olin so insistent in regards to the woman in his bed?

He knelt beside the pallet and pressed his lips to her forehead, the technique his mother used when checking for fever, but the gesture caused Una to growl. "You overprotective hunk of fur." He straightened and Una began to purr. "You are a strange Semita." He always wondered why Una, unlike the rest of her species, took to humans, but he was grateful she did. Una saved his life, and now the life of this woman.

There was a special quality to the blond-haired beauty before him. Even unconscious she possessed an undeniable air of royalty with an angelic glow that made her appear surreal. He wet a piece of cloth and laid it across her forehead. Did she have mystical powers like Olin? If she did she would not be lying here struggling for breath and burning with fever.

He wet another cloth and rubbed it over her bare shoulders, but no lower. Something about her frightened him, and he knew exactly what that something was—carnal attraction. A mesmerizing fascination pulled at him, stirring passion deep within his soul, causing thoughts he had no right to have about a woman he had never even met.

She was the embodiment of the term his people used when they referred to a beautiful, tempting woman—Sutae. It meant, "My precious love", and she was precious. Her shiny golden hair, still damp, spread provocatively across his pillow. He inhaled her sweet feminine scent which he could only liken to wildflowers in the meadows.

Little did Olin know he would listen to anything she had to say, a thought that sent shivers through him. Was he vulnerable because he was lonely? Did he crave another being to talk to? Or was it because she was the most delectable creature on the face of the planet? Whatever the reason, he would have to use every technique he knew for self-control to stop his masculine cravings for the woman who so boldly intruded on his life.

CHAPTER SIX

Shayla opened her eyes and focused on a torch. From all appearances she was in a cave. When she slowly sat up, a cloth fell from her forehead onto a fur cover. When the heavy animal skin slid to her waist, she realized she was naked and quickly pulled it back up. Who undressed her?

Hazy memories of falling and her body being battered while she rolled down the treacherous mountainside formed in her mind. At that moment she thought she would die. Was she dead? No because pain engulfed her and she gasped for breath which caused her ribs to ache unmercifully. Dark bruises were visible on her arms, and judging by the way she felt, her entire body was one giant bruise.

How had she gotten here? No sooner had the thought crossed her mind when a man stepped into view from the shadows. She sucked in her breath. Realization hit. Whoever he was he must have been the one to undress her and see her naked. The tall, muscular man had bronze skin, and exuded a warrior's power from the top of his long dark mane to the tips of his fur boots. His piercing blue gaze raked over her, and she shivered with the sick realization he had undressed her. He was intense, yet he had a kind face, considering the set of his square jaw, narrowed eyes and pursed lips.

"How do you feel?"

His deep melodic voice vibrated through her. "Better, thank you." He stepped closer and she shivered, but she was not cold at the moment. "Who are you?"

"My name is Rydor."

"I owe you my thanks. You saved my life." Out the corner of her eye she saw something gold fly through the air. She screamed when the large creature landed on the bed. Mouth agape, she stared at the mountain cat and terror seized every muscle in her aching body. In a flash Rydor was at her side, his large hand clamped firmly over her mouth.

"Please, Sutae, do not be afraid. This is Una, my pet Semita who saved your life. She is only concerned for you. Do not scream, you'll scare her."

Shayla nodded. He removed his warm hand from her mouth, but remained kneeling next to her. His muscles flexed beneath the snug, leather tunic and pants he wore, and she found it difficult to remove her gaze from his raw, powerful physique. "I'm sorry if I upset Una."

"She will be fine, but do nothing to betray her trust. Una is loyal, but she is still a wild beast."

"I'll remember that." Shayla met his gaze for a long moment before he turned and stood. His leather clothes were held together with laces, the hand stitching the most perfect she had ever seen. The woman who made his clothes must be a true craftsman. "Where is your life-mate?"

"I live alone."

It seemed odd his tone became sharp at the mere mention of a mate. "I'm sorry, I just assumed..."

"Assume nothing."

"Why did you call me Sutae?" Color flushed his tanned cheeks. Had she made a mistake asking such a simple question?

"Because I do not know your name."

"I am Princess Shayla D'Par of the Zared tribe, only child of Ruler Nuri." He remained emotionless, even his penetrating eyes did not reflect a hint of emotion. What was going through his mind? "What tribe are you from?" Rydor paced the width of the pallet several times before he stopped to face her, arms crossed over his chest, legs spread and firmly planted.

"I belong to no tribe."

"Everyone belongs to one of the three tribes. I know you're not of the Zared tribe, so you must be Quelan or Voltran." Anger flared in his eyes, and she became acutely aware of her nakedness and the fact she must be in his bed. She clutched the coverlet tighter to her neck. "It matters not where you're from."

"Why have you come?"

It seemed Rydor was a man of few words. "I am looking for a Kiah Master." He took the news without blinking, unlike the others she had approached. "I met a gray-haired man with a long beard in a tavern. He told me the warrior I was looking for lived on Spirit Mountain."

"Indeed."

"Do you know the man I speak of?" He nodded. "Is he a friend of yours?" A hint of mischief replaced the anger in his gaze, yet he seemed reluctant to answer. Rydor did not appear to be the kind of man who could be pushed into anything, so she decided to back off. He started to leave. "Rydor?"

He stopped and turned. "What, Princess D'Par?"

"My clothes?"

"Of course."

When he walked away, she could not help evaluate him from the rear, and found every inch of him pleasing to her eye. Too pleasing, if she were honest. As a warrior he seemed an excellent specimen, and as a man he was most tempting. Of course, she had only seen him walk, but she had no doubt his physical prowess would prove superior in battle.

Rydor made every Zared warrior pale in comparison, including Arden and Rance, which were the fittest and most virile of her tribe. She was not normally impressed with the physical appearance of any male, but this particular man piqued her curiosity and made her stomach flutter.

The shuffle of his soft boots signaled his return so she quickly laid down and pulled the cover up to her chin. She wished she could hide the heated blush on her cheeks when he stopped beside the bed.

"Your clothes, Princess D'Par."

She took the garments from his outstretched hand, accidentally brushing his fingers with hers. Rydor stood ridged while she felt herself melt. She had to get a grip on herself. For some reason she was confident this man could pass the test; and, if he did, they would have a long journey together. It could simply be wishful thinking on her part, yet Rydor seemed different. Deep inside her soul she sensed he was a man of integrity, bravery and honor.

"I will prepare supper."

He disappeared around a corner and Shayla let out the breath she'd been holding. She slipped the blue tunic over her head and winced at the pain in her ribs. She pulled on the matching leggings before she attempted to stand. Her legs were shaky and sore, but she walked slowly across the stone floor which was cold on her feet. She hurried in the direction Rydor had gone, anxious to learn more about the provocative man who could prove to be her Kiah Master.

When she turned the corner, she stared in amazement. The large cavernous living area dwarfed the well-crafted wooden furniture, complete with a couch, two chairs, a low table, and at the far end, a dining set. It was crude next to the palace, but it suited Rydor. She had no idea how long he had lived here, but it was quite a nice home. She ran her hand over the surface of the chair's back, astounded by the smoothness.

She stood on one of the many fur pelts spread over the floor and curled her toes in the fuzzy softness. Rydor was bent over a raised cook area he had created out of stones, and once again she found herself more pleased with his appearance than she should be.

Thoughts of her mission pushed all wayward notions from her mind. She was royalty, and her betrothal to Eaton was next to official. So why did her body stir at the mere sight of Rydor when she really didn't know him? She had spent time alone with Eaton, shared kisses with him, touched him, but never experienced sensations like the ones Rydor provoked by his very presence.

He turned abruptly and caught her stare. His gaze caused her legs to wobble, and she lowered herself onto the chair she had admired before she fell faint. Without hesitation he rushed to her and grabbed her hand.

"Princess, are you all right?"

How could she tell him his concern was only making matters worse? She could not admit the truth. He would think her a wanton woman. "I'm just a bit weak." His deep blue gaze searched her face in a worried manner. "I'll be fine, really. And please, call me Shayla."

"As you wish." He stood, scooped her up into his arms and walked toward the table in the eating area.

"Put me down!" It seemed odd to protest while savoring the feel of his powerful arms around her. This was ludicrous. She must have hit her head in the fall. It was the only explanation for such lewd thoughts. Beads of sweat formed on his forehead, which seemed odd since he carried her with ease. He set her on the chair next to the table.

"Food will do you well," Rydor mumbled, returning to the stone hearth.

A few moments later, he placed two large wooden bowls full of stew and a loaf of bread on the table, along with a platter of cheese. She frowned. More strange looking stew. When this was over, she would never eat stew again. The aroma was tempting, but then she had not eaten in at least one sun- cycle, maybe more. She had no idea how long she had laid in the forest, or in Rydor's bed. She picked up a spoon and hesitantly stirred the brown concoction. It took courage to lift the first bite to her lips.

"It is not poison."

Rydor sounded offended, so she tasted the stew, surprised by the delicious flavor, hearty and zesty, but the meat still remained unidentifiable. It was best not to think about it while she ate. She was starving and certainly had no desire to upset him by not eating his cooking. "It's very good, Rydor."

"Humph."

A typical male response. She ripped off a piece of bread and dunked it into the gravy the same as he had done. Rydor's cooking was far better than what she'd eaten at the taverns during her travels in the Badlands. But the silence was deafening, and she had a few burning questions to ask the stranger. "Did you see my Esroth?"

He shook his head.

"How long have I been here?"

Rydor stopped eating and looked up. "Not long, why?"

"I must find my Esroth. The Kiah Rod is in the saddle bag and I cannot lose it."

"I'll look for him in the morning."

"No, we must go now." He looked at her with a very disgruntled look on his face and she knew she had made a big mistake.

"It's dark and the storm still rages."

"That doesn't matter. I'll go myself." Shayla stood a little too fast which caused her injured ribs to scream in protest. She sucked in a deep breath. "How do I get out of here?"

Rydor pointed to his right and she walked in that direction. She followed a short tunnel then stopped in front of a large opening that revealed nothing but a dark, stormy sky. They must be high on the peak to have such a view. The moment she moved closer to the opening her heart raced hard and fast. She peered down, gasped and took a quick step back.

The drop was too great to measure without enough light. How had he climbed the sheer rock wall carrying her? It was not possible. She turned and stomped back to Rydor, who sat at the table calmly eating. Taking her seat, she scowled at his nonchalance. "How did I get here?"

He took a bite before he answered. "I carried you."

"That's not possible. There's no way you could have scaled that cliff carrying me."

Rydor dropped his spoon and stared. "How would you know what I am capable of?"

He had a point. "I don't, but I know what I saw."

"Why is this Kiah Rod so important?"

Was he playing games with her? Surely he had heard what was going on among the three tribes? Everyone on the planet had been educated about the Kiah and the Ultimate Battle during the later part of their education. "I know you live a secluded life here, but don't pretend you have no comprehension of the Kiah."

"What happens among the tribes is of no concern to me."

"You claim allegiance to no tribe, but you live on Zanthus, as we all do. Would you allow the Voltrans to enslave us all? Surely you're not that shallow." She stared into his expressive blue eyes. "Or is it because you're Voltran and want them to win?"

"What do you want from me?"

Shayla took another deep breath to calm herself. Rydor's anger was palpable, and she did not know how far he could be pushed before becoming violent. She did not want to risk alienating him on the chance he might be her Kiah Master, so she decided to approach the subject with a bit more diplomacy. "Do you have family members living in one of the tribes?"

"No."

"Anyone you care about?"

"No."

So much for diplomacy. "Surely you have compassion for human life, do you not?"

"Of course."

"Then, out of that compassion, will you help me find my Esroth and take the test?" She had his full attention, but he still remained a cold, immovable force, void of emotion. Could she penetrate his invisible wall enough to elicit a response? "My people's lives depend upon my finding a Kiah Master to defend them."

"Why is there no Zared warrior to fight for your people?"

"I wish there were, and you know very well I would not be here had I found any of them worthy."

Rydor stood and began to clear the table. "What makes you believe I am worthy?" He turned to face her. "That is why you came, right?"

Shayla nodded. "As I said, the man in the tavern sent me here. I don't know him, but I believe him."

"He is wise."

"Then you will take the test?" He was quiet while he considered her request, his expression full of doubt and reprisal. Rydor was a strange man. Dangerous looking, but at the same time kind and aloof. His silence pushed her toward anger, and his defensive stance reminded her he was in control. She was in his home, partaking of his hospitality, asking his assistance, and she was not an invited guest.

"I will consider your request."

"That is all I ask."

"Return to my pallet. Rest. I will wake you at first light."

"Thank you, Rydor. I appreciate your kindness." Shayla stood. "I owe you my life. I truly thank you for saving me."

"I could do no less."

"Well, I thank you." She turned and headed back to his sleeping chamber. She wrapped her arms around her ribs to hold them together. Physically she had never felt worse, but at last she had hope.

CHAPTER SEVEN

Rydor paced the width of the cave. On each pass he glanced outside while he waited for the twin suns to rise. Sleep evaded him. Shayla's request and Olin's words consumed his every thought, which forced him to face demons he had worked so hard to forget.

It was not his intention to toy with her regarding the Kiah, but he had to be sure her intent was honorable, and that she had not been sent by the Voltrans. His father knew he had potential to become Kiah Master should the occasion arise. Damek and Turic believed him dead, but the moment he touched the Kiah they would learn the truth, of that he was certain. If he took the test and she found him worthy, he would have to fight against his own tribe, and possibly face his younger brother, Turic. Granted, he had a score to settle with his father and brother, but he could never kill them. The thought of taking a life still sickened him.

He was a coward. Any normal warrior would relish the opportunity to fight, to right a wrong. Revenge appealed to him, but not if he had to take a life in the process. Murder, no matter what the reason, was a deed he could not perform. Not for Olin, not for his people, and not for Shayla.

Why, after all these annual-cycles, had his peace been disturbed? He was happy here, alone, living in harmony with nature, answering to no one but himself. How could he allow the wishes of another to violate his code of ethics? Yet how could he deny the request?

He raked his fingers through his hair. It was an impossible decision with only one choice. He was sure his father's malfeasance had been transferred to Turic. By now the man had most likely turned his brother into a ruthless warrior with evil intent. Could he, Rydor Celon, coward son of Damek, fight a battle to stop his tribe's dominance?

Even at sixteen he'd known about the Voltran's desire to rule all of Zanthus. Voltrans never accepted peace. They were warriors, always pushing the limits to start skirmishes and wars, but total control was not possible with useless fighting. They needed to win the Ultimate Battle.

"Rydor?"

He turned to face the woman who had disrupted his life. Blaming her was futile, she was but a messenger. No matter how he wanted to deny it, it was his father and brother who pledged to destroy life on Zanthus and enslave the inhabitants for their own selfish purposes. "I have considered your request and will take the test."

She relaxed and a smile crossed her face, a smile that melted his very soul. "Follow your heart," Olin had said, but the man neglected to reveal how the visitor of his prediction would affect him. The next time Olin appeared, he had a few choice words for the wizard.

"I knew you would make the right choice."

"You know nothing." Even as he spoke the words, he regretted them, yet he felt the need to push her away. It would be far too easy to become close to Princess D'Par and he did not trust himself around her. There was no time for a foolish mistake. She was here for only one reason, and he had to maintain proper distance.

"I'm sorry to intrude. I'll leave you alone." She turned to leave, but stopped. "I regret this as much as you do."

Rydor moved closer, her delicate scent spiraling through him. "Never apologize for doing your duty. I understand your position." He stepped past her and removed their parkas from the tree rack. "You will need this."

She took her coat and slipped it on. "Before we leave I'll need my boots."

A deep laugh rumbled through him, and it felt good. "A minor oversight on my part, Princess D'Par."

"One which surprises me. I never imagined you the kind of man to forget anything."

"Only what I choose to forget." He reached into a recess high on the cavern wall and grabbed the top of her leather boots. "You're fortunate they're dry."

"From the looks of it, not for long. Does it always rain on Spirit Mountain?"

Rydor glanced out at the heavy mist that fell like a cloud of doom. "Often, but not always." She smiled at him and his body responded too easily to her charms. "Follow me and stay close," he instructed while she slipped her boots on. "There are dangers here you know nothing about."

***

They had been walking for hours, up and down places better suited for Granbees, those lithe little six-legged creatures with suction cups for feet. Rydor was at home here, but why not? The entire mountain was his backyard. He knew exactly where he was going, and he searched thoroughly, but they had yet to find her Esroth.

Rydor strode like a king surveying his kingdom, but she felt nothing like a princess. She was cold, wet, her ribs ached and her feet hurt. Traipsing through the forest may be an enjoyable activity for Rydor, but she'd already experienced enough to last a lifetime.

Without warning, he stopped on a ledge and she ran into his back and lost her balance. He grabbed her arm and pulled her to him. Even through their parkas, she was aware of the hard, muscular warmth of his body and his undeniable warrior's strength. "Thank you."

"Be careful. Una is not here to save you."

Shayla glanced around. "Where did she go? She was right behind us."

"Una has hunting of her own to do. She will return. Now, let me concentrate."

She took a step back and watched him close his eyes and take deep, measured breaths. He stood in silence for several minutes before turning to face her.

"Your Esroth is just over the hill behind us."

"How do you know that?"

"I sense his vibration."

With that announcement, he headed back up the slope at breakneck speed. He did not stop to consider that her legs were shorter than his, and still sore from all the bruises. He had maintained an impossible pace all morning and she wondered what drove him like a man possessed. He was not in a hurry last moon-cycle, but now he considered the quest for her Esroth to be of the utmost import. Men.

The wet ground made the climb difficult, but she did her best to keep up, yet he pushed on. She knew her search for a Kiah Master would not be easy, but she never expected this. Enough was enough. She stopped and leaned against a rock to catch her breath.

Behind her she heard twigs crack and gravel crunch. Rydor was far ahead, so what in the name of Zanthus was approaching? She slowly turned. Wide-open jaws with double rows of teeth confronted her. Saliva dripped from razor sharp incisors while black protruding eyes froze on her. The creature had a tall, lizard-like body with high spines along its back, and talons long enough to pierce straight through her. The monster lifted a clawed foot and moved closer. One scream and she was dinner.

The pounding of hooves distracted the creature, its tongue darting in and out. She did not dare move or make a sound.

"Here!"

By the Gods, it was Rydor, and none too soon. The monster stepped beside her, its gaze fixed on the plateau above. She heard the whoosh, then an arrow pierced the creature between the eyes, green fluid spurted from the deadly wound. Her heart nearly stopped when the creature lunged forward, but it fell to the ground at her feet with an agonizing groan.

She stood frozen, her mouth agape, barely able to comprehend how close to death she'd been.

"Are you all right, Princess?"

She turned and found a terrified expression on Rydor's face. "I'm a bit shaky, but—"

He picked up her hand and pressed his lips to her skin. "Please forgive me, I will never let you out of my sight again."

A shiver ran down her spine when she realized his terror was for her and had nothing to do with the creature. His heated blue gaze raked her from head to foot, and she suddenly felt warm, a welcome relief from the cold panic that gripped her moments before.

"What is that?"

"It's a Thadirum. They thrive on Spirit Mountain with so many animals to eat."

"Do they eat people?"

"They're not particular what kind of flesh appeases their appetite."

Shayla swallowed hard. Rydor was right, there were dangers here she knew nothing about, yet she was not sure she liked his statement about never letting her out of his sight again. He was an excellent protector, but she did not trust him. Or was it herself she could not trust?

"Come, your Esroth awaits."

Rydor slipped his arm around her waist and all but carried her up the hill. It felt good to lean on his strength, yet the sensations that assaulted her had nothing to do with safety. He held her tightly while he pulled her up the steep slope. She wished, for a moment, they were not wearing parkas so she could better feel the contours of his body since his chest was pressed tightly against her side and back. She had seen him enough to know those muscles were well-toned and hard. She should probably be ashamed for wanting to touch and explore him, yet she longed to feel him.

She shook her head, unable to believe such thoughts crossed her mind. They were definitely not thoughts a princess should have. Her mission was of utmost importance to her people, and she had no right to betray the trust they bestowed upon her. It was her duty to find a Kiah Master and return him to Terita to represent the Zared Tribe in the Ultimate Battle, not to find solace in a stranger's arms.

The moment they reached the plateau she saw her Esroth, still saddled, the leather case sticking out of the bag. She sighed, never more relieved to see an animal in her life. She hurried to him, threw her arms around the Esroth's neck and gave him a hug.

"Please, Princess, I sense danger. We must go."

Shayla nodded. Rydor had been right about everything so far and she had no reason to doubt his warning now. He grasped her waist and lifted her onto the Esroth as if she weighed nothing. His foot pressed into the stirrup and in one fluid motion he was seated behind her. His strong thighs rubbed against her backside and it was quite distracting. He surprised her when he lifted her, slid into the saddle, then settled her on his lap. Now she could barely breathe.

He prodded the Esroth into a cantor and headed in the direction of the cave. His powerful chest against her back, and his arm around her waist felt reassuring while they galloped along the edge of the bluff. She silently cursed herself for allowing so many improper thoughts about Rydor to cross her mind, but how could she stop when his body rubbed against hers so intimately?

Why was a man like Rydor living on a mountaintop, alone? What was he running from? Certainly something in his past had forced him into the life of a recluse. Pictures of every conceivable crime flashed in her mind. The Rydor she'd seen so far did not seem capable of murder, or any other breach of the law. What was his secret? His breath caressed her neck when he tightened his hold. His strength poured through her. He guided the Esroth around trees and through streams. Maybe his only crime was causing too many women to fall in love with him and refusing to life-mate any of them?

Would this ride never end? Rydor's hard body against hers sent a tumult of emotions to race through her—emotions she did not want to acknowledge. What kind of a Princess was she to allow the nearness of a stranger affect her? These were feelings she should have only for her betrothed, but Eaton never stirred her blood like the long-haired warrior at her back.

She recognized the meadow they entered and sighed when he reigned the Esroth to a halt by the entrance to his cave. He lifted her down, but pulled his hands back as if he could not stand to touch her. It was for the best he felt that way. There could never be anything between them. She was a Princess, destined to mate with the warrior of her father's choice, as custom dictated. Yet she could have sworn she saw something in the look he gave her, exactly what that look was she could not say, just something that intrigued her.

Rydor led the Esroth into the cavern and tied him to a stalagmite in a large alcove. "I will feed him later."

Shayla reached for the saddlebags but found Rydor's large hands clasp hers. She gazed up at him and tried to read the look in his foreboding blue eyes. He was a contradictory mystery. On the outside he appeared gruff, but she sensed a softness within his soul. She prayed she was right, because if he passed the test her people's lives would be in his hands.

"I will carry your bags." Rydor untied the leather straps and tossed the saddlebags over his shoulder. "After you, Princess." He lifted his arm and pointed to the stone hall on his left.

She remembered the way and walked briskly because his heated gaze on her back sent shivers through her. Surely he would not insist on spending every moment with her. He did say he would not let her out of his sight again. He had a way of making her feel self-conscious and more aware of him as a man than she should be.

He grabbed her arm and she spun to face him. His touch sent more shivers up her spine. "What?"

"I thought I should warn you before we enter the main room. We have company."

"I thought you lived alone, and that no one else had ever survived the climb up the mountain."

"Olin is different."

"Olin?" A half-smile crossed Rydor's lips, and she knew he was fond of this Olin, whoever he was. Of course she wondered how he knew the man was here, but he probably employed the same technique he used to find her Esroth. She did not understand his ability, however it obviously proved handy at times.

They passed through his sleeping chamber, maneuvered the hall then entered the main room. A gray haired, gray bearded man with a floppy velvet hat sat at the table drinking wine. "I know you!"

"Yes, my dear, you do. We were not formally introduced." He rose and stepped closer to the woman. "My name is Olin. Glad to see you have come."

"You're the man from the tavern."

"Guilty." Olin glanced at Rydor and smiled. "I see you have taken good care of Princess Shayla D'Par."

"How do you know my name?" The mischievous twinkle in his eye made her uncomfortable. He seemed to know even more than he was saying. "Why did you disappear so quickly at the inn?"

"This quest is yours. I only guided you."

Rydor frowned. "Why are you here?"

"Don't look so sad, my boy. I've come to witness the test." Olin chuckled. "You didn't think I'd miss such an event, did you?" He walked to the sofa and took a seat. "Bring the rod. We have much work to do."

There was something about Olin she liked, even if he seemed a bit—odd. She reached into the bag that still hung across Rydor's shoulder and removed the leather case. Rydor had an anxious expression, but she saw that same look on every man's face who had taken the test. She prayed Rydor would prove to be the chosen one, that her search had finally reached a fruitful end.

Rydor set the bags on the table then stepped to the center of the room and knelt before her on the fur pelt. Even in such a humble position he looked powerful. She removed the rod and held both pieces in one hand.

"Oh my," Olin said. "We have more work to do than I thought."

"What do you mean?" Shayla tightened her grasp on the two round, black crystals.

"Before the Kiah Master can fight the Ultimate Battle, he must first mend the rod."

Shayla studied the old man. "Is that possible?"

"Anything the mind can conceive is a possible reality."

She glanced down at Rydor to see if he understood Olin's statement. He raised an eyebrow and grinned. Rydor understood Olin, but she was not sure she understood either of them, but the moment was at hand. She laid the rods across Rydor's outstretched hands.

"I am Kiah Master. I am worthy."

She held her breath as the fate of her people rested in Rydor's grasp. He tightened his hold on the Kiah and raised the pieces over his head as if offering them to the heavens. Her gaze followed the dark crystals. Both halves of the rod began to change color in his grasp. Words escaped her as she watched the black crystal turn dark emerald green.

The reality of the man before her came into focus. He was indeed the man she so desperately searched for. Of all the warriors tested, he was the only one who caused a change in the rod. Before she began this search, the Zared Elders told her to follow her heart when choosing and to remember she had little time. Whoever she chose needed to hone his skills with the rod and understand his powers.

The elders did not tell her what to do if she was physically attracted to the man. How could she hear what her heart was saying when her body screamed for his touch? Such thoughts were futile, but she could not deny the desire he evoked by his presence.

Both halves of the rod remained a deep green color and she silently praised the proof sent by the Gods. She had been led to this place by forces she might never understand, and those same forces whispered in her mind to accept Rydor.

She laid her palm on the top of his head and prepared to say the words she had waited so long to say according to ancient legend. "You are my Kiah Master. You are worthy to fight in the name of the Zared tribe."

Rydor lowered his arms. "I will serve you well, my Princess, and will defend the Zared honor in the Ultimate Battle."

"Rise, warrior." She pulled her hand back. "I give you the Kiah, to protect with your life, to keep with you until victory is ours."

He stood and bowed. "It will be as you order."

Silence hung heavy between them, the air hard to breathe. She felt bonded to him in some unexplainable way. His deep blue eyes appeared troubled. Had she sensed what he was thinking, or were they her thoughts? So much responsibility rested on Rydor's shoulders. His life, the lives of her people, and the very survival of Zanthus.

She wished he would quit staring at her, his gaze searing through her. He held her spellbound. Was it the power of the Kiah, or the man? She felt an unshakable dynamic pull toward his undeniable masculinity.

"Come, let us celebrate."

Shayla was glad Olin broke the interminable silence, but she shook her head. "I don't feel like celebrating."

"You should, my dear." Olin took her hand and led her to the table.

When she glanced at Rydor who now stood firmly in the center of the chamber, it made her believe he was no happier about the turn of events than she was. She had always assumed the warrior she chose would be thrilled by the honor, but every muscle in his body was tense and his expression grim.

"Come, my boy, join us." Olin poured three glasses of wine.

Shayla sat and watched Rydor stride to the table, his skeptical gaze on Olin. If he was so reluctant to accept his position as Kiah Master, why had he taken the test? The dark and mysterious warrior was a man of few words.

Olin held up his glass. "A toast." He studied Rydor, then Shayla. "Please, join me in a toast to the future."

She picked up her wine and Rydor did the same. What kind of mystical bond existed between these two men? Olin called Rydor "my boy" and "my son", but somehow she knew he was not Rydor's father. They all touched glasses and sipped the tangy, sweet wine.

"There is much you both must learn over the coming weeks, and I will watch with interest as you discover things you never knew possible."

Rydor grimaced. "I fear there's something you're not telling us."

"Your beliefs will be put to the test." Olin sat on the chair across from Shayla. "Let us examine the so called dictates from the Gods."

"So called? How dare you!"

"Bear with me a moment, Princess. You must open your mind and consider everything on its own merit. Trust nothing, question everything."

Rydor's hands turned to fists. "Get to the point, Olin."

"You must work on your patience if you're to be the victor." Olin chuckled. "There are rules for the Ultimate Battle, and you must follow them, or you will surely fail."

"I know of only one rule—winner takes all." Rydor picked up his goblet and took a sip.

Shayla sighed. "The legend states that the wisdom of the ages will descend on the warrior who believes. Knowledge and love are the tools against evil, the catalyst that binds. The rules are none, the rules are all, but only the purest heart will find victory."

"Exactly, my dear, but do you know what that means?" Olin shook his head and patted Shayla's hand. "I will guide you."

"Will you return to my home with us?"

"No. You will remain here with Rydor until the battle is to begin."

"That's not possible, I must return to my people. My father..."

"Your father has no part in this. You must concentrate only on helping Rydor prepare."

Shayla was shaken by the seriousness in the old man's eyes."I don't understand."

Rydor crossed his arms over his chest. "Olin never speaks clearly."

"How are we to prepare if you don't tell us?" Shayla stood. "I cannot stay here."

"Do you want the Zared Tribe to win?"

"Of course, but..."

"Then you will become Rydor's Focus. Each of the three tribes have a Kiah Master, and each Kiah Master must have a Focus. The better the Focus, the better the warrior's ability." Olin took another drink.

Rydor groaned. "How does this work?"

"The two of you must learn to communicate on the psychic plane, the fourth dimension. Do not think for a moment that this battle will be a physical one." Olin chuckled. "I see doubt in both of you. Physical strength is necessary, but it is not the most important attribute."

"Olin, you're talking metaphysical mumbo-jumbo again, and I for one want to hear no more." Rydor turned and walked away.

Her eyes followed his proud, powerful form while he left the area. Where was he going? She turned back to Olin. "Why doesn't Rydor want to discuss this?"

"Rydor is a complex man."

"You seem to know him well." He nodded. "Please, explain to me how a battle can take place in the fourth dimension. I don't even know where that is."

"The fourth dimension is where our souls go when we die before moving on to other realms. It is where we go when we astral travel, a place where communication is free, the truth cannot be denied, and everyone conjures their own reality."

"Conjures their own reality? How is that possible?"

"Thoughts are things, and simply thinking something can make it real. For example, if you envision a large building, you will find a large building. If you imagine monsters, you will find them. Do you understand?"

Shayla suddenly felt a need to escape. Olin's philosophy was beyond her understanding. "Who are you?"

"Olin the Wizard."

"I've heard stories that wizards once existed, but I had no idea..."

"Forgive me, Princess, I have said too much. Just tell Rydor he is to practice his meditation and learn to connect with you the same as he does the animals."

"I don't think he will listen to anything I have to say." She saw a smile cross Olin's face an instant before he turned to a puff of smoke and disappeared into thin air.

"Olin?"

CHAPTER EIGHT

"You and Brina are doing well." Damek slapped Turic's back with his open palm as he passed his son. He seated himself on the large, throne-like chair in his private quarters. "By the time the battle arrives, your united strength should surpass the other two teams of Focuses and Masters by quite a margin."

"I heard through my sources that Ruler Sinead has chosen a Master named Mandel and his Focus is Akela." Turic crossed his booted feet on the edge of the low table and slouched lower on the couch. "I've instructed my spies to learn more about these two."

Damek ran his fingers through his hair. "And what of our sources in the Zared tribe? What have they learned?"

"Only that Nuri's daughter, Shayla, has left on a quest to find a worthy Master." Turic laughed. "Can you believe that no Zared warrior could pass the test?"

"We have nothing to fear from either of them. You and Brina have a strong bond." Damek ran his hands over the rich, upholstered arms of his chair with a big smile on his face. "You know how both tribes subscribe to the old dictates of not mating with a woman without the blessing of a legal union. And we both know how mating increases power between Master and Focus."

"We do." Turic massaged his temples."Father, I sense someone is touching a Kiah Rod. Who and where I don't know.

Damek scowled. "The headache is starting again?"

"Yes, but the sensation is stronger than in the past."

Damek looked at his son who appeared to have searing spikes were ripping through his head. He even doubled over while he gripped the sides of his head with his hands. "Don't tell me you're going weak on me."

"I've never felt this intensity before."

"You knew when Mandel took the test and passed. You've known every time Mandel and Akela have practiced."

Turic straightened. "This vibration is different. It's not coming from those two Quelan weaklings."

Damek hated to see the debilitating effects this had on his son, but it would be worth the pain when he gained total control of the planet. They would all be happier then. "Tell me what you see!"

"Fog, a mountain, a large man, a beautiful woman. It's not clear."

"Damn you! Try harder."

"The man has long dark hair, blue eyes. His soul is troubled, he has doubts. There are scars...wait...damn the Gods! It's..."

He watched his son fall to the floor reeling in pain, every muscle clenched. What was going through that boy's head? "Who do you see?"

"Rydor lives, and he's passed the test!"

Damek cursed long and hard and heard Turic do the same. Rydor was the only man who could ever threaten him. How could this be! He was so sure his son was dead! "Those fools! I'll kill every one of them myself!" Damek walked to where Turic grappled on the floor and kicked him in the ribs. "You will stop Rydor. I cannot believe those idiots didn't bury his miserable body in the Badlands where no one would find him. They will pay!"

Damek watched Turic take a deep breath and pull himself together. The grip on his mind had obviously loosened. He shook his head. "Call a council meeting immediately." Damek glared at his son. "I don't care what you have to do or how you accomplish it, but you will destroy Rydor. Do it now, or on sacred grounds. It matters not as long as the bastard is destroyed—forever!"

***

There was no response. Only a wizard could vanish like that, and know the things he knew. Olin's words left little to draw on except esoteric theories. Claustrophobia settled in, and she headed down the short hallway to the large opening. She leaned against the cold stone wall and took a deep breath while she sank to the ground. She clutched her knees to her chest and tipped her head down.

The scent of rain wafted on the cool afternoon breeze and caused the air to become heavy and overbearing. So much ran through her mind, especially thoughts of her father who would be sick with worry, but there was no way to send word. He trusted her, so did her people, and she prayed she would not let them down.

Footsteps echoed through the cave at a rapid pace. She looked up and gazed down the hall. Her heart raced when Rydor rushed in with a bow in one hand and a cutter in the other.

"I'm sorry, Princess D'Par, I never meant to leave you alone. I thought Olin was with you."

"He just left."

"I vowed to protect you." Rydor bowed his head.

Shayla laughed. "Has anyone ever climbed up the face of this cliff?"

"No human, but there have been creatures."

She had momentarily forgotten the threat of the mountain's wild inhabitants. "Why did you leave, Rydor?"

"Some things I cannot answer."

"You mean you won't answer." He walked to the opposite wall and leaned against the rocks. His heated gaze pierced her very soul. "I don't know how we're to work together when you won't even be honest with me."

"What did Olin say to you?"

"That I must serve as your Focus, and you must learn to connect with me like you do the animals, and work on your meditation." He shook his head and his grasp on the weapons tightened. His disgruntled frown set her teeth on edge. "Am I that distasteful to you?"

"It's not you, Princess, it's me, I'm a..."

"What?" She waited for his reply, but he remained silent. His long black hair, damp from the heavy mist, lay across his wide shoulders. He'd changed into a leather vest and pants, but he wore no shirt. His arm muscles flexed when he widened his stance. He filled the tan leather pants like no man she had ever seen. He looked like a warrior from head to toe, yet he did not appear to have the heart for battle.

His arms were badly scarred, and what little of his chest was visible above the front laces revealed similar marks. Someone, or something, did a thorough job on him. It was a wonder he survived such an attack. "Who are you, Rydor? What troubles your soul?" She watched his breathing quicken, and an angry flame sprang to life in his discerning gaze. He appeared to fight demons so horrifying he would never be free.

"My soul is not your concern." He sat on the floor and crossed his legs.

"If I'm to be your Focus I must know you as well as you know yourself." She stood, walked across the cold stone floor and knelt at his feet. "I beg you, confide in me. My people's lives are in your hands, and the very future of Zanthus."

"Why did you come? Why choose me? I have never done anything heroic. I'm not capable of such deeds."

Shayla laid her hands on his knees and he tensed. Why did her simple touch cause such a reaction? "Olin sent me up this God-forsaken mountain." Rydor squinted and his mouth formed a thin line. "He told me to come alone, but before I could question him he was gone. I didn't see him leave, and everyone thought I was crazy because they never saw him at all.

"He helped me through a fog that tried to consume me with its repugnant odor and cries of the damned. I survived swarms of insects that tried to eat me alive. It was as if someone placed an invisible, protective cocoon around me, and I was saved. Then there was the terrible winds that blew so hard I couldn't walk, and it howled until I thought my head would burst. Then suddenly it stopped."

"You nearly died by that stream."

"Olin didn't save me from that, you did." The hard look on his face softened, and she took a deep breath. "You saved me for a reason, Rydor."

"Una saved you."

"Una didn't carry me here, or keep me warm. Nor did Una undress me." She could swear he blushed, so she reached out with one hand and cupped his cheek. "Admit it, you care what happens."

Rydor dropped the cutter and placed his hand over hers. "I will not blame you if you search for another Kiah Master, one more worthy than I could ever be."

"Why do you doubt yourself?" The heat of his hand on hers quickened her pulse and made her stomach flutter. Why did she have such a compelling need to get closer, to know more? He opened his mouth to speak, but she silenced him with her fingers. "You do not owe me an explanation. Your past belongs to you. All I ask is that you trust me and follow Olin's instructions."

Shayla pulled her hand back and stood. "When do we begin?"

"Now."

Rydor shifted his position to face the opening and sat cross-legged. He rested his hands, palms up on his thighs. He closed his eyes, head erect, chin slightly up. His breathing became measured and controlled while he slipped into his own world. The change was remarkable. She had never seen him so relaxed and confident.

Before her sat a man who held the planet's future in his hands. It was difficult to trust Rydor, a man who claimed no tribe or family. What had he wanted to tell her? Maybe it was for the best he stopped, since she did not need any more reasons to worry. He had to be a first born son in order to possess the power over the Kiah.

Something moved behind her and she turned and sucked in a deep breath. It was Una. She just returned from her hunt and she licked her whiskers while she sauntered to Rydor's side to lie down. Rydor was so immersed in his own world he did not move a muscle when the animal joined him.

Una was beautiful, but it was difficult to accept such a giant cat that everyone claimed to be a killer. The man and his beast made quite a picture. They belonged together. Could Rydor be as close to her as he was to his pet? If what Olin said was true, she would have to win the warrior's confidence, and that was exactly what she planned to do.

***

Rydor tried to clear his mind. He never had trouble meditating before, but he was alone before. Shayla's presence was like the sun, warm and inviting, which made ignoring her difficult. If she would have come searching for a mate and a life of solitude, he would have been more than happy to comply. Shayla was the most beautiful and desirable woman he had ever seen. He almost laughed considering his contact with the outside world ended sixteen annual-cycles ago, but there was nothing wrong with his memory of what other women looked like, and none of them compared to Shayla.

Instead she came for a warrior. He agreed to take the test because Olin asked it of him, and he owed his life to the wizard. Shayla's plea for her people also affected his decision, along with the sadness in her big brown eyes. She was so unlike him, light where he was dark, and the difference went deeper than hair and skin. Her soul was light where his was black. It was the dichotomy that separated them and brought them together.

Shayla was loyal to her tribe, he claimed no allegiance. His family believed him dead, and it was for the best. However, his participation in the Ultimate Battle would expose him, and his existence would never again be the same. Even if he proved himself not to be the branded coward his tribe banished, he would never be accepted by his people, nor could he accept them. He was a man without a family, without a tribe, without an identity.

He felt Shayla's presence behind him. Revenge had consumed him even though he knew no good would come from a confrontation, yet the pain remained just under the surface of his visible scars. He disgraced his father and paid the price, now destiny demanded further payment. Did

Olin and Shayla realize what they asked?

If he opened his mind, she would learn of his physical desire for her and possibly his darkest secrets. He couldn't allow her access. She would think him weak to lust after her, a woman he didn't know. He felt her presence by him and it took great effort to keep his body from responding to her. He'd been alone too long and he had normal male desires. How would he ever be able to work closely with Shayla and keep himself under control?

After several deep breaths, a calm passed through him. He was strong enough to control his lust, but his burning need for revenge was another matter. The answers he sought would be sent to him from somewhere beyond. He needed guidance of the highest order to overcome recriminating thoughts. If he were to help her people, he had to quell all anger toward the Voltran Tribe. A warrior with a confused mind was useless. It would be difficult to fight against them after being trained for sixteen annual-cycles to fight for them.

Why did it have to be so complicated? He exhaled and cleared his mind. No higher council could penetrate as long as his mind ruled his instincts. He had to concentrate to hear the quiet, because it was out of the quiet that wisdom descended.

Receding footsteps allowed him to breathe easier. Shayla interfered with his meditation, but he instantly felt lonely. He could not push her image from his mind. Her beauty astounded him, her body excited him, and her intelligence intrigued him. Her perfect face floated in his mind's eye and he simply allowed her to be and focused on her innocence.

Visions formed behind her, and his brother and father invaded the serenity. Shayla's face contorted and her image began to fade. It was as if Damek and Turic robbed her of her life force. "Shayla!" He regretted saying her name out loud, but he could not help himself. They laughed while they inhaled her essence. He silently cried for Shayla. Turic was now a man with an evil black aura that matched his father's.

He heard the cheers of many voices he could not see, but he knew it was the collective voice of the tribe. His heart ached. They enjoyed the destructive evil Turic and Damek represented.

"Rydor?"

The sound of Shayla's voice pulled him from his vision. He opened his eyes, stood, then turned to face her. Long blond curls gently framed her worried face. He was beginning to understand what they were up against. "Sutae."

"You called my name. Is something wrong?"

Rydor reached out and ran his fingers down the silky strands of her hair. "It was nothing. I'm sorry to alarm you."

"You saw something in your meditation." She took his hand in hers. "Tell me Rydor, please. If we're to work as a team you must learn to share your feelings and thoughts."

"It's too soon."

"Come, I've fixed dinner."

She led him into the main chamber, her hand clasped around his. The warmth of her touch pushed away the ugly, icy premonitions of his vision. She was right, they would have to share, but he was not ready. Or was it because he did not know how? For sixteen long annual-cycles he had kept his emotions to himself. He did not even admit to Olin how he felt about his family and what they did to him. Although he had the distinct feeling that the wizard knew.

"Please, sit." Shayla sat across from Rydor and filled his plate with sliced cheese, bread and cooked vegetables. "What did you see that caused you to call my name?"

"I feared for your safety, that's all." He laid cheese on a piece of bread and took a bite. "Go no place without me." He studied her questioning gaze. "It is imperative, Sutae. You must promise."

"If it makes you feel better, I promise. But..."

"There are evil forces at work. Forces you don't understand."

"And you do?"

"I'm afraid I do."

Shayla shook her head. "Tell me what we're fighting against. As your Focus, I must know how to help you."

"Help me? I need no one's help."

"That's not true and you know it. Just because you've lived up here all alone is no reason to think you can stand alone. Olin explained..."

"Olin is not always right." Rydor rose from his chair and began to pace.

"Maybe I should call him and see what he thinks."

"No."

"Why are you being so stubborn?"

"I am not a Kiah Master."

Shayla stood and stepped in front of Rydor as he crossed the room. "You took the test. You turned the Kiah green. You have the power."

"I have nothing. And if you put your faith in me, you too will have nothing."

"You must not doubt yourself." Shayla took his hand, but he pulled away. "Why are you afraid of me?"

"You're a Princess. I have no right touching you."

"But I touched you." She picked up his hand. "There is nothing wrong with a simple touch."

Nothing about Shayla was simple, especially her touch. Only his mother had shown him tenderness, and he did not know what to make of Shayla's gestures. All he knew was the way she made him feel. She confused him since the main emotion in his life continued to be hate. "I know Zared customs and..."

"No Zared is here to judge or condemn." She smiled. "What would your tribe think?"

He felt his jaw tighten and his temples throb at the thought of where he came from. "You said it didn't matter."

"Not to me, but it matters to you."

"Nothing matters."

"Nothing? Surely you don't mean that."

Rydor saw tears well in her eyes. She tried to blink them back, but one escaped down her cheek. Instinctively he wiped it away with his finger. The last thing he'd intended to do was hurt her. How could he ever make her understand? "Please, do not cry."

More tears rolled down her face, and he noticed she was shaking. He touched her shoulder with his hand, and she pressed her body against his and sobbed. One arm slid down her back, his other hand threaded through her hair and he pulled her close to him. Her breasts heaved against his chest and her heart beat rapidly against his thin leather vest.

"What have I done?" He rubbed her back, but she suddenly pushed away and looked up at him. Her watery eyes pleaded for something he did not know how to give.

"I'm sorry. I didn't mean to cry. I'm usually strong." She pressed her forehead to his chest. "I haven't cried since I lost my mother five annual-cycles ago."

"You have a big responsibility. It's not easy being in a position of power."

Shayla looked up at Rydor. "I have no power, but the man I life-mate will. My tribe puts no faith in women. We aren't allowed to hold high positions."

"But they sent you to make the most important decision they've ever faced. Is that not faith?"

"The elders had no choice, it was written by our forefathers and dictated by the Gods." She wiped tears with the back of her hand.

"Then your Gods are smarter than I gave them credit for." He tilted her chin up with his finger. "You are brave and intelligent. I pray I won't let you down."

"How do you feel about all this?"

Rydor shook his head. "It's best if we don't discuss it."

"I need to understand you, including your fears, if I'm to be your

Focus. Olin said you had to concentrate, and you can't do that if you don't trust me or yourself."

"I trust you, Princess."

"Then trust yourself. Let me help you. Work with me. Don't shut me out. This is too important."

He released her and stepped back. "I understand the importance of your mission."

"Do you? Do you know the Voltrans have cut off not only our water supply, but the supply to the Quelan Tribe as well? They want to force our submission even before the battle. They want to control the entire planet, Rydor."

"The three tribes of Zanthus have survived separately for two hundred annual-cycles, each governing themselves."

Shayla sighed. "You have been on this mountain too long. The Voltrans have been causing trouble for over twelve annual-cycles, and it's getting worse. We can no longer trade with them, nor can the Quelans. Each tribe has something the other needs, but the Voltrans are determined to take everything. They want total dominance and will stop at nothing to get it."

"I didn't know the situation had gotten so bad." Thoughts of his father and brother in his vision passed through his mind, and he knew what it meant. Their evil had to be stopped. He could not imagine life on the small planet of Zanthus if the Voltrans ruled all. They had no regard for life. He had known it then, as he knew it now.

"Rydor? What are you thinking?"

"The Voltrans must be stopped."

Shayla laughed. "At least on that we agree." She stepped toward him. "Are you ready to fight?"

"You're a very persuasive woman, Princess Shayla D'Par."

She threw her arms around his neck and hugged him tight. Every muscle in his body tightened in response. Why did she have to touch him? Did she not recognize he was a man with desires of the flesh? It was torture to feel her against him, yet his arms circled her and held her tight. He should push her away, but every ounce of him begged for her, and he reveled in sweet anguish.

A quickening in his groin forced him to end the embrace. He walked back to the table and began to eat, suddenly starved for what he could never have.

CHAPTER NINE

Shayla returned to her seat and picked up a piece of bread. She worked hard to control her breathing since the feel of his body still affected her. Rydor was not a man a woman could ignore. A heated blush invaded her cheeks. She had never wanted to touch a man before, but Rydor had a charisma that begged her.

She felt foolish for crying, and even more foolish for throwing herself at him. It must be Olin's spells. How else could she explain her shameful behavior? "Tell me about Olin."

"He's a wizard. You've met him, what do you think?"

"I sense he's very fond of you. Like a father."

"Better than a father, Olin doesn't judge."

"I see what you mean." Was he saying his father was judgmental? Or was she looking too hard for clues to his family and a past he wanted to hide? At this rate she would never learn much about her Kiah Master.

"Olin can be frustrating at times. He talks in circles."

Rydor's head turned toward the hall, and she glanced in that direction to see Una strut in and flop down at his feet. "Una is devoted to you."

"Una is a free spirit. She does as she pleases."

Rydor reached down and scratched Una behind her ear and Shayla smiled. The cat began to purr and tilt her head as if asking for more. "How long have you been living here, with Una, and Olin popping in and out?"

Rydor grinned. "Sixteen annual-cycles."

"That's a long time." The burning question remained; why would a man choose to live in such isolation? He wanted her to believe he enjoyed the serenity, but she had seen the haunting anguish in his eyes.

"At least you have Olin."

A puff of smoke appeared in the empty chair. "Did I hear my name?"

"You did. Join us." Rydor poured his mentor a glass of wine.

Olin took a long drink. "I see you two are getting along better."

Rydor cleared his throat. "To what do we owe this visit?"

"I wanted to tell Shayla that her father has received word she has found a Kiah Master and that she is well."

"Thank you, Olin." Shayla let out the breath she'd been holding. "Is my father well? How are my people?"

"Your father is worried, but fine. Your people are anxious and scared." Olin set his glass down. "There is nothing I can do to alleviate the situation. Only you and Rydor can accomplish that."

"Did you see my father?"

"I delivered a message to your bodyguards, who took it to your father."

"I can't thank you enough. I was concerned for Arden and Rance's safety. Last I saw them they were engaged in battle."

"With who?" Rydor pushed his plate away and glared at Olin. "What do you know of this?"

Olin took a deep breath. "Shayla, do you remember the three warriors who attacked you in the desert?" He watched her nod. "They followed you. They wanted the Kiah Rod for themselves."

"What did they hope to gain? They took the test and had no powers."

"Credits my dear. They knew your tribe would pay any price to get the Kiah back."

"One of them broke the rod, but it was the tall, white haired warrior who tried to rape me." Rydor slammed his fist on the table, and she wished she had omitted their failed attempt to violate her. The look on Rydor's face frightened her. His eyes turned dark and wild which sent shivers up her spine. She had seen many emotions come and go, but this was the first time he looked violent enough to fight. He rose to his feet, both hands fisted, biceps bulged and forearms strained.

"Easy, my boy. Shayla wasn't harmed." Olin took another drink.

"Rydor, please, sit down." Shayla put her hand on his arm. "It's over, and I'm fine. I shouldn't have said anything." She watched him sit, but his guard was up and he refused to relax.

"What kind of a world is this, where a man attacks a woman?"

"I'm afraid I haven't prepared you very well, my son." Olin removed his floppy hat and set it on the floor. "I should have told you about the violence and evil, but I'd hoped it wouldn't be necessary."

"How long has this been going on?" Rydor shook his head. "I don't remember men like these when I lived..."

"Let me explain. Two annual-cycles after you arrived here, the Voltrans began sending warriors into the countryside to stir up trouble. They killed and robbed travelers, both men and women. I know when you were a boy there was very little crime, and offenders were dealt with swiftly and severely. The Badlands were originally named for the desolate lay of the land. Now it stands for the criminal element that calls that region home."

She had forgotten how many changes Zanthus had seen over the years. "Rydor, they will not stop unless we stop them."

"Forgive me for protecting you, my boy." Olin set his glass on the table. "Now you see the necessity of fighting."

Rydor raked his fingers through his hair. "Why must violence be used to stop violence?"

"It doesn't. The Ultimate Battle was devised to alleviate an all out war where thousands of lives would be lost. Is it not better for a few lives to be lost than thousands?"

"Three Kiah Masters, one victor." Rydor crossed his arms over his chest.

"And three Focuses." Olin grinned. "Do not underestimate the role of the Focus. They will fight their own battle while supporting their Master."

"How dangerous is that?" Rydor's gaze turned to Shayla.

Shayla smiled at Rydor, his concern touching, but misplaced. "I will do whatever is necessary to save my people."

"Good." Olin cleared his throat. "What about you, Rydor? Have you decided to cooperate fully and completely?"

"Yes."

"Good, good. But you cannot hold back from Shayla. She must know you to help you."

Rydor scowled at Olin. First he was a man with little emotion, now he could barely control his anger, but she knew in her heart, he would protect her with his life. She smiled at Rydor. "Why don't you talk with Olin while I clean up."

Rydor rose and started toward the hall that led to the opening. "Come, Una."

Shayla laughed when the oversized cat rolled on her back, front paws bent, looking like a helpless kitten with no intention of going anywhere. "We'll be fine, won't we Una?" She bent and patted the animal's powerful chest, laughing at Rydor as he walked away shaking his head, mumbling something about loyalty.

***

Olin conjured two chairs, sat, then patted the one next to him. "Sit, my boy."

"You created very soft chairs." Rydor ran his hands over the cushioned, upholstered fabric.

"I'll leave them for you and Shayla. You will have much to discuss, and I know this is your favorite place, especially at sunset."

"It is, but that's not why we're here. Tell me what I'm to do."

"You must open your mind and heart to Shayla. A bond between you is imperative and cannot be broken. Your spirits need to join if you intend to defeat the enemy."

"How can I do that and keep my secret?"

"I'm not sure you can. However, if you place that secret behind a door and lock it, she will not be able to look behind that door. But I warn you, that can be dangerous."

"Why?"

"Your enemy will use your weakness against you. He will reveal all, tell all, lie, anything to break your resolve and your Focus." Olin shook his head. "Don't look at me like that. Yes, I said break your Focus, and I mean that literally."

"I will not let that happen."

"Your desire to protect Shayla is honorable, but to do so requires far more than a desire. You know Turic and what he's capable of. And if you don't prepare Shayla for what she might hear, you weaken her ability as your Focus. For if she falters during the battle, Brina will destroy her."

"Brina is Turic's Focus?"

"You're surprised?

Rydor shook his head.

"I know you have a history with her, which is why Shayla must know about your past. Brina will tell Shayla what you refuse to, and more. She'll say anything to confuse and cause doubt in Shayla's mind and heart. You absolutely cannot afford that. Brina is a very convincing woman."

"As I well know." Brina's betrayal was fresh in his memory. It felt like last sun-cycle. She was the only woman he had ever been with. He was young and stupid, he thought she truly wanted him, but it had been nothing but an emotionless, drug-induced mating. "I will consider confiding in Shayla."

"Don't wait too long, my son."

A lifetime would not be long enough. How could he possibly share his humiliation with Shayla? His entire past was as repugnant as fighting his own brother in the impending battle. The thought of harm coming to Shayla boiled his blood. He never finished his warrior's training, but he needed to pull from the limited knowledge he had. "Tell me, Olin, why does my brother have such strong powers? I was always told the powers belonged to the first born male of a family."

"The rules are none, the rules are all."

"Don't give me that! There must be an explanation, and I want it."

"Some things must be accepted on faith."

"Then my faith is not as strong as it should be."

"Another facet of your training that requires work." Olin chuckled. "Can we move on?"

"Fine. How does this battle work? Do we use the Kiah as swords?"

Olin laughed. "Definitely not swords!"

"Then what is the purpose of the crystal rod?"

"It channels energy, both good and evil. It magnifies vibrations and enhances powers."

"If I'm a coward, I will become a bigger coward?" Rydor laughed. "So the Gods do have a sense of humor."

"Definitely, and don't forget that. You'll need to master every emotion known to man and God, if you're to win."

"That may be, but I am starting out handicapped, or have you forgotten I have been presented with a broken rod?"

Olin patted Rydor on the shoulder. "You will mend the rod and restore your power. Don't look at me like that. As I've told you many times, anything is possible."

"When will I perform this...miracle?"

"When the time is right, not before."

Rydor grinned. "You put my mind at ease when you're so specific."

Olin grinned."I thought as much."

He laughed along with Olin. Although he wanted to know more, he trusted Olin's wisdom concerning such matters. Olin had yet to be wrong, but the wizard demanded blind faith and that was difficult to fathom. "I've had a disturbing vision. Damek and Turic tried to steal Shayla's essence, and they appeared to succeed. Voices cheered at their evil."

"Heed the warning. Power is not a gift only to the worthy. The test of the Kiah was not to determine if you had honorable powers, only if you had power. Evil is a viable power and very real."

"I will be fighting my brother."

"And all he stands for. Are you ready to face what that means?"

"How long do I have to prepare?"

"Forty sun-cycles."

Rydor closed his eyes and visualized his brother. They resembled each other and shared the same blood, but that was where the similarities ended. "Do I have to kill Turic?"

"Only your soul can dictate your deeds."

"Why is this battle so important to you? You're a wizard, nothing can hurt you, you have your own powers."

"That's true, but I can do no good in a world full of evil. If people's souls are possessed by the dark forces, they cannot hear me or see me. What kind of an existence would that be? For them, or for me? No, my boy, our only hope is victory."

"Why can't you be my Focus?"

Olin chuckled.

"It is written the rules are none, the rules are all. Therefore, you could stand by me."

"I will be present, but I can do nothing. It's up to you and Shayla, for reasons you will learn."

"Why did she have to choose a branded coward? I refused to kill an old man to become a warrior. What if I can't..."

Olin held up his hand. "Do not judge yourself so harshly."

"You know what they did to me." Rydor ripped open his vest and exposed his scarred chest. "This is the mark of a coward."

"Only to unenlightened people." Olin stood. "Hear me, Rydor. You know it took more courage to stand up for what you believe than to senselessly kill an old man. We have never discussed this before because I wanted you to accept your choice, and in the process accept who you are."

"I wish I could." Rydor studied the brilliant red and gold of the sunset. If only Zanthus were as peaceful as the sky. He would fight Turic, but what price must he pay? Could he take his brother's life? He wished he had no powers, that Shayla had never come, and he never had to face his past again.

That was not exactly true. He could never really live until he resolved his past, and Shayla was the only light he had seen in his life of darkness. He would face his brother and father. He would lay his life down for Shayla, a woman he would always want, but could never have.

Rydor sensed Shayla's strong presence enter the chamber. Her vibratory level was high, and he would recognize her scent anywhere, sweet and stimulating. How could he focus with her by his side when she commanded his attention to the point of distraction?

"I'm sorry, I didn't mean to interrupt." Shayla turned to leave.

"No, my dear," Olin said as he stood. "Please, take my seat. It's time for me to go."

In an instant Olin was gone, and Rydor found Shayla taking the seat next to him. The thin fabric of her tunic brushed his arm when she sat. His jaw clenched along with every muscle is his body. If Shayla could read his mind she would run far and fast. He respected her position as Princess, respected her as a woman, but it did not stop him from wanting her in a most carnal way.

"Did Olin clear things up?" she asked, crossing her legs and clasping her hands in her lap.

"He warned me of the danger to you as my Focus."

"I'm not afraid, Rydor. I may be a woman, but I'm very capable. It's a risk I'm more than willing to take. Surely you can understand."

"No, I don't. You're a Princess, you must be protected, not put in danger!" He wished he hadn't sounded so angry, but he was. Women had no place in battle, especially not one as fragile and beautiful as Shayla.

"You are a warrior, Rydor, and in a sense I am too. My duty is to my people, no matter what the gamble to my personal safety." She turned to face him. "I will be at your side, and we will not discuss the issue any further."

He bit back a heated reply and whispered, "As you wish, Princess D'Par." Regardless of his fears, she was royalty, and he pledged his services to her. "I have never gone against my word, nor will I."

Shayla nodded several times. "Why do you live here?" Her hands fidgeted in her lap. "What are you hiding from?"

The woman was persistent and he could not hide from her beautiful brown eyes. She carefully assessed him and her eyes were filled with doubt. "I agreed to help you. I did not agree to reveal my past."

She smiled. "As you wish, Kiah Master."

"Do not call me that!"

"Why? It's an honor bestowed by the Gods." She looked into his eyes. "And by me."

"It's a curse." Rydor stood and marched out of the chamber. He should not be so touchy about his past, but to him the subject was closed. Olin might say they needed to know each other, to bond as one, but there had to be a way around that. He well knew they could not completely bond without revealing their darkest secrets, and he had been no help at all.

While he walked down the hall he thought just how sullen and stubborn he acted. Attitude aside, he never should have treated the princess like that. She did not deserve his nasty attitude. Far more important issues were on the line than his past. His father was evil, no doubt, and had to be stopped. Personal feelings aside, he had to fight for the good of the people of Zanthus. Although his personal revenge might well be satisfied in the process.

CHAPTER TEN

Rydor sat under the luna tree next to the hidden entrance, the full moon bathing the meadow in subdued light. He closed his eyes and controlled his breathing, but he could not shake the sinister impressions in his mind. The only way he could discover the source of his discontent was to meditate. He forced Shayla, Olin and all other thoughts from his mind and waited. Slowly colors formed, danced and grew brighter. Then a cloud descended and Turic's face replaced the peaceful scene. Turic stared at something, or someone with a furrowed brow and a lustful expression on his face.

What Turic saw remained blurry, but it appeared to be someone in a bed. It was difficult to focus through the foggy vision. He concentrated and willed the clouds to lift so he could see who Turic focused on. When things became clearer he panicked. It was Shayla! He had to get to her before Turic did something terrible. What the evil man could do in a vision he was not sure, but whatever it was could be lethal.

He stood and made his way back into the cave, through the winding corridor to his sleeping alcove. The instant he stepped in the chamber a malevolent force tried to overtake him. He closed his eyes and focused on his brother. The only way to help Shayla would be to face his foe. Then he heard Shayla silently screaming his name. He sent her a mental message to stay calm and let him handle the situation.

In the torchlight he saw Turic's dark shadow hovering over Shayla, holding her in place. "Get up, Shayla, now." He reached for her, but a cold, invisible force prevented him from touching her. Una's claws slashed through the air and her growl deepened. "Shayla, answer me!"

A searing pain shot through his mind and he heard the word "coward" spoken clearly. "Turic! Leave now!"

"Still the coward, still running, but you can't run from me. I will have your head and her body!"

"No!" Rydor reached for Shayla again. This time he used his mind to form a pathway through the icy wall. He pushed forward until he reached Shayla and lifted her into his arms. The moment he cradled her to his chest the cloud disappeared, and his brother's evil presence vanished.

"Rydor?" Shayla mumbled weakly. "What, or who was that?"

"Shhh. It was nothing." She clung to him tightly. It was a strange sensation being viewed as a protector. He wished he deserved her appraisal. He had already failed her too many times, but it would be the last.

"Don't treat me like a child. I felt his evil. I saw him and he looked like you."

"I would never hurt you, Sutae."

"Shutting me out *is* hurting me."

Shayla's warm, tempting body trembled in his arms. The depths of her eyes searched his face. He did not want to lie to her, yet he was not ready to explain his family. If he told her he was the son of the most hated man on the planet, she would never trust him again.

"Rydor, I must tell you something." Shayla pulled back and sat up on the bed. "Sleep evaded me, so I just tossed and turned, trying to get comfortable. Then all of a sudden Una let out a loud, deep growl that actually shook the pallet. I sat up and looked around. The torch light made weird, eerie shadows on the walls, which kind of scared me. But then I felt a strange tickle in my mind, then a malevolent presence seemed to consume me."

He took her hand in his and felt her entire body shake. She was truly scared, and he could not blame her. Turic had that effect on nearly everyone. "It's okay, Sutae. Take your time. I'm right here."

Shayla nodded. "Then at the foot of the bed there was a fuzzy outline of a man that began to form. My first thought was Olin, but it felt evil, so it could not be Olin." She looked into Rydor's eyes. "I hate to say this, but as the vision cleared that shape began to look like you. He had long, dark hair that laid on his shoulders, but his eyes glowed with evil. He just stood there, then he reached out and grabbed my arm. I was horrified." She covered her mouth with her hand for a moment. "That's when I screamed your name."

"My sweet Sutae, I am so sorry you had to go through that." Gently he guided her to lie flat on the pallet and pulled up the fur blanket. Her flawless beauty shone like a beacon. He wanted to touch her face, kiss her lips, bury himself in her softness. Instead he reluctantly pulled away.

He could bring her nothing but unhappiness and heartache.

Shayla grabbed his arm. "Don't leave me."

The terror in her eyes was as real as his desire. He did not trust himself to be so close, not this moon-cycle. Every masculine instinct said to pull her close and never let go. "It isn't proper for me to stay with you."

"And who is here to tell us no?" Shayla ran her fingers through the length of hair that hung over his shoulder. "I'm not asking you to do anything improper, just hold me till I fall asleep."

"I cannot deny your request, Princess." Rydor laid down beside her and held out his arm. She snuggled close and rested her head on his shoulder. His arm wrapped around her, and she laid her arm across his chest. Her breasts pressed into his ribs and with each breath she took he felt their firmness tighter against him. Of course he wanted to protect her, but how could he stop the hunger that welled inside and begged for release? He had lived sixteen annual-cycles without a woman, never knowing how badly he wanted one. Not just any woman, he wanted the beautiful Princess D'Par.

***

A heavy weight pressed on Shayla's back and she opened her eyes, fearing the terrible evil she felt before. Instead she found Una's paw on her, then felt the roughness of her tongue on her neck. She smiled. Una no longer scared her, in fact she had a true fondness for the cat.

Rydor lay beside her, eyes closed, breathing even. He was still asleep, but his grip on her remained tight, as though he were afraid to let her go. She tried to sit, but he pulled her back.

"Going somewhere?"

"I thought you were asleep."

"You thought wrong."

"Una wants us to get up." She barely got the words out when Una bounded over her and landed with a thud on Rydor's chest." Does Una always wake you like this?"

Rydor groaned and opened his eyes. "Usually. She likes to test my alertness."

"Look," Shayla pointed to a puff of smoke that began to take human form at the foot of the pallet. Her first instinct was panic after last moon-cycle's visitor, but this cloud seemed friendly.

"I'm glad to see you two getting along so well."

Shayla smiled. "Good sun-cycle, Olin."

Rydor quickly rose to his feet and cleared his throat. "It was necessary to protect the Princess. An evil entity threatened her last moon-cycle."

Olin nodded. "That's why I've come. We must take action before it's too late."

"Let's talk over breakfast." Rydor rolled off the pallet and walked toward the bedchamber entry. "I'm suddenly famished."

"Come, my child." Olin offered Shayla his hand.

He helped her to her feet and walked her to the dining table where she took a seat across from Rydor's usual place. Olin sat at the head of the table like royalty, a serious look on his face.

They had slept in their clothes, but that did not stop her cheeks from burning. Never had she spent the moon-cycle in a man's arms, but she had to admit it felt good. Her father and the elders would have a stroke and lay heavy punishment on her; but they were not here, and for that she was grateful.

Rydor placed three cups of tea on the table and settled into his chair. He looked more somber than she had ever seen him, if that were possible. She took a sip and watched both men exchange strange looks. They spoke without words, and that annoyed her. She hated secrets. "If you two have something to say, say it."

Olin ran his finger around the rim of the cup. "Last moon-cycle you met the enemy, and he is getting stronger by the sun-cycle." He looked into Rydor's eyes. "I saw him with his Focus. She is a woman to fear."

Rydor nodded. "Brina."

Shayla saw a spark of recognition in Rydor's blue eyes. How did he know this woman? Maybe he knew her by reputation, but he definitely knew who Olin was talking about. "Why is she so dangerous, Olin?"

"The woman is as evil as Turic Celon, Kiah Master for the Voltran Tribe. They have bonded in the most important way."

"How is that?" Shayla immediately regretted the question when Rydor raised an eyebrow and rolled his eyes. Olin simply smiled.

"They have mated."

Rydor stood. "You don't expect Shayla to mate with me, do you?"

Rydor's question caused her heart to race. The thought was not unpleasant. In all honesty she was more attracted to Rydor than she should be, but it was forbidden for her to mate with anyone other than her life-mate, and that would most likely be Eaton. She already decided not to let anything stand in the way of Zared victory, but she never considered what Olin proposed.

"I expect nothing. The two of you will decide what needs to be done to win the Ultimate Battle. However, you must become much closer than you are if you're to defeat Brina and Turic."

"We have time." Rydor returned to his seat.

"You have only three sun-cycles left before you leave."

"There are thirty-eight sun-cycles before the battle. Why so soon?" Rydor poured more tea.

Shayla heard reluctance in Rydor's voice. She knew he loved his solitary life on Spirit Mountain, but he seemed extremely hesitant to leave. His home would still be here when he returned, especially with Olin's protective spells in place. "Olin, how will we know when we've become closer?"

Olin smiled. "You will feel yourself melding with Rydor, thinking like Rydor, sensing his feelings, knowing his desires, as he will know yours."

That thought terrified her. It was one thing to long for him, it was another for him to know about her lustful thoughts. She lowered her head. They did not have to be bonded for her to know his gaze was fixed on her.

"Turic and Brina's strength grows with each bonding. They are of like mind, and want the same thing. But that should be no surprise."

She looked up at Rydor who appeared to be well acquainted with Turic and Brina. He offered no explanation for his familiarity, which confirmed the tribe of his birth. "You're Voltran, aren't you?"

"I told you," Rydor said loudly. "I claim allegiance to no tribe."

She had suspected all along. He had the characteristic dark hair and bronze skin of the Voltrans. Some Quelan and Zared men also had the dark look, but there was a proud air that surrounded Voltrans, and Rydor certainly carried that arrogance, even though he tried to hide it.

"I will return in three sun-cycles to check your progress. And I expect progress, Rydor. Promise me."

"I promise, but..."

Olin disappeared in his usual puff of smoke and Rydor looked like he had just lost his best friend. Maybe he had. Obviously Olin had never asked Rydor to do anything against his will, and she had the feeling this was a bigger test than she imagined. Rydor would soon have to face whatever he was hiding from.

"Where shall we begin?" Rydor stared at her as if he had no idea what she was talking about. He was being difficult, and she was not in the mood. "You know what I mean. Don't play stupid."

"I would not do that."

"I want to know what you will do." He shook his head at her. In his own way he was saying he did not want to talk. He was good at that. How could she reach him? If he did not want to share, he would remain silent the way he was right now. The man had to have a trigger, something to make him talk. At some point he had to open up, or they would lose the battle.

"Come, we will meditate."

CHAPTER ELEVEN

Hours passed while they sat cross-legged, face to face in the opening of the cave. How could he concentrate with Shayla so close? Maybe Olin was right. If they mated, it would clear the air of all the sexual tension between them. He opened his eyes to find her staring at him. Did she desire him, or was he just the warrior she felt obligated to sleep with to win her cause? If the beautiful princess wanted to mate with him, it had to be for Rydor the man not some misconstrued sense of duty. "Go get the Kiah Rods."

Silently she rose and walked into the chamber. He took a deep breath. Emotions rushed his mind. The thoughts were not precise, but the meanings were clear. They were Shayla's thoughts, and fear was the primary force. He concentrated and sent her a calming message, shocked when he heard her mental reply, "It won't help."

"Indeed." His gaze fell on the passageway the moment she entered with the leather case in hand and a serious look on her face. She resumed her cross-legged position and held the Kiah toward him. He accepted the case and smiled. "You heard me."

"Of course I heard you. But if you think words will ease my worry, you're wrong. You can tell me over and over, but until you get serious about this training and do like Olin says, I won't rest."

"I sent the message to your mind and you heard me." Anger turned to joy in her beautiful brown eyes. He wished that joy was for him, however her only concern was making him into a Zared Kiah Master. It was for the best. Shayla could never love a Voltran coward.

"What does this mean?" Shayla clasped her hands in her lap and sighed.

"We have the ability to communicate telepathically." Rydor opened the case and took out both pieces of the rod with his right hand and grasped them firmly. The cold crystal began to warm and black lightened to a deep emerald.

"You changed the color again."

Her amazed expression held an innocent sense of wonder. He wished she knew more about the crystal than he did. He stared intently at the rods. Deep shades of green began to pale, and the slight warmth of a moment ago became warmer against the palm of his hand. "Take the rod."

Shayla grasped both pieces and instantly dropped them on the blanket. "They burned me!"

Rydor took her hands in his and examined her palms. Red marks formed where the rod had touched her skin. "I'm sorry. They were only warm to me. I thought you should feel the sensation. I never meant to…"

She smiled. "It's all right. I'm glad you showed me. Now we both know you can wield the power of the Kiah."

He stood and paced. Doubts ran through his mind so fast it was impossible to sort them. Shayla had no idea he would be fighting his brother, and she would be fighting the woman who seduced him as a young, naive warrior. How could he tell her and destroy what faith she had in him? She believed he could save her people, and for both of their sakes he would try.

"Rydor? You're pulling away again." Shayla stood and stepped in front of him. "Every time we make one ounce of progress, you stop. Now, let's start again. Please."

The Princess was right. He could no longer run from her or his obligation. Savior of the planet was not a title he wanted, but that was what Shayla needed. He returned to his place on the quilt. It was time to get serious and take their relationship to a higher level.

"Tell me about your people. Tell me everything that has happened on Zanthus the past sixteen annual-cycles. I must be prepared."

"That's a tall order, and I'm far from an historian." She met his gaze. "All right. Where do you want me to start?"

"What caused the Voltrans to initiate the Ultimate Battle?"

"Greed. Their ruler, Damek Celon, and his son, Turic, began making raids on us and the Quelans. They've engaged in subversive tactics. Poisoning water supplies, jamming communications, destroying power centers, and committing acts of terrorism as warnings to cooperate. They've murdered and raped." Shayla took a deep breath. "Ask me what they haven't done, the list would be shorter."

"I see." He knew all too well what the Voltrans' capabilities were, and how far they would go to gain control. No one knew Damek's mind like he did. He had seen his father's diabolical side many times, and it was not a pretty picture. The man was maniacal with no heart or soul.

"Do you? I doubt that. Until you've seen the human suffering the man has caused you won't know. You've been on this mountain, protected from the insanity of the real world."

"I have lived in the real world, which is why I prefer my mountain."

"Well life here hasn't prepared you for what's to come."

"You doubt my abilities?" This was the moment he'd anticipated. Somehow he knew she would see through him, to his soul where all his indiscretions resided.

"No, of course not."

"Now is the time to take your Kiah rods and find another Master, one more suited to your needs." Her hands found his and a warmth greater than the rods crept through him, and a desire too strong to deny. "You owe it to your people to bring them the best warrior."

"And I plan to do just that. You are my choice, unless of course you..."

"I gave my word. I'm only offering you a chance to change your mind." He tried to pull his hands from hers, but she held fast.

"I have made my choice." Shayla released her hold. "We will not discuss this matter again. Agreed?"

Rydor nodded. She was one stubborn woman. He had given her every opportunity to take her rods and select a more qualified Master to fight her battle. Part of him wanted her to leave, and part of him wanted her. If she left, he would have to return to life as it was before she entered his solitary kingdom. In the short time since she arrived he had grown accustomed to her. Without her, there would be no smile to brighten the darkness of his existence. "We have much work to do before Olin returns."

"I don't know Olin like you do, but I'd hate to see him mad. He could turn us into animals or something." Shayla laughed. "What does a wizard do when he's really angry?"

Rydor smiled. "Let's just say an animal would be the best you could hope for." He watched her dark eyes sparkle with laughter in the morning sun while the urge to kiss her grew stronger. It may not be a good idea, but the burning need to feel her lips against his nearly overpowered him.

"Do it," she whispered.

"What, Sutae?"

"For such an astute warrior you're...you're..." Shayla leaned forward and pressed her lips to his.

She threaded her arms around his neck. His heart pounded, his groin tightened. Her lips felt softer than flower petals when he gently brushed them with his. Kiss me, Rydor. He heard her plea as clearly as if she had yelled it through the entire valley. His tongue found hers and she slowly moved closer until her firm breasts rested hot against his chest.

Shayla's embrace brought back a memory he'd locked away, one he never wanted to remember, but the feelings she stirred were not familiar. Brina may have seduced him, but he had felt nothing, even under the spell of the aphrodisiac. He performed, nothing more. This was different. Every muscle in his body tightened and anticipation danced in his stomach.

He pulled her onto his lap and threaded his fingers through her silken hair, then down her back while he held her tight against him. This princess may be forbidden to him, but he did not want to stop. She made him feel worthy. With Shayla in his arms, he did not question his courage, his manhood, or his reason for living.

He deepened the kiss and searched every crevice and tasted her honey sweetness. Her breathing quickened along with his and her fingers twined in his hair. He needed her, by the Gods, he needed her. His hands found her forearms and he eased her back. He had to separate from her or her maidenhood would be gone.

She did not meet his gaze, and he wondered if he scared or embarrassed her? Olin suggested mating would strengthen their bond, but he could not take the risk. A Zared Princess and a Voltran outcast was an unacceptable relationship to both tribes. Not that he cared what his people thought, but Shayla held a royal position of honor. He would do nothing to shame her or her family's name, even though his body ached with longing, and his heart cried for fulfillment.

***

The sun-cycle flew by and Shayla was exhausted. She never knew meditation took so much energy. Or was it Rydor who drained her power? She laughed to herself while she finished setting the table for the evening meal. If anyone had told her she had special powers, she would have called them insane. She had learned to hear Rydor's voice as clearly in her mind as if he spoke aloud.

Heat filled her cheeks just thinking about the kiss they shared. She never felt anything so passionate or exciting. Rydor tempted her in ways Eaton never had and never could. She had tried to make herself feel emotion for Eaton, but it never happened. It was hard to understand how she could have worked so hard and failed with Eaton, when it took no effort at all to burn with desire for Rydor, a man she barely knew.

What bothered her was that Rydor started to know what she was privately thinking, not just messages she meant to send. In fact, the first thing he responded to was her thought of "Kiss me." Of all the messages he could read it had to be that one! She should have been embarrassed, but at that moment it was exactly what she wanted. Her father would be appalled, and Eaton would challenge Rydor in the warrior's ring. Eaton would be entitled if he knew Rydor had kissed her. Men's egos were too fragile, and the barbaric way they preferred to settle disputes was primitive at best.

Knowing Rydor could read her thoughts was disturbing, but she had read his as well. This new ability might help her learn his secrets. They had talked about the progress on Zanthus over the years, and she told him about her people, yet he told her nothing about his past. He remained the dark warrior who called himself Rydor.

He claimed no family name or tribe. It seemed he wanted her to believe he was born on this mountain, although she knew he had been raised a Voltran. It would take a lot of explaining to the council to justify why she chose a Voltran to fight for the Zared Tribe. The council would have to accept him since they were the ones who put the decision in her hands.

Una bounded into the main living area, a strange fuzzy creature clasped in her powerful jaws. Shayla opened her mouth to yell at the mountain cat when Rydor strode in with a skinned animal in hand. She pointed at Una. "I will not have her eating that...that thing in here."

Rydor grinned. "Una, out."

The lanky cat rose, growled, then walked down the passageway toward the only useable exit. "Thank you." Shayla stared at the bloody-looking prey Rydor held with pride. "And what am I supposed to do with that?"

"Nothing. I will cure the meat."

"Cure it?" He gave her a look she was learning to hate. It was the expression he assumed every time he did not want to explain things to her.

"Do your people not cure meat?"

"We have coolers, butchers and chefs. I really don't know what they do to meat. I prefer not to eat much meat." He narrowed his eyes and let out a long, exasperated breath as he passed in front of her. "It's just that I don't like the thought of an animal sacrificing his life for my dinner."

She wrinkled her nose while he poured some kind of oily herb mixture over the carcass and rubbed it in with his hands. Then he tied all the legs together with a crude rope and turned to leave. She followed him down a passageway she was not familiar with. "Where are you going?"

"You ask too many questions."

She cursed under her breath while they walked down the passageway, the sound of her boot heels echoing off the gray rock walls. Rydor's animal skin footwear traversed without a sound, and his long strides put more distance between them than she felt comfortable with in the near darkness. She was out of her element here, but she refused to show fear.

Abruptly he disappeared to the right. Her steps slowed and the oppressive silence closed in on her. She glanced at the natural curved ceiling Mother Nature provided, barely able to discern the shape of the rocks high above. Something flew at her head and brushed her hair. She screamed and covered her eyes.

Before she finished the second scream, two strong arms circled her body, her face pressed against the soft leather of Rydor's tunic. "I'm sorry." She fought back tears.

"It is I who owe you an apology, Princess."

Her head tilted back, but he held her as if she were a piece of broken china. A shiver coursed up her spine and she trembled. He smiled that familiar, knowing smile she found attractive, yet frustrating. She felt silly and began to giggle.

"I vowed never to let you out of my sight. I failed you." Rydor shook his head. "Are you all right?"

She could not stop laughing.

"Shayla?"

His concern touched her, but for some reason her laughter would not subside. Her stomach hurt and tears rolled down her cheeks. Never had she felt so giddy, even as a child. The walls spun, Rydor's face blurred, and darkness swept her away.

CHAPTER TWELVE

Rydor cradled Shayla's limp body in his arms, his heart pounding. He carried her back to his pallet and laid her on the fur coverlet. He knew it would happen, but there was no reason to alarm her. She would have thought him sick if he had run around asking her how she felt all the time. The altitude of Spirit Mountain caused temporary delirium. He suffered it himself a few sun-cycles after he arrived here. It took from one to four sun-cycles at the peak, and this was sun-cycle four. He was surprised it took Shayla this long to succumb.

In her present state she could wander off into the wilds of the unforgiving mountain. The dangers were too numerous to even think about. He had to stay beside her until she recovered. If Olin had not nurtured him during his ordeal, he would not be alive. He and Olin spent many moon-cycles laughing about his bout with delirium. Some of the things he said and did were hysterical. There were also rampant emotions and hatreds that erupted that nearly destroyed him.

It would not be easy keeping Shayla under control. The moment she woke she would have renewed vigor, and if she reacted like he had, she would return to her childhood and experience fantasies and fears beyond imagination. He would learn things about her she never wanted anyone to know, which was a burden he had to bear in silence.

"Where's my father?"

"He's not here right now." Her eyes sparkled with the exuberance of a little girl, and her voice reflected a childish tone.

"Who are you? I haven't seen you before." She giggled. "Want to play a game?"

"It's time for your nap." The distress would pass easier if he could get her to sleep. She laid back and closed her eyes, her long lashes still damp from tears. A healthy blush invaded the fair skin of her cheeks while she lay still, but her rapid breathing drew his attention since it caused her breasts to rise and fall seductively. She was far from a child.

A smile creased the corners of her mouth, and he listened while she mumbled, "I want to play a game." When she opened her eyes, they were full of impish mischief. He sat next to her on the bed and touched the back of her hand. Before he could take his next breath she quickly rose and jumped on his lap. Her arms wrapped around his neck, her pert little nose buried in his cheek.

Then he heard her in his mind. Confused messages, childish thoughts mingled with womanly desires. Then she sent mental pictures. He saw her playing with a pet of some kind, but a large man reprimanded her and escorted her back inside what looked like a palace. Visions of classrooms and other children her age came and went.

The next image she sent shocked him, an image he was not prepared to see. It was of a warrior, blond, tan, virile, handsome and definitely in love with her. It was difficult to tell if she shared the man's feelings, but the warrior seemed completely devoted to her. A twinge of jealousy surged through him, a feeling he never experienced before.

Shayla wiggled closer against him, and he felt her breast against the thin leather of his tunic. Then he saw himself through her eyes and marveled at her perception of him. She thought him stronger and more capable than the fair-haired man of her tribe. It was odd seeing himself, but he liked the way she admired him.

Shayla pictured him kissing her, carrying her. His arms circled her waist and he pulled her close. Their lips met and her hands tugged on the laces of his tunic until they fell free, and she pushed the leather from his shoulders. Next he began to undress her. No, this was going too far. She was not in her right mind and he would not take advantage of her.

Rydor settled her back on the bed and stepped back. He took a deep, slow breath and tried to calm his out of control heart beat. How could the woman excite him with a mere thought? Unfortunately, he joined in her illusion, enjoyed the intimacy, but it made him want so much more. They were dangerous thoughts, but most of all, forbidden. "Olin!" he yelled. "Olin, you'd better show your old wrinkled face this instant!"

Where was the odd little wizard when he needed him? Olin said he would be back in three sun-cycles, but with Shayla in the condition she was, he would never make three sun-cycles with his sanity intact. He was a man too long denied the company of a woman and he no longer trusted himself. "Olin!"

"Why are you shouting?" Shayla protested. "If you don't stop this instant I shall summon my father."

In a flash she was off the pallet and running across the cold stone floor. Rydor gave chase and grabbed her around the waist from behind. She kicked and screamed at the top of her lungs. "Shhh," he whispered in her ear, but it had no effect. She made so much noise Una leapt into the air and raised a paw. When Una's paw came down, one of her claws dug into his leg. "You're supposed to protect me, you stupid cat!"

An unexpected silence enveloped the chamber. Shayla fell limp in his arms and Una rolled onto her back, paws in the air and slid into an instant deep sleep. "What the...?"

"You called me, didn't you?"

He cradled Shayla in his arms and turned to face the unmistakable voice. "Your arrival is none too soon."

"Actually, it is too soon. You were supposed to bond with the princess. You know, get close—intimate?"

Rydor laid Shayla on the pallet and pulled the cover over her. Thank the Gods she was sleeping. "What did you do to her?"

"A simple sleep spell. And one for Una before she added to your battle scars." Olin laughed. "Where's my wine?"

"Will she be all right alone?"

"Of course. Now come, my boy. You know I only visit because I like your wine so well."

"You like any wine too well."

Olin followed him to the table. Rydor grabbed a bottle and two glasses then sat across from his mentor. "Shayla has delirium."

"I put her into a healing sleep."

"Why didn't you do that for me?"

"Some things make a man stronger."

Rydor tapped a finger on the table. "And a woman wouldn't grow stronger?"

"There isn't time. I was going to allow you to stay another two sun-cycles, but it's time to begin your journey to Terita, home of the Zared people."

"I'm to take Shayla home?"

"Isn't that what you want to do? Get rid of her?"

Rydor took a healthy swig of wine. For some reason the idea no longer appealed to him. "What of the battle?"

"The Zared Elders will escort you and Shayla to the Holy Temple of Caelum."

"Are you sure? I thought the only humans allowed to set foot on those hallowed grounds were the High Priests."

"It is the only place the Ultimate Battle can be fought. Only the participants, tribe Elders and High Priests are allowed."

Rydor scowled. "What about wizards?"

Olin chuckled. "I will watch, but of course no one will see me."

The worried look on Olin's face unsettled him even more. "What's bothering you?"

"I said I will watch, but I can do nothing to help once the battle begins. It is solely up to you and Shayla to defeat the dark forces." Olin refilled their glasses. "You must bond so completely with Shayla that you become as one. Whether you mate with her or not isn't an issue, although it would help immeasurably."

Rydor shook his head. "Don't start with that nonsense. It can never be."

"Be that as it may, you must become one mind, and allow nothing to separate you. It is imperative. I can't stress this strongly enough. Brina and Turic have already achieved such a bond. They are united in a way that defies definition. Do not doubt their power for a moment.

"You have experienced a very mild visit from Turic. Heed my warning, he will strike again, many times before the battle begins. He will try to wear down your resolve, break your confidence, and work to separate you and Shayla. It's the only way he can gain an upper hand."

"I will protect Shayla with my life."

"Don't let it come to that."

Rydor traced scratches on the wooden table with his finger. He planned to defeat the enemy once and for all. Turic and his father would go down. His father would *not* win this time. He had much to prove to the Voltrans, to himself, but most of all to Shayla. She put her faith in him, and he would win for her. "When do we leave?"

"Shayla won't wake till morning." Olin winked. "She'll be ready to travel then. I have provided you with an Esroth and saddle. However, your mode of transportation once off the mountain is up to you and Shayla. Remember, the rules are none, the rules are all. Never forget that."

"I won't. And—thank you for helping Shayla through the delirium."

Olin laughed long and hard. "I couldn't have you screaming my name all moon-cycle, could I? Besides, we don't have time to let her recover naturally. I can't help with the battle, but I won't leave you stranded along the way."

"Thank you, my friend."

"Thank me by bonding with that beautiful princess in there and defeating the two most evil men on the planet." Olin leaned against the back of the chair. "How's the mind-melding process going?" Olin studied Rydor's reaction. "Better than I hoped from the looks of it."

"We have learned to communicate, if that's what you mean."

"Far more than that, I think." Olin chuckled. "And it's about time. You are slow for one so young and healthy."

"I feel old."

"When you reach my age you will be old, not until."

"Shayla and I cannot work together. It's impossible."

Olin smiled. "You make a powerful team, but you're not yet strong enough together." He took another drink. "Until you become totally honest with her, your unified strength will suffer the consequences."

"We haven't had enough time to work together."

"Patience, my son. It will happen."

Olin set his glass on the table and disappeared into a puff of smoke. Rydor returned to Shayla who slept peacefully in his bed. He laid down beside her and pulled the fur cover over them both. He turned on his side and slipped his arm around her tiny waist. She felt so small, so fragile, but he knew her strengths.

Shayla was one beautiful woman with the heart of a warrior. She moaned softly so he tightened his hold and pulled her closer. Her backside fit snug and perfect against his groin. Olin said she would sleep all moon-cycle. He would get up early and prepare for their journey. If he stayed in the pallet too long he might have to face her wrath for sleeping next to her.

Rydor closed his eyes and thought only of how Shayla felt in his arms. Her sweet scent teased his senses. He never knew how complete a woman could make him feel, and tried to visualize her as his life-mate, sleeping by his side every moon-cycle. He was tired and began to dose off with thoughts of protecting his sweet Sutae.

Pleasant dreams faded to nightmares. Shayla was tied between two trees and Turic stood in front of her. His brother reached out and grabbed her tunic so he could rip it from her body. "No! Leave her alone."

"What's the matter, brother? Don't want to see your whore naked?"

"Enough!" Rydor tried to rush Turic, but for some unexplainable reason his feet would not move. He was constricted, stuck to the ground, unable to budge even the smallest muscle.

"This isn't a dream, you know. I could kill you right now and take Shayla's favors, and there's nothing you can do about it."

He watched in horror as Turic's hand grabbed the top edge of Shayla's tunic and ripped it from her body. She wore a thin garment underneath, which was no barrier to his evil brother's lustful eyes.

"There, have a good look before she becomes mine. You aren't man enough for her!" Turic removed the drawstring that held her leggings. The fabric slithered down and pooled on the ground.

"You will never have her!" Rydor gritted his teeth and took a deep breath. This was a dream, yet it was real. Olin's words of warning ran through his head. This was the fourth dimension, where the rules were none, the rules were all. He was not sure how it worked exactly, but the battle had begun. Sacred ground or not, Turic meant to defeat him here if he could.

Turic's hand reached for the thin straps that held Shayla's undergarment in place. The thought of his brother touching her sent waves of adrenaline through his veins. He closed his eyes and visualized the invisible bonds Turic had placed on him melting away. With that thought he was able to move. He rushed Turic, who spun to face him and held up his right hand.

The moment he reached for Turic's neck he hit an undetectable barrier. Pain shot up his arm. Then he realized anything Turic could do, so could he. When Turic turned toward Shayla, he envisioned an unbreakable glass barrier that surrounded and protected her from Turic's assault.

Turic's hand connected hard against the invisible shield and he yelled a curse to the Gods. Rydor smiled, quite satisfied by his newfound ability. This battle of wits would prove most interesting.

"You're a fast learner, for a coward. But you won't win." Turic stepped back from Shayla. "Once Brina unleashes her talents against that princess of yours, you'll rue the sun-cycle you agreed to become a Kiah Master."

"No, brother. It will be you and Brina who will regret your decisions." Rydor laughed. The expression on Turic's face was priceless. Neither Turic, nor his father, could accept even the slightest defeat.

"Laugh while you can. It will not be this easy next time. That I promise." Turic raised his arms, snapped his fingers and disappeared.

"Good riddance." Rydor mentally removed the shield around Shayla and rushed to her. He gently caressed her cheek. "Are you all right?" She nodded, and he let out the breath he'd been holding. He concentrated on the ropes and trees that held her and pictured them gone. At once she was free and he took her hand in his. "Let us return."

"Where? I don't know how we got here, or where we were before."

"It's best that way." Rydor wrapped his arms around her and pictured them lying on the pallet the way they were before Turic decided to pay them a visit. With that thought, reality returned. Shayla moaned and twisted in his grasp. She tried to rise, but he gently eased her back.

"Rydor, I had a dream. It was awful. There was a man and he…"

"Shhh, Sutae. Sleep. It was only a dream." She relaxed in his embrace and the warmth of her skin reassured him she was real and safe. One thing he learned was that the dangers that lay ahead were far greater than he ever thought possible. He'd experienced a mere sampling of his brother's powers. Turic was potent, and Rydor had no way to measure Turic's true potential, or how much it would increase when he linked with Brina.

He was grateful for Turic's little demonstration. Now he had a better idea how to prepare for the impending battle. Brina and Shayla would play key roles, and he was beginning to see the need Olin had stressed all along. No one had a better command of the esoteric elements of the universe than Olin, and he had many questions for the kindly wizard

CHAPTER THIRTEEN

"Shayla."

Slowly she opened her eyes to Rydor's form kneeling beside the pallet. She blinked several times to clear her vision. His long, dark hair hung on his shoulders and framed the strong masculine contours of his ruggedly handsome face.

For some reason Rydor looked different, more at peace, yet with a determination she had not seen before. Maybe it was the smile on his face she was not accustomed to seeing. She propped herself on one elbow and took the cup of fruit juice he held out to her. Her eyes opened wider when she sipped the tangy sweet nectar that teased her pallet. "It's good." She licked her lips.

"Drink it. You'll need the energy. We're leaving as soon as you're dressed."

"Leaving? I don't understand."

"It's time."

"But..."

"Have faith, Sutae." Rydor stood and left the room.

Shayla smiled. When he called her Sutae she heard a passion in his voice that she really liked. What had changed? Her mind was blank. She desperately tried to remember what she was doing before she went to sleep. It seemed impossible. A dull ache throbbed behind her eyes when she stood.

Her hand touched the silky fabric on her stomach. She looked down, surprised to find herself clad only in her undergarment. Undergarment? Had Rydor undressed her? No, she must have done it herself, but she had made a point to sleep in her clothes since her arrival. Something was wrong here, but she had no idea what it was.

If she were the drinking kind, she would swear she had one too many glasses of wine. The vague memory of laughter stuck in her head. Rydor was nice, but far too serious to evoke uncontrolled merriment. There must be an explanation, but her head hurt too much to think.

The idea of riding an Esroth this sun-cycle did not appeal to her. She shed the last remaining garment and quickly washed with the warm water in the basin by the bed Rydor had thoughtfully provided. A cold chill ran down her spine, and it was not because of the temperature. It was the eerie kind of chill of someone watching her.

She swiftly dressed, unable to shake the persistent feeling that she was not alone. Had Rydor invaded her mind? She shook her head, grabbed her pack from the floor and tossed it upside-down on the bed. The contents spilled all over the fur cover, but she easily found her brush and ran it through her tangled hair.

The sinister sensation persisted, and she knew it was not Rydor. She glanced around the chamber. Her shadow danced on the stone wall of the cavern from the torch light behind her. Maybe Rydor was right to insist they leave now. The tranquility she had found in Rydor's cave no longer seemed to exist.

There was no time to braid her hair, so she tied it back with a clip, then shoved the rest of her belongings back into the saddlebags. All she had was a couple changes of clothes, a few personal grooming aids, and her com-unit. Once off Spirit Mountain she could contact her father and he would send a cruiser to pick her up.

Shayla put on her parka, tossed the bags over her shoulder and headed down the stone corridor toward the rays of sunshine at the end. She wondered what happened to the blue tunic and pants she'd worn last sun- cycle? She had not found them in the sleeping chamber, and she certainly did not take her clothes off anywhere else. Another fact that did not make sense. It made her wonder how Spirit Mountain earned the name.

Rydor stepped in front of the opening, arms crossed over his chest, legs apart. He looked every bit the warrior. His hunting bow and arrows were secured behind his back, and a wide blade hung from a leather sheath on the front of his belt. His weapons may be crude next to Rance and Arden's, but he looked fierce and competent.

"I'm ready." He took the bags from her shoulder and secured them with the ties on the back of her saddled Esroth. She grabbed the saddle horn, placed her left foot in the stirrup and hopped several times, unable to mount the tall animal. Not again. Fear of ending up in the dirt the same as she had in front of the Black Heart Inn made her cringe. She certainly did not want Rydor to witness her incompetence. When she hopped again, she felt a strong hand on her bottom that pushed her atop the beast. "Thank you.,"

Rydor mounted his Esroth ."I will lead. Stay close."

"Where did that Esroth come from?"

"Olin."

She nodded, then prodded her mount to follow his. Was there anything the wizard could not do? Many times she had wished for her own personal wizard, everyone did, but wizards were only intriguing elements in fairy-tales. No one she knew had ever seen one, yet Rydor lived with one.

Rydor was not much for conversation this sun-cycle, but that was fine. Her head hurt, and for some reason her wrists were sore. How could she not remember what happened last moon-cycle? The blank space in her memory bothered her. She stared at the furry vest Rydor wore over his long-sleeved leather tunic and wondered if she had gone insane?

Confused memories of last moon-cycle flew through her mind. She wanted to ask him what happened, but she didn't want to sound stupid. After all, she was there, she should know, but her mind was a fog.

I will explain when we make camp.

She didn't want to wait that long, but she had no choice. The realization of his mental message poured through her. *Stop reading my thoughts!*

Then read mine. We must practice, time is short.

What had come over him? She wasn't sure she liked the change. She had begged him to be serious, but she had not planned on this bonding stuff to be so personal. The thought of Rydor being privy to her every thought terrified her to the bone. He would learn of her attraction to him, and she could not face the ramifications. Her betrothal with Eaton would take place after the battle, and she had no say in the matter. Her father would choose, and she had to obey.

After a deep breath, she concentrated on Rydor. It took a few moments, but then she saw sky, water, wet clothes. *What kind of a message is that? Don't tell me it's going to rain.*

Good. Now, stay alert. I will send you messages throughout the sun-cycle, and I want you to answer each time in the same manner.

Rydor, what's going on? She found it hard to believe he had suddenly become serious. She shifted in her saddle and wondered if he heard her.

I heard you, and yes, I'm dead serious.

It's about time! She could swear she heard his laughter in her mind. *Glad you're amused. Is there anything I can think that you won't hear?*

Of course. Simply block what you don't want me to hear.

And how do I do that?

Divide your mind. Think of one side as open to me, the other as closed. Only place thoughts you want me to hear in the open side. Try it.

If she were to maintain her sanity she had have to learn the technique. No one had the right to her every thought, especially not Rydor. She mentally built a wall. One side for her, the other for him. That might be a bit simplistic, but she was new at this. In her imagination she stepped into her side. *What happened last moon-cycle?*

She waited, but heard nothing. Had it worked? She hopped the imaginary wall. *Did you hear that?*

Did I hear what?

Never mind. At least she could keep him out of her private thoughts, and that was a relief. However, it would be difficult to remember what side of the wall to be on before thinking. Her people's lives depended on her ability to control her mind. It was simple. She would mentally sit on top of the wall and go to one side or the other before thinking. Right now she hopped to her side.

Where Rydor was concerned, nothing was simple. He remained a mystery, a very tempting mystery. All the inappropriate thoughts and desires she had for him would dissipate when they left the mountain. When she returned to her comfort zone, she would put Rydor in the proper perspective. Here, in his domain, she was surrounded by the overpowering sense of him, and Olin's spells must be partially responsible.

The caw of a large bird circling overhead was a pleasant distraction. She had never seen a bird with such brilliant yellow and orange feathers. He abruptly dove, then soared higher into the cerulean sky. In her mind she moved back to the top of the wall. *What kind of bird is he?*

A Perdair. Be glad he isn't interested in us. They can be lethal.

Shayla laughed. She hadn't meant to ask Rydor a question. Obviously straddling the wall did not work. *Thanks for the warning.* She slipped to her side of the wall. Would this telepathic process ever become second nature, or would it always be a struggle?

The terrain became rocky and thick with thorny underbrush that scraped her legs while Rydor blazed a trail where none existed. He constantly glanced over his shoulder to check on her. There was a rustle in the bushes. She pulled her Esroth to a stop. She mentally slid to his side of the wall. *Rydor!*

Abruptly he turned and stopped. *I hear it. Stay calm.*

The sound of leaves and twigs crunching beneath feet rapidly grew closer. Shayla's breath caught in her throat. Her heart pounded so hard every vein in her body pulsed. Something hairy flew from the brush and landed in front of her. "Una!" she shrieked, "you scared me to death." Shayla heard the sound of Rydor's deep laughter echo through the canyon beside them.

"She says she will not be left behind."

Shayla smiled. Rydor was happy to see his cat, and she might have been as well if the animal had not ambushed them. The warrior and his Semita were quite a devoted team. "I don't mind her coming along, just tell her not to scare me like that again."

Rydor chuckled then nudged his mount into a fast walk. She should have known Una would follow. Wherever Rydor went, Una was close behind. She had grown fond of the furry beast. He was the pet she was never allowed as a child.

Her father's face formed in her mind's eye as she followed Rydor down the hill. She had not been able to communicate with her father since she set foot on Spirit Mountain. Olin said he sent him a message, but she knew he would worry himself sick until he heard her voice. Her com-unit malfunctioned the first moon-cycle she made camp. She had not known then about a wizard who had placed protective spells around Rydor's mountain, and that those spells could disable electronic equipment. Better Olin's spells than Voltran interference.

This was indeed Rydor's mountain, his private domain where he was king. She saw it in his eyes and every muscle of his body. He loved nature. What would he do when he faced her world? She feared he would be unhappy and it would be her fault. He could lose his life because of her. No. She refused to think such negative thoughts. Rydor would be the victor, and when this was over, he would return to his beloved mountain with Una. He belonged here, in his world, where he was comfortable with the serenity that would drive any other man insane.

She missed her home and all it afforded. Servants, plush gardens, and the grandeur of the royal palace. And there was Eaton, the man her father planned to announce as her life-mate. Her unexpected trip postponed all official functions, and she was glad. She was not ready to life-mate any man. When she did take a mate she wanted passion, and that was a missing ingredient with Eaton.

The terrain became steeper and her Esroth's hindquarters swayed back and forth as he made his way down the steep incline, and the drag of his hooves caused rocks to tumble. She was not used to this type of travel, yet there was a part of it that appealed to her. Serenity. The three sun-cycles she had spent on Spirit Mountain before Rydor found her had been terrifying, bringing nothing but hopeless desolation. The moment she met Rydor everything changed. He touched dormant feminine emotions, and stirred a desire she should not acknowledge, because if she did, all would be lost. One indiscriminate mating with Rydor would force her father to inflict the worst punishment possible—banishment. The very idea was too much to think about.

She was the one forcing Rydor to take the test. Since he was her Kiah Master, it was her duty to insure his safety. No easy task. Once he set foot on Zared soil she would be lucky to keep him alive if he was indeed a Voltran, since any Voltran found would be killed.

The prophetic ancient scrolls each tribe kept in their temple foretold of three Kiah Masters and their Focuses. When the sacred temple vaults in Caelum were opened, everyone learned the time and place of the battle. It also said only first born sons possessed the power of the Kiah, but little else was known about the event.

Don't worry.

Shayla turned her gaze from the tree-lined horizon to Rydor, who was glaring over his shoulder at her. I'm not worried. She scowled. *How did you...*

I sensed your feelings. He grinned. *You're the one who said we need to be honest with each other if we're to bond.*

"Can we stop?" He rode a few more feet then dismounted by a cluster of boulders. In three strides he was beside her. He lifted her from the saddle and placed her feet on the ground. He took her hand and led her to a flat rock where they both sat. "Thank you." She studied his penetrating blue eyes, but it was the heat of his hand that warmed her all over.

"Do you remember last moon-cycle?"

She shook her head. "I've tried. However, this morning while I bathed, I felt as if someone were watching. It was an eerie, evil sensation."

"You felt Turic Celon."

"How do you know?" Rydor frowned and she felt his every muscle tense. She did not need to touch his mind to know his gut reaction to the man. "Why does the mention of his name make you so angry?"

"He's the enemy."

"I think he's more than that to you."

"What he is to me matters not."

"You're one stubborn man." Rydor's resemblance to Turic Celon was uncanny. They could well be related, cousins maybe, but Rydor insisted on his code of silence. "Olin warned us about keeping secrets from each other."

"Then tell me yours."

"You know who I am, where I come from, my family name, my tribe. I know nothing about you, yet you talk about secrets?"

"Are you promised to anyone?"

"You're asking if I've chosen a life-mate?" She averted her gaze, not sure how to honestly answer. Her father hadn't made the official announcement to the tribe Elders, but she knew he'd chosen Eaton. "There is no man I love, if that's what you want to know."

"You're a woman. It is your father who must choose your mate. Has he done so?"

"Not yet, but..."

"There is a man, isn't there?"

"Yes. His name is Eaton. He's our Ruling Warrior. That's the highest position in the Zared Defense League."

Rydor stood and paced, arms crossed over his chest. "You have feelings for this...Eaton?"

"We're friends. I admire and respect him." She almost laughed as Rydor kicked dirt while he silently strode from side to side. Was he upset, or jealous? He could not possibly be jealous, they barely knew each other. Of course they had kissed, but a kiss was not a lifetime commitment. She opened her mind to him. *Do you have feelings for me?*

She waited for a response, but he acted as if he had not heard her. How was that possible when earlier he picked up every private thought she had. "Are you angry?"

"I have no reason to be angry."

Livid might describe his reply. She wished Olin would appear and work his magic on Rydor. A spell to loosen his tongue and insure complete cooperation would be good for a start. Then again, if she knew his secrets she might have doubts about her choice of a Kiah Master. Many times the more she knew about some people the less she liked them and she could not afford to have that happen with Rydor.

"Are you hungry?" Rydor opened his saddlebag and removed two sticks of dried meat. He stepped toward Shayla and placed a piece in her hand.

"Thank you." She took a small bite, pleasantly surprised by the flavorful, salty taste. "I've never had this before. It's good." A little tough, she decided, but good. Even her compliment did not rouse a reply from the surly warrior. "Rydor, please, tell me what's bothering you." She caught a glimpse of his scowl before he turned his back to her.

Then she heard his jumbled voice in her head, a message she was sure he did not mean to send. One word registered loud and clear, *coward.* Was he referring to her? She wanted to press him for answers, but he obviously wanted to hide his secrets. She could only hope that he would confide in her before the battle.

"Where are we going?" Her breath caught in her throat when he turned. He assumed the universal warrior's stance, legs slightly apart, hands clasped behind his back, head held high, chest out and not one ounce of emotion on his face. She had seen that stance and expression thousands of times before, but Rydor made her pulse race and her breathing rapid. To say he had no affect on her would be a lie.

Shayla stood. "It's too soon to go to the Temple of Caelum."

"Our journey will meet with many delays."

"Who or what can delay us?" He shook his head at her. She hated the way men thought all women were naive. "You're talking about Turic Celon?"

"There is much you don't understand, Sutae."

Her heart skipped a beat at the endearment, but she refused to fall for his sweet-talk. "Then explain it to me. I'm not stupid."

"Never have I thought that. Why would you say such a thing?"

"Now who's being naive?" Shayla grinned. "The men of my tribe do not afford the same importance to women as men. They have loosened a bit over the years, but a woman still cannot hold a position on the council or become ruler."

"All the tribes hold to that rule, but I do not agree with their thinking."

Shayla's eyes widened. "Then you're one of a kind." Rydor's brow furrowed at her comment.

"So I've been told."

"You don't need to sound so gruff. I meant that as a compliment."

"Time to go." Rydor took her hand and led her back to the Esroths.

The heat of his touch seared through the fabric of her leggings when he helped her up onto the saddle. His hand lingered on her leg several seconds after she was seated. There was a sadness in the depths of his eyes. What secret tortured his soul?

CHAPTER FOURTEEN

Rydor was relieved this sun-cycle had ended, camp was made and dinner eaten. If only he knew how to pass the time till daylight without thinking forbidden thoughts about Shayla, he might be able to relax.

"I'm going to the stream to bathe."

"Not alone."

"You certainly can't come with me."

He smiled. "Of course not. Keep an eye out and call me with your mind if you see or hear anything out of the ordinary."

Shayla picked up her bag and headed down the slope filled with thick brush and trees, obstructing his view. Propriety be damned, he was not about to allow her out of his sight. Wild beasts roamed the mountain, but the beast he feared most was Turic, who could attack at will.

Following at a safe distance, he stopped when she reached the bank of the river and ducked behind the thorn bush in front of him. Shayla looked in his direction first, then surveyed her surroundings. She set her bag on the bank and removed the leather vest he had loaned her, then her tunic top and leggings.

The setting sun cast shadows across the ravine, yet Shayla's ivory skin glistened like the finest jewel in the near darkness. She peeled the one remaining undergarment from her body, stuffed everything into the bag, then stepped into the water. He smiled when she jumped back and shivered, her silhouette highlighted by the rising twin moons.

The snow-fed river was cold, but he was sure if his arms were around her, neither of them would notice. His fingers itched to roam the curves of her sensual body. A quickening in his groin reminded him he wanted far more than to touch. It was torture to feast his eyes on her untouched body, knowing she could never be his. His hands fisted at the thought of that warrior, Eaton, claiming her.

She inched her way into the water, stooping to dunk the bar of soap. She worked up a lather and he wished it were his hands moving up and down to spread it over her perfect body. He turned his head and fought his desperate need for the fair Princess Shayla D'Par.

Olin said if they mated, it would help them bond better for the battle, but the battle was not on his mind. It was simply his selfish desire to satisfy the basic needs of the flesh with the one woman he could never have. He knew the customs of Zanthus, and the Zared tribe was even more formal in their life-mating practices than the Voltrans or Quelans. Life-mating outside of one's tribe was never accepted. Even if it were, no father would choose a coward for his daughter.

A twig cracked and his attention was drawn back to the water. Una had joined Shayla by the river, but only for a drink. He heard her giggle at the cat and it warmed his heart. The sound of her laughter healed his troubled soul. It was precious moments like this with Shayla that allowed him to forget, just for a moment, about his past and the implications it held.

"Una, no!"

Una bounded up the slope and proudly presented him with Shayla's saddlebag. "Bad girl. You must love getting me in trouble!" Una licked his hand while he petted her head. Then his head nearly exploded when he heard Shayla scream, *bring me my clothes!*

He glanced toward the water. *As you wish.* He picked up the bag and began his descent only to have his head ring with another scream. *What's wrong?*

Turn your back!

I cannot back down the hill. He could, but he certainly did not want to. The overwhelming feeling of embarrassment made his skin tingle. Shayla's emotion was so strong he stopped in his tracks and immediately turned his back. It was no easy task to maneuver around boulders, trees, fallen logs, and avoid ankle-breaking holes dug by the underground inhabitants of Spirit Mountain. But he would do anything for her.

That's close enough. Just drop the bag.

Rydor laughed. *You sound like a highwayman.*

Your cat is the thief. And I'm not so sure you didn't put her up to it!

He wanted to turn his eyes on her naked beauty, pull her into his arms and never let go. Instead he dropped the bag. *Get dressed before you freeze.* The rustling sound behind him said she wasted no time covering the body he wanted so badly. She stepped in front of him, still adjusting her clothes. When he held out his hand to help her she looked stunned.

Hesitantly she placed her hand in his and he smiled. He closed his fingers over hers then pulled her closer so he could lean his forehead against hers. "I was going to ask if I could borrow your soap, but I'd much rather hold your hand." She pulled away from him and he immediately felt the loss.

"Of course." Shayla picked up the scented bar from the riverbank and threw it at him. She turned and started to climb the hill.

"Wait here. It's not safe for you to be alone."

She turned. "There are only two people on this mountain, what could possibly hap..."

The agonizing wail of an animal echoed through the canyon and terror marred her features. "Trust me when I tell you it's not safe." He removed the fur-covered vest, then pulled off his leather tunic. He noticed when her gaze became riveted to the scars on his chest. She looked shocked and appalled, but walked closer.

"What kind of an animal did this to you?"

"The worst kind." He flinched when her hand touched the widest scar across the center of his chest.

"I'm sorry. Did I hurt you?"

Rydor shook his head. "No one has ever touched them before."

"There are so many. I don't know how you survived." She smiled. "I hope Una wasn't responsible."

"Quite the contrary." He turned his back to her, removed his pants, grabbed the soap and dove into the dark, menacing depths of the river.

***

Shayla's stomach lurched at the sight of Rydor's badly beaten back before he disappeared under the gloomy depths of the river. The sight of his magnificent form, so badly marred made her see him in a new light. Whatever kind of creature did that to him had obviously left him near death.

Fingers of darkness consumed her soul and the musty dampness of the forest filled her lungs. She slowly sank to the ground, sensing strong emotions churning within Rydor, emotions he obviously did not want to face or talk about. He was a very troubled and complex man. How could she reach him when he locked the door to his heart?

During their ride they had practiced their mental communications, but she had found a door, locked and chained, forever closed to her. She could only wonder what terrible secrets he hid. She'd tried to approach that door with her mind, but he pushed her back with a force stronger than any she had ever encountered.

Rydor had told her to put anything she did not want him to know behind a door and lock it, but the only thing she needed to keep locked away was her physical attraction to him. Was he hiding similar feelings? No, that was wishful thinking on her part. He was acting only as her Kiah Master, nothing more. Yet she had seen a spark of desire in his eyes even though he tried to hide it.

Her experience with men was very limited, but she had seen Eaton look at her during their walks in the gardens. Poor Eaton. He did desire her, yet she felt nothing for him. She tried to feel pleased when Eaton slipped his arm around her, or stole a brief kiss. Instead she had wanted to run from Eaton and put as much distance between them as possible. There was just something about that man that bothered her—something she could not put her finger on.

With Rydor she found the opposite, and it annoyed her. He had not admitted to being a Voltran, but all the signs were there. Since he wasn't Zared he would have to keep his tribe affiliation neutral, the way he claimed it to be. Her father had to accept her choice of Kiah Master, but the situation would become extremely difficult if Rydor truly was Voltran.

The sound of water splashing caught her attention and her gaze locked on Rydor. He slowly rose from the river. First his shoulders, then his upper body. Sparkling rivulets coursed down his powerful chest and mingled in the dark matt of hair in the center. His belly button emerged. Another few inches and he would be totally exposed. His sensual gaze held hers for the longest moment. She turned her entire body because she did not trust herself to keep her eyes closed. She wanted to see him completely naked walking toward her, but it was not proper. She laughed. Nothing about her and Rydor was proper.

"What's so funny?"

His deep, sultry voice sent chills down her spine. "Nothing."

"Then you're laughing at me?"

"At us really." She heard him dressing and sighed in relief. "You must admit, we're a strange team."

"So are Una and I, but I don't laugh at her."

"You know what I mean. You're a reclusive mountain man, and I'm a Princess who can't find acceptance as a woman." She heard him laugh. "Now you're laughing at me."

"Never."

He slipped his hands under her arms and pulled her to her feet. She turned to face him. He was fully dressed and, for some shameful reason, she wished he were still naked. Her cheeks burned from the inappropriate thought, and her stomach fluttered unmercifully.

"I sense there's something you want to ask me, Sutae."

How she melted when he called her that, his voice so gentle and caring. When his lips came closer, all she could think about was wanting to kiss him. "Has Olin taught you how to cast spells?"

"Why would you ask?"

She could not answer without revealing lustful fantasies a Princess should not have. "I just thought it would come in handy during the battle if he had."

"Wizards never share their secrets."

"What about warriors? Do they share secrets?"

"Rarely." Rydor put the soap back in her bag then slung it over his shoulder.

He slipped his arm around her waist and helped her up the hill. The man's strength amazed her. He nearly carried her up the slope as if she weighed less than the saddlebag. Then she heard him in her mind.

You smell good.

His head lowered and she felt his lips on the side of her neck and his warm breath on her skin. She shivered. *So do you.* She should not have sent him that reply, but it was true. They reached the crest of the hill, but he kept his arm tightly around her. He dropped the bag then pulled her close. Her arms slid up his back under the vest, the soft leather of his tunic smooth against her palms.

You're cold. Let me warm you.

She wanted to respond to him, to make his embrace last all moon-cycle, but to encourage him was not fair. She had no right to let him believe she could give herself to him in the way he wanted. Reluctantly she pushed him back and the moon-cycle's chill replaced his warm body.

"Maybe we should turn in for the moon-cycle."

"Are you tired?"

"A bit." Shayla picked up a fur cover from inside the makeshift tent Rydor had erected and wrapped it around her.

She sat on a large rock by the fire he had made earlier and watched him stoke the dying embers to new life. The crackling of burning wood and the smell of smoke created a very cozy setting. "I've never camped before."

"You don't travel?"

"Of course, but I've always stayed in diplomats' quarters or at an inn."

"It's been a long time since I've given thought to how the outside world operates."

"Make me understand why you've stayed on this mountain for so long, isolated, away from your family and friends."

"I have no family or friends."

"You have Olin."

"Olin is different."

"I must agree with that." It was comforting to see a smile tug at the corners of his mouth. "You should laugh more often. Laughter is good for the soul. I'm sure Olin has told you that."

"He's told me many things."

"You love him like a father, don't you?" At the mention of the word father, Rydor recoiled. "You're lucky to have Olin as an advisor." She smiled. "Too bad we all can't have our own personal wizard to guide us. Zanthus would be a happier place."

"Only if you have a lot of wine."

Shayla laughed. "He does like his wine." He stood then sat next to her. The warmth of his thigh against hers made her heart beat faster. "Will we see Olin again?"

"When you least expect it."

"So I've noticed." Shayla placed her hands on the sides of her head. "I feel dizzy."

"It's the altitude. You body needs to adjust."

"But we've been going downhill. It should be getting better, not worse."

"Such is the mystery of Spirit Mountain."

"You never seem affected. Why?"

"After sixteen annual-cycles, my body is well adjusted." He placed his hand over hers and lowered it, clasping her fingers. She tingled all over. Why did his slightest touch make her yearn for more? She felt lost in his mesmerizing gaze and did not have the will to pull away. Olin's words played in her mind, and she wondered if his mating suggestion was the cause of her wayward longings. "Did Olin place a spell on me?"

"Only a sleep spell to ease your sickness."

"Nothing more? Are you sure?"

"Why do you ask?"

"I don't feel like myself." The moment she said that she regretted it because she had no intention of explaining.

"Who do you feel like?"

"You're toying with me, Warrior. You know very well what I mean." She pulled her hand from his, unable to deal with his touch any longer.

"What will your father think of me?"

She mentally shook herself. He had a way of changing the subject and catching her unprepared. "You are my choice for Kiah Master and he will respect that."

"But will he respect me? He knows nothing about me."

"Neither do I, but I respect you."

Rydor stood and put more wood on the fire. "Only because you have to."

"That's not true. I can tell you're an honorable man with a kind heart. That's all I need to know." Rydor gave her a disbelieving glare. He knew she wanted to know more about him, but she had no desire to make him angry by prying into his past. She could only pray he would tell her when he was ready.

"Indeed." Rydor groaned. "If you knew me, you wouldn't have such nice words to say."

"Really. And I suppose you're going to tell me you have an ugly side, that you're dangerous—maybe even a murderer."

"I wish it were that simple." Rydor stood, grabbed more wood and dropped it on the fire.

Shayla watched red-hot embers rise into the dark sky then disappear as if they had never existed. She had been away from Terita and her father for seventeen sun-cycles, but she felt like the burnt-out embers— like she never existed. Terita seemed like another planet next to Spirit Mountain, but the problems she left behind were real.

What had been happening in Terita in her absence? With no way to communicate, she could only guess. The minute she got off this god-forsaken mountain she would call her father. She had promised to keep in touch, and he was bound to be furious, not to mention Eaton. A sad realization washed over her. She may have thought about Eaton, but she had not for one moment missed him.

A twinge of guilt gnawed at her. She should miss the man her father had chosen as her betrothed, instead she enjoyed being away from him. Eaton was a fine man, above reproach. Loyal, devoted and genuinely good. She had known him her entire life and loved him as a friend, not a mate.

She glanced at Rydor bent over the fire and that familiar tingle assailed her stomach. He raised to his full height, stretched, and every muscle bulged beneath the soft leather of his clothes. She silently cursed her attraction to Rydor, yet she could not deny the way she felt every time he was near, and he was too near.

Her father had raised her to think proper, act proper and speak proper. And here she was, in the wilderness, alone with a warrior that made her think everything improper. She wanted to believe it was Olin's doing. It would be easier that way.

Shayla stood and walked to the tent. She crawled inside and tried to make herself comfortable when the discomforting realization hit. One tent and two bedrolls so close they overlapped. She turned on her side and faced the tanned hide wall. She heard a rustling and held her breath when the small shelter filled with Rydor's presence.

It would be a long moon-cycle with him beside her. His breathing was fast, and she found her own breath coming as rapidly as his. By the Gods, how had she gotten herself in this predicament? If Eaton had proven worthy, her problems would be over. Instead she had to come to terms with Rydor and fight her body's desire for him. She could not betray Eaton, her father, or her people, which struck fear in her heart. Before this was over, she was sure to betray one of them.

CHAPTER FIFTEEN

Rydor tossed and turned, unable to find a comfortable position. He could deal with the hard ground, it was the princess next to him that caused his unrest. His life had been so simple before she arrived. Now he had to face his past and his growing affection for Shayla. His Sutae, a woman he could lose his heart to, but could never have.

He had been out of touch with the outside world for many annual-cycles, but he knew the rules had not changed. He played dumb to her questions and comments, but he knew all too well what was going on off the mountain.

Power. It was always about power. He fought against his father because of the rules. He saw no point in taking a life so another could gain power. Especially not an old, defenseless man who had a right to watch his grandchildren grow and prosper. The price had been high, but he would do it again.

He closed his eyes and thought about his mother, a gentle woman who had died too young. His memory of her was fuzzy. The last time he saw her was when he was barely six annual-cycles. He was never told how she died, but he last saw her by the river with his father, who had seemed extremely angry. He always believed his father killed his mother, but never knew why. His mother truly loved Damek, even if the man did not deserve her devotion. Damek on the other hand loved no one.

After her death, Damek became even more evil and controlling. Nothing made him happy. Even becoming ruler of the Voltran tribe did not satisfy his lust for blood. Damek took Turic under his wing, claiming his wife had given birth to a first born male who was a sissy. It was as if Damek knew all along he would fail his test of manhood. So be it. The past never changed, but he could have an impact on the future, a future no one on the planet wanted to face if Damek became the ruler.

Rydor turned on his back. Shayla moaned and rolled toward him, her arm draping across his chest, her head coming to rest in the crook of his arm. Her hair sprawled over his skin, the clean scent tickling his nose. How could he ignore her when she was so close? Everything about her tempted him to the limits of his endurance.

All pleasant thoughts of Shayla ceased, and Turic's evil filled the small confines of the tent. He tightened his arm around Shayla and forced his mind to tune into his brother's vibration.

Brother dearest, nice of you to welcome me. Turic laughed. *I see you're sleeping with your little whore. Too bad she won't let you do more than hold her.*

Rydor wished Turic's visit was a physical one so he could make him pay for insulting Shayla. Olin's insistence he have patience was all that held him back. *What do you want?*

Just checking on your progress. I don't see much, but I didn't expect much from a coward.

In the darkness Rydor saw a slight haze floating above their feet on the makeshift pallet where they lay. *Think what you like, Turic. I will destroy you.*

Really? And you hate me so much you refuse to even call me brother. He laughed. *What will Shayla say when she learns your family heritage? That you were disowned for being a coward?*

She trusts me.

But will she in the future? Once I tell her the truth, she will change her mind.

So tell her, or are you the coward? Rydor sensed the irritation in Turic, but his features were hazy in the cloudy apparition.

I'll tell her when it serves me. Since you're a coward, I know you'll never tell her. Turic laughed. *I'll enjoy watching you sweat each suncycle, wondering when I will.*

As quickly as Turic arrived he departed, but he left behind the desired effect. So far Shayla was not aware of his identity. She had no memory of Turic's assault, but that could change. She had sensed when Turic watched her, but how long this little charade could remain secret depended solely on Turic, a man with no scruples.

If he told Shayla, she might not trust him to fight honestly for her tribe. Admitting he was a Celon still put a bitter taste in his mouth. Of course his father had disowned him, and over time he realized it was exactly what he wanted. Now to even mention the family name along with his felt like an even bigger disgrace. He no longer had a last name.

Gently he rolled Shayla off him and eased out of the tent. He put more wood on the dying fire and stared at the tiny fingers of flames as they reached for the fresh wood. Sleep would not come this moon-cycle. Between Shayla's temptation and his brother's visit, he could find no peace. Why did it have to be so difficult?

"Rydor?"

Shayla's voice sent a cold chill through his body. She was so vulnerable, so trusting. He hated to destroy her confidence, but if he kept his secret it would surely destroy them both.

"May I join you?"

She walked over to him and sat on the flat rock by the fire. He had to admit he was glad for her company. "You should be sleeping. We have a difficult journey ahead."

"I got cold." She scooted closer to Rydor. "It was warmer with you next to me." Shayla looked into his eyes. "Why did you leave?"

"I needed some air." A dip in the cold river was more like it. Once Turic left, all he'd wanted to do was hold Shayla tighter, closer than he ever had. His protective instinct mixed with strong masculine desires had become a most dangerous combination.

"I had another dream about that man, the one you said was Turic. He scares me, Rydor."

"I wish I could say you have nothing to fear, but he is the enemy, and never underestimate him."

"How did he become so evil?"

"He learned from the master."

"And that would be his father, Ruler Damek Celon?"

Rydor nodded, unable to say more.

"We have followed Damek's career from his sun-cycles as a warrior to his rise in politics. Each position he filled had been vacated due to a death. We suspect he was responsible for creating his own advancement. What we don't understand is why the Voltrans allowed him such free reign. Or should I say, tolerated his reign of terror?"

Shayla brought up questions he had asked himself a thousand times. If he elaborated more he would spill secrets best left buried.

"We also kept a close eye on his son, Turic, who's now their Ruling Warrior. He's the one responsible for all the attacks and sabotage. Not to mention countless rapes and murders." She looked into Rydor's eyes. "We know Damek had another son born an annual-cycle before Turic. It's said he died from some unknown illness, but that's all we were able to learn. All records of his existence burned in a fire, which was before the time the Voltrans were the threat they are now. Our sources weren't even able to learn his name. It's a shame to die so young."

Rydor bit his tongue. For all intents and purposes, he had died young and in shame. With Olin's help, and many annual-cycles of self-examination, he was a different person. Unsettled hatreds were impossible to forget. He had buried his feelings long ago, until Shayla arrived with the shovel to dig them up. "Has there been attempts by your people, or the Quelans, to stop Damek and Turic?"

"Of course, but our sources haven't been able to learn of their plans early enough to set a trap."

"You won't need to worry much longer. The Ultimate Battle will end his power struggle once and for all." Rydor squeezed her trembling hand. "Tell me about your father. What kind of a ruler is he?"

"Of course I'm biased, but he's very fair. Maybe not as open-minded as I wish he'd be, but he tries to understand and sympathize with the plight of his people."

"What of the elders?"

"The council isn't as forgiving as my father, but they listen to him."

"And what is your role as Princess?"

"Not what I wish it were. I entertain diplomats, but I'm forbidden to attend meetings. Sometimes I feel like nothing more than an ornament."

"Because you're a woman?" He saw the sadness in her face and knew all too well what it was like to be shut out. "That prejudice could change after the Ultimate Battle."

"Everything will be different. All three tribes will become one, with the victorious tribe choosing the ruler. But I don't see the men in charge suddenly giving women rights they've never had."

"You believe if we win that your father will be the chosen leader?"

"It's possible." Shayla crossed her legs and pulled the fur cover around her. "No one can predict what will happen. All we can do is pray for our victory."

"And if we're not the victors?"

"Then my second choice is for the Quelan Tribe. They're not that different from us. But the Voltrans—never!"

"I agree." He said more in that simple statement than she would ever know. Her gaze was on him looking for more. He raised her hand to his lips and kissed her soft skin. She sighed, and emotions swam in the depths of her eyes.

"I did not leave my home to meet defeat, and you have not risked your life on this mountain in vain.

"We will stop the Voltrans, Sutae."

***

Shayla fidgeted in her saddle. She had been on her Esroth for almost three full sun-cycles, a fact her sore muscles screamed about. The tall trees of the forest thinned as they entered a beautiful valley. Wildflowers, tall grass and a variety of blissful hopping creatures with pointed ears, plump bodies and long, wide flat tails filled nature's expanse.

As usual, Rydor had said little, but he sent mental messages to keep her on her toes. She was proud to say she had mastered the wall thing and was able to keep him out of her private thoughts with little effort. Only a couple of slips this sun-cycle, and that was progress.

The sun began to wane, but its warmth still penetrated her skin. It was nearly time to stop and make camp, which brought a wide smile to her face. Her posterior was in dire need of a rest, and she had come to enjoy the moon-cycles spent in Rydor's arms. They always fell asleep separately, but by morning their arms and legs were tangled, and her head lay on his chest, his arm curled protectively around her.

Something magical seemed to happen between them in the moon-cycle. In her dreams she felt so close to Rydor, as if they were one. Yet in the sun-cycle, he became a stranger. Shayla sighed. She found it harder and harder to deny her attraction to Rydor. He was a man that excited her beyond words, and it was not because he was her Kiah Master.

One glance at Rydor sitting tall in the saddle said it all. His proud countenance, magnificent body, and tender but tortured soul set her heart fluttering faster. No, it wasn't the Kiah Master she lusted for, it was the mountain man himself. He pulled his Esroth to a stop next to a cluster of large boulders that formed a half circle. "Are we camping here?"

"Of course you are!"

That voice was different from Rydor's, but she knew it well. Shayla glanced to the top of the tallest rock to see Olin in all his grandeur. He looked as he always did in his floppy purple hat and matching robe tied with a sash at the waist.

"Will you two join me for supper?"

"Are you cooking?" Rydor asked as he dismounted.

Shayla shifted her weight to the left stirrup and swung her leg over the animal's back. Before her right foot found solid ground, two strong hands grasped her waist and lifted her down.

"We'd love your company, Olin!" She glanced over her shoulder at Rydor who tried to hide a smile. "Is that smile for me or Olin?"

"What do you think, Sutae?"

She did not dare answer for fear she would be wrong, but the look in his devilish blue eyes said it was her. He stepped away and walked toward Olin. She followed him and laughed when Olin popped off the boulder onto the grass in the blink of an eye.

Olin spread his arms, mumbled several odd sounding words and nodded his head. Instantly a feast appeared on a fine table set with china, crystal goblets and gold utensils. "Wow." She took a seat on one of the chairs Olin had so kindly provided.

"I know, I know."

"What?" Olin gave her the funniest smile she'd ever seen.

"Rydor doesn't like me to use my magic like this, but you're both tired, and I thought a treat would be nice for a change."

"I will not argue your gift." Rydor sat across from Shayla while Olin took his seat at the head of the table.

"Shayla, my dear, has Rydor been good to you on this journey?"

"It all depends on your definition of good." She smiled when Olin laughed and Rydor scowled. "He's been a gentleman, if that's what you want to know." More than a gentleman she wanted to add, but Olin did not need more fuel to needle Rydor.

"Your visits always have a purpose, Olin. What is it this time?"

"Rydor, my boy, don't be so anxious. I missed you both and wanted to see how things were going."

"Fine." Rydor groaned.

Shayla glanced at the clearing to her right and saw the unmistakable fog bank. "Is that..."

Olin smiled. "It is, but I will remove it long enough for you to pass, but that won't be till the sun rises. In the meantime we need to discuss what lies ahead."

"Do you still want us to go to Terita?"

Excitement coursed through her at the thought of seeing home and her father again, but she did not want to show Rydor how anxious she was.

"Yes, but don't take the direct route, it's too dangerous."

"Why?" she asked.

"The Voltrans are not the only ones who want to see you fail."

"I hadn't thought of that." It had been simple-minded of her to think the Quelans would not try something. Of course they wanted to win. Each of the three tribes wanted to save themselves and claim victory. "Winner takes all. I can't think of a better reason to stop an opponent."

"When you leave the mountain, trust no one except yourselves. That applies to friends, family and strangers as well."

"Understood." Rydor dug into his food and took a bite.

Olin touched Shayla's arm. "Princess, I know this will be hard for you."

"Are you telling me not to trust my own father?"

"I am."

"He would never do anything to hurt me or betray his people."

"Not consciously, but he may lose his objectivity. His perspective is different than yours." Olin leaned toward her. "Allow no obstacle to come between you and Rydor."

Shayla nodded. She could not believe Olin thought her father would interfere. Such an idea was ludicrous and would never come to pass. Nuri sent her to find a Kiah Master, and she had. He would be proud of her success and would support her choice. "You have nothing to worry about where my father is concerned."

The wizard pulled his hand back. "Remember my words, fair Princess."

For the first time, she understood Rydor's occasional irritation toward Olin. He spoke in innuendos, yet how could his advice be ignored? The magic man had proven right so far, but he could always be wrong, and where her father was concerned, she knew he was. She tasted Olin's conjured food, then took a sip of wine. "Your magic is better than my cooking."

"Better than Rydor's as well, but he insists on doing things the hard way." Olin chuckled. "He says he can't count on me to show up in time to feed his hunger."

"I said I can't depend on you to show up. I said nothing about my hunger."

"So you did."

Rydor shook his head. "Now tell us what we need to know."

"Rydor, give him time, enjoy the meal. It's wonderful."

"Don't become spoiled, Princess."

Shayla smiled. "I'll try not to."

"If you two are finished, I have some news." Olin took a sip of wine. "The Quelan tribe has chosen Mandel for their Kiah Master and Akela as his Focus. Since they're the smallest tribe, they will fight the Voltrans first. This will give you both an opportunity to study their technique."

"How will that help us?" Shayla picked up her fork.

"It might not help at all, but any insight you gain can only work to your advantage. I have seen Mandel and Akela work together."

Rydor took several bites and waited. He laid his fork down and cleared his throat. "Are you going to tell us, or are you waiting for me to ask?

"Patience still escapes you." Olin grinned. "As a team they are no stronger than you and Shayla. They too adhere to the moral code of not mating without legal sanction. Right now, neither the Zared nor the Quelan team can defeat Turic and Brina."

Shayla took a deep breath. "Olin, tell me about Brina."

"She is strongly bonded to Turic. I wouldn't call it love, but they have a very potent lust which never goes unsatisfied. With each joining they gain power, which is why they will go undefeated."

"So if Rydor and I...join, we will gain power?"

"Absolutely. But that is your choice."

Rydor shoved his plate away. "There must be another way. I cannot believe the Gods would dictate such nonsense."

"Maybe it is man who has dictated nonsense."

"He has a point, Rydor. It is tribal law that a woman and man be life-mated before they join."

"What are you saying, woman, that you'll mate with me? Here? Now?"

Shayla hung her head. What was she trying to say? Saving her people was the priority, everything else was secondary. Still, it was difficult to go against rules that had been crammed down her throat her entire life. Yet being in Rydor's arms felt right, and it had nothing to do with crystal rods and battles.

"Children, please. Don't do this to yourselves. Your decisions will become clear with time. You still have thirty-four sun-cycles to decide." Olin laughed. "Now, finish your supper. It took me all sun-cycle to prepare."

Rydor laughed. "All sun-cycle? You only snapped your fingers or mumbled a spell, or whatever you did. It took but an instant."

"Yes, but it took all sun-cycle to remember the spell. I'm getting old, you know. Not the wizard I used to be."

"But a wizard all the same." Rydor pulled his plate back in front of him and picked up his fork. "No food should go to waste."

"That's my boy. Shayla, eat. You need your strength."

They finished their meal in relative silence. Only Olin seemed amused with the irony of the situation. She and Rydor had life altering decisions to make, yet the kindly wizard chuckled and made light, as if there were nothing to it. Did he know something they didn't? Probably, but she knew he would never tell.

"Well now, that's better. Since you're finished I must go. However, I will leave you with something to think about."

As Olin turned into a puff of smoke so did everything else. Her head spun and she felt as if she were floating through the air. As quickly as it began, it was over. There was something soft beneath her. She ran her hands over silky fabric. Her fingers touched something warm. The fog instantly cleared and her shock was total.

"Olin has really done it this time. I'm sorry." Rydor sighed.

She and Rydor were lying on a high bed beneath a fine canopy, the rich fabric matching the bed covers. Sitting up, she laughed and crossed her legs in front of her. "He certainly left us something to think about." Sixteen candles flickered, eight on each side of the bed held by tall, golden candelabras. Rydor got out of bed and pulled his pillow onto the floor. "I will sleep down here."

Shayla rolled to the side of the bed and glared down at his prone form. He'd closed his eyes, rested his arms over his chest and crossed his booted feet. "You don't look comfortable."

"I'm fine."

"Why would you want to spend another moon-cycle on hard ground when this bed is more than ample for two? Besides, there's more room now than in the tent."

"It's not proper."

"Was it proper to sleep in your arms the last three moon-cycles? What's different now?"

Rydor rose to his knees and looked her in the eye. "Everything."

"Why? We've done nothing improper. Please, Rydor—"

He grabbed her shoulders. "Don't you understand? There's nothing proper about the way I think about you, and if I spend one more moon-cycle holding you I'll..."

"What?"

"Fulfill Olin's wish."

"Oh." Rydor's lips eased closer, and she felt a tingle in her abdomen. Her pulse raced, and her breath caught in her throat when he kissed her. His arm slid behind her neck, and he held her immobile, his tongue slipping into her mouth, tasting and searching.

Rydor's hand shook, but her entire body trembled. He eased himself onto the bed beside her, then rolled her on top of him as he deepened his assault. His tongue roamed every recess while his hands slid up and down her back. Rydor had the strength of ten men, but he touched her as if she'd break.

He rolled over and pulled her with him. Hard muscle rested on her chest. He kissed a trail down her neck, moaning deep and low. Her body was on fire. She wanted him as only a woman could want a man. Her fingers threaded through his dark hair. He nibbled at her breast through the fabric of her tunic. She wanted his lips on her bare skin.

Her hands traced the hard sinew of his shoulders. He tensed beneath her touch and stopped all motion. He pushed away and got out of bed. He paced, his shadow moving with him on the silken tent wall in the candlelight. "Rydor, what's wrong? Is it me?"

"I cannot violate your maidenhood and bring shame to your family name."

"I thought you were making love to me." He shook his head and mumbled words she did not understand. "Rydor, stop that irritating pacing and talk to me!"

He halted. "There's nothing to say. I'm not the gentleman you told Olin I was. There's lust in my soul."

"Is that bad?"

"Don't play with me."

"I am not playing." She hopped off the bed and stood in front of him, her arms threading around his neck. "Do you want me?"

Rydor buried his head in her hair. "May the Gods forgive me...I do."

"The gods don't have anything to do with this."

He stepped back.

"Maybe we can't fight destiny." She inched closer to him, but he took another step back. "Are you afraid of me?"

"Only of what I might do to you."

"You wouldn't do anything I didn't want you to, would you?"

"No."

"Then don't be such a coward." She reached for his arm, but he wrenched away and stormed out of the tent into the darkness. Tears rolled down her cheeks. She'd thought he wanted her. How could she have made such a stupid mistake? She threw herself on the bed. It seemed the fragile bond between them was lost. She wanted a man she should not have, and she was willing to give herself to him. Now he rejected her.

All those moon-cycles in his arms meant nothing to him. How could she have thought they were getting closer? Was she really that big a fool? What had she said to send him out into the moon-cycle like a man possessed? So many questions. She was sick of not knowing the answers, and even sicker for offering herself like dessert to a man who was not hungry.

CHAPTER SIXTEEN

Rydor lay in the grass staring at the stars, wondering when he had lost his senses. He almost made love to Shayla. Why had she been so willing? Was it to save her people, or did she have feelings for him? She was right. He was a coward. Some things never changed. The scars on his body were nothing compared to the scars on his heart.

Would the Princess D'Par sacrifice herself for the good of her people? Of course she would. He would be a fool to think she felt anything for him, especially love. Shayla was a princess fulfilling her duty. Love was an emotion he was never fated to have. Shayla said they could not fight their destiny, and she was right. She belonged with her people and he belonged on his mountain.

Love. It was a stupid emotion that made a man look ridiculous, especially when that love betrayed him. He knew betrayal well. Yes, he once loved his family, and look where it got him. Flogged and left for dead.

He had no intention of opening himself to that kind of pain with Shayla. Yet something deep within screamed it was already too late. What he felt for Shayla rocked him to his soul. His emotions were out of control—not good for a warrior.

Tomorrow they would leave the protection of Spirit Mountain and venture into the world that wanted him dead. Maybe he was dead already. When Shayla said the word coward, he recoiled, unable to prove her wrong. He was what he was. Why she thought him any kind of warrior was beyond him. He did not deserve the faith she had placed in him.

A low growl moved closer. "Una, where have you been?" The cat flopped down next to him and purred. He rubbed her full belly. "Glad hunting was good for you. Wish I could say the same." The peacefulness of the meadow closed in on him. Una growled and looked behind him. Before he could turn, he felt the vibration of someone he had not seen in a long time.

My handsome warrior. It's good to see you again, even if I can't touch your body.

Rydor stood and faced the apparition that touched his mind in a melodic voice. *Brina. I wondered when you'd come.*

How could I stay away? She glanced toward the tent. *I've seen her. She's not your type, Rydor.*

What is my type?

"I am. Remember how I stirred your blood? How we shared passion with our bodies for hours on end? I know you haven't forgotten. It was too good to forget."

Brina's filmy presence still held her physical beauty. Long flowing red curls, flawless skin, and curves made to entice men to madness. She wore a white gown cut low in the front. She always dressed to show off her finest assets.

You like what you see, don't you? I could offer you so much more than that...princess you left crying in the tent. What's the matter, Rydor, didn't you find her as tempting as me? Brina laughed. *I was your first and your last. Which makes me hard to forget.*

Go back to Turic's bed.

She floated closer. *Aah, but you excite me more. I had you when you were just a boy. Maybe it's time to see how you pleasure a woman with a man's body.*

Rydor sensed Shayla behind the rocks. This game of Brina's was meant to tempt him and anger Shayla, and no matter what he said, he was caught in the middle. He could explain to Shayla later, right now he had to let Brina think she'd had some success. If Turic thought sending Brina gained them more than his visits, he would send her; and she was less of a threat to Shayla. *You do tempt me, Brina. But I cannot make love to a ghost.*

Oh I'm very much alive.

Doesn't Turic satisfy you?

He does, but I want to have you. A woman must compare before she's sure.

Come back when you have a body I can touch and feel.

We will meet in the flesh, that I promise, and it will be a meeting you will never forget."

I could never forget you, Brina.

See that you don't. And don't waste your time with that poor excuse of a woman. She could never please you.

Rydor smiled as Brina faded into the moon-cycle. Only when she was completely gone did his skin stop crawling. He turned slowly, knowing Shayla was behind him, a look of betrayal written all over her face.

"So, you leave my bed for another woman? You disappoint me."

He grabbed her shoulders and pulled her against his chest. "I never meant to disappoint you, Princess." His mouth took hers with a passion that surprised him. He could barely restrain himself. His hand slid lower down her back and found the roundness below her waist. He pressed her abdomen against his need. She gasped at the contact, but he did not release her. He deepened the kiss, his other hand moving to the middle of her back. He applied pressure and groaned at the feel of her firm breasts against his chest.

She responded with a whimper, her arms holding him as tightly as he held her. He jerked his head back. "By the Gods woman. You're..."

"As good as Brina?"

"That witch can't hold a candle to you." This time her mouth closed over his, and it was her tongue that found his and danced erotically, sending new surges of desire to his swollen manhood. He pulled her down with him onto the soft grass. She was beneath him, trembling. "Is this what you want?"

"How can you ask?"

His hands slid under her tunic and found the soft mound of her breast. "Because there is no going back. Once we join, you will never be looked at the same, not by me or those you love."

"How will you look at me?" She closed her eyes. "I don't want you to look at me differently. I..."

"You will become my Sutae, my precious love. I will cherish you and protect you."

"You won't think less of me?"

"On the contrary. I will think more."

She pulled him down, her mouth seeking his with a fervor that took his breath away. Shayla's desire was as tangible as his. He should not be surprised, he had sensed it all along, yet the reality overwhelmed him. His hands found the bottom edge of her tunic and he pulled it up. Shayla stopped kissing him long enough for him to slip it over her head.

"You can still change your mind."

"Do you want me to?"

Her voice was a husky whisper that excited him even more. "No. But I thought you'd be angry about Brina."

"You said what you had to." She touched his cheek with her palm.

"I know you well, and I heard distaste in your voice."

"You're all I want." He loosened the waist-string of her leggings, eased the pants down her legs and exposed her skin to the moonlight. He then slid off her boots, pulled the garment free and tossed them over his shoulder.

He bent and pressed his lips to her ankle, then inched his way to her knee and up the inside of her thigh. She inhaled deeply and whispered his name when he came close to her womanhood. He knew she was a virgin, and he should move slowly, but he could not wait much longer.

Shayla's skin glowed with moonlit radiance. He never wanted her more. His hand slid one strap then the other of her undergarment off her shoulder. She shook beneath his touch. "Don't be afraid, Sutae, I won't hurt you." He wiped a stray tear from her cheek. "Do you want me to stop?" She shook her head. "I will not ask you again, so be sure of the sacrifice you make."

"I am making no sacrifice, only following my heart. Love me Rydor, please."

***

Shayla blinked back tears. She felt emotionally confused and physically excited all at the same time. Rydor's hands pulled her undergarment down her body inch by tormenting inch. He stopped when he reached her waist, studied her bare breasts and caressed her with his gaze.

Tremors rippled through her abdomen when he lowered his head and sucked a nipple into his mouth. Her back arched and she grabbed his shoulders. She should be embarrassed having a man touch and kiss her for the first time in places reserved only for a life-mate, instead it was magic. She reveled in the pure sensation of skin against skin.

He moved his assault to the other side, his hand covering the dampness left behind from his kisses. Her mouth found his ear, and she ran her tongue over the soft lobe. He moaned, and she felt the power of a woman. She held him in her arms and sensed his vulnerability. Words formed in her mind and his familiar touch calmed her.

You're so beautiful, Sutae.

Her breath caught in her throat when he peeled the undergarment away and recklessly tossed it aside. She had never been so naked. His hands traced her every curve and she could swear she heard him purr like Una.

I will remember this moment always.

As will I. But first there is something I must do. She pushed him back, and he rested on his knees and she rose to hers. Grasping the bottom of his tunic, she pulled it up over his head in one fluid motion. Her hands followed the contours of his chest and the wiry mat of hair in the center tickled her fingertips. As her hands moved from side to side, she felt the thin ripples of his scars, scars that made him who he was. Rydor inhaled deeply when her hands slid lower down rock-hard muscles to the tie at his waist.

You play with fire, little one.

I am not playing. Before she could change her mind, she pulled his leather pants down. This time it was her turn to gasp. He was all male, and more than ready to prove it. Her eyes feasted on forbidden territory.

Touch me.

It was a simple request, but she hesitated, all those proper lessons of the past haunting her, screaming no. Her heart raced when she looked him in the eye. *You're beautiful, Rydor. More perfect than I imagined.*

How can a man so scarred be perfect?

Be proud of who you are and how you got here. Perfection is in the heart and the mind. To me you are perfect.

His mouth found hers in a rush of passion. Every movement he made sent chills up and down her spine. He eased her back to the grass, kissing her neck, then her breast, then her mouth. His erection pressed against her for entry. She wanted him, needed him.

He straddled her, his powerful form perched above. *Now is not the time for patience, warrior.* She had not meant to be so bold, but her body was on fire for the man she wanted since she first laid eyes on him.

I have been patient too long already.

She saw it in his eyes. They were both sending thoughts they had always kept guarded. Their minds seemed as naked as their bodies. He pressed against her and found her slickness. *Oh, Rydor, will it hurt?*

Love always hurts.

He smiled, his eyes full of compassion. She knew he spoke about emotional scars, not the brief physical pain she anticipated. *Love doesn't always hurt.* Her heart cried for his tortured soul.

He pressed into her until she thought she'd rip apart. His breath came rapidly, but she held hers, waiting for him to continue. *I'm so afraid.*

Never fear me.

With one deep thrust he consumed her virginity. She exhaled when the brief tinge of pain subsided and she became acutely aware of his thickness inside her. He moved with an exacting rhythm she followed easily. Then he picked up the pace, faster and deeper. A moan escaped her lips, and she found him in her mind. His thoughts entered in a jumble and mingled with hers. She could not separate what belonged to him or to her. They were joined in every way possible.

Close your eyes and follow me.

She saw him in her mind, naked and beautiful. He offered his hand and she accepted. The moment they touched, a surreal sensation overtook her. She soared into the sky, flying, floating, Rydor by her side. He pulled her to him and thrust himself inside her. How can we make love in two places at once?

The physical and the spiritual have joined. We are one on Zanthus and in the fourth dimension. Our love knows no bounds.

Rydor pressed harder and faster, sending waves of delight through her body. It was a dizzying sensation. Her physical body and her ethereal body could both feel him. It was like being two people feeling the same thing. How it was possible did not matter. All she wanted was Rydor, and he was hers.

Time had no meaning. It was as if they just joined, then it seemed like hours, then he entered her anew. There was no reality. She floated between her physical self and her spiritual self, but no matter where she went, he was inside her, with her, holding her.

Then her mind became a fog, and she felt herself fall through the stars, spasms of ecstasy gripping her body moments before Rydor's hot seed spilled into her. She gasped for air and clung tightly to the warrior who stole her heart. His movements slowed but they remained one, lying naked in each other's arms on the lush grass of Spirit Mountain.

He rolled onto his back, breathing rapidly, but he did not let go of her hand. The moon-cycle air was cool, but her body was still on fire from the feel of him. "I've never felt so..." Mere words could not describe what she just experienced.

"What do you feel, Sutae?"

"Complete, so satisfied, so happy." She rolled toward him and kissed his chest. "What about you?"

"It was more than I imagined. Words fail me."

She reached for her clothes, but his hand grabbed her arm as he rose to his knees.

"No. You will lie naked in my arms this moon-cycle." He cradled her to him and stood. "Do you have an objection?"

All she could do was shake her head. The magic they created left her light-headed. She was grateful he was carrying her to the bed in the tent. If she had to walk, she would probably fall from exhaustion. He was right, there were no words or explanations for what they just shared. All she knew was that she wanted more. She never dreamed something so forbidden could be so good.

CHAPTER SEVENTEEN

Rydor smiled while Shayla walked stiffly to her Esroth in the early morning light, Una nearly stepping on her heels. "Are you sore from riding?"

"Yes, but it's not the Esroth's fault."

She blushed and her cheeks turned redder than the rising sun, but she never looked more beautiful. Their joining caused changes in her he found exciting. Her eyes sparkled with happiness, and her expression had the knowing look one lover gave to another. Everything about Shayla was special.

He walked up behind her and lifted her onto the saddle. "One sun-cycle you must learn to mount unaided. I'm growing too fond of feeling your backside." She laughed, and his heart swelled with pride that the angelic princess belonged to him in every sense of the word. Reluctantly he released her and walked to his own Esroth.

"Rydor!" She rode up beside him. "Do I look different this sun-cycle?"

"Of course you do."

"You're looking at me differently, just like I thought you would."

She bowed her head. He reached over and tipped her chin up with his finger. "You have already forgotten what I said?" She shook her head. "Then what is this long face about?"

"Everything has changed...everything will change...I don't know, it's..."

"I feel it too, Sutae, but trust in us. Together we will defeat all enemies." At that she smiled, but he sensed her fear. There were obstacles waiting to destroy them. He may not be a solid believer in the Gods, but he prayed they would survive and not be torn apart.

The Esroths shied when they entered the fog, and Una gave an uneasy growl. Eerie mist swirled around them and rose to form a low ceiling. A clear path lay before them, and he nudged his mount into a comfortable cantor. He kept a keen ear on the beating hooves behind him. This was no time to lose Shayla.

It did not take long to break free of the transition area and exit into the sparsely vegetated desert of the Badlands. He pulled to a stop and waited as Shayla rode safely through and stopped by his side. Together they watched the heavy haze descend from above to seal the zone between Spirit Mountain and the rest of Zanthus.

"Will it ever be the same?" Shayla whispered.

Rydor shook his head. "Never." That admission hurt more than Shayla would ever know. Everything he had found comfort in lay behind him, and the uncertainty of the future loomed ahead. Even the special bond he and Shayla shared was on that mountain. Was their love strong enough to hold them together? They had not spoken the words, only shared the feeling, but it was real.

"Rydor? Are you all right?"

He tightened his grip on the reins and spurred his Esroth along the trail. They rode in silence for several minutes before his warrior's instincts detected danger ahead. *Follow me, and do not speak out loud.* He led them away from the trail down into a gully. Once in the dry creek, he stopped and helped Shayla dismount.

What is it?

We're being watched.

By who?

Two men. Wait here. He pulled the cutter from the sheath at his waist then climbed out of the shallow gulch. Voices drifted on the breeze, deep, excited voices. He stood and walked toward the riders that rapidly approached in a swirl of dust.

Do not move, Shayla.

"You there!" one man yelled.

Both riders halted their Esroths and looked down on him. They were warriors dressed in fancy gray uniforms meant to impress and intimidate.

"Where is she?"

"She?"

"Don't lie to us, we saw her."

The bigger of the two jumped down and reached for him. Rydor grabbed the man's arms and wrestled him to the ground. He placed a foot on the man's chest. "Never call me a liar."

An arm grasped him from behind. He dipped one shoulder and flipped the man to the desert floor. Rydor flashed his cutter when both men rose to their feet.

"We can talk about this, stranger. Just tell us what you did with the woman."

"Why?"

"You don't know who you're dealing with."

"Don't I?" Rydor circled the uniformed men. "You are Zared warriors." He touched the cutter to the silver braids on their shoulders. "Of some rank. Now, state your business."

Rydor, don't hurt them.

Stay out of this, Shayla.

"We're here to escort Princess Shayla D'Par home."

"I see. Who sent you?"

"Ruler Nuri, her father. We are her personal guards. I am Rance and this is Arden. We have her best interests at heart. You must believe that."

"I believe nothing without proof."

Shayla, join me. It took but a moment for her to reach them. Instead of stopping beside him, she rushed past and hugged the man he had been talking to. *Shayla!* His stomach knotted and his hands fisted. He would kill them both if they laid a hand on her. *Shayla, get away from them!*

"Rydor, it's all right. They're my personal guards. They brought me here. They saved my life more than once while I was looking for you." She walked to Rydor and took his hand. "Rydor, please meet Arden and Rance. Two of the finest guards a princess could have."

He scowled. Why did the idea of any man in her life bother him so? He was not the jealous kind, but then, how would he know? Shayla was the first woman he had ever had real feelings for, and they were so new he was not used to them.

"Rydor. Grasp their wrists in the traditional warrior's greeting." *And stop acting like that!*

Like what? He did as she requested and extended his welcome to them both.

Like a jealous fool.

I am not! I'm only protecting you.

"Arden, Rance, meet Rydor, my Kiah Master."

"Our pleasure, Rydor, and please, accept our apologies for the misunderstanding."

Rydor saw both men draw a weapon from a holder on their belts and aim at something behind him. He glanced over his shoulder and saw Una bound toward him. A blue beam of light blew a hole in the earth just behind the cat.

He spun on Arden and Rance and knocked both of them to the ground. Shayla screamed. "Do not harm the Semita. If you do I will personally rip you both limb from limb. Is that clear?"

"Rance, Arden, Rydor! Stop this insanity. Get up, all of you." Una sauntered over to Shayla and sat next to her. "This Semita is called, Una. She belongs to Rydor. I'm fond of her as well. You will guard her as you guard me. She is bound to cause a stir, and it's your job to see to it she isn't harmed."

Arden and Rance scrambled to their feet, snapped to attention, bowed their heads and mumbled in unison, "Yes, Princess."

As for you, my diligent warrior and self-appointed protector. Go easy. You can't bully your way in my world. There is an order to things here, and I hate to tell you, you're not in charge.

Perhaps I should return to my mountain.

Only if you insist on being a rough and tumble mountain man. She raised an eyebrow and looked him in the eye.

As you wish, Princess. She was right. He did not fit into her world, and if he were to function at all he must adjust to their ways. Taking orders was a foreign idea, but he would concede to please Shayla.

"Arden, how is my father?"

"He is well. Worried about you."

"As you can see, I'm fine. I will contact him immediately. Where's your com-unit?"

"Not working."

"Then I'll get mine." She turned and headed toward the gully.

"Princess, wait. You don't understand. All communications have been jammed by the Voltrans."

"How long have they been jammed?"

"Since the sun-cycle we lost you."

Shayla laughed. "And I thought it was Ol..."

Do not speak Olin's name. It is not safe or advised. He makes himself known only to those he sees fit. You will look like a crazy woman talking about a man no one else sees.

Sorry, I forgot. I've already had that experience once.

She silently laughed. *You know, this private communication stuff is fun. Look at them, they have no idea we're talking.*

"Princess? Is something wrong?"

"No. Let's get out of here and have a hot meal at that horrible inn."

"The Snake Eye?"

"None other."

They all mounted their Esroths and quickly made their way to the Snake Eye Inn. Una kept pace with them, which made Arden and Rance nervous. She hoped they would adjust to the cat quickly because it would take all of them to keep Una safe. They all secured their mounts at the hitching rail along the side of the inn. She watched Rydor whisper something in Una's ear and the cat scurried off into the brush. They all walked together into the Snake Eye and made their way to a table in the back.

Shayla had never felt more uncomfortable in her life. She and the three men who cared about her shared a meal in a dark corner of the Snake Eye Inn. It was a good thing the utensils were dull. Sharp objects were not a good idea with three jealous warriors in close proximity. Arden and Rance sized Rydor up, and he glared at them as if they were demons from beneath the planet.

Rydor was unusually quiet. He'd changed the moment he left his mountain. She knew he would. It was difficult to tell if the change was for the better. So far it was not.

Rance put his fork down and wiped his mouth with the lap-cloth. "When do we leave?"

"In the morning." Three pairs of eyes glared at her. "Is there a problem?"

"Yes," Rydor grumbled. "It's not safe here."

"You know, I actually agree with you," Rance added.

"Fine. We'll take the solar cruiser to Terita now," Arden suggested.

"No," Rydor argued.

"Rydor." He was irritating her with his mountain man routine, but he never looked more handsome in the light of the single candle that flickered in the center of the rough-hewn table.

Rydor glared at Shayla. *Remember Olin's warnings. Trust no one. Do not take the conventional route, it isn't safe.*

But it's faster than by Esroth. We could travel non-stop and be there by the end of tomorrow's sun-cycle. Wouldn't that be safe?

Are there not weapons to shoot your cruiser from the sky?

The same weapons that can shoot us off our Esroths! Come on, Rydor, be reasonable. Besides, when Turic and Brina wanted to find you they just showed up. They can do that anytime, anywhere.

You're right, Sutae, which is why we need to travel alone. Only we can fight them, your guards would only interfere.

He frowned and she ground her teeth. His blue gaze darkened. He looked ready to pounce on something. His stare became a warning that was hard to ignore.

I am not unreasonable.

She wanted to disagree, but it would not be wise. *What should we do?*

Follow our hearts.

Shayla sighed. *Then I want you to hold me in your arms and kiss me.*

As you wish, Princess.

Don't you dare! Not here, in public, in front of my guards.

But I never refuse a princess.

"What's going on between you two?

She couldn't hide her smile when Rydor glared at Arden for his rude intrusion into a conversation he had no idea existed. "Nothing is going on. I was just thinking about how we should proceed."

Rydor leaned his arms on the table and faced the two men. "We will proceed without your services. I do not mean that as an insult, only as a necessity. There are things we cannot explain."

Arden stared at Rydor. "It is not up to you to dismiss us. Our duty lies with Ruler Nuri first and Princess D'Par second. We will not allow either of you out of our sight. Our orders stand."

Rydor, it's no use to argue with them. I've tried that before when I set off to find you. However, Olin may be able to aid us. What do you think? Shayla took a relieved breath when Rydor nodded his consent. "Arden, Rance, let's not debate the fact right now. We'll get rooms for the moon-cycle and all leave together in the morning. Rydor, will you agree?"

"As you wish, Princess."

"Good, then it's settled."

Arden stood. "I'll make the arrangements."

"I'll help," Rance said.

Shayla waited till her guards were busy talking to the innkeeper before she squeezed Rydor's hand under the table. "Thank you." He returned the gesture, then inched his hand up her arm. It was hard not to smile, but she feared someone might see the amorous response she had to hide.

"I look forward to holding you in my arms this moon-cycle."

"I'm afraid that won't be possible. I must keep up appearances."

Rydor grinned. "I can be discrete."

"I'm sure you can, but the risk is too great." His hand left her arm, and she suddenly felt empty. Had they spent their last moon-cycle together? Would he ever make love to her again? Damn proprieties. All her life she had worried about her place and position, what people would think and how they would judge her.

"Don't worry. We will be together."

"You can read my mind that easily?"

"Only when I'm having the same thoughts." *We're bonded now. We can't be separated.*

I pray you're right.

Rydor leaned back in his chair. *Trust me.*

Arden and Rance returned to their seats, a grim look on their faces. "Is something wrong?"

"There's only two rooms available," Rance grumbled.

"We'll make do." She bit her tongue before she blurted out that she and Rydor would be happy to share a room. That behavior would not be tolerated. Too many people would see them, and that information would be worth a great deal of money to the media. For all she knew there were journalists drinking at adjoining tables, waiting for a scoop. She cringed thinking about the headline, "Wayward Daughter of Ruler Nuri Found In Barbarian's Arms."

Not that Rydor was a barbarian, but if he were assessed by his appearance, it would be accurate. His long dark hair hung past his shoulders when most men wore theirs short. Handmade leather clothing wasn't the fashion statement of the sun-cycle, not even for the outlaws of the Badlands. She would have to secure a wardrobe for him and see that he made a proper impression when he met her father.

"Princess?"

"I'm sorry, Arden, did you say something?"

"I asked if you're ready to retire?"

"Yes, of course."

The four of them climbed the rickety wooden stairs to their rooms. Rance opened her door and handed her the key. Rydor stood by the wall, lost and rejected. Or was he simply feeling out of place and angry? Happy did not explain her mood either. "Good-moon-cycle."

Three male voices echoed hers as she slipped inside the rustic accommodations. She closed and locked the door behind her then settled on the bed. A hot scented bath and clean clothes would be heaven, but not a reality. Soon she would be home, her royal wardrobe and personal quarters waited, yet the sacrifice would be great.

No longer could she sleep in Rydor's arms and lie in his bed. Tears welled in her eyes. They may have bonded, but he was still as forbidden as he was before. Why did life have to be so cruel? Finally she had found a man she could love, a man she wanted to be with, but a man her father would never give permission to life-mate.

Tears rolled down her cheeks. All may not be lost, but the intimacy she and Rydor had shared on Spirit Mountain was gone. Their lives would forever change, and there was no going back. A future without Rydor promised a dismal existence. Their time together may have been short, but it was the most special time of her life. She did not want to be without him. They had not been separated since he found her by the river, and that was the way she wanted it. There was only a thin wall between their rooms, but it seemed as if she were locked in a dungeon.

"Shayla?"

She lifted her head and saw a fuzzy form materialize in front of her. "Olin?" she mumbled, sitting up on the bed. "I'm so glad you're here."

"None too soon from the looks of it. What has Rydor done now?"

A smile pulled at the corners of her mouth. "It's not Rydor. My bodyguards will not let us continue to Terita alone. Rydor says we must travel together, without them. I don't know what to do. I knew you'd help."

Olin grinned. "I see a spark in your eyes that was not there last time I saw you."

Shayla laughed. "You are a wise old wizard, and you know exactly what that spark is."

"I do." Olin sat on the chair next to the bed. "I still don't understand what took so long."

"Some things can't be rushed, even with magic."

"How are your mental communications?"

"Very good. And if you ask Rydor, he'd probably tell you too good." She laughed. "I used my ability to tell him things I didn't want my guards to hear. We held a complete conversation and no one was the wiser." Shayla leaned forward. "It's kind of fun actually."

"I'm glad you find it amusing, my child, but it is serious business. Then again, you know that."

"Olin, I'm worried about Rydor. He's having trouble adjusting to the outside world. After being on that mountain so long, he's...he's..."

"Stubborn?" He chuckled. "I've known that as long as I've known Rydor. Don't you worry. He's a survivor, among other things."

"He's an amazing man."

"That he is, and don't forget it." Olin reached out and took Shayla's hand. "There will be times you're tempted to doubt him. Keep the faith—the feeling you have in your heart this moment."

"I'm scared it will change."

"Fear is an enemy. Never give fear your energy, it's counterproductive and creates negativity. Think positive, visualize the outcome you want."

"That sounds so simple."

"The simplest things are the most difficult. With that said, I'll tell you the plan I have devised to get you and Rydor safely on your way, alone."

CHAPTER EIGHTEEN

Rydor paced the confines of the small room. He had never had claustrophobia before, and it was a feeling he hated. Rance and Arden lay on the two cots against the opposite wall. They stared at him as if he were a creature from the deep. There was no forgiveness in their eyes. He sensed they suspected something was going on between him and Shayla, but they had no idea how far it had gone.

Warriors were always combative, it was their job. He had no desire to fight them, only escape. The plain wooden walls closed in and made the loneliness in his heart deepen. All he could think about was Shayla in the next room, alone.

Turic's threats were still real. He could sense Turic's presence if he appeared to Shayla, but she was behind a locked door. Walls, locks, rules, lies, betrayal. Those were the reasons he rebelled in his youth, reasons he still rebelled against. Some things never changed.

Worst of all, he had seen the way Rance and Arden looked at Shayla. They adored her. He saw it in their eyes, heard it in their voices, and that did not please him.

"Sure you don't want the bed, Rydor?" Arden asked.

"No."

"Then lay on the hard floor and sleep. I can't take any more of that incessant pacing."

Rydor gritted his teeth and bit back a heated reply. He hated taking orders, especially from them. Shayla's saddlebags were on the floor, and he stopped in front of them. He lay down, slipped his cutter into her bag then used it as a pillow. It was as close as he could get to her this mooncycle.

Making love to Shayla was a special gift he would cherish forever.

She made him believe in himself, and restored his self-worth which stirred emotions he never knew possible. Caring about a woman was something he had been denied, another gift Shayla had given him.

The rhythmic snoring of Rance and Arden hummed through the room. He wanted to go to Shayla; no, needed to go to her. He rose to his feet and made his way to the door. Sliding the safety-bolt to the side, he quietly slipped out.

He stared at her door. His blood raced just thinking about her. The risk no longer mattered. He wanted her, and have her he would. With one finger, he quietly tapped. The wait seemed forever, then he heard the metal bar slide to the side. Hinges creaked while the door slowly swung open. He stepped inside and pulled her into his arms.

When he bent his head to kiss her, she pulled back. "What's wrong, Sutae?"

"I cannot kiss you until you bring my saddlebags in here. We must have the Kiah with us, as always."

"One kiss before I go." He pulled her closer, but her hands pushed hard against his chest. "Do you refuse me?"

"Never. I will kiss you all you want as soon as you bring me my bag."

She was acting strange. "Is this a game?"

"You could say that. Now go get the bag. I want my kiss. Please, hurry."

"As you wish, Princess."

She stood at the door while he entered his room. Arden and Rance still slept soundly. He picked up the bags, quietly closed the door and returned to Shayla. "What kind of guards do you have that sleep so soundly? I could have killed them, or you, moving in and out. Yet they didn't stir." He secured the bolt on Shayla's door.

"Are you going to babble about my guards, or are you going to kiss me?"

He smiled. "A bit anxious, aren't you?" She nodded. "I'm not in the hurry I was before. I think I'll take my time." He walked to the bed and sat, her bag in his hand.

Shayla rushed to him, pushed him back and lay on top of him. Her firm breasts pressed suggestively against his chest and he knew it would be hard to resist her for long. Her lips rested against his, but he did not respond.

"What's wrong Rydor? Do I not please you?"

"I thought this was a game."

"In a way it is."

"One should never rush a game."

"There are times it's advisable."

"Not this kind of game." She looked at him as if he were crazy, but he saw the spark of desire in the brown depths of her eyes. He reached up and cupped her firm breast in his hand and her nipple hardened instantly, the outline clear against the thin fabric of her nightgown.

Blood coursed through his veins. He wanted this woman here and now. He felt his manhood thicken, and he swallowed hard. If this was playing, he could hardly wait for her to get serious. "I believe you've turned into a vixen."

"Are you trying to insult me, Mountain Man?"

"I could take that as an insult."

Shayla pressed her lips to his and fire brewed in his veins, but he resisted and held her back. "What's your rush, sweet Princess?"

"For a man with no patience, you're certainly trying mine."

Rydor tensed when he heard footsteps in the hall.

"Kiss me now or lose me forever!"

Her urgency was great, and he could no more deny her wish than he could stop breathing. He kissed her with an all-consuming passion, deep and sweet. Her tongue teased until the room seemed to spin. He felt dizzy and light-headed, the same way he felt when they made love on two levels.

A chill raced over his back. The air turned sweet and misty, laden with the pleasant aroma of the Taber flower. But that could not be. Taber flowers only grew in tropical oases, and they were far from such a place.

Shayla moaned when he threaded his fingers through her hair. A bird cawed overhead. His eyes flew open and his head jerked back. He scrambled to his feet and stared in awe. "Explain this!"

"Olin."

"I should have guessed." He glanced at Shayla lying in soft Lufa grass, her blond curls glowing in the moonlight against the plush green beneath her. He dropped the saddlebags. "Why didn't you tell me you'd seen him?"

"And ruin the fun?" She giggled.

"Fun? We haven't begun to have fun yet." He knelt beside her and untied the lace of her tunic before pulling it over her head. His breath caught in his throat when he realized she wore nothing underneath. The tightness in his groin grew stronger. With haste, he pulled off her boots and leggings then buried his head in the warmth of her breasts.

"Aren't you going to ask what Olin said?"

"I'm busy." His mouth closed over her breast, his tongue teasing her nipple. She was soft and delicious, everything he had ever wanted. He lost himself in her flesh, joining with her mind and her body. It mattered not where they were as long as they could share their love. He slipped inside her, lost in the world that was theirs alone.

Here there were no rules or locks, no restraints or inhibitions. He could make sweet, passionate love to her till the sun shone on their naked bodies, and he intended to do just that.

***

Shayla blinked several times in an effort to stop the bright light from stinging her eyes. It was too early to get up since she'd been asleep barely an hour. Rydor's performance all moon-cycle was nothing short of miraculous. She'd never have guessed something so wonderful could last so long.

Now she was starving and wanted a good meal followed by a long nap. She lifted her head from Rydor's shoulder and perused his exquisite body stretched out next to her. With one finger, she lightly traced the largest of the scars across his chest. Who could have done this to him? She'd seen marks left by animals' claws, but these lines had the distinct mark left by a warrior's whip.

Rydor stirred slightly under her touch. *You're magnificent, my love.* She started to get up, but he pulled her back.

I heard you, Sutae, but it is you who stirs my blood.

A quick glance below his waist, and fire invaded her cheeks. *You couldn't possibly want to...*

Couldn't I?

Shayla laughed and pushed herself free of his grasp. "Not until we've eaten."

"Food is more important than I am?" He chuckled. "You disappoint me."

"One of us must stay rational." She loved the seductive grin he gave her. "People die from starvation you know, and I don't plan to be one of them. Besides, if you keep up this pace we'll need all the strength we can get."

He propped himself up on one elbow. "If it's food you want, you shall have it."

"I'm afraid we don't have any supplies."

"We did leave in a hurry."

She watched Rydor pull on his pants and boots, then stomp off into the dense foliage of the oasis, mumbling something about spells and wizards. At least he had a smile on his face.

She quickly dressed and studied the surroundings. From the looks of it, they were in one of the many remote oases about two hundred megators from Terita. Ever since she left home all she had wanted was to return. Now the idea held little enticement. She would rather live in the wilderness with Rydor than have the comforts of the royal palace.

The bond between them deepened each sun-cycle. She now had a strength she never before thought possible. Their combined strength made them capable of things she had never before done, or even dreamed about. Mental communication and traveling out of her body while making love were new and exciting adventures. It had become second nature to be in his mind and have him in hers.

Pain suddenly throbbed in her head. She heard a woman's voice. A foggy mist took form in front of her. Long red hair came into focus, then a flowing white gown cut low in front. The woman's refined features cleared and there was no mistake. "Brina!"

"So, you know who I am."

"You know I saw you when you came to Rydor."

"I thought you'd be gone by now. Especially after learning that Rydor and I were lovers."

"Never assume anything about me, Brina. And I don't believe you and Rydor were lovers."

"Indeed, then I shall show you."

Like a hologram, she saw Brina and Rydor naked in each other's arms, coupling frantically, touching intimately. Even their moans sounded real. Her stomach turned. She felt numb, betrayed. She thought Brina lied that moon-cycle she appeared to Rydor, but the proof was there in front of her.

Then Olin's words flooded her mind. He had told her the enemy would do or say anything to weaken them. "You lie. You were never with Rydor."

"Believe what you like, but I know that Kiah Master of yours in ways you never will."

Shayla took a deep breath. "You're wrong, Brina. I know him better than you can imagine."

"You've coupled?" Brina laughed. "Now it is you who lie! You're a princess, promised to another, you would never risk your royal status!"

"Wouldn't I?" Shayla closed her eyes and sent a vision of her and Rydor together in the tent. "See what happened after you left? Your little visit was a failure. Now go back to Turic and see if he can please you. Rydor belongs to me, and I'm not the sharing kind."

"Really? He was used goods when you had him. Besides, Rydor could never surpass Turic. Not in or out of bed."

"We'll see, won't we?" Shayla took a step toward the woman's apparition. "You don't scare me."

"And you're a fool for trusting a Voltran coward to fight for the Zared Tribe."

"Rydor is no coward."

Brina laughed long and hard. "Ask him!"

Before Shayla could say anything more, Brina was gone, and with her went the ache in her head. She slumped to the ground, her body shaking. Brina was as evil as Turic. This encounter was meant to intimidate and frighten, and she expected future attacks which would be even worse.

Only Rydor could tell her if he had been with Brina. Somehow she could not imagine such a mating, but recent lessons had proven anything was possible. Worst of all Brina called Rydor a coward. What possessed her to throw that insult? She wrapped her arms around herself and rocked back and forth. The air was warm, yet a cold chill penetrated right down to her bones.

"Shayla!" Rydor rushed to her side and wrapped his arms around her. "What's wrong?"

"Brina."

"She was here? Did she hurt you?"

"She just came with insults and threats." Shayla held his arm, her hands still shaking. "I don't know how to fight her." She looked into Rydor's eyes. "Help me, Rydor. Teach me how to be your Focus. We can't lose, we just can't."

He softly brushed his lips over hers. She felt like a failure. There must have been something she could have done to intimidate Brina. Instead, she'd fallen into her trap. "Rydor, I'm so sorry. I've made such a mess of things. Brina called you a coward and I wanted to kill her, but all I did was look like a defenseless fool. I convinced Olin to send us here and I forgot Una. Now she'll never find us."

Rydor wiped teardrops from her cheeks with his fingers. "You have done well. This was your first meeting with Brina. You'll be more prepared next time. As for Una, she will find me." He gave her a long, tight hug then stood. "Now, I shall retrieve our breakfast."

"Hurry." Her hunger returned with a vengeance. She was glad Brina had come. Now she had a better idea what she was up against. Brina had obviously lied about being with Rydor, and about him being a coward. This was no time to doubt Rydor and she would insult him if she asked him to deny Brina's accusations.

"Here. Eat. We have much work to do. This sun-cycle you will learn to astral travel at will."

Rydor handed her a piece of fruit he had sliced in half with his cutter. "What do you mean?"

"Remember how we left our bodies while making love? Well, you can do the same while meditating. We too can pay a visit to the enemy, and I believe it is time we did. But first you must master the travel part."

"Are you saying I can go anywhere I want by just thinking myself there?"

"Yes."

"I could even see my father?"

"Yes. In fact that might be the safest first try."

"You'll go with me?"

"Of course. I'd never let a novice go alone."

Shayla ate quickly. The thought of seeing her father calmed her shaky nerves. This was the first time they had been separated for so long. She was a grown woman, and in Rydor's company so she certainly was not lonely, but she missed her father all the same.

Rydor peeled more fruit and handed it to her, along with berries and nuts. She knew he preferred meat, but there were no edible creatures within megators. She watched him crunch the Mora nuts and smiled at him. "I'm still worried about Una."

"It's a good thing she's not here, considering the cuisine." Rydor wiped his hands on the grass. "Are you ready to begin?"

"Let's do it."

"Okay, sit like this." Rydor crossed his legs and laid his hands on his knees, palms open. "Breathe slowly. Concentrate only on your breathing. Close your eyes, and think of nothing but each breath you take. When you're totally relaxed, you'll feel yourself float up out of yourself. Then picture yourself with your father."

"I won't lose you, will I?"

"No, Sutae, you will not."

She'd seen Rydor do this many times, but it was more difficult than she thought to concentrate on nothing but breathing, especially with him next to her. Rydor was all she could think of.

Think of nothing. You must ignore me.

How did you know I was thinking of you?

Your vibrations are strong. Since we've joined, I sense you faster and deeper.

You can read my mind now?

Your private thoughts are safe, but I can detect moods in them, like anger, fear, love.

She shut out Rydor and all her feelings. One breath at a time. In, out. In, out. A light feeling came over her, and she drifted above herself. She glanced down and saw herself sitting in the meditative posture with Rydor by her side. Then she pictured her father's study.

Instantly she stood before his desk. Nuri was bent over a stack of papers, three of his advisors sat before him. "Father?" He didn't hear her. She didn't think he would sense her presence. Rydor appeared next to her. My father doesn't know I'm here.

Only a person highly attuned to the metaphysical can sense us.

You look as solid to me as he does.

Because we're on the same plane in our ethereal bodies, but we view the physical world as well.

Can I touch him?

He won't feel it. Rydor took Shayla's hand in his. Only those on our plane can see and feel us.

So if Turic and Brina were here, we could speak to them and touch them?

He nodded. They would be on our plane. The biggest danger is if they attack our physical bodies while we're here. But I'll explain that later.

She watched her father sign several documents. In the sun-cycles she'd been away, he'd changed, and that frightened her.

Ruler Nuri stood. "Is there any news about Shayla?"

"No. All communications are still disabled."

"Damn the Voltrans." Nuri poured himself a glass of water and took a drink. "Send four of our best warriors to check on Rance and Arden. Put Eaton in charge of the assignment. He's been worried about Shayla. If anyone can bring them back, it's Eaton."

"Yes sir."

"Go, all of you. I need to be alone."

Shayla watched his advisors leave. Nuri returned to the large chair behind his desk and sat. There were circles under his eyes, and his skin was overly pale against the dark blue material of his clothes. How she wanted to reassure him all was well. She glanced at Rydor, but he showed no emotion. How do we get back?

Rydor didn't have to answer, the thought of leaving was all it took. She immediately felt heavy being back in her physical body. A hand touched her arm and she opened her eyes.

"You did well for your first time."

"I hadn't planned to come back so fast."

"All it takes is a thought."

"I found that out."

"Anything you want to do, or create, only takes a thought in the fourth dimension. That is the key element to remember. Whatever you need, just think it."

Shayla smiled. "Can I make Brina disappear by thinking her gone?"

"I wish it were that simple."

"Nothing is ever simple." Rydor took her hand, the warmth of his skin the only comfort to her troubled mind. "How will I be able to remember all this?"

"You will. We have thirty-two sun-cycles to practice."

She prayed she could become adept in that amount of time. At least Rydor was more accomplished, but, as his Focus, she needed to be equally as strong. She had to handle Brina while Rydor matched wits with Turic, and Brina had quite a head start on her. "What about the Kiah Rod?"

"Olin said it only magnifies our strength."

"Let's see what it does." Shayla pulled the leather case from the saddlebag, opened it and handed both pieces to Rydor. "Let's pay a visit to Turic and Brina."

"I think we should check out our other competition first."

"I forgot about the Quelans."

Rydor smiled. "They fight the Voltrans first, and should they win, we would fight them. It's doubtful, but it could happen."

She watched with interest as Rydor matched the two pieces together in front of him. "Do you think it's possible to mend the Kiah?"

"I don't know."

"Olin said before a Kiah Master can fight the Ultimate Battle, he must first mend the rod. Anything the mind can conceive is a possible reality."

"Your memory is good, Sutae."

"But I have no idea what it all means." Rydor raised one eyebrow and grinned, the same as he had when Olin first imparted that tidbit of wisdom. "So, let your mind make it whole."

He closed his eyes and held the two pieces together over his head. The dark black turned emerald, slowly lightening several shades. It looked like one piece, but when he lowered his arms and separated his hands she sighed. "Try again."

Several more tries yielded the same results. His expression took on an agitated scowl, and the green glow faded to black once again in his grasp. She reached out and touched his arm. His muscles shook, and she sensed frustration and failure in his darkening mood. "Don't worry. You'll succeed. There must be a trick to it you haven't figured out yet."

Rydor stood and walked toward the edge of the large hot spring a short distance away. He obviously needed to be alone. She pulled the saddlebag closer and laid down on the soft grass to use it as a pillow. Their moon-cycle of passion had taken its toll, and it was past time for sleep.

CHAPTER NINETEEN

"Brina, my pet." Turic stroked her red hair with his hand. "Tell me about your visit with Shayla."

"She tried to tell me she and Rydor coupled."

"You don't believe her?"

"I'm not sure. I didn't sense any increased powers in her, but then Rydor wasn't close enough for me to detect any changes in him."

"It matters not if they've joined. They cannot defeat us."

"What about the Quelan team?" Brina slipped her arms around Turic's neck.

"They're no threat at all. We will destroy them so fast they won't know what hit them."

Brina laughed. "Of course we will. No one can touch us."

Turic kissed her and she moaned softly. "What did Shayla do when you let her view your past?"

"She froze like a scared animal, and I detected jealousy, an emotion I will use against her. She's weak, and so is Rydor. I think a visit from you in the near future will send her packing back to daddy."

"Maybe. I do have a few plans for the princess." Brina squinted and while she stared at him her lips turned down. "What's the matter, my pet? Jealous?"

"She's not woman enough for you, my most capable lover!" Brina laughed.

"And you are?" Turic chuckled. "A bit overconfident, aren't you?" Brina glared at him as if she wanted to scratch his eyes out. "I love it when you're angry." He threw her down on the bed and lay on top of her. "Maybe I should teach you a lesson."

"Make it a long lesson."

Turic laughed to himself. Brina was a fool. She actually thought he had feelings for her. He took pleasure in her body, but he cared nothing about her. If he knew his brother, the coward was falling in love with Shayla, and he planned to use that to annihilate him. Rydor's downfall had always been caring about others too much.

He nibbled Brina's neck and enjoyed the power he held over her. She melted in his arms. Brina was good for sex, and she was a compatible Focus; but when this was over he wanted nothing to do with her. He missed the other women in his life. Damek made him promise to bed only Brina till the battle was over so their power would not be diluted.

She squirmed when he grabbed her breast. He wondered what it would be like to have Shayla beneath him like this. The princess did have a certain appeal.

"Turic, that hurts," Brina complained.

He slapped her across the face. "Don't ever criticize me!"

***

Rydor pulled off his boots and pants and jumped into the mineral spring. The bubbling hot water soothed his body, but not his mind. He failed to mend the rod and had no idea how to accomplish the feat. Olin said it could be restored, but neglected to mention how. Where was that sneaky old wizard?

He tilted his head back, rested it against a smooth rock and closed his eyes to the afternoon sun. Shayla was sleeping, and he needed this time away from her. Was he still a coward? Could that be the reason he failed to mend the rod? Shayla had too much faith in him. The time had come to tell her he was a branded, outcast coward. Brina already told her part of his past. Shayla in her innocence had not believed her. In time the evil woman would prove it to Shayla somehow, and he wanted her to hear it from him, not the enemy.

The same held true with the coupling incident with Brina. Even if it was not mutual, it happened. But how could he tell Shayla about being with Brina, and admit to his cowardice without telling her who was responsible for it all—his father?

Damek put Brina up to the drugged seduction. He had been afraid his first born son wasn't a man, and he thought bedding a woman would remedy that. How wrong he was. All Brina accomplished was cementing his resolve to defy his father in every way possible. He hadn't let the man down during his warrior's training, that was a matter of pride. It had been his denial to complete the rite of passage that sent Damek over the edge.

The true essence of a man could always be seen in the face of adversity, and his father revealed it to him full force. Not one lash of the whip did he regret. How could a father put his own child through so much pain? Physical and mental pain—both hurt. The physical pain healed, but the mental issues never did. All he had to hold on to was his own integrity. Something Damek and Turic knew nothing about. It could well destroy him again, but he gladly took the risk because somewhere, somehow good had to triumph over evil.

Zanthus had to be saved from Voltran evil, and Damek was at the core. Turic had learned his lessons well, but without Damek's strength and support, he doubted his brother could become ruler. Oh, Turic was wicked enough, but so far he did not have the support of the Elders. Then again, things may have changed since his departure from the tribe.

A visit to Turic and Damek was in order. He had to learn for himself the condition of his Tribe. The Voltran people were not at fault. They were only following their leader, no matter what a bad mistake that proved to be.

Rydor took a deep breath, the fragrance of flowers heavy in the steamy air around him, their scent reminding him of Shayla. She was so sweet, so good, so loving. May the Gods forgive him for defiling her. He never should have corrupted the purity of the princess. There would be a price to pay for such a deed.

Shayla was Ruler Nuri's only daughter. How could he face the man knowing what he had done? It would take all of Shayla's courage to stand before him considering the sacrifice she made. Then there was that warrior, Eaton. What would he do when he learned he would not life-mate a virgin?

Instead of Shayla convincing him he was not a coward, she proved it true. If he had any courage at all he would have resisted her womanly charms. Olin tried to push them together, and he successfully resisted for a time. Then weakness set in and he gave in to lust. No, it was more than that. He truly cared about her and wanted her people to be victorious. The moment he took her, it was to satisfy selfish pleasures of the flesh, but he also hoped to mend his broken heart.

Shayla had tempted him from the moment he picked her up in his arms and carried her to his home. He felt possessive of her, yet she was not a prize to be won. She belonged to another, and he knew the rules as well as the next man. He committed a punishable crime and the sentence belonged to Ruler Nuri. Punishment did not matter to him because Shayla was worth any sacrifice. His only regret was the humiliation she would face because of him.

A warm essence touched his mind, and he knew Shayla approached.

He could feel her anywhere. Time alone was refreshing, but he missed her. How could two people become so close in such a short time? As Olin would say, some things are beyond explanation.

"Rydor, may I join you?"

He turned, shocked to see her naked. "You're so beautiful." She smiled at him and his heart beat faster. Shayla bent toward him, and he lifted her by the waist into the bubbling pool.

"This is heavenly. I haven't had a hot bath since I left Terita."

"Do you miss your home?"

"Of course."

"And Eaton?" An immediate frown told him he just made a mistake. He had no right to question her. She had a life before she met him and would have one after he was gone.

"I told you before, I have no feelings for him. Why don't you believe me?"

"I heard what your father said."

"I never said Eaton didn't have feelings for me, but I think of him as a friend. We went to school together. We've known each other our whole lives." She threaded her fingers through his wet hair. "You have nothing to worry about."

Her words held little consolation. Even if there was nothing between her and Eaton, he would lose her in the end. Nuri would see to it. Inter-tribe life-mateings were forbidden. No, they were doomed from the beginning.

"Don't look so sad."

Rydor let go of her waist and drifted to the center of the pool. The situation was impossible. He had to stay close to her as his Focus, he wanted her as his lover, but it was all temporary. They were fooling themselves to think otherwise. Didn't she realize that?

She floated toward him with a seductive look in her eye. How could he withstand her temptation when his body craved her touch? This had to be the most depraved trick the Gods could play. He should be strong and hold on to his resolve to do the honorable thing, it was the only way to keep his sanity. Every time they coupled he craved her more, felt her more, needed her more. Her arms threaded around his neck, her breasts pressed against his chest, the triangle of hair between her legs rested on his thigh. His erection was immediate, and he knew he could never turn her away. Was it cowardly to take advantage of her? No. Not when he loved her.

There, he admitted it. He loved her more than she would ever know. Never had a woman taken his heart, but Shayla stole it so fast he never even noticed when it actually happened, only that it did. Coward or not, he loved her, wanted her, and would have her. He entered her and moved, slow at first, then with an urgency without reason. As many times as they mated during the moon-cycle, he never got enough of her. Then she was in his mind.

Their thoughts mingled with an intensity stronger and more potent than before. He steadied his feet on the sandy bottom a moment before he drifted with her out of his body into the bright lights above. They soared higher, each breathing heavily, pressing deeper and faster. He could hold his seed no longer when she gripped him in ecstasy.

He held her tight as they floated in the dimension above. *Sutae, you please me so.*

Then why do I sense regret?

I'll never regret one moment with you.

Nor I.

But what about when you return to your father and Eaton?

I don't want to think about that.

Come with me. Let's travel together.

Rydor held her tight and visualized the Quelan capital where he sought their Kiah Master, Mandel and his Focus Akela. They were sure to be somewhere under protection within the palace's walls.

Look Rydor, someone is there! She pointed straight ahead. Rydor, stop! We're naked!

And you've never looked lovelier. Even in her ethereal body she blushed a bright shade of crimson. He looked her up and down one last time before visualizing her in a royal blue flowing gown, low cut so he could take pleasure in her cleavage, tight around the small waist he liked to hold, but with a long flowing skirt to enhance her graceful moves.

Oh my. This is...a bit risqué?

It's perfect. He smiled. *You've never been more beautiful.*

Now it's my turn.

Shayla ran her hands over his shoulders, and he felt her touch down to his toes. She stared for the longest time before clothes appeared on his body. *A uniform?*

A Zared warrior's uniform. And I must say, you fill it out nicely. Gray is your color. In fact, you're the best specimen I've ever seen, and I inspect the troops regularly.

You do?

With my father. It's part of my duties. She laughed. *Sorry, I forgot to give you rank.*

On his shoulder appeared several silver braids and some kind of medal on his left collar. *I hope you gave me a high rank, I hate taking orders.*

I did, and I even gave you a special medal.

Should I ask what it's for? She giggled at him with a knowing look.

Let's just say no other Zared man has such a medal.

He loved it when she played little games, but if he continued, they would never reach their destination. *Let's continue before you have the wrong thought.* She smiled and took his hand. *Have you ever met Mandel or Akela?*

I saw Mandel once at an official banquet.

Good. Picture him in your mind.

In a flash they were in the palace garden. Two people sat beside a fountain keeping a proprietary distance between them.

That's Mandel. He's handsome, isn't he?

Rydor groaned. *Akela is a fine looking woman.* Shayla slapped his shoulder, and he smiled. *No woman compares to you, Sutae.*

I don't believe you.

Trust me.

Look, Rydor, he's picking up the Kiah Rod.

He watched with interest to see how the rod reacted in another Master's hands. It turned green, but not as light in color as he had turned theirs. Rydor concentrated on the vibrations of the two people. They were trying to communicate, but they were not on the same level. Their thoughts clashed instead of mingled. *Do you sense it?*

I feel discord, not harmony like we share our thoughts.

Exactly. If they don't progress rapidly, they're doomed. He saw compassion in Shayla's gaze while she studied the woman with long, brown hair. *What is it?*

It's like looking at myself when we first tried working together. She glanced at Rydor and touched his shoulder. *I suppose we both looked as lost.*

Rydor slipped his arm around Shayla's waist and they watched Mandel handle the Kiah, but the hint of green drained, leaving only the cold black color between his fingers. *Did you notice they haven't sensed we're here?*

Shayla slipped from Rydor's grasp and moved closer to the woman. *Akela, you have company.* She touched Mandel's hand. *Look at me, Mandel.*

"I just felt a cold chill. Did you feel it?" Mandel asked Akela.

Akela shook her head. "Maybe we should quit for this sun-cycle and try again tomorrow."

"No. We have to keep working on this. If we don't we'll never succeeded."

Shayla returned to Rydor's side. *I can't watch any more.*

No sooner had Shayla slipped her fingers between his when he felt warm and wet. He opened his eyes and laughed. "You really must quit leaving in such a hurry. It makes my head hurt."

"Mine too. I'll have to work on that."

"I've never seen two people more finely dressed bathing together."

Rydor turned abruptly. "Olin. Nice of you to pop in."

"I've brought someone with me."

Olin snapped his fingers and Rydor found Una leaning over the rock behind him licking his face. Shayla laughed.

"Thank you. I was afraid Una was lost."

"She was wandering aimlessly around that place you call an inn. Una terrorized everyone, but I did enjoy watching the expressions on your guards' faces. They really didn't know how to handle her. I decided I'd better deliver her in person before someone got hurt."

"Enough Una, enough!" Rydor commanded. The cat's paws came down on his shoulders, and she continued to lick his cheek. "I'll pull you in, you demented cat!"

"You missed her and you know it." Shayla laughed.

"Do either of you know how ridiculous you look fully dressed in that water?"

Rydor ducked below the surface to get away from Una's fervent welcome. He grinned when Shayla tried to adjust the front of her wet gown to cover herself better.

"I hope you've done more than play in the fourth dimension."

Shayla gathered her gown and climbed out of the water. "We've seen Mandel and Akela."

"And what did you learn, my dear?"

"Rydor and I are more advanced, but I'm not sure we're ready for Turic and Brina."

"Brina paid Shayla a visit. She held her own." Rydor was proud of the way she defended him to Brina, even if she had been wrong in her assumptions.

Shayla cleared her throat. "I wouldn't say that exactly."

"You didn't let her get the better of you. I watched the encounter from the hill." Rydor pulled himself from the pool. "Don't look so surprised. I vowed to protect you." He learned his lesson well about leaving Shayla alone for more than a few seconds.

"You certainly didn't come to my rescue."

"What would you have learned if I had?"

"Children, that's enough. I get the point."

He hated when Olin referred to them as *children*, but at Olin's age, there was not much of an argument to make. "Is there a reason for your visit?"

"Do I need a reason?"

Rydor and Shayla both nodded.

"Very well, I came to warn you. The Voltrans have launched a search party. They want you both."

Rydor grinned. "I assume they're not coming to safely escort us to Terita."

"Don't jest about this, Rydor. They mean to kill you and Shayla. As I told you, I cannot assist you in the battle, but nothing says I can't offer a helping hand along the way."

"We appreciate your help, don't we, Rydor?" *Be nice, we need his help. Quit scowling like that and agree with me.* Shayla nudged his shoulder with hers.

I'm not sure which is worse, agreeing with you or Olin. I have the impression neither of you trust me, or my ability to keep us safe.

I trust you implicitly. But you're no good to me dead. You seem to think you're invincible. I hate to break it to you, but you're not!

My only concern is for you, always remember that. It doesn't matter what happens to me.

Well, it matters to me, you stubborn Mountain Man!

"Children, children. Stop this foolishness."

He can hear us?

"Yes, Sutae." Shayla's cheeks reddened, a sight he had grown very fond of during the recent sun-cycles.

"If you two don't mind my interrupting your lover's spat for a moment, I have news from Terita."

Shayla gave Olin her full attention. "Tell me, please."

"Your father has sent a party of four warriors, headed by Eaton and Turic to look for you. You must not return with them, it's imperative you heed this warning."

"We knew about the detail Nuri sent, but why can't we return with them?" Shayla wiped water from her cheeks with her hands.

Olin adjusted his floppy hat. "And how do you know that?"

Rydor groaned. "A little practice traveling in the fourth dimension."

"Good. No, excellent. I was hoping for such progress. But it's obvious you don't have all of the details. One man in that detail is working for the Voltrans."

"I can't believe what I'm hearing. Eaton selects his men carefully, he would never..."

"Shayla," Olin stepped closer, "you never know who your enemies are, especially with so much at stake. And don't rule out a move by the Quelans either. They want victory as much as anyone. The winner of the

Ultimate Battle will hold the entire future of Zanthus in their hands. It's an enormous responsibility, and in the wrong hands, a complete disaster!"

"So it's already begun." Rydor sat on the grassy river bank.

Olin nodded. "I'm glad you understand. When I told you the rules are none, the rules are all, even I didn't realize all the implications. And if the Voltrans have their way, there won't be a need for battle. They want to get rid of their competition and eliminate any chance for failure."

"I knew Turic would try something underhanded. He already has, but this?"

"Not Turic." Olin shook his head. "Damek."

"I should have known."

Shayla placed her hand on Olin's arm. "If we're being bombarded from all sides, how are we to survive the next thirty one sun-cycles?"

"That's why I've come. I have placed a protective spell around this oasis. You'll be safe here from physical attack since no one can even see you, but I'm afraid there is no spell to repel psychic attacks."

Rydor raked his fingers through his hair. "You want us to stay here till it's time for the battle?"

"I wish that were the case, but I can only afford you a few sun-cycles."

Shayla's eyes grew wide and Rydor knew her thoughts. Once they left the oasis, they would be ripped apart by her guards, her father and their mutual enemies.

"Use this valuable time to cement your bond. Place your trust in each other. Perfect your communications so that no matter the distance, you're still receptive to each other. This skill is more important than you realize."

The implication of doom resounded in Olin's warning. Shayla looked terrified and he had to admit his words scared him as well. "Why must we leave here?"

"There are obstacles in Terita you must face. It's out of my control."

"Are you talking about the elders? My father, or our enemies?" Shayla sat next to Rydor on the grass.

"Destiny." Olin waved his hand and smiled when a silken tent appeared.

"It seems you're getting better at this, my friend."

Rydor walked inside the elegant shelter. The same bed he and Shayla shared that first moon-cycle was in one corner, a carved wardrobe in the other, a table full of food supplies and three chairs were in the center. He smiled at the large carafe of wine and three glasses. When he turned around he found Olin and Shayla. "I suppose you want a drink?"

"One before I leave would be nice."

Shayla smiled at Olin. "How do you do all this?"

"He's a wizard, remember?" Rydor laughed and handed them both a golden goblet of wine.

Olin held up his wine. "A toast...to destiny."

CHAPTER TWENTY

The past four sun-cycles had been like a dream to Shayla. Working and sleeping with Rydor had never been better, but his mood had slowly turned dark. It was as if he were two men; one devoted to her, and another who wanted nothing to do with her.

Rydor cooperated with their mental exercises, but he was now obsessed with physical fitness. He did sit-ups and push-ups like a man possessed. He even found a heavy log that he used as a weight, lifting it repeatedly, holding it over his head until sweat ran down his brow.

The physical training was effective, every muscle in his body rock hard to the touch. He picked her up and carried her to bed each moon-cycle as easily as she plucked and held a flower. His stamina increased, and he was about to wear her out completely, but she never tired of his affections.

The moon-cycles were filled with passion, but he had yet to tell her he loved her. She never felt closer to him, but at the same time he seemed to slip farther from her. There was still that place in his mind he kept under lock and key. She lowered the wall she had erected to keep him from her secret thoughts in hopes he would do the same. Instead, his wall grew stronger and higher. He obviously had something he would never share—something that might separate them forever.

Considering his withdrawal, she felt like a fool for showing him her loving feelings. She did not keep her love a secret, but when would he be completely honest with her? It hurt to know he held back. Every effort she made to convince him to open his heart failed miserably. Whatever secret he protected must be devastating. Secrets like that were dangerous and destructive. Now she wondered if she even wanted to know about that dark place in his soul that tortured him, yet she feared without that knowledge the enemy would destroy them both.

"Shayla, are you ready?"

With a nod, she joined him outside by the hot spring under the bright, twinkling blanket of stars. She sat on the soft grass and folded her legs in front of her and rested her hands, palms up, on her knees. This was the moment they had both prepared for, a visit to Turic and Brina.

"Are you sure we're ready?"

"We'll know soon enough."

She closed her eyes and fell into meditation. The process was easy now. They had practiced so much it was second nature, especially after several trips to see her father and visits to check on Mandel and Akela's progress.

When she began to lift from the physical to the second realm of existence her heart began to race. She was very comfortable with Rydor by her side. This journey belonged to him, she was only the observer. Whenever they traveled together like this, one person controlled the destination and the return, the other followed, and this she knew was some sort of test for Rydor.

She sensed serious apprehension in him, but he had not been to his homeland in over sixteen annual-cycles. It was sure to be a shock. Would she know if he found his family? Rydor's emotions were harder to read than hers.

Turic's face formed in Rydor's mind; and, in an instant, they were in a bedroom somewhere in the royal quarters. She covered her mouth with her hand to hide a gasp. Before her was Turic and Brina, engrossed in the throes of coupling. The embarrassed blush she expected to experience did not happen. There was something different about Turic and Brina.

The couple seemed oblivious to their presence, yet at some level she suspected Turic was cognizant they were there. That was it, Turic did not care if they saw him mate with Brina. In fact, he seemed proud of it. With that thought, the room began to fill with the essence of evil. Then she saw a bucket of water form over the couple an instant before its contents spilled over their sweaty bodies. Brina screamed and Turic groaned.

"Very funny, Rydor," Turic said without turning.

"I am not amused by your incompetent show of affection for Brina."

"Then I shall amuse you by taking Shayla into my arms."

Shayla's jaw dropped when Turic and Brina slumped to the floor. She watched in amazement as their ethereal bodies rose from the physical to join them on their plane. Turic, naked as the sun-cycle he was born, walked toward her. Instinct took over. Shayla erected a stone wall between them and Turic groaned when he ran his toe into the rocks. With little thought, she conjured a loose pair of pants to cover his blatant nakedness.

"Too much man for you, huh?" Turic laughed. He turned his gaze toward Rydor. "I see you're wearing a Zared uniform. Now you add traitor to your title of coward."

"You would know better than I about being a traitor."

Brina approached Rydor slowly, not stopping until she pressed her naked body against his. It took every ounce of control Shayla had not to kill the woman on the spot. Instead she conjured a robe to cover the brazen hussy, then pushed her back with her mind. Brina looked surprised, but she was too cool to let her emotions show.

Brina turned from Rydor and strode to Turic's side. "So, the enemy has come to see how it is done. Learn anything?"

"Not from you." Rydor took Shayla's hand in his and squeezed.

"I taught you plenty." Brina grinned. "And don't tell me you've forgotten."

Rydor winced when Brina replayed the coupling scene between them again for his benefit. He tightened his grasp on Shayla's hand, his muscles quivering in anger. She may not know his secrets, but he did not hide his mood any better than his desire.

"As you can see, you weren't very good. I had to do all the work." Brina looked straight at Shayla. "I do hope he's gotten better." She tilted her head back and laughed.

Shayla swallowed hard. If she were to win a war of wits with Brina she had to control every emotion the woman tried to evoke. "Why would you care about Rydor's ability to bed a woman? What I saw when we arrived proved to me you're not very particular." Turic's face contorted and Shayla anticipated retribution, but was not prepared for the metal cage that suddenly appeared around her.

"A bitch like you should be locked up!"

Rydor turned his angry blue gaze on the bars and they melted before her eyes. He looked like a man driven by demons. A cutter appeared in Rydor's hand an instant before he moved toward Turic.

"I'll cut your tongue from your mouth. No one abuses the princess!"

Turic laughed. "Maybe I should call her a whore. She is one now, isn't she? Or weren't you man enough to take her?"

A cutter appeared in Turic's hand, the blade twice as long as Rydor's. Then Rydor pushed her aside and Turic lunged violently at him

The two men struggled for control. Turic's knife slashed at Rydor's throat. From the corner of her eye she saw Brina, but she was too late to dodge the rope that wrapped around her neck. She struggled as Brina tightened the noose. Shayla gasped for air and thrust her elbows back into the woman's stomach.

Brina groaned, but held tight. Then Shayla remembered all those sun-cycles of practice. She visualized the very same cord tied around Brina's arms and legs. For a moment the woman was stunned, but she quickly removed the bindings. They both paused at the sound of Rydor's angry voice.

Rydor held Turic, his cutter poised at his enemy's neck.

Turic looked up. "Kill me, coward!"

"I will not make it easy for you. We will meet on sacred grounds and decide this as prescribed."

"You don't have the guts."

Shayla grabbed Rydor's outstretched hand and instantly they returned to their physical bodies by the hot spring. Reality returned with a vengeance. She was dizzy and a bit shaken, but otherwise in one piece. "Are you all right?"

He nodded. "Your neck." His fingers traced the welt.

"How could my physical body show this?" Shayla shivered at the thought of what could have happened but did not.

"I don't know."

"It's all so strange—so much I don't understand."

Rydor stared at her with an odd expression on his face. "What?"

"The mark has disappeared."

Her hand moved to where the rope had ripped her skin. The pain subsided along with the welt. "That woman is evil."

"They both are, but then they serve the most demonic leader Zanthus has ever known."

"Rydor, I know you're Voltran." She took a deep breath. "It doesn't matter. You're nothing like the Voltrans I've known, and you're certainly not like those evil Celons, Damek and his son Turic. Your family isn't evil like theirs." She looked into his blue eyes and saw a fiery rage welling deep inside him. "We won't discuss your family, if that's what you want, but at least admit to me that you're Voltran."

"Why does it matter who and what I am?"

Shayla hung her head. She wished it did not matter, but it was crucial. She could picture them both standing in the council chamber answering to her father. Not a pretty picture. Every Zared and every Quelan hated the Voltrans and all they stood for. How could she convincingly explain to her people that Rydor was different, that he would fight for them?

"I know what you're thinking." Rydor stood and walked to the edge of the hot spring. "I don't need to admit what you already know."

She rose and moved to his side by the steaming water. "The truth is not always what we perceive it to be. I know you're Voltran, but I also know you're still hiding something terrible from your past." She slipped her hand under his arm. "When I present you to my father I plan to tell him what an honorable man you are."

"Your opinion may change. Then what will you say?"

"Why are you doing this?" He glared at her and a chill ran down her spine. There were times she knew him as well as herself, and there were moments like these when he was a stranger. "Don't pull away from me, Rydor. Trust me, please."

He turned and took a step back. "I do trust you, Princess."

Whenever he called her Princess it was to put distance between them. "You've changed these past sun-cycles and it scares me."

"You're wrong. I haven't changed. You're just seeing the real me, and you don't like what you see."

Tears burned at her lids, but she refused to cry. "I see a loving man who cares what happens to the people of Zanthus, a man who is willing to risk his life so others may live in peace."

"Then you're blind." He shook his head. "You give me far too much credit."

He turned and walked away. "Don't! I love you.," If Rydor heard her words he did not believe her. Why? She slumped to the ground and gave in to the pain in her heart. He was right, love did hurt. The real question was why did he consider himself not worth loving? He turned away her love like a man doomed to be alone, never to love a woman. That was not possible. Nobody shunned love like that. It was not normal, and she refused to accept his attitude.

How could he hold her in his arms after making love then turn a cold shoulder when she asked a simple question? It was obvious there were some questions he refused to answer and all the answers were hidden behind that tall wall in his mind she was not allowed to breach. A warm tear trickled down her cheek. If she failed to pull Rydor from his despair everything could be lost.

"Now is no time to lose faith, my dear."

She jerked her head up. Olin sat on a fallen tree a few feet away, a smile on his face. With the back of her hand she wiped tears from her cheeks while she walked toward the wizard. She sat next to him, sniffling, ashamed he found her in such a state.

"He can be difficult, but this is no time to doubt him."

"I'm not strong enough. I'm sorry. I just..."

"Now, now," Olin said, handing her a handkerchief. "What has he done to hurt you so?"

"He won't confide in me. Every time I ask about his family, or mention the fact he's Voltran, he walks away. I'm losing him, Olin, and I don't know what to do."

"Love him."

She stared at the wizard. "Have you lost your mind? He's a Voltran and I'm a Zared Princess. We can't love each other, it's forbidden."

"He's a man and you're a woman, it's destiny."

"How can you be optimistic? There's no possible way to work this out. No. Besides, he's changed. When I first met him he was kind and understanding. Now I see a man consumed with hate, and he won't tell me why. How can I help him if I don't know what's destroying him?"

"That's the secret of love, my dear. You don't need to know. Love heals all, and Rydor needs much healing. It's simple really."

"Simple? Nothing has been simple since the sun-cycle Damek issued the challenge." Shayla shook her head. "I always thought I was capable, that I could rule my people as well as my father, or any man. But they're right. Women are weak and have no place in positions of power."

"You are feeling bad this moon-cycle!" Olin chuckled. "You have much to contemplate, my dear, and only you can resolve this problem. We each create our own reality. Create what you want for your people, as well as for you and Rydor. Then trust that creation to become reality. The future is in your hands."

"Olin, you must know that Rydor is impossible! I thought we were getting closer, but he has pulled away from me and moving further all the time. I've tried, I've really tried." She wiped a tear from her cheek and looked Olin in the eye. "What can I do? You know him better than anyone. How do I unlock the secrets he insists on keeping from me? We'll never beat Turic and Brina if he can't be honest with me." More tears escaped and ran down her cheeks.

"Oh my dear princess." Olin handed her a soft cloth. "I do know Rydor very well, and he is a stubborn pupil." He watched her shake her head. "Okay, a very stubborn pupil. But the one thing I do know is that you can, and will, break through that barrier. Patience, my dear, patience. I know it's difficult. If it were easy anyone could do it. But fate has chosen you, and I know you are the right person for the job. You have many special abilities, use them."

She opened her mouth, but he was gone. Olin was full of answers she didn't understand. Trust, reality, love, patience, it all added up to sacrifice. She already sacrificed her virginity to the one man who found his way to her heart and soul, the same man who now rejected her. Why did she have to partner with the most stubborn man on the planet?

Olin actually thought this arrangement would work. Right now that prospect was out of the question. She'd tried to reach him on every level she knew, yet failure was the only outcome. Whatever he was hiding must be devastating, at least to him. She knew how secrets could destroy a person, she had seen it happen before.

Hopeless was the only feeling she had right now.

CHAPTER TWENTY ONE

"Look what you've done, my boy! Shayla is down there crying her eyes out over you and here you sit, stubborn and alone, watching her from a distance. Distance does seem to be the problem here. Secrets create distance you know."

Rydor stopped petting Una. "Olin. I should have known you'd show up. If you hadn't interfered, we wouldn't be in this mess."

"You're right, you'd both be dead."

Rydor glanced at Olin's haggard face. He appeared overly tired and worried. "I didn't mean to sound ungrateful."

"Then don't. I placed a very special life in your hands. It's no accident she found you."

"You taught me long ago there's no such thing as an accident."

"Then why do you continue to second guess yourself? Have I not proven to you time and again to trust in fate?"

"You have, but..."

"There are no *buts* where trust is involved. You know that." Olin sat next to Rydor on the rock.

"I've hurt Shayla in ways I never should have. I'll never be able to...to..."

"To apologize for loving her? My dear boy, no apology is needed where love is concerned."

"I do love her. I'd give my life for her."

"Then what's the problem?"

"It's complicated." Rydor watched Shayla from his vantage point on the hill. He'd picked this spot for his private get-away place because he could see everything she did. Shayla lay in the grass, crying. This was his fault and he had no excuse. He would never forgive himself. She deserved better. Surely Eaton could satisfy her without driving her to tears.

"No, Rydor, it's simple. You're the one making it complicated."

"I saw my brother and I wanted to kill him."

"Good. I'd hate to think you'd lost all emotion and common sense."

"I thought I was over the hatred, but it's as strong as ever."

"And that's the reason you punish yourself and Shayla?"

Rydor stared at the ground. Olin was not telling him anything new, but life never seemed to work the way it should. "I do not want to involve Shayla in my battle with the Celons."

"Really? Do you honestly believe they're separate issues?"

"Of course."

"Then you're a fool."

"I'm a fool for trying to protect her from evil?"

Olin cleared his throat. "You must realize that the two of you will be fighting that very same evil as a pair. You cannot fight as one unless you tell her of your past. Is that really so difficult?"

"I've never told anyone. Including you. You just knew."

"That I did because I witnessed your punishment by your father. I was assigned to you by the Wizard's Council that very day."

"There's a Wizard's Council?" Rydor laughed.

"Now now my boy, everyone has a boss."

"Really?"

"Really. Now, back to you and Shayla. I have told you your strength is when you meld as one, something you cannot do if you refuse to let her in. Now think about this, and think well because your life and Shayla's life depend on it, not to mention every other life on the planet. If you want total evil to preside over all of Zanthus keep your secret. I can offer no further help!"

A gust of wind blew his hair while Olin's departure left him speechless. For the first time in his life, he wished Olin had not paid him a visit. In the past the wizard always helped, but there were no solutions for two people who would never be allowed to love each other, no matter how much they wanted to. No, it was best this way.

How could he spend another moon-cycle in her arms, making love, caressing her body under the stars when it was so wrong? Better to suffer the heartache now than to fool themselves into thinking they had a future together. Even so, he would love her till the sun-cycle he died, but he did not want to tell her and ruin her life-mating plans with Eaton. Even that might be too late if Eaton learned they coupled.

Una growled. "Not you too." Suddenly the cat bound down the hill toward Shayla. He ran after her, the thick tropical vegetation slapping at his face. Whatever threatened Shayla, he prayed he was not too late.

Pushing aside vines and branches, he heard Una's battle groans. She was pitted against something fierce by the agonizing sounds in the clearing ahead. Shayla screamed. His heart raced faster. *I'm coming*!

The moment he stepped into the clearing he saw Shayla, frozen like a statue, watching in horror as Una fought for her life with a Semita bigger than herself. He skirted the two animals and made his way to Shayla's side and pulled her into his arms.

Do something, Rydor, she's going to die!

It was suicide to interfere with nature, but he couldn't let Una be ripped to shreds. He pulled the cutter from its sheath and headed for the dueling pair. Claws flew wildly ripping flesh. The metallic smell of blood tainted the air. He took a deep breath and lunged for the unfamiliar cat.

Una's teeth were in the animals neck, but she let go the moment she realized he'd come to help. He sent the cat a quieting message. As if by magic, the intruder retreated. Una limped to him, blood running down her leg. He stroked the mane around her neck and she licked his cheek.

Is she all right?

She'll be fine. It's only a scratch.

Una sauntered from his grasp and, to his astonishment, meandered over to the big cat who lay like a king under a nearby tree.

"She's licking his face!"

"Of all the..." Rydor was so stunned it took him several seconds to realize what just transpired. He ran his fingers through his hair.

"What?"

He watched in silent agony as Una traipsed off into the jungle with the male Semita. "I interfered in the mating ritual." He might never see his faithful cat again.

"How could you have known? I don't know anyone who's witnessed such an event between the mountain cats and lived to tell about it."

"Now you do."

"Will she be all right? I mean, they won't fight anymore, will they?"

"No more fighting, only...you know." A faint smile curved her lips, and the familiar blush colored her cheeks in the glow of the full moon. "Sutae, I'm sorry."

"For what? Leaving me alone, or turning your back on me?"

Apologies did not come easily and she was making this one particularly difficult. "Both."

"Did you see Olin?"

It didn't surprise him that Olin visited her as well. The old man was fond of her. "Was he full of advice?"

"As usual." Shayla turned and walked to the tent.

Rydor followed her inside and sat across from her at the table. Had she accepted his apology? He reached for her hand, but she pulled away. "What did Olin have to say?"

"Nothing much."

Now it was Shayla who shut him out. She was behaving the way he expected, but it was not what he wanted. It was nonsense to quarrel with her. He gave up his home to be with her and agreed to fight his own brother to save her people. How much more could he do?" Talk to me, Sutae."

"Why? I thought you liked secrets."

Her voice was angry, but he deserved her wrath. He was a coward once again for thinking he could push her away. There was no easy way out. The love he had for her already made her a part of him.

She rose and walked to the bed, crawling in fully dressed. He stood, pulled off his tunic and reached for the covers.

"You will not sleep with me this moon-cycle."

Shayla's cold glare said more than her words. He grabbed his tunic from the floor and left. If she wanted to be alone, he would grant her request; but if she thought it was over between them, she was mistaken.

His love for her might lead to disaster, but he would never abandon her. It could be the bravest decision, or the most cowardly he ever made, but his choice was made. Shayla was his and he intended to keep her, whatever the cost. She might fight him, but he would win this battle.

He laid in the grass not far from the tent and watched Shayla's shadow. She undressed, her silhouette revealing the womanly curves he knew so well. Even now his body yearned for her. He had learned contentment while holding her close, loving her body, and touching her mind.

Good-moon-cycle, Sutae. He waited to hear her sweet voice in his mind, but only a dark void met his search. The wall she used while learning to communicate was back in place, and higher than before. He could break that wall as easily as she built it. He would respect her privacy for now, but she could not keep him out forever.

***

Shayla bolted upright in bed. The early morning light penetrated the thin cover of the tent. Her hand caressed the empty space next to her. She had tossed and turned all moon-cycle. It was lonely without Rydor by her side, but if he wanted it this way, so be it.

Olin's advice churned in her mind. Rydor did need to heal. There was so much she still did not know about him, and might never learn. She prayed his secret would not destroy them during the Ultimate Battle. The only hope was that Turic and Brina had no knowledge of what tormented Rydor. If they did, it could mean the end of them both.

She slid out of bed, quickly dressed, then walked to the table. After a glass of juice, she grabbed the Kiah and went outside. She made an important decision during the moon-cycle, and it was time to tell Rydor.

Rydor squatted at the edge of the hot spring and splashed water onto his face. Her heart raced as she approached. He looked so powerful, so alive, so sensual. Everything about the man excited her, but sexual gratification would never be enough. She wanted his heart, his undying love, but most of all his trust.

All moon-cycle she considered her options. Stay here, alone with Rydor, or return to her people. She longed to spend these last sun-cycles wrapped in his arms without a care for the outside world, however Rydor's withdrawal made that an impossibility. She could no longer stand to look at him with desire and have him turn his back to her.

Rydor was a man of great passion, and she loved that side of him, but his dark side overshadowed his every thought and deed, his pain too great an obstacle to overcome. Her plan would anger him, but there was nothing he could say to change her mind. "I'm leaving for Terita."

He stood and turned to face her. "Fine."

"That's it, fine? Where's the argument?"

"I do not wish to argue with you, Princess. If it is your wish to return home, I will take you."

Something changed since last moon-cycle, but what? Rydor was strangely calm, too willing, his temper far too subdued. It was as if he had given up. Never had she seen him so distraught.

She turned and walked toward the dense foliage, his footsteps close behind. His silence was more irritating than the thick jungle growth that threatened to swallow them in their immense leaves and vines.

Huge green plants covered the moist jungle floor, others grew thick and long, hanging from tall trees. She pushed aside a fuzzy leaf and forged through the maze. A vine caught her around the neck. While she struggled to free herself Rydor's strong arm reached over her shoulder, cutter in hand. With one flick of the blade the clinging plant fell to the ground.

"Follow me. It's safer."

She would not argue. He moved past her, hacking a path with his blade. It was easier with him in the lead, but progress was slow. Maybe she should have waited for Olin to help them. After all, he put them here. Anger had made her decision and she now questioned the wisdom of her choice.

Guilt reared its ugly head. She had no right to be angry at Rydor. He was here because she asked him to help. He saved her life more than once, left the comfort and serenity of his home and was about to risk his life for the Zared tribe even though he was Voltran. If his people caught him, he would be executed as a traitor.

She selfishly demanded everything of him, yet he asked nothing of her. How egotistical could she be? The moment he entered Terita he would fall under scrutiny by her father, the council and her people, yet he was willing to fulfill the obligation she forced on him.

Whatever his secret, it belonged to him and she had to respect his wishes. Rydor seemed willing to face adversity for her, the least she could do was trust him. This was their time to bond, to prepare for battle. There were enough enemies to pull them apart without them turning on each other.

As Rydor's Focus she had to remain totally committed. Winning the Ultimate Battle was all that mattered, not his past. As Zared Princess she found a Kiah Master. Now she had to deliver him and convince the council not only to accept Rydor as the Zared Master, but her as his Focus.

Bonding with Rydor proved to be the most exciting and rewarding experience of her life, and she had not one moment of regret. If Rydor were Zared, she would beg her father to choose him as her life-mate, and she was sure he would.

Instead, she had to face Eaton, knowing she betrayed him by bonding with Rydor. In her heart, she did not view it as betrayal since she never had feelings for him. However, as Princess, she would be judged harshly for her decision should anyone discover she bonded with Rydor.

Leaving the oasis without cementing that bond one more time would be a mistake. Her heart ached just thinking this could be their last opportunity to couple, to hold and cherish each other. Never being intimate with Rydor again made her heart ache. She was determined to make one last memory with him.

They emerged into a small clearing. Her breath caught in her throat. A tranquil lagoon fed by a magnificent waterfall lay before her. Water cascaded into a glimmering pool surrounded by lavender flowers and soft yellow grass. She walked to the edge and looked through the clear ripples to the smooth sandy bottom. Perfection barely described what her eyes feasted upon.

The oases on Zanthus were all nestled around the foot of the desert mountain range, the cold snow pack feeding the rivers that flowed to the warmer climate. She was glad tribal disputes over ownership had prevented development. Beauty like this should never be disturbed. All the Zared and Quelan efforts to claim the oases would become a moot point after the battle because one tribe would rule all.

Rydor waited a few steps away, assuming the warrior's stance, his body tense but poised. His long dark hair blew in the tropical breeze, and he never looked stronger or more desirable. *Come to me.*

In three strides his chest pressed against her breast. He took a deep breath, the hard muscled planes of his chest molded deeper into her while her hands moved up his tempting contour. Her heart beat rapidly, anticipation tingled through her. *Make love to me, Rydor. I need you.*

His lips quickly found hers. Her mind filled with Rydor's essence. His thoughts and hers meshed into one rush of emotion so strong it buckled her knees. His arms folded around her. She felt euphoric, protected and loved.

He guided her to lay on the soft matt of grass. She dropped the Kiah and held his broad shoulders, her nails digging into the soft leather of his tunic. The only vision she concentrated on was her love and how much she wanted him.

I love you too, Sutae.

You heard me? He kissed her deeper, and groaned. *Don't ever leave me, I need you so.*

It is I who need you, my precious.

Love drummed like a steady pulse in her blood. It throbbed through her veins, filling her heart so full she wanted to scream. He loved her, he said so. She never dreamed he would speak those words. The sharing was wonderful and free.

Rydor pulled her tunic over her head, kissed each breast then nuzzled his head between them. His tongue traced a trail to the drawstring of her leggings. He undressed her as he had many times, but with an urgency that sent chills down her spine.

She now lay naked to his gaze, the hunger in his eyes so real she wanted to cry. He stood to undress, his hands shaking ever so slightly while he pulled off his boots and removed his pants. *You're magnificent.* Slowly he knelt by her feet, his body hot, his desire strong and full. She expected him to drive into her, instead he nibbled at her toes, then her ankles.

Her stomach quivered as Rydor kissed his way up her calves to her knees. He continued up the inside of her thigh. His hands parted her legs and his tongue found her most sensitive part. She gasped at the sweet sensations he invoked and reveled at his expertise and control.

The stubble of his beard tickled and sent fantastic sensations while he continued his assault. His hands slipped under her and held her firm. Her fingers threaded through his hair. What he did to her was delicious, but she wanted to feel him inside her. She pulled his head up, and he eagerly followed her lead.

His strong form slid higher till their mouths met in a hard kiss. He pressed into her and she gasped, his masculinity hot and slick. He filled her with himself, but he filled her mind as well. The familiar experience of leaving her body left her even more breathless than usual.

Together they floated up above the waterfall that pounded a graceful rhythm next to their physical bodies. This was as close to heaven as two people could get, as close as a man and woman could be. They were one. One mind, one body, one love, strong and everlasting.

Rydor thrust deeper and faster, but there was a softening in his mind. She felt a flutter in her head, like the soft wings of a butterfly. Then she saw the door he kept locked momentarily fade. Behind the barrier he'd so carefully protected she saw a young man strung between two trees being beaten to death. Deep red blood covered a bare, bronzed chest. Even the man's head was bleeding from the brutal, attempted scalping. A pain beyond human endurance coursed through her causing her stomach to turn upside down.

The door reappeared and Rydor groaned. He sent her love with his mind and pleasured her with his body, but the brief glimpse of torture stayed with her. There was no mistake the young man was Rydor. He still bore the scars on his body and in his heart. She wished with all her being she could make him forget the tragedy of his youth. Vehemently she sent compassion and all the love she possessed, and she sensed he accepted her humble offering.

If this moment could last for eternity, Rydor might be able to mend his tortured soul. No human should be made to suffer such pain. The ethical man he had become could never have matured out of a boy who deserved that kind of treatment.

She glanced down at their physical twins, sweat dripping from Rydor's brow, yet in the fourth dimension all that existed was pure thought and emotion so intense it was all—all there ever was, all there would ever be. She wanted to stay and soar with Rydor to the ends of Zanthus.

Power surged through her. It was as if they could defeat any enemy, rule any tribe, and find the happiness they both wanted...together. Here nothing mattered. If a Zared and a Voltran found solace and peace in each other's arms so be it. The moment was all there was. Rydor's hard body thrust against hers, his sensual movements sending waves of delight so intense she cried out in complete satisfaction. Rydor pushed to his climax, spilling his seed into her receptive body. They lay entwined. Time had no meaning, the line between the physical and the esoteric blurred. She cherished him on both levels, holding on to what was hers, to what might never be again.

CHAPTER TWENTY TWO

Rydor pulled Shayla through the cascading sheet of water to the edge of the lagoon. The chilly water did little to cool his fevered desires. No matter how many times they made love, it seemed that was all he wanted to do, but there were other pressing matters they both needed to consider. It was time to get out of the water, but Shayla kept pulling him back. "We have to get dressed. We have work to do."

"No. I want to stay."

"Sutae, I wish we could."

"Maybe we should wait for Olin to transport us."

"It's time we go. I feel it."

"Things will never be the same. I'm afraid, Rydor." She grasped his arm. "They'll take you from me. I know they will."

He smiled. "We can never be separated. Our minds have melded and can find each other whenever we wish."

"But what will I do without you next to me? The moon-cycles will be long."

"You will do what you did before I came into your life."

Her eyes narrowed and her lips pouted and he nearly laughed. "Do not make faces at me, my sweet."

"You don't understand. My father won't let you near me. He'll only let..."

"Eaton?" She hung her head, unable to meet his gaze. "We must have faith in our destiny."

"You sound like Olin."

"He's a wise man." Rydor pulled himself from the water then grabbed her arms and helped her out. She gazed at him with a pleading look in her brown eyes. "He could be right."

"I want him to be right, but I know the way of the Zared Council."

"Am I not Kiah Master? They cannot keep my Focus from me."

"Possibly, but..."

He silenced her with a kiss and a pat on the rear. "You'd better get dressed if you're to meet your father."

Rydor slipped on his pants and reached for his boots, unable to take his eyes off Shayla's perfect, graceful form. She was the love he always wanted but was afraid to hope for. He refused to lose a woman who was embedded in his soul. If it took moving the heavens for her, he would gladly find a way.

The future may be risky, fraught with danger, and challenges beyond imagination, but he was sure of one thing—he would have Princess Shayla D'Par even if he had to kidnap her. Fate had not sent him this far, and brought him a love so deep he could not exist without it, only to lose it all.

He was anxious to witness how strong a bond she had with her father. Parents held a certain power over their children, but the relationship lovers shared remained special and untouchable.

A rustle in the jungle made him turn. Shayla opened her mouth. He silenced her with his hand and pulled her behind a rock. They waited in silence. He felt her heart beat heavy against her chest while the unknown enemy approached.

CHAPTER TWENTY THREE

Rydor picked up Una's vibration, but he sensed the cat was not alone.

What is it?

Una and her mate. Sure enough, both Semitas wandered down to the lagoon for a drink. Rydor laughed.

What's so funny?

He bent his mouth to her ear. "Una has the same satisfied look in her eye as you, my love."

"Ooooh." She slapped his arm.

"I love it when you get rough." He growled and she slapped him again.

"Take that back."

"Never. I want to see that look forever." And he did. If he had his way, Eaton would never lay eyes on the fair princess again, let alone touch her. The thought sent a jealous rage through his veins. He would fight any man who laid claim to his Sutae.

The odds of staying with Shayla for life were slim, but he might as well die trying since his existence would be worthless without her. Until they met her father and the council head on, they had no idea where they stood, and it was time to confront that obstacle. "How far are we from Terita?"

"On foot—I don't know. About three hours by cruiser."

"It's mostly desert, isn't it?"

"Half the way."

They had no supplies and no way to carry water. He had to count on Olin not to let them die of thirst. Olin said he'd help until the battle, and he was relying on the wizard.

"I don't want to go." Shayla adjusted the top of her tunic.

"It's time to meet the enemy."

"My father's not the enemy."

"It was a figure of speech." Or was it? Ruler Nuri could very well prove to be his enemy. Shayla put too much faith in people, especially those close to her, but he learned his lesson at sixteen annual-cycles of age. Betrayal came from within the ranks, the more intimate the person, the deeper the deception.

Damek taught him well as the perfect example of what to expect. Shayla may think her father had her best interests at heart, but he was a man of power and he had to protect that power. The sweet princess was merely a pawn in his game. He could be wrong. Power may not corrupt everyone the same as it had Damek, but it certainly made a significant difference. Hopefully Nuri would stand at his daughter's side with full support of the council.

He took Shayla's hand and led her into the last remnants of the jungle. Her hesitance to leave their private paradise was palpable, but he forged on through her doubt. Olin said there were lessons to learn in Terita and he wanted them over and done. He was ready for what lay ahead.

Una and her companion trotted behind them. He felt like the father of the bride—he'd gained a new pet. It would take many sun-cycles before Una's mate would consider warming to him, if at all. Semitas were like humans. They life-mated forever. From here on out he'd either have two mountain cats at his side, or none. Una's loyalty belonged to the male, so there was a substantial chance he might lose her.

Ahead he saw the familiar fog of Olin's spell. Shayla stopped abruptly and pulled him back. "What?"

"I'm not going through that fog. Call Olin and have him remove the spell."

"No. We're on our own." She started to object, but he silenced her with one fingertip. "It's time to trust me. We cannot rely on a wizard to save us at every turn." She reluctantly nodded, and he continued toward the magic veil.

The moment they entered the haze, a howling wind pushed them back, eerie sounds ringing in their ears. Shayla's hand shook in his. He pulled her close and slipped his arm around her waist. Progress became difficult against the invisible force. Olin's spell was strong, but he was determined to get through.

Shayla held the Kiah Rod tight against her breast. Her hair blew in his face. He pulled her forward one step at a time. Why couldn't Olin concoct a spell that did not include them? Knowing Olin, it was all part of the greater plan, another annoying facet in the scheme of things.

Hurry, Rydor. My ears can't take any more.

He sheathed his cutter then turned, but when he looked at Shayla she swayed back and forth then began to fall to the ground. He scooped her into his arms since she could not walk. Her added weight actually aided his steps against the turbulent wind that fought against them. Just when he thought his idea of walking through the spell was a bad one, the wind turned to his back and all but pushed him free of its grasp. Bright sunlight covered him again, and the rocky desert lay before him in all its desolate splendor. He eased Shayla to the ground, but kept a steadying arm about her waist.

He felt her regain her footing and she seemed to be in control once again. That was the Shayla he loved, the fighter who never quit. He looked at her and all he thought about was how damn cute she is. Or should he say, beautiful, or gorgeous? The term did not matter, her face said it all

"I never want to go through that again!"

"There will be no need." He kissed her on the cheek and she smiled. "You're beautiful when you smile." She blushed and he grinned. After all they had done together, she still blushed at the smallest compliment and slightest touch.

"Come, we have much ground to cover." He took the leather case and tucked it under his arm. She held his hand and walked by his side. It felt right to be with her, and he silently vowed to keep her by his side for eternity.

The megators dragged on, the dusty red desert floor hot and unrelenting. Shayla held her complaints even though she had to be as thirsty as he was. Una and her companion followed a safe distance behind, the male not sure if he wanted to be near humans.

Shayla leaned into him. Her dry lips were beginning to crack, her steps slowing. He surveyed the area and found no safe shelter. They were exposed, a vulnerable position to be in, but they had to take the chance since there was no alternative. He stopped and helped her sit on the ground. "I'm sorry. This is hard for you."

"I'm fine. Just sit with me. Hold me."

He joined her on the pebbly sand and pulled her onto his lap. Her hair was soft against his neck. Resting his chin on top of her head, he inhaled her delicate scent, sweet and fresh. He wished they were back at the cave instead of heading for Terita where he was not welcome. May the Gods be merciful and not make Shayla pay for loving him.

The hum of engines overhead pulled their attention to the sky. Three large air-transports approached, all with the official Quelan emblem on the side. There was nowhere to run or hide. They would have to make a stand and hope for the best.

Rydor stood and pulled Shayla with him. "Say nothing, Sutae. Maybe we can convince them we're lost travelers."

"They're landing. Be careful, Rydor. You're only one man."

The cruisers touched down and several men poured out and rushed toward them. The soldiers were armed with weapons he had never seen before. Sixteen annual-cycles was a long time to be away from technological advancements, but he knew the simple pressure of a finger on the trigger could kill them both.

"Drop your weapon and let go of the woman."

Rydor took a deep breath. Against his better judgment, he pulled his cutter free and tossed it off to the side, but he refused to let go of Shayla. "Who are you to harass innocent travelers?"

The man in charge stepped forward. "As Quelans we own this territory and you're trespassing."

"The Zared Tribe holds claim to this land."

"And who are you to make such a declaration?"

Shayla tilted her chin up and thrust her chest out and he began to panic. *No Sutae, do not tell them who you are, and do not act like a princess!*

"Tell me who you are woman, now!" The man turned toward his men. "Take that case from her and bring Mandel and Akela here."

Rydor, they'll know who we are!

Block your mind to them, you know how.

I didn't think they could communicate with us mentally.

They can't, but they can sense our powers. Just do as I say. He watched the Quelan Kiah Master and his Focus step forward. They looked determined, deep in concentration. Mandel stepped in front of Shayla and pulled the leather case from her grasp.

No! Stop them Rydor.

The moment he reached for the Kiah in Mandel's hand, a guard rushed him and held a weapon to his temple.

"If you don't cooperate, we'll kill you both." The man turned to Mandel. "Are they the Zared team?"

Mandel opened the case and looked inside. "They have the rod, they must be."

"Don't give me maybes! You're a Master. Tell me now!"

Two more cruisers landed behind them and five men rushed at their backs, weapons drawn. Shayla turned in his grasp. "Eaton!"

He watched one large warrior lead a group of soldiers toward them. It only took a moment for them to arrive and he knew exactly who that man must be.

"Princess, are you all right?"

"Oh Eaton! I'm so glad to see you." Shayla brushed dirt off the seat of her pants. "I've been better."

Eaton moved closer to Shayla, weapon in hand, his men behind him. "What is the meaning of this?

"Border patrol."

"Really? And you must bring your Kiah Master and his Focus to patrol a border that isn't yours?"

"Nor yours."

"That may well be, but you will withdraw and let us take these two people with us. And," Eaton took a step closer, "you will return our Kiah Rod."

The man nodded and Mandel handed the case to Eaton.

"Your rod is as useless as your Master." Mandel pointed to Rydor. "And if she's his Focus, you're all in trouble."

"Enough!" Eaton aimed his weapon between Mandel's eyes. "Either you give the command to retreat this instant or you'll be searching for a new Kiah Master."

"Fine. We'll settle this at the battle once and for all. Until then, take your miserable Master and Focus with you, but stay clear of our territory."

Eaton backed toward Shayla. Rydor knew better than to turn his back on the enemy so he waited for them to board their craft. He turned and assessed his competition. The blond-haired man was formidable, an effective officer, but he did not like him. Whether that was an honest judgment, or a jealous one he could not say, but there was something about Eaton's vibration that set his teeth on edge and riled his warrior's instincts.

The war party finally departed in a noisy whirl of dust. Eaton was the last man he wanted to see, but his intervention proved most convenient. In a heartbeat Eaton turned and pulled Shayla into his arms. Rydor's blood instantly boiled.

"Oh Eaton, I'm so glad to see you!" Shayla threw her arms around Eaton's neck and hugged him. "My father, how is he?"

"Worried about you, but otherwise, well."

Shayla pulled her arms back. "Aah...Eaton, I'd like to introduce Rydor, Zared Kiah Master."

Eaton extended his arm in greeting which left Rydor no choice. They grasped forearms in official warrior tradition, but Eaton eyed him very skeptically. This man could prove to be a bigger problem than he imagined.

"I'll see to your safe return, Princess." Eaton led her to his craft, two guards close behind. He looked back over his shoulder. "Rydor, you ride in the other vehicle."

And so it began. If Eaton thought he could pull them apart, he was sadly mistaken. Rydor watched the warrior help Shayla to her seat and shut the door. His hands fisted at his sides. Shayla gave Eaton a warm smile and a hug. He tried to rationalize why. Eaton's timing had been perfect, and he managed to pull off the rescue without incident, yet there was something wrong with this picture.

One of Eaton's men tapped him on the shoulder and pointed to the open door of the craft. He stepped inside, settled on the seat and fastened the safety harness. Both conveyances lifted off the ground, red dust swirling about the windows.

The ride was smoother and faster than in annual-cycles past. There had been so many improvements to transportation he barely recognized the vehicle. His lifestyle may have remained the same, but Zanthus had moved forward. Progress was good, but the reasons for advancement scared him. Better weapons to kill with, and faster transportation to get there. It was the same old story.

Power struggles never ceased. The Quelans and Zareds could not even agree over a border. Considering their bickering, it was a wonder the Voltrans had not claimed the area in dispute. Under the circumstances, none of that mattered.

Shayla and Eaton were in the back seat of the cruiser ahead. They followed close enough for him to see Eaton slip his arm around Shayla's shoulders through the back dome window. He gritted his teeth and suppressed the urge to rip the man apart. Now that Eaton had become a reality instead of a faceless name, he needed to adjust. The idea drove him crazy, but he would behave himself—for Shayla's sake.

It would be impossible for him to take Eaton and all of Terita by storm then claim the princess as his possession. She belonged to her father, her people, and to Eaton once Ruler Nuri made his announcement. He would do his part not to upset Shayla until the battle was over. After that, he planned to claim her as his mate and made no promises about breaking laws or tradition. She was his, and he would have her.

The terrain below eased from barren desert to lush farmlands, green and yellow replacing dull red rocks. In all his annual-cycles, he had never been to Terita. Voltrans had never been welcome in the Zared capitol. The Voltrans produced and sold power to the planet, while the Zareds provided food and the finest gems mined from the abundant sea that bordered the Teritan peninsula.

Damek called the Zareds spoiled and soft, his opinion based on their civilized way of life. How could an evil man see worth in anyone that went out of their way to preserve human life? Of course his father never cared much about anyone's life except his own. Damek bad-mouthed the Quelans for the same reason. The man would never understand kindness or compassion.

As a Voltran he would be judged the same as the man he despised, all Voltrans were. It was his curse. There were times he wondered how he could possibly have been born to a race of people he so strongly disagreed with. He tried to fit the mold of a Voltran warrior, and his failure nearly cost him his life. How could he forget that failure when he wore the scars.

Olin always said he had been saved for a purpose and he would soon discover exactly what that meant. Loving Shayla was the only blessing he had ever had, and now even that pleasure would be taken away. May the Gods have mercy on them both.

CHAPTER TWENTY FOUR

Safely in her personal quarters, Shayla quickly bathed and dressed for her meeting with the High Council. She wished she could have a moment alone with her father first, but she had been told in no uncertain terms that was not possible.

Many times since she left on her adventure she dreamed of being back in the palace with all the comforts it afforded, but without Rydor by her side, the joy was gone. Where had Eaton taken him? It was time to put their communication skills to the test. *Rydor, where are you?*

Sitting in a hall in front of two large doors. There's a guard on each side of me, as if I were a criminal.

I'm on my way. She ran the brush through her hair, twisted it up on top of her head and slipped a gold comb in to secure it firmly. It was the first time she had worn her hair up since she left Terita. Many things were expected of a princess here which made her miss the freedoms she had while alone with Rydor.

She hurried out the door and headed for the council chambers where Rydor waited. This meeting with the council was critical. It was up to her to smooth ruffled egos and ease the tension that was sure to mount when they learned Rydor was a Voltran.

The long halls that led from her private quarters to the government wing seemed unending. She and Rydor had only been separated a few hours, but it felt like an eternity. Turning the last corner, she saw him on the bench, tapping his foot, arms crossed over his chest, eyes narrowed, lips pursed tight. Her heart raced at the sight of him, and her mind wandered to the times they were naked and close.

The Royal Guards saluted when she stopped in front of them. "Please excuse us. I need a word with Rydor—in private."

"Sorry, Princess. Our orders are to stay with him."

"Very well." She sat next to him on the hard marble bench and fought the urge to take his hand in hers for strength. His eyes revealed her thoughts exactly, desire mixed with a fear of what may happen. She could plainly see in the set of his jaw that he did not appreciate their separation any better than she did.

Why didn't you send them away?

They only answer to my father. I have no authority. I'm little more than a decoration.

What have you done to your hair, Sutae? And what are you wearing?

There are rules I must follow. She straightened the long skirt of her high-necked, long-sleeved dark burgundy gown. *I'm sorry you don't like the way I look.*

You're always beautiful to me.

Shayla felt a familiar warmth flood her cheeks. She glanced at Rydor. A smile tugged at the corners of his mouth. She wanted to kiss him and assure him everything would be fine, but she could do neither. *When we go inside, let me do the talking. Just answer their questions, but don't offer any additional explanations.*

I *won't embarrass you.*

That's not what I meant. Rydor still wore his hand-made leather tunic, pants and boots. *Didn't Eaton offer you a change of clothes?*

Not exactly.

What was Eaton up to? He knew better than to let anyone face the High Council without proper attire. Eaton wanted to demean Rydor, but little did he know that was not possible. Rydor carried himself with dignity, and she had no doubt the council would see him for the man he was, regardless of how he was dressed. Personally, she loved how the soft leather hugged his body and defined the muscled planes and valleys of his well-toned physique.

The double doors to their left swung open and the page announced the council was ready to see them. Rydor stood and offered her his arm the way any gentleman would. She accepted graciously, resting her hand on his forearm. Two Royal Guards fell into step behind them as they entered the formal chamber and stood before the immense curved table.

The uniformed page snapped to attention. "The Princess Shayla D'Par and Rydor to address the council."

Shayla curtsied and Rydor bowed before the twelve man council. Every Zared priest on the planet sat in the gallery seats that ran parallel to the front podium, along with distinguished politicians and their aids. Anyone who could wrangle an invitation was there, which left no empty seats.

Ruler Nuri nodded. "I'm delighted you have safely returned to us, my daughter." He stared at Rydor. "Please state your family name for the council. It isn't proper to address you simply as Rydor."

"I claim no family name or tribe affiliation."

"That's not possible. State the last name you were born with, whether you claim it or not."

"With all due respect, I will not."

Shayla cringed at the disturbing looks the council gave, but her father seemed most displeased of all. No one ever denied the ruler's request. *Rydor, please answer him.*

I'm sorry, I cannot.

Nuri cleared his throat. "We will investigate you, Rydor. It's best you tell us now."

"A man's past belongs to him. I ask you to respect my privacy."

"There is no privacy when it comes to national security." Nuri shook his head. "Shayla, please, give us a full report."

"As you wish. My search was long and arduous as I'm sure Arden and Rance have reported."

"They told me how you risked your life to climb Spirit Mountain. You went against my orders."

"I apologize, but it was necessary."

Nuri tapped his fingers on the dark polished wood table. "Why?"

Shayla glanced at Rydor. *What can I tell him?*

Let me explain.

No. You must not speak until requested to do so. We have to adhere to protocol.

"If the council will indulge me for a moment." She waited as the members each gave her a nod of consent. "You are all aware of what the legend of the Kiah says, and the advice of the Priests. It was my duty to find a Kiah Master who could pass the test. I was guided to that location by a very wise man who insisted I go alone."

One of the council members stood. "Tell us who this wise man is and why you obeyed him."

"Councilman Merrick," she acknowledged, "the man did not give me his name, only specific instructions which I could not ignore. Until that moment, my search had been futile. I could not ignore his words." Merrick sat down with a frown. He was one member of the council who was never satisfied. She never really liked him, even if he was supposedly her future father-in-law. He didn't look like Eaton. He had short, dark brown hair streaked with silver, but he and Eaton shared the same arrogant attitude.

"Page," Nuri called. "Admit our Chief Warrior."

Shayla sighed. This was bad enough without Eaton in the room. She had her fill of him in the cruiser. He had purposely sat in the back seat with her so his men would not see him grope her. She did not welcome his physical advances, and now he disgusted her to the point of making her nauseous. Rydor was the only man she wanted to touch her. Eaton touched her as if he knew she and Rydor had bonded. Eaton's advances were rough and demanding, not slow and gentle like before she left. Fear coursed through her. Was her love for Rydor so obvious they could look at her and know? She prayed not. Rydor stood statue still next to her, strong and unshakable.

You're doing fine, Sutae.

I need your arms around me.

Nothing would please me more.

It was hard not to smile. Footsteps echoed behind them. She tilted her chin up and took a deep steadying breath. Eaton marched past them and laid the leather case on the table before her father.

Nuri picked up the case. "Rydor, I know you took the test once, but we must witness your abilities for ourselves. Shayla, please initiate the test."

Shayla stepped forward and removed the Kiah from the case. Loud gasps filled the chamber.

Merrick jumped to his feet. "What is the meaning of this!"

Another councilman rose. "Explain immediately!"

A shiver ran down her spine as all twelve council members grumbled their disbelief. Several of the men rose and rushed toward her father. Shayla cleared her throat and summoned courage she did not feel. "There was an unfortunate accident when I gave the test to three men, who can only be described as undesirable."

"We're doomed!" Merrick yelled.

"Order." Nuri slammed a gavel on a block of marble in front of him. "Everyone to their seats." He waited a moment. "Did Rydor take the test with the broken rod?"

"He did."

"Fine." Nuri stared at Rydor. "You will take the test again...now!" He waved an arm at Shayla. "Proceed."

Rydor, I'm sorry.

Do not worry, Princess. We have overcome obstacles larger and more dangerous than this.

She turned and walked toward Rydor, the broken rod in her hands. He knelt at her feet, his blue eyes filled with love. *Don't look at me like that, they'll see!*

Love is hard to hide.

"Is there a problem?"

"No." Her father's agitated voice made her tremble. She laid the rod on Rydor's outstretched hands. His fingers closed around the black crystals that immediately turned emerald. Her heart raced when she heard his voice.

"I am Kiah Master. I am worthy."

Rydor raised the rods high over his head and they turned pale green. Pride swelled in her as she listened to the surprised mumblings of the council. She knew they would change their minds about him once they saw his ability. Rydor closed his eyes and both pieces glowed as blue as his eyes.

Rydor, your powers are greater. Look!

He tilted his head back and viewed the crystal. *It is you who have given me the ability. Now, before you raise suspicion, finish this little demonstration.*

"You are Kiah Master. You are worthy. Fight in the name of the Zared Tribe."

He lowered his arms. "I will serve you well, my Princess, and will defend the Zared honor in the Ultimate Battle."

"Rise, Warrior. I give you the Kiah to protect with your life, to keep with you until victory is ours." With her back to the council, she smiled and winked at Rydor as he stood.

Be careful, Sutae, your desire is showing. And do not blush, it's a sure sign of your affection for me.

Stop that! If I blush it's all your fault.

Nuri cleared his throat and she turned to face him.

"It seems you've chosen well. Rydor does indeed have powers."

Eaton stepped forward. "May I address the council?"

"Of course."

"Ruler Nuri, esteemed Council Members. Councilman Merrick requested a physical examination of Rydor. He wanted to be sure he was fit. Excluding his numerous scars, he appears to be in good physical condition. However, our medical team found a problem with his blood test."

"Is he sick?" Nuri asked.

"He's a Voltran!"

Shayla cringed at the obvious pride in Eaton's announcement. She feared this issue would be raised, but not by Eaton. The councilmen again grumbled loudly to each other. Her father slammed the gavel.

"You will explain this, Daughter!"

Be careful, my love. Don't risk yourself for me.

I promise, Rydor, I'll make them understand. "Have you not seen Rydor pass the test with your own eyes?" Shayla watched them nod. "I chose this man not only because he has the power to wield the Kiah, but because he is good at heart. He has saved my life more than once. He has safely returned me to my home. He has agreed to be our Kiah Master, even if it means fighting against the Voltrans. Rydor claims affiliation with no tribe or family. He has sworn his fealty to me and the Zared people when he took the test. What more could you ask of any man?"

Her father and the council quietly stared. Satisfied she made her point, it was time to break the news. "I trust him implicitly. So much so, I have agreed to act as his Focus."

The silence was more deafening than the council's disturbed chatter. The color drained from her father's angry face. She had seen him like this before, and he was unpredictable in such an angry state. One of the councilmen started to speak, but he held up his hand to silence him.

Nuri stood. "You will do no such thing! Your job was to choose a Master, not fight by his side. I will not have it. That's final!"

Shayla's heart was in her throat. She did not know whether to scream or cry. How could he make such an announcement?

Easy, Sutae, it's my turn now. "May I address the council?"

"Please, and you had better have a good explanation. No one endangers the life of the Princess. Do you hear me—no one!"

"Ruler Nuri, esteemed Council Members, and honored guests. I would never risk the safety of Princess D'Par. I would lay down my life to protect her, as would any Zared Warrior. However, you must take into consideration the function of a Focus. Kiah Master and Focus must possess the ability to communicate without words on the same vibratory level and complement each other with their skills. The proper Focus is as rare as a competent Master."

Councilman Merrick stood. "Be that as it may, Princess D'Par is spoken for. We cannot allow her to spend time alone with you."

"I only request the princess be allowed to serve as my Focus. I said nothing about being alone with her."

Eaton cleared his throat. "If I may speak frankly?" Nuri nodded. "When I found them they were about to be captured by the Quelans." He grinned. "So much for laying down his own life. I for one, don't trust any man who won't reveal his family name or take pride in his tribe. He does not even have the manners to dress properly for an audience with the High Council."

"I found it inappropriate to wear a Zared uniform for this occasion, which was all I was offered. Once you have given your approval Ruler Nuri, I'll be honored to wear the uniform, if it is your wish."

"Shayla also confided," Eaton began, taking a step closer to Nuri, "that Rydor has touched her inappropriately."

"Is this true?"

The look in her father's eyes scared her. If a Zared was accused of an unofficial coupling with a woman, the usual consequence was an immediate life-mating ceremony. But Nuri would never order that between her and Rydor. Rydor was an outsider and she had been promised to Eaton, even if the official decree had not been announced. "Eaton lies. I said no such thing."

"You dare call my son, the Chief Warrior, a liar?" Merrick protested.

Shayla's hands fisted at her sides, her heart pounded and her mouth went dry. "Councilman Merrick, I would be the liar if I called him less." She had tried to like the Merricks. Now she held nothing but contempt for them. Eaton and his father seemed more like Damek and Turic. How many fathers and sons did she and Rydor have to fight?

"Shayla D'Par, you will apologize to Councilman Merrick and his son. Now!" Nuri demanded.

"I will do no such thing, and I cannot believe you would ask me to."

"I did not ask. I ordered."

Sutae, do as he says. It's not worth it.

Eaton disgusts me. I hate him!

I'm relieved to hear that. I saw him put his arm around you and was afraid you liked it.

Oh Rydor, I...

"Well?" Nuri coaxed.

"My apologies to you both. I must have been mistaken. My error." *Rydor, I hate this!*

Be patient, my love.

How can I be patient when they want to separate us? No, I can't stand it. I'm going to tell my father we coupled. He'll have no choice then. He'll have to let me...

"Ruler Nuri, I will work with whatever Focus you wish." He glanced at Shayla. "And please forgive the princess, she has been through much these past sun-cycles."

Shayla stared at Rydor. *Why? How could you do that?*

My only concern is you. As you told me yourself, this is your world, and you have to survive in it. I am the intruder here. This reception wasn't as bad as I had anticipated.

My father refusing to allow me to be your Focus isn't bad? What are you thinking?

You don't want to know.

She wanted to slap him and kiss him at the same time. Her emotions were being pulled in every direction. Loyalty to her father, love for Rydor, and contempt for the Merricks. It could not possibly get much worse.

"If I may," Councilman Burlay said as he stood. "I have listened quietly, and I'm abhorred by the dissension I've witnessed. We are about to face the greatest challenge in the history of Zanthus. It is a time to pull together, not rip each other apart. I detect jealousy in our Chief Warrior's accusation, and I believe Councilman Merrick speaks as a defensive father rather than a Councilman. We have judged Rydor by accident of birth. I have known many Voltrans who are as honorable as any Zared."

Nuri scratched his head. "Do you also have an opinion as to who Rydor's Focus should be?"

"Considering the magnitude of Rydor's task, I believe he should have the Focus of his choice. We cannot afford failure. None of us will be safe if the Voltrans win the Ultimate Battle. Especially those in positions of power."

Shayla sighed. Finally one Councilman had taken their side. She had always been fond of Zane Burlay. He was a man who took pride in weighing all his options before making a decision. He had proven it again, which was why he was the highest ranking member and her father's top advisor.

"Rydor," Nuri said, looking the man in the eye, "who do you want as your Focus?"

"Princess Shayla D'Par. We have practiced our skills and work well together."

"I will consider your request, but I make no guarantee. I need time to consider the alternatives." Nuri stood, tapped the gavel and announced, "This meeting is adjourned."

"Shayla, I'd like to speak with you in my office." Nuri turned toward Eaton. "Take Rydor and find him something appropriate to wear, then assign him a room in the guest wing."

Eaton saluted his commander. "As you wish."

Shayla's heart sank when Rydor left the chamber with Eaton. Her courage thrived with him next to her, and her body ached for him. This would be the first moon-cycle without him close since they met. How quickly she had learned to rely on him and crave his loving touch.

"Are you coming?"

She turned to see her father waiting impatiently by the open door of his office. With a nod, she walked into his private domain where life altering decisions were the order of the sun-cycle. Every eye in the room was focused on her so she hurried into the office and closed the door behind her.

Nuri sat behind his desk and motioned for Shayla to sit in the chair before him. "I want to know what kind of a relationship you have with this Voltran."

"You mean Rydor, our Kiah Master?"

"You know what I mean. Explain yourself before I lose patience."

Time away from her father caused her to see him with a new perspective. She had always believed him to be kind and understanding, but so far he had not acted very kindly. "I do not consider him a Voltran any more than he considers himself to be one. Our relationship, as you put it, is as Master and Focus."

"I've always known when you lied, and that same look is on your face now."

"Why would I lie?"

"To protect a lover?" Nuri leaned against the tall back of his chair. "There's more to what you're telling me, but I won't press you. Just know that I plan an announcement to the people this very moon-cycle. They have a right to know you've found a Master to defend us, and that you will life-mate Eaton the moment the battle is over."

"I will not life-mate Eaton. I find him repulsive."

"You didn't until Rydor came into the picture."

Shayla concentrated hard to stop a heated blush. She did not dare give her father the slightest hint of how she felt about Rydor, which was a difficult task considering he was all she could think about. "My journey matured me in ways you'll never understand."

"Be that as it may, I do not want you seeing Rydor. I will assign him a new Focus."

"Do you want us to lose?"

"I'm not intimidated by the Voltrans."

"You should be. I've seen Turic and his Focus, Brina. They are a force to be reckoned with. I have an advantage over anyone else you choose, because I've already confronted them."

"How is this possible?"

She shook her head. "We met in the fourth dimension."

"This is nonsense."

"Then you'd better consult the priests if you don't believe me."

"Shayla, why do you fight me?"

"Because I have firsthand knowledge of what's to come. And if you're a wise and just ruler, as I've always known you to be, you'll allow me to act as Rydor's Focus."

"You're too strong-willed for a princess." Nuri smiled. "I love you, Shayla. What I do is for your own good. Don't you see?"

"I love you too, but it's for the good of the Zared Tribe I beg you, not for myself."

Nuri shook his head. "You're a good daughter and princess. I could ask for no better, but I cannot give my permission for you to be Rydor's Focus. The subject is closed."

"Did you not hear Councilman Burlay's plea?"

"He has reasons to be sympathetic to the Voltrans, which is why I put no credence to his words."

"But..."

"I will not argue with you. I have decided. Now, I suggest you prepare to address the people. And I want to see joy on your face when I announce Eaton as my choice for your life-mate."

She nodded to avoid saying something she would deeply regret. Never before had she questioned her father's decisions, but this time he had gone too far. The very idea of defying him sent chills of terror down her spine, yet she knew she would. Her heart and soul belonged to Rydor, and she couldn't bear to be with another man. Somehow she had to stop this insanity.

CHAPTER TWENTY FIVE

Rydor paced the confines of his assigned room. Of course Eaton put him in the farthest location possible from Shayla. Little did the conniving warrior know it could not stop him. He could see Shayla any time he chose in the fourth dimension, and he would.

He had not planned to fight Nuri and the entire council. Except Burlay. Thank the Gods one man had the presence of mind to question the paranoia of the moment. He could understand the council's reluctance to accept a Voltran, but to deny Shayla as his Focus was foolhardy.

It seemed some of the council members had hidden agendas, but he remembered well how politics worked. One man could easily persuade the masses. He could only hope that man was Burlay rather than Merrick, even if it were a bit premature to decide who his allies might be.

The door opened and Eaton stepped inside carrying a large box which he tossed on the bed. "What's this?"

Eaton bristled. "Ruler Nuri instructed me to supply you with the proper wardrobe, which I have done."

Pushing the lid aside, Rydor inspected the contents. At least Eaton did not bring him a uniform. Instead of the official Zared gray, all the shirts and pants were black. "Colorful."

"Don't be snide with me. I know what you're up to, and you will not succeed!"

"You want me to lose the battle?"

"You will win the Ultimate Battle, but you will lose the fight for Shayla's affections. I'll personally see you never touch her again."

He smiled at Eaton, pleased when anger flared in the man's eyes. "Indeed. You're quite sure of yourself."

"Ruler Nuri backs me. You're nothing to us and never will be."

"Really." Rydor stepped closer to Eaton. "You're a fool if you think you can force Shayla to love you."

"I don't care about her love. You're the fool if you think love matters."

"You'd be satisfied to claim her as your life-mate and never lay with her?"

Eaton laughed. "You really are deluded. I will claim her in every way, whether she's willing or not."

It was déjà vu. Eaton possessed the qualities of the Celons, qualities he despised. How could Eaton have fooled Ruler Nuri and Shayla for so long? He wanted to destroy the self-confident warrior, but it was too soon to let him know the lengths he would go to keep Shayla. "Sell your soul for power, I don't care."

"I think you do." Eaton shoved a hand against Rydor's chest.

"Think what you want." Rydor's arm muscles tightened. He wanted nothing more than to wipe the sardonic grin off Eaton's face with his bare hands; but if his plan were to succeed he had to be patient. After several deep breaths, the urge to beat Eaton senseless still remained.

"I'll be watching you. Try anything and I'll reassign you to the prison wing."

"Throwing your power around again?" The crazed look in Eaton's eyes revealed the man's despicable nature. "You don't scare me."

"You should be scared. I can destroy you."

Rydor chuckled. "Others more powerful than you have tried."

"I will succeed where they failed."

"We'll see what Ruler Nuri thinks about the way you treat the Zared Kiah Master and his Focus."

"You're too much of a coward to tell him. Besides, he'd never believe you." Eaton gritted his teeth. "And Shayla is not your Focus, or have your ears failed you as well?"

"I have no intention of telling Nuri. You'll betray yourself. And Princess D'Par will be my Focus."

"Never." Eaton stomped to the door. "Get dressed. You will be presented this moon-cycle to the people as their Kiah Master. Try and look the part."

Eaton opened the door, stepped outside then slammed the door behind him so hard it shook the windows, then Rydor heard the lock slide into place. He was no better than a prisoner. Eaton was a force to be reckoned with, but he had no doubt he could best him in any battle. No man would ever again call him a coward. Eaton may have had his moment of private fun, but he would reveal the man for what he was, a power monger who was using Shayla as a pawn.

It was too soon to make any obvious moves. Before he could devise a plan, he had to learn more about his surroundings and his enemies. Nothing would keep him from Shayla, not Eaton, Nuri, nor the High Council.

There was one man who might help, Councilman Burlay. He had been a sympathetic ally so far, but only time would tell if he dared confide in him. He believed Shayla when she said her father was a just and fair man. Nuri completely destroyed his belief when he refused to allow Shayla to be his Focus.

Why did so many Zareds refuse to see he could not win the Ultimate Battle without the proper Focus? Had they all gone insane, or were they too absorbed with their own selfish needs? They sent Shayla to find him, and now that he was here, they treated him like the enemy. Something was terribly wrong.

"You're right, my son. Much is wrong in Terita."

The smoke cleared and Olin appeared in one of the two chairs in front of the polished marble fireplace. "I've missed you. What took you so long?"

Olin conjured two goblets of wine in his hands and gave one to Rydor. "Sit and have a drink. You need to calm yourself. Eaton has ruffled your feathers."

"I don't like him, and I certainly don't trust him." Rydor took a sip. "You said someone in Eaton's command worked for the Voltrans. I suspect it's Eaton himself."

"No. Eaton works for his own cause. There are others that want the Voltrans to win. They are very misguided, but they believe they'll be greatly rewarded once the Voltrans are victorious."

"I miss Spirit Mountain."

"You miss Shayla and the love you've found with her."

"We're being tested, but we will survive this."

Olin smiled. "You're very astute, Rydor, and you're learning patience, which is long overdue. But be careful. I cannot stop what is already in motion."

"Care to explain?"

"I wish I could. I'm a wizard, not a mind reader." Olin smiled. "That's your job, remember?"

"All too well, I'm afraid."

"Good. You will soon learn who your allies are. I know it's difficult for you to trust others, but you cannot fight alone. So many forces are at work, on so many levels."

Rydor groaned. "I had no idea there was such dissension within the government. I thought all I had to do was fight Turic and Brina not every person in Terita."

"While you lived on Spirit Mountain in solitude, the Voltrans have been busy. They infiltrated Terita long ago, securing allies in the upper echelon, and the common people as well. So beware. As I've said before, trust no one until you're sure. Even then, be wary."

"I'm not good at diplomacy."

"Oh, but you are. I observed you before the council. You did well, my boy."

Rydor lifted an eyebrow at his mentor. "You're as sneaky as ever."

Olin laughed. "How do you think wizards become so wise?" He magically refilled his glass. "I will not desert you, but there is little I can do from here on out. It's up to you and Shayla."

"That's a laugh. They won't let me near her."

"You're in her heart and in her mind. You've bonded on levels few have known."

"I pray it's enough."

"Have faith." Olin emptied his goblet. "I must be off. Take care of yourself, and watch your back."

In a misty whirl Olin faded from sight. Where did he always rush off to? Some sun-cycle he would learn the wizard's secrets, but for now he wanted to speak to Shayla. Actually he wanted to hold her and feel her soft body against his. The pain of separation already gripped him, which only served to strengthen his resolve to keep them together. *Shayla? Can you hear me?*

Oh, Rydor. Thank the Gods! Eaton is here with me and he won't leave.

Rydor quickly assumed the meditative position on the floor and concentrated. He had to go to Shayla. It took every ounce of will to clear his mind enough to leave his body and travel to her in the fourth dimension. Practice paid off because the simple thought of protecting her sent him soaring to her private quarters.

She looked terrified. Eaton held her by the wrist and she was trying to wrench free, but his grasp remained tight. *I'm here, my love.* All he could do was place an invisible barrier between Shayla and Eaton. He sent Shayla all the strength he could. *Step back.* She did as he requested.

Eaton tried to move closer to Shayla, but his fourth dimension energy held him back. That success gave him even more power. Shayla was able to pull free of Eaton's grasp and he watched a smile cross her lips. Eaton fiercely scowled when he pushed against air and moved his hands with no success. He looked like a mime paid to make people laugh.

"I forbid you to touch me!"

Eaton groaned. "What kind of witchcraft is this?"

"Get out before I show you more."

"You'll pay for this!"

Eaton turned and made a hasty retreat. It was amusing to watch the Chief Warrior defeated twice in a few short minutes. *Are you all right, Sutae?* She nodded, a tear running down her cheek.

I want to see you so badly.

Then join me. You know how.

It seemed forever before Shayla could complete the process to free her spirit and join him. She wrapped her arms around his neck and buried her head in his chest. Without their physical bodies touching, the sensation of touch was severely diminished; but it was all they could hope for. *I love you, Sutae.*

Oh, Rydor, I'm so sorry for all of this. I never thought my father would be so unreasonable, and the council wouldn't even listen to me!

What about Councilman Burlay?

I'd almost forgotten. He did speak for us, but he's only one man.

It starts with one. He hugged her as tightly as his ethereal body would allow. *Is Burlay a man we can trust?*

Right now he's the only council member I'd trust. I've known him since I was a child. He's been like an uncle to me.

Are you sure?

Do you doubt my word?

He tilted her chin up with one finger. *I don't want to, but you told me your father was a just and fair ruler, yet I saw no evidence of your claim.*

Shayla pushed him back. *I can't believe you said that! My father will see you as I do soon enough. Just give him time.*

We have no time left. The moment he sensed her doubt, she disappeared into her physical body.

What happened?

Negative thoughts and doubts clouded your mind and interfered with the energy that put you here. But that wasn't all. What caused her abrupt departure was her doubts about him. The knowledge hurt, but he pushed it aside. *Rest, my love. This moon-cycle will be a trial, but you must cooperate with your father and Eaton. Do not let them down. Proudly play your role as princess. Let no one suspect your true thoughts.*

How can I look favorably upon Eaton when it is you I want in my bed?

And it is I you shall have. Until then act your part and have patience.

You're sounding more like Olin every sun-cycle.

I'll regard that as a compliment.

Shayla smiled. *As you should.*

Rydor willed himself back to his body. He certainly did not need Eaton to burst in while he was gone. That could spell disaster. The threat of anyone attacking the physical body while the soul astral traveled could result in death.

CHAPTER TWENTY SIX

Shayla glanced in the mirror for the twentieth time. She looked the part of a royal princess, but she did not feel much like royalty. The blue gown she wore was the same as all her gowns, high neck, long sleeves, floor-length flowing skirt. It was proper...and boring. Memories of the seductive gown Rydor imagined for her sent a heated blush to her cheeks. So many women wore dresses just like that when they came to parties at the palace, but she could never deviate from the sedate style required of her.

Rydor had shown her freedom and taught her how to love. She would cherish those memories forever, but she prayed to have more than memories to keep her warm during long moon-cycles. Life without Rydor was not worth living.

She would see Rydor in the flesh in a few moments, but she had to keep her distance and act indifferent toward him. That task required the performance of her life. Not to touch him, or smile at him would be next to impossible. She longed for the peace, serenity and privacy of Spirit Mountain.

A loud knock on the door startled her. Her hand flew to her chest as if she could quiet the rapid beat of her heart. "Enter."

Arden and Rance stepped inside. "We have come to escort you to the balcony for the presentation ceremony."

"Have you spoken with my father?"

"Ruler Nuri has been in conference with Eaton and Councilman Merrick."

That comment did little to help her dark mood. "Let's go." Shayla walked through the open doorway into the hall. Her loyal guards fell into step behind her, the heels of their knee-high, military style boots echoing in the long, chilly hall. It was ironic how cold the palace seemed. All the time she spent in a cave high on a mountainside she never felt cold. Rydor generated so much heat, he could make her sizzle just walking into a room.

She stopped and turned toward the guards. "Have you seen Rydor?"

"No, Princess. Eaton allows no contact with him. Strict orders. Guards have been placed at his door for his protection. Eaton wants no harm to come to our Kiah Master before the battle."

"Will you do your best to keep me informed?" She watched them nod. "I want to know everything that's going on in the palace. It's important to me, as well as private. Can I count on you?"

"We understand completely. You can depend on us to be discrete."

"Good. Thank you." She turned and finished the long walk in silence. Ahead she saw a crowd gathered, sure her father was at the center. When she drew closer, the people stepped aside and she cringed at the sight of Eaton at her father's side.

Eaton bowed. "Good evening, Princess." He raised. "You're lovely, as usual."

"Well," Nuri began, "are we ready?"

Councilman Burlay stepped forward. "The people are assembled in the courtyard as you requested, and anxious to meet their Kiah Master."

"Good. Proceed."

Shayla clasped and unclasped her hands while the Zared anthem played through the city's speaker system. They still held to old traditions where the royal family was concerned. If only the song could go on all moon-cycle she would not have to take Eaton's arm and pretend she was thrilled to be promised to him.

The melodic strain ceased and Nuri's official page announced them. She took her father's arm and walked at his left side, Eaton next to her. Rydor followed with Councilman Burlay. *I can't do this, she screamed in her mind.*

You can, and you will. For us. For your people.

I'm a coward, all I want to do is run!

Never say you're a coward. Hold on to your pride and dignity.

Oh Rydor, I want you to hold me. I can't stand this pretense.

Nuri stepped to the stone rail and held his right hand up until a hush fell over the crowd. "Esteemed citizens of Terita and every member of the Zared Tribe. It is with pleasure I come to you this moon-cycle. I have two reasons to celebrate my joy with you. First, I want to announce that Princess D'Par has returned safely, her mission a complete success! She has found a Kiah Master with great power, and he is here. I present Kiah Master, Rydor."

Rydor stepped forward and stood at her father's side. Nuri grasped Rydor's hand and held it in the air. The enormous crowd roared for what seemed like an eternity. She was happy her people accepted Rydor at face value, but the undercurrent on the balcony was palpable. She sensed mixed emotions, but there were so many people assembled behind them, she was unable to discern who was sending the negative vibrations.

Rydor, do you feel it?

Yes, but I don't know who has the most adverse thoughts.

Too many minds and emotions.

Nuri brought Rydor's arm down and let go. "Rydor has pledged his fealty to the Zared Tribe. He will win the Ultimate Battle and free us all!"

Again the crowd roared their approval for several long moments.

"We are fortunate. Our princess has served us well."

There was a time she reveled in her people's approval, but not this moon-cycle. A bittersweet euphoria swept through her. So close to Rydor, yet they could not touch. Proud her people applauded a man so worthy, but she dreaded what was to come.

Nuri silenced the gathering. "Now, one final decree. I have chosen Eaton Merrick as my daughter's life-mate. The ceremony shall take place immediately following the Ultimate Battle!"

Shayla's legs shook, her heart beat heavily in her throat. It was done, there was no going back. No royal mating had ever been cancelled once the official decree was made. She was doomed to a loveless life with a man she despised. Nothing could be worse than this. The deafening jubilant roar caused tears to burn at her lids. She blinked them back, along with an overpowering urge to grab Rydor and run as fast as they could to their mountain.

Nuri bent his head to Shayla's ear. "Smile for your people. Look happy." He presented Shayla to Eaton.

Eaton took her hand then slipped his free arm around her shoulders. Her stomach turned. Her father gave her a commanding glare and she forced a smile, waving at the awesome assemblage below. From the size of the gathering, every man, woman and child in Terita and the surrounding areas had crammed into the sprawling public courtyard.

Help me, Rydor!

Have faith in our love, Sutae.

She couldn't even answer him, it was too painful. A quick glance at Rydor and her pulse quickened. The sight of Rydor clapping in honor of her betrothal made her sick. Would this ever end?

"Thank you, thank you. The Princess and I are pleased you approve. Let there be celebration this moon-cycle for the Zared people and the future of Zanthus!"

The happy screams and shouts of emulation made her head spin. Eaton took her by the arm just when she thought she might faint. He half dragged her back inside toward the main ballroom.

How could she face a celebration when her life had just been destroyed? Her father had assured her before she left he would choose a man she approved of, yet Eaton was at her side. Maybe he misunderstood? No, that was not possible. She told him in his office after the Council appearance that she would not life-mate Eaton under any circumstances. Before her departure she agreed with his choice, but he was well aware that things had changed. The problem was he did not like the change. She pleaded to be Rydor's Focus when she should have argued harder against being Eaton's life-mate. It was a mess with no way out.

Eaton tightened his hold on her arm. "You could look more pleased, my dear."

She forced a smile and tilted her chin up. She behaved only because Rydor had insisted she play the part. She would give everything she owned to be back at the Oasis with Rydor. Thinking about lying naked in the soft grass by the waterfall sent a warm blush to her cheeks and a smile to her lips. She glanced at Eaton. He seemed pleased at her genuine look of happiness, luckily he would never know what prompted the happy reaction.

Her father entered the ballroom first, she and Eaton right behind. Rydor, Arden, Rance and Councilman Burlay in the rear. While they descended the wide, sweeping stairway to the main floor, the guests stopped and paid homage to their leader. Men bowed and women curtsied while the entourage made its way to the podium table to begin the feast. Once they were seated, a hearty round of applause filled the immense ballroom.

Nuri stood, the crowd quieted. "Please, dance, eat and celebrate our good fortune."

She was seated between her father and Eaton, Rydor on the opposite side of Nuri next to Councilman Burlay. Rance and Arden stood behind keeping a watchful eye on everyone. They had been her guards for many annual-cycles. She trusted them to help her and to protect all of her interests.

"Dance with me?" Eaton held out his hand.

"Of course." He helped her to her feet and led her to the dance floor. With a wide grin he slipped an arm around her, the other hand taking hers. They whirled past several other couples who grinned, nodded and winked their approval.

She graciously smiled and nodded as she should, hating every minute of the endless torture. Eaton seemed pleased about their upcoming nuptials and all the attention it brought. She would never be able to return his enthusiasm. He told her during their school sun-cycles together that he cared about her, and he claimed he did now as well. Now it was obvious he cared more for the power of her position than her. She kept the happy mask on her face for fear she might cry.

I believe you're enjoying yourself too much, Sutae.

As they twirled past the podium, she caught the look on Rydor's face. He reminded her of a little boy who had just lost his favorite toy. *That would be true if it were you in my arms.*

Is it proper to ask for a dance with you?

You must first ask my father, then Eaton.

"You're ignoring me," Eaton protested.

"Never. What gave you that idea?"

"You were looking at him."

"Rydor?" She laughed. "I was looking at my father. I've missed him. We haven't had much time together."

"Nor have we."

"It seems we'll have a lifetime to bond."

"That we will, my dear."

The music ended and they returned to their seats. A feast was laid before them, but she lost her appetite long ago. The mood of the evening did not seem to effect Rydor's fondness for roast meats and fresh fruits. He ate as if it were his last meal. Eaton on the other hand was too busy watching Rydor to attend to his stomach.

Councilman Burlay asked permission to dance with her and she gladly accepted. Once on the floor, safely away from the podium, she whispered, "Thank you."

"You looked as if you could use a diversion."

Burlay was an excellent dancer and a safe partner. He reminded her of Rydor with his slicked back dark hair and mature good looks. She felt more relaxed than she had all evening. "I want to thank you for your support. No one else possessed your audacity for truth and common sense."

"I spoke my mind and meant every word I said."

"But can you convince the others that Rydor is an honorable man?"

"I believe I should get to know him a bit better first. However, I'm impressed by your faith in him. I assume you two had lots of time to become acquainted?"

"We did." Shayla bit her lip before she said how acquainted they were. She wished her mother was still alive to council her about love.

She hated keeping her relationship with Rydor a secret when all she wanted to do was shout it to all of Zanthus. Her thoughts went straight to when Rydor held her tight, skin against skin, mouth to mouth.

"I see by the blush on your face it went quite well."

Damn. She knew her cheeks were as red as the napkins on the tables. Why did she always have such a reaction? It was a curse to be sure.

"It's all right, Princess. I've known you since you were a child. Believe it or not, I want you to be happy, and I know Eaton is *not* the man for the job."

"You are wise, Councilman Burlay."

"No, just observant." He smiled.

"What do you mean?" Fear gripped her throat and it was hard to believe he knew her secret.

"Love is a wonderful and glorious emotion, but very hard to hide. I once felt as you and Rydor."

"But you've never life-mated. What happened?"

"It's a long, tragic story. Just suffice it to say the woman I loved was taken from me by fate."

Shayla knew exactly what he meant and how painful the realization was. She saw sadness in the depths of Burlay's dark blue eyes. "I'm sorry it didn't work out for you."

Burlay twirled Shayla. "Which is why I will do all I can for you."

"It's already too late. The decree has been made. It's official."

"There's a first time for everything." Burlay smiled. "There are many policies which need changing."

She laughed. "And you're just the man to make those changes. However, this situation is beyond hope." The music stopped and Burlay walked her back to her seat where Eaton all but slobbered over her return. He was overplaying the part of a doting suitor, and she could not bring herself to cooperate.

After a few bites of dessert, she stood. "I'd like your permission to retire." She hung her head in hopes Eaton would cooperate.

"Not until I have my dance."

Her head jerked up. Rydor stood before her. He bowed then offered her his hand. Eaton's gaze bored into her, which kept her from smiling on the outside, but her heart leapt for joy at Rydor's touch. She pretended to be apprehensive by glancing at Eaton, who gave his nod of approval.

Keep your required distance, Rydor. We can't do anything to attract undue attention. We're both the center of attraction at this little fiasco.

I thought you knew me better than that, Sutae.

She held back a chuckle at his wayward grin. They reached the floor and Rydor placed one hand on the small of her back. She carefully placed her fingertips on his shoulder and their free hands found each other, fingers twining together. She followed his lead around the floor. "Where did a mountain man learn to dance?"

"On a mountain?"

"Sure, I can picture it now, you and Olin, arm in arm."

"No, Una and I."

Laughter slipped out, but she quickly extinguished it. She glanced at the podium, grateful Eaton held a deep conversation with her father, neither of them noticing. "I'm worried about Una. Will she find you?"

"She won't come into the city. She might wait on the outskirts. Then again, she might return to the jungle with her mate. You know what love can do to a woman."

Stop it this instant! I'm having enough trouble keeping up appearances without you making suggestive remarks!

"Speak to me, Sutae. I love hearing your voice."

Some things are better kept between us.

Like making mad passionate love under the stars and beneath waterfalls?

You know very well what I mean. A tear slipped down her cheek. *Rydor, you know I love you, please don't make this so hard. I don't want to hurt you, but if you insist on acting like we can share a future you'll be hurt.*

I told you, love always hurts. "The palace is lovely, Princess." *And so are you, but I like my choice of gowns better than yours. I prefer more skin to show.*

"I'm glad you like it." Shayla nodded at several of her friends who made a point to waltz close to them. Rydor was being impossible. She longed to have him hold her like this, but it only made things more difficult. Neither of them was satisfied by the casual contact of dancing. "By the way, how did you ever get my father's consent to dance with me?"

"I'm devastated. You have no confidence in my powers of persuasion."

"Quite the contrary, I find you most persuasive." He spun her twice then pulled her close, her breasts pressing against the thin fabric of his shirt. The contact was only for an instant, but heat rushed through her. "Most persuasive indeed."

That wasn't even a good sample of what I want to do to you. Shall I show you more?

Not if you want to stay alive. Now keep your distance, Eaton is watching.

I don't fear Eaton, or your father.

You should. Shayla felt his mind close to her. He closed and locked his mental door to her. What had she said to make him withdraw? They approached the podium and he ended the dance. His fingers maintained the polite, acceptable hold on hers as he escorted her back to her seat.

"Thank you for the dance, Princess, and thank you, Eaton for your permission. I'll not bother you again." Rydor paused by Nuri. "Thank you for the celebration and the dance with the Princess, but I wish to return to my quarters."

With a heavy heart Shayla watched Rydor leave, two guards right behind him. Tension abruptly sprang between them when she said he should fear Eaton and her father. He must have thought she doubted him. His assumption could not be farther from the truth. If Nuri or Eaton suspected Rydor had made love to her, they might kill him. The only consolation was they needed him alive, at least until the battle was over.

"I believe this is our dance?"

Fighting tears, she took her father's hand and performed her duty as the happy bride to be. If only Olin could appear and cast a spell to make everything all right again. It would take more powerful magic than even a wizard could provide.

CHAPTER TWENTY SEVEN

It had been a long, sleepless moon-cycle without Shayla. He had not even tried to visit her in her mind. She did not trust in him, or their love if she believed he should fear Nuri and Eaton. Had he not proven himself to her a thousand times over?

Rydor sat on the edge of the garden wall and waited for the assigned Focus to arrive. The note Nuri sent early this morning said to meet a woman named Jasmine. She was supposed to be a psychic with telepathic abilities. That remained to be seen. The sun's rays warmed his aching muscles since he spent most of the moon-cycle exercising to relieve the tension in his body. Little good it had done. He ached for the woman he loved, and nothing would change that except holding Shayla in his arms.

"Rydor?"

He rose to his feet. "Jasmine. Nice to meet you." The cut of her pink gown revealed flawless olive skin and way too much cleavage. She wore her dark brown hair swept up on the sides, the back flowing to her waist. Jasmine was beautiful, and he felt she was sent to seduce him as well as become his Focus.

"You're thinking I'm attractive and you'd like to get closer." She took his hand. "It's all right, Rydor. Nuri has given us permission to become as close as necessary. He knows that mating will increase our powers and has no objections. In fact, he suggested I stay in your room so we have ample opportunity to bond."

"Why don't we work on basics first."

"What did you have in mind?" Jasmine sat on the garden wall and crossed her legs.

Rydor sat on the ground and assumed his meditative position.

"Please, join me." He inwardly groaned when she sat next to him, her knees touching his. Closing his eyes, he searched for Jasmine with his mind. She was reaching out for him, but he found her vibratory level almost painful. *Can you hear me, Jasmine?* He heard nothing but static on the psychic plane. "You must concentrate and speak to me in your mind."

Distorted words and half-sentences gave him a headache. *Try harder.* He doubted she heard him since nothing changed.

"I'm doing better, don't you think?"

"Speak only with your mind, Jasmine." The discord between them only got worse. She was sending messages, but nothing made sense. A test was in order. *I want to sleep with you.*

She sat straight, eyes shut, lips clamped tight, but he received no sensible reply. He was sure she'd be all over him if she'd received the message. *This is not working. You can never be my Focus.* "Did you hear what I said?" He opened his eyes and stared at her.

Jasmine laughed. "Of course. You said I'm doing fine and you're anxious to continue. Right?"

He nodded and closed his eyes, but all he could see was Shayla's face while she danced with him. Shutting her out might have been a mistake, but he had reached the saturation point. One more sexy look from Shayla, and he would have swept her away to the nearest dark corner. He did what he had to do, leave her with Eaton, a thought that turned his stomach.

Time dragged on and on as Jasmine babbled nonsense in his head. The woman meant well. It was not her fault Nuri decided she should serve her tribe as Focus. Nuri mistakenly believed psychic powers and telepathy were the only necessary qualifications. How could he get any of them to understand the fragile balance necessary between Master and Focus?

Rydor?

Jasmine?

Who is Jasmine?

He laughed. Shayla sounded jealous and confused. *Ask your father, he sent her.*

Obviously this isn't a good time to speak to you.

It couldn't be better. Where are you?

Jasmine's hand found its way to his lap and rested on his thigh. He shuddered when she moved her fingers closer to his groin. She pressed her body into his and ran a hand up his arm. He kept his eyes closed, but they opened when her lips met his cheek.

I'm watching you from my window.

By the Gods! He glanced at the building beside them and saw the outline of a feminine figure on the third floor. Jasmine wrapped her arms around him now that he faced towards her and planted a kiss on his mouth. He grasped her shoulders and pushed her back. She fought against the move and knocked him to his back, then lay on top of him.

And I don't like what I see. What's going on down there?

How on Zanthus could he begin to explain this? He laughed to himself, making sure Shayla heard him. *I'm playing the same game you have to play with Eaton.*

That's different. I've been pledged to him.

Well, your father has pledged Jasmine to me.

He did not!

Not in so many words, but he told her to bond with me and to share my room. If that doesn't please you, feel free to have a word with him. Careful not to hurt Jasmine, he freed himself from her grasp. "I think we've accomplished enough for one sun-cycle."

"But we've only just started. Why don't we go back to your room and..."

"No." He stood and walked away, relieved to put the amorous Jasmine behind him. *I miss you, Sutae. Isn't there someplace we can meet?*

We both have guards assigned to us, it's not possible.

Be creative. He waited for an answer, but her presence in his mind was gone. It was possible to speak to her no matter where she was, but he did not want to interfere if she was working on a plan to get them together.

***

Turic tapped his fingers on the table. Brina was late. She knew better than to keep him waiting. He was anxious to receive word about Rydor and Shayla. Damek ordered them not to make further contact with the pair until the battle. Pity, it was just getting interesting.

"Sorry, Turic." Brina stepped into his office.

"Close the door." He seated himself on the sofa and motioned for her to join him. "What did Merrick have to say?"

"Don't I even get a kiss first?"

He gave her a quick peck on the cheek. "Now tell me."

"You can't stand not knowing what your brother is doing. Or is it Shayla?"

"Don't start with me." Turic grabbed her arm and squeezed. "I'm losing patience."

Brina wrenched free and rubbed the red mark. "Fine. Two of the three contacts have checked in. Rydor has been presented to the people as Kiah Master, Shayla is to life-mate Eaton immediately after the battle." She laughed. "Of course we know that's not possible. If I don't kill her she'll rot in a Voltran dungeon."

"I'll handle Shayla. Now tell me the rest." He smiled at Brina's frown. Yes, he had plans for Shayla. Her jail would be his bed. At least until he got bored with her.

"Rydor is working with Jasmine just as we planned. She's doing her best to look like she's cooperating, although I believe she finds Rydor a bit too attractive."

"But will she kill him?"

"As soon as she has the chance. She's just been assigned to him."

"Has my brother been denied Shayla's company?"

"Nuri responded even more harshly than we anticipated. His moral standards are..."

"Well above ours, my pet." Turic laughed and slipped a hand inside the front of Brina's low-cut gown. "So they have no contact at all?"

"None."

Brina groaned as he fondled her breasts. "Excellent. We can't have them growing stronger." Turic pulled Brina on his lap and unfastened the top of her gown. It fell to her waist. Brina never lied when he touched her lovingly. He gently cupped a breast in each hand. "Have you heard from Arden?"

"Yes, but he hasn't learned much. Hmmmm, that feels wonderful."

He eased her down on the couch. She wrapped her legs around his waist, her breathing grew ragged. It gave him a sense of power to know how Brina lusted for him, but he still wanted other women in his bed. He hated being loyal to just one when there were so many others waiting for his attention.

***

Shayla used every argument in the book to get her father's permission to go into the marketplace to consult with her seamstress. She insisted every woman needed a special gown for her life-mating, as well as something appropriate for the Ultimate Battle.

It had been hard to pretend she cared about the upcoming ceremony to Eaton, and even harder to act as if she cared about what she was wearing when the future of Zanthus and the survival of her tribe were at stake. He must think her shallow and self-centered, but it was a small price to pay.

Arden had escorted her by himself since she gave Rance an even more important assignment. Arden stood next to her, hands clasped behind his back. He was a very competent bodyguard, and he wanted everyone in the quaint shop to know.

She listened to her seamstress babble about cuts and fabrics, business as usual. "Cindra, could I see the bolts in the back. The ones here don't please me. And I'd like to try on the gown you were working on before I left."

"As you wish, Princess. Follow me."

Shayla stood and walked toward the door behind the counter, Arden followed nearly stepping on her heels. "Arden, you'll have to wait here. I'll be fine."

"Princess, my orders are not to leave you alone."

"You certainly cannot go into the dressing room with me. Now, do as I say." He grumbled, but remained in the lobby while she walked out of his sight into the back area.

"Everything is as you requested. I hope it meets with your approval."

Shayla opened the door and peered inside. "Everything seems in order. Make sure I'm not disturbed—for any reason. Keep Arden informed, I don't want him rushing back here. I'm counting on you." Cindra had taken care of her clothing needs since she was a child. They had developed a close relationship over the annual-cycles, and she was counting on the loyalty of that friendship.

"Don't worry about a thing, Princess. I understand completely."

She stepped into the cubicle then closed and locked the door. Two strong arms wrapped around her waist and she sighed. The moment she turned, Rydor's lips were on hers, tasting and searching as if for the first time. It felt so good to be held again, to be kissed and cherished.

His hands worked on the covered buttons that ran down her back. Before she knew it her gown was sliding to the floor. He had no patience for her undergarment. One hard tug and it lay at her feet, the thin straps ripped from the silky material.

I thought I'd never see you again.

Oh Rydor, that could never happen.

He pulled back and looked her in the eye. "Your father will never allow me in your life."

"He'll change his mind, you'll see."

"Don't be a fool. No one in Terita even wants a Voltran in their midst, let alone life-mating their princess."

"Anything is possible, Rydor. Remember what Olin said about..."

Rydor pressed his fingers to her lips. "Then Olin is a fool as well."

"Don't do this, not now. We may not have another chance to be alone together. I took great risk to arrange this."

"Maybe you shouldn't have."

He turned from her and perched on the small bench. She moved to him and sat on his lap, naked to his gaze. Wrapping her arms around his neck, she kissed him long and hard, but his response was not what she expected. "Look at me."

His gaze bore into her, and she felt heat prickle her bare skin. Her desire had never been greater than it was this moment. "I love you, Rydor. I want you, here, now. Would you refuse a princess?"

He eased her to the floor then quickly undressed. There was no tender kisses or gentle explorations with his tongue. He plunged into her and moved with an urgency she'd never sensed in him before. It had seemed like an eternity since they'd bonded, but that did not explain his hurry.

She imagined being with him over and over in her mind. This was *not* her vision. Tears slid from beneath her closed lids. Rydor was bonding with her and doing everything right. He was not hurting her, but he was not loving her, nor were they soaring into the fourth dimension and bonding with their ethereal bodies and minds. It was a purely physical sensation. Something was absent, and she missed the depth they had come to enjoy.

What's wrong? She waited, but his mind was closed. This may not be the first time he shut her out, but she hoped it would be the last. On the dance floor they were surrounded by hundreds of people, and she understood his reluctance to communicate. But here? Alone? How could he tune her out when they lay flesh to flesh?

She wanted to plead with him to love her the same as before. He became a different person, cool and aloof the moment he set foot in Terita, Where was the man of Spirit Mountain? Maybe Rydor was a free spirit that could never be tamed. Or was it his past returning to haunt him? She wished it were that simple, but she feared it was something deep inside him that refused love. She grasped his cheeks with her hands and pulled his lips to hers. He kissed her back, but it seemed empty and shallow.

Rydor finished his service. That's what it was since he was only here physically. Her heart ached and tears rolled down her cheeks. He glanced at her while he quickly dressed. She was losing him, and she had no idea how to get him back.

Without a word he opened the door, checked the empty hall, then slipped out. She clutched her gown to her chest and released pent up tears from the last few sun-cycles. Time was running out for them both.

Olin and Rydor had repeatedly told her to hold on to her faith, but faith always hung by a very fine thread that she now felt slipping through her fingers and out of her grasp.

CHAPTER TWENTY EIGHT

Rydor stood in the dark alley and waited for Rance. His little tryst with Shayla had been torture. How could he have hurt her so? Their meeting had been pre-arranged and he was supposed to leave her doubting him. He wanted her so badly that taking her in that ridiculously tiny dressing room did not bother him. There had been no time for love, nor was it the place, but at least he got to see her and touch her. He hated the fact that he hurt her, but through it all he cherished every moment, every touch. The sweet scent of her body still lingered on him and he silently wished he could go to her now and explain.

"There you are." Rance walked up to Rydor.

"I hope you know what you're doing because I just hurt the princess, and if it's for nothing, I swear I'll..."

"Easy, my friend. We both have Shayla's best interest at heart."

"When did you change your mind about me?"

"I told you, last moon-cycle when I learned about the plot."

"Why trust me?"

"You wouldn't be here if you didn't care about Shayla, and you have no reason to betray her. You may very well lose your life in that battle. I'd call that reason enough."

"Are you sure of what you heard?"

"Merrick told Arden to be sure Jasmine stayed with you. He insisted, actually. He told Arden to use whatever means necessary to insure Jasmine's success with you."

"I don't understand why." He did, but he wanted to hear it from Rance.

"He wants to be sure Shayla stays away from you. He will do anything necessary to insure the life-mating between Shayla and Eaton.

You know that."

"By doing that he's insuring the Zareds will lose the Ultimate Battle."

Rance shook his head. "I have a suspicion the Voltrans have promised him a position in the new government should they win. Merrick doesn't care how he obtains power. You and Shayla are merely pawns in his bid for power. And I'm afraid Ruler Nuri is also in danger."

"So am I." Rydor stepped toward the end of the building and looked up and down the street. "Who can we trust to help us?"

"At the moment, Councilman Burlay, possibly."

"Do nothing without being sure. It would be safer to do it on our own. I can't talk to anyone. I am a Voltran and what Councilman would trust a Voltran?"

"I'm afraid one already has."

"Merrick?"

"That's my guess."

"There's much we don't know." Rydor motioned for Rance to walk with him. They made their way down the nearly deserted street. Only a few women rushed home with packages, but there were no men or guards visible. "I'll do my part with Jasmine." He stared at Rance. "You do your part to keep Shayla and Nuri safe. How many men can you gather that you actually trust?"

"Enough. Leave that to me. Whatever you do, you must tell Shayla it's over between you. She needs to be convincing. I know her well, but the others know her even better. If it isn't real, our plan won't work."

"I understand, but I don't like it. I've hurt her so much already."

"Shayla's acting abilities will never fool Merrick and Eaton. It has to come from the heart. She'll understand once it's over."

Rydor groaned. "I hope you're right."

"You know I am." Rance's hand moved to his weapon when a group of men turned the corner. They passed without incident. "Burlay wants to meet with you tomorrow. As First council to Nuri, it's expected."

"I look forward to it. I'll know then if he can be trusted."

They continued their walk back to the palace but guilt gnawed at him. He would do anything for Shayla, but hurting her was never part of the bargain. She gave him the most precious gift a woman could give— first love. Would he ever have the opportunity to make her understand?

At least Turic and Brina had left them alone. He doubted they would show up in Terita, but with those two, nothing could be left to chance. The threat of a possible visit bothered him, but they would have to attack on the psychic plane and he would feel their presence immediately and go to Shayla. She was strong and handled Brina well; but now that he made her doubt their love, Turic would gain a substantial advantage.

The words in the legend turned in his mind, "Knowledge and love are the tools against evil, the catalyst that binds. The rules are none, the rules are all, but only the purest heart will find victory." That left hope as long as he and Shayla could hold on to their love. This plan had just become extremely dangerous.

***

Rydor sat in the waiting area outside Burlay's office. It had taken the Councilman four sun-cycles to meet with him. Rance had been wrong that moon-cycle. He hoped that was all Rance had been wrong about. If there were other mistakes they were doomed.

He was tired. Sleepless moon-cycles fighting off Jasmine had worn him down. All the physical exercise to work off anger and frustration had done nothing more than create exhaustion. The woman was relentless. She turned down-right livid when he shunned every advance she made. He was surprised she had not resorted to drugs like Brina had all those annual-cycles ago. The possibility still loomed over him.

There had been no contact between him and Shayla since their meeting at her seamstress' shop. Her hurt must be far deeper than he thought. She was probably waiting for him to make the first move, but it was not possible. Nuri, Eaton and Councilman Merrick had to see real tears and anger, nothing else would convince them. The price of love, as always, was high.

"Rydor, the Councilman will see you now."

He looked up at the woman who now opened the door for him to enter. "Thank you." He rose from the chair and walked into Burlay's executive suite. Burlay stood and extended his arm across the immense wooden desk. Rydor complied with the traditional warrior's greeting, carefully honing in on Burlay's vibration.

"I'm sorry for the delay, but it was necessary." Councilman Burlay took his seat and gestured for Rydor to do the same.

Rydor sat in the soft, curved back chair and rested his arms on the dark green upholstery. "What is this meeting for?"

"As Nuri's First Council, it is my job to report to him exactly what kind of man you are. You will be representing us in the Ultimate Battle as a Zared, and..."

"Aren't you a little late, considering there are only fourteen sun-cycles remaining?"

Burlay laughed. "Oh, what I wouldn't give to be young, impatient, and passionate once again." He pointed to a decanter on a tray. "Care for a drink?"

"No, thank you."

"All business. I like that." He poured himself a glass of juice, took a sip then set it aside. "I've spoken with Rance and we've come up with a plan."

Rydor's hands fisted. How dare Rance make a move to enlist Burlay's help without consulting him first? He hated to suspect everyone, but Rance just joined the ranks of suspicious again.

"We believe Shayla must be your Focus, however, no one but the three of us can know. I'm working out the details of how to get Jasmine out of the picture."

"I'd be eternally grateful if you could at least get her out of my room. She's quite insistent we bond."

"Done." Burlay pressed the button on his com unit. "Doctor Gravin? Burlay here. I want you to give Jasmine Presard a complete physical examination. Keep her in the med unit until you're done, which should take at least eight sun-cycles, right? You heard correctly, eight."

Rydor could not hear what the doctor was saying, but he was sure Burlay's request was out of the ordinary. The silence dragged on. Maybe the doctor refused to cooperate, or worse, could not be trusted.

"I knew you'd understand, my friend. Yes. Everything is fine otherwise. No. There's no further need to examine Rydor. Thanks." Burlay ended the communication. "You will have no further problems with Jasmine, however, you will have to practice with her a few hours each sun-cycle for appearances. We don't want to raise suspicions."

"Why are you doing this?"

"That is a long story."

"I have time." Rydor crossed his legs and leaned back in the chair.

"I suppose I can tell you. It's not exactly a secret. I confided in Nuri long ago." Burlay cleared his throat.

"I was in love with a Voltran woman when I was about your age. We bonded, even though we knew it could never be." Burlay exhaled slowly. "We were so much in love. We'd even thought of leaving our respective tribes and making a home together in the Badlands."

"What stopped you?"

"Besides the fact that is no place for a woman?" He watched Rydor nod. "She became with child."

"And you didn't stand by her?"

"I couldn't, she was promised to another, someone with power. And I don't need to tell another Voltran what would have happened to her, and the child."

"They'd both be killed."

"Exactly. I loved her too much to let that happen, and I always wanted a son." He hung his head for a moment then looked Rydor in the eye. "Several annual-cycles later she was killed, and our son died after that. I don't admit this to many, but I've been a broken man ever since. I can't tell you how much I loved that woman."

"Who was she?"

"I'm sorry, Rydor. I'll take her name to my grave. Even in death I would do nothing to cause her shame. She suffered enough because of me."

"Why tell me this now?"

"Because you and Shayla are in the same position, and I don't want you to make the same mistakes I made."

"Nothing has changed, inter-tribe life-mateings are still forbidden, regardless of social rank. I couldn't ask Shayla to abandon her father and her position to run off to the Badlands, or anywhere else. No, we're as doomed as you and your lover were."

"Don't be so quick to judge. If you win the Ultimate Battle, all three tribes will be combined as one. A new government will be put in place, a new ruler, and..."

"Voltrans will still be Voltrans, and Zareds will still be Zareds. Attitudes don't change that easily. There will be mass resentment about. Three tribes trying to function as one will not change minds and moralities quickly."

"In time it's possible."

"I'm a realist, Councilman. Dreams are for children. If I succeed in battle, the hierarchy of the Zared government will assume power. Yes, they will elect a new official leader, but I'm sure they'll restore Nuri to that position. Why change what works?"

"I can convince him to..."

"Shayla is to life-mate Eaton right after the battle. You'll have no time."

"Are you giving up?" Burlay took a sip. "I can see by the look on your face you don't want to. Work with me, let's see what we can do. Give it a chance."

"By the time this is over, Shayla won't want to look at me let alone become my life-mate. There are secrets in my past she will learn. Turic and Brina know them well. They will use them against me. Even my success in battle will depend on Shayla's ability to ignore my past."

"Surely there's nothing that bad."

"There is. I only pray it doesn't destroy us all. The last thing I want is to have the Voltrans in power. Of course, I'm a dead man either way."

"We would do you no harm, you know that."

"If I lose, it will be because I'm dead. If I can't have Shayla, I might as well be. Like I said, either way I lose."

"And you're still willing to sacrifice all for her?"

"I can do nothing less."

"You're an honorable man, Rydor, just as Shayla said you were. Zanthus must not be ruled by the Voltrans. Of course, I want the Zareds to win, so I will do everything you wish to insure your success. You call the shots."

Rydor studied the man and honed his senses to pick up moods and ambitions. Burlay's vibrations were stable and well intentioned. As hard as he tried to find duplicity, there was none.

All his instincts verified Burlay was a man of his word. "I have no choice but to trust you with my life, Shayla's life, and the future of Zanthus. But be warned, if you betray me I'll kill you."

"Excellent! I'd have it no other way. Now, join me for a drink."

CHAPTER TWENTY NINE

Shayla pushed food around on her plate. This dinner with Eaton had been nothing but torture, which left little hope for the rest of their life together. Where was Rydor? She had not seen or heard from him since they made love at Cindra's shop.

That bonding could not be called a special experience like all the other times before, but it was all she had to hold on to. When her father complained about Rydor's refusal to bond with Jasmine it was difficult for her to hide her relief and happiness. Councilman Burlay's order that Jasmine undergo extensive physical and psychological testing made her father furious, especially since he ordered Rydor and Jasmine to remain sequestered together until the battle. The idea of Rydor holding Jasmine in his arms shook every jealous bone in her body. She thanked her lucky stars for Burlay's interference.

"You're not eating, my dear."

"I'm sorry, Eaton, I'm just nervous."

"About our life-mating?"

She nodded. It was hard to lie to Eaton, he knew her too well. "And the battle."

"Aah, yes. Three sun-cycles isn't long. I do hope Rydor and Jasmine bond well, our lives depend on it." Eaton laid his fork on the plate. "How is Rydor as a lover?"

Shayla felt the blood drain from her face. She clasped her hands in her lap so Eaton would not see them shake. "I wouldn't know."

"Really? In all the time you were alone with him, he never touched you?" Eaton chuckled. "Not much of a man then, I'd say. If I had you all to myself, you would know what it's like to have a real man."

She wanted to strike back, but he was baiting her. Eaton was slick, but she refused to fall prey to his prying comments. "Like I told my father, we only worked as Focus and Master."

"I'm not stupid, Shayla. I've seen the difference in you since your return. You've changed. A man knows when his woman has been unfaithful to him."

His woman? That was a laugh, considering what had transpired between her and Rydor, but that was a secret she would never admit, especially not to Eaton. "How could I be unfaithful when we haven't life-mated yet?"

"You know the rules better than I." Eaton stood and walked to Shayla's side of the table in the exclusive crowded eatery. He bent his lips to her ear. "Don't play games with me. Now, it's time to return to the palace where you will give me the rewards due a life-mate."

She stood and leaned toward him. "You'll be rewarded when you are my mate, not before." The angry look on his face sent chills down her spine. This Eaton was not the same man she knew before her quest. She was fond of him then, now her emotions ran close to murder.

How could a man turn into a monster in such a short time? Or had she finally seen the real Eaton? She missed Rydor so badly her body ached and her mind grieved. They had been one—lived as one and loved as one. Now they were two and it hurt.

Eaton helped her into the back of his chauffeured cruiser and got in next to her. He pressed his body against hers and slipped his arm around her shoulders. Her skin crawled. He nibbled at her ear, and she thought she might lose what little dinner was in her stomach. There had to be a way out of this. "I don't feel well, Eaton."

"Shall I take you to the med unit?"

"Please, I'm really sick."

"Must have been something you ate. I'll have a word with the manager."

"No, it's just me. I haven't felt well for several sun-cycles now."

"Driver, to the med unit, fast."

He pulled her head to his shoulder. She did not dare fight him. If the truth be known, she had not felt well since her separation from Rydor. A constant feeling of queasiness seemed to live in her stomach sun and moon-cycle. Spending so much time with Eaton must have upset her more than she realized.

The moment they pulled to a stop, the med staff rushed to the cruiser. When Eaton helped her out her head spun. Bells rang in her ears, her heart raced, her knees buckled, and she felt herself fall a split second before blackness consumed her.

Eaton caught Shayla in his arms and placed her on the transport bed.

He followed the staff inside to the exam area. A privacy curtain was pulled around Shayla and doctors rushed to her side.

"What are you doing here, Sir?"

The voice made Eaton turn. "Arden. I could ask the same."

"I've come to pick up Jasmine. Her tests ran three sun-cycles longer than they should have."

"Is anything wrong with her?"

"Nothing. That's the point."

Shayla opened her eyes to several people in white jackets, masks and gloves, a bright light nearly blinding her. She closed her eyes again, but there was no mistake about whose voices she heard on the other side of the thin partition.

Eaton cleared his throat. "I didn't realize you and Jasmine were friends."

"I'm here officially on orders from Ruler Nuri. I'm to take Jasmine to Rydor's quarters where they're to stay sequestered until we leave for the battle."

"It's about time."

"Sir, why are you here?"

"Shayla and I were at dinner and she took ill."

"Really? It seems odd she'd become sick on Terita's fine cuisine when we ate at the raunchiest inns in the Badlands. And who knows what that barbarian fed her while she was up on that mountain."

She'd known all along her guards would not accept Rydor, but Arden sounded as if he hated the man. What was going on? Everything seemed surreal. She was in good hands medically, yet she was terrified.

Doctor Gravin scanned her with the diagnosis bar. He looked perplexed, his mouth curved downward as if he found something so terrible he could not put it into words.

"Princess D'Par," the doctor said as he studied the digital read-out. "You're..." he glanced around, "free to get dressed. I'll discuss the findings in my office."

She nodded to Dr. Gravin and he promptly left. The assistant helped her into her gown then escorted her down the hall. Eaton and Arden talked by the entrance like old friends rather than a superior officer speaking to one of his men. The sight struck her as odd, but she continued into the doctor's office. He sat behind his desk, an overly serious look making him appear older. Was it just her, or was everyone around her in a strange mood? First Eaton, then Arden, now the doctor. The ability to detect changes in attitudes had developed since working with Rydor, but she never expected to feel them so strongly without him. She was obviously not as calm as Rydor when it came to reading another's vibrations. "What's wrong with me?"

"I...ah..."

"Just tell me. You've been my doctor since I was born. It can't be that serious. I only felt a little sick to my stomach and dizzy."

"Shayla, my dear, I'm afraid it is very serious."

"From the look on your face, I'd guess you're going to tell me I'm about to die."

Gravin grinned. "There's no threat to your life, only your reputation."

His words began to sink in, and she felt the cursed blush warm her cheeks. "Say it."

"You're with child. Approximately twenty-eight sun-cycles."

All she could do was shake her head. She'd been a fool to ignore the symptoms. As princess she was required to life-mate as a virgin, so no birth control was allotted to her. Her betrayal to Eaton would certainly become obvious. "Must my father know?"

"By law I'm required to report to him any visits you make to the med unit and the results of my findings. You know that, Shayla. And you also know I can't hide it from him. The moment I scanned you, the findings went into your record; and if he caught me lying, well..."

"I'm sorry, Doctor Gravin. Do your duty. It's my problem."

"I couldn't stop the flow of information through the computer even if I tried. It's I who am sorry. I know what this means."

The good doctor had no grasp of the situation. She and Rydor were both doomed, but her fear was even greater for their child. Princess Shayla D'Par would go down in history with many firsts to her credit. She prayed her failure as princess would at least save Zanthus from Voltran control.

An obtrusive buzz stopped her thoughts. She watched Gravin answer the call, knowing deep in her heart it was her father. Then she heard his angry voice through the speaker demanding her to appear before an emergency council meeting within the hour.

CHAPTER THIRTY

Rydor stood several feet from her in the council chamber, Jasmine at his side. It was late and everyone in the room had an angry air about them, some more agitated than others.

Eaton was seated at the center of the table next to her father, Merrick next to him. Burlay sat next to Merrick, the rest of the somber council members on each side. The High Priests and all the other government officials filled the gallery. Emergency meetings of the council were rare, but when one was called, everyone attended.

The only vibration that had any sense of calm belonged to Burlay. Even Rydor looked as if he wanted to kill someone. *Rydor?* His blue gaze fixed on her, sending a chill down her spine. He looked more handsome than ever dressed in black, his long, dark hair secured in a queue at the nape of his neck. *Do you know why you're here*? He just stared. *Please, talk to me.*

Rydor carried the broken Kiah in his right hand. It was his to protect, and she was sure her father had insisted. It hurt to see him with the beautiful, brown-haired Jasmine next to him as his Focus. The woman clung to his left arm with a death grip. Had they bonded? Was that why her hands were all over him?

The gavel slammed and Nuri stood. "I will waste no time. Distressing news has just come to my attention." Nuri glanced around the room, his gaze finally resting on Shayla. "Princess D'Par has brought disgrace to herself and her family. She has lost her virginity and is with child."

Everyone murmured, quietly at first, but their shocked remarks became louder until the room exploded into chaos. She searched Rydor's face for a reaction, but he maintained the same cold demeanor. Jasmine released her hold on him and inched away. Even a seductress like her did not want to be too closely associated with the man who violated the princess.

Why didn't you tell me?

At last he spoke in her mind, but even his reaction was one of bewilderment and anger. *I only found out an hour ago when Eaton took me to the med unit. I fainted at dinner.* The loud obtrusive chatter in the room made it difficult for her to even hear Rydor, and it felt impossible to think.

Eaton told your father?

He didn't have to. All my med visits are automatically sent to him. I'm sorry to put you through this.

The gavel slammed again and order returned to the room. So many pairs of eyes bore into her. She had committed the biggest sin in the history of Zanthus. No Zared Princess had ever brought disgrace to the royal family. She longed for Rydor to hold her and tell her everything would work out, but this was beyond his control, and hers.

"What do you have to say for yourself, Princess D'Par?" Nuri asked.

She took a deep breath and tilted her chin up. "Would it matter what reasons I had?" Heads shook. "I didn't think so. And since you've already judged me, I have nothing further to say."

Nuri groaned. "You will explain yourself to this council!"

"Fine." She took another steadying breath. Where was Olin when she needed him! "You sent me to find a Kiah Master. I did. You all know that Master and Focus need to bond. We did." The condescending looks bore harder on her and Rydor. He took it like a warrior, but her entire body began to shake. "What Rydor and I did was for the good of the Zared Tribe, nothing more."

Eaton stood. "And I'm to believe this nonsense?"

"Believe what you will. I can do no less than try to save my people."

"So," Nuri interrupted, "you're saying you have no feelings for this Voltran?"

Shayla glanced at Rydor who stood emotionless. This was the hardest thing she would ever have to do, but to protect him and his child, she would bear the blame. "I do not love Rydor, nor do I have any feelings for him. I did what I did solely to insure our success in the Ultimate Battle. It was my duty."

The council mumbled to themselves, but Eaton stood fast, teeth bared, hatred in his eyes. Was Rydor the victim of his anger, or was she? It was hard to tell. Knowing Eaton, it was both of them. This was all her fault. If she would have just gone back to her room and given Eaton the favors he wanted, this little secret would never be out. At least not until after her life-mating to Eaton.

The thought of Eaton claiming the baby as his made her even more sick than standing in front of these people admitting she had coupled with Rydor and had no feelings for him. Nothing could be farther from the truth. If Rydor stood a prayer of getting out of this mess unscathed, she had to stick to her story.

"And you, Voltran," Eaton began, "what do you say?"

"I care nothing for Princess D'Par. It is as she stated."

"We must decide what to do about this matter before the people gain knowledge," Merrick said. "It is unprecedented."

"I say we abort the child. I will life-mate her even though she betrayed me. It's the best offer you'll get." Eaton leaned back in his chair.

The council was out of control, all members talking at the same time. Her father appeared pale, Eaton had a satisfied grin on his face, and she felt faint. In a flash, Rydor stepped toward the council table. War glistened in his eyes.

"You will do no such thing!" Rydor gripped the Kiah tighter.

Eaton jumped to his feet. "You have no say in this. Shayla belongs to me!"

"It is *my* child she carries. I'll kill anyone who lays a hand on her, and you are first on my list."

"And you're a coward!"

Rydor placed a piece of the rod in each hand and lifted them over his head. Slowly he pushed the ends together. When they met, he let out an anguished cry. Shayla's mouth dropped open when the rod glowed bright crimson. Rydor groaned and tiny sparks bounced from his fingertips to the Kiah. She was as stunned as everyone in the room. Only Rydor's heavy breathing could be heard over the deadly silence that fell heavy over the room.

"I am not a coward. And no one will touch my child. I will kill the first person who tries."

Her heart filled with pride. No matter how Rydor felt about her, he would protect their child. *Thank you.*

Our child deserves a chance to live. Rydor lowered the rod.

"Then kill me, you bastard!" Eaton leaped over the table and lunged at Rydor.

"No!" Shayla screamed. Rydor tossed the rod to her an instant before Eaton knocked him to the floor. Both men rolled, body over body, arms and legs tangled, grunts and groans echoing off the high domed ceiling. She had never seen either man so enraged. Her heart raced. Eaton managed to pull his lazer weapon, but Rydor knocked it across the floor. Suddenly the blade of a cutter gleamed in the light.

Eaton thrust the knife toward Rydor's neck, but he was able to block the deadly blow with his arm. The black sleeve of his shirt was cut and blood soaked the fabric. Rydor flipped Eaton backwards in the air with a vengeance, then jumped on top of him, wrestling the cutter from his grasp. Rydor held Eaton's life in his hands.

"Stop this at once!" Merrick yelled.

Guards rushed Rydor and pulled him off Eaton. Each man took an arm and held it behind Rydor's back. Thank the Gods both men were alive. She watched blood drip from Rydor's arm to the polished floor behind him. If only she could do something to help him. The Kiah felt warm in her hand. She glanced at the rod and gasped. Rydor had mended the rod in his emotional rage!

Eaton sneered. "I knew you were too much of a coward to kill me."

Councilman Merrick rose to his feet. "Ruler Nuri, I have learned from a reliable source certain information about Rydor you should all know."

Shayla cringed. How could it get worse than this? She eased the Kiah to her side and let the folds of her skirt hide what only she seemed to know. It might be the only defense Rydor had once Merrick finished. Whatever the man had to say was bound to be one more nail in Rydor's coffin.

"By all means, Councilman Merrick. Address this council." Nuri took his seat and yielded the floor to Merrick who left the podium and walked toward Rydor.

Merrick stopped a few feet from the Kiah Master and looked him in the eye. "Your name is Rydor Celon, son of Damek Celon!"

Shayla held her breath while Merrick circled Rydor, ignoring all the shocked murmurs in the chamber. She prayed this was another of Merrick's tricks to make himself and Eaton look important, but the gnawing ache in the pit of her stomach knew different. Everyone gasped when Merrick ripped open the front of Rydor's shirt, silver buttons bouncing on the floor.

"Guards, remove his shirt!" Merrick ordered.

Rydor's magnificent torso was bared to everyone's eyes. To her he never looked better, but she sensed the repulsion of those viewing his scars for the first time. He did not look her way, nor did he speak. Words were of little use.

"These are the scars of a Voltran coward. He refused the warrior's rite of passage. He would not perform his duty in order to become a warrior. His father disowned him and his tribe inflicted these wounds, wounds befitting a coward. Everyone believed him dead until our unfaithful princess found him."

Shayla's legs weakened and her head swam in an effort to absorb the varied vibrations she had learned to read. Merrick's announcement numbed her. She did not need her mental abilities to know the intent of those in the chamber. Now she knew what was behind Rydor's locked door. He'd betrayed her!

How could he have kept a secret that could destroy them? It all made sense with alarming clarity. That last moon-cycle on Spirit Mountain when he stormed out of the tent after she said the word coward. There were other times the word had come up, each time his reaction was the same. She should have guessed when she noticed the resemblance between Rydor and Turic. All the clues were there, she had just been too blind to acknowledge them. No wonder he refused to give his family name.

"I say kill him!" Eaton shouted.

Councilman Burlay calmly rose to his feet and held up his hand to silence the noisy crowd. Shayla overheard several of the priests' comments and was thankful they were not allowed to participate in the discussion. It seemed everyone shared Eaton's desire to extinguish anyone with the name Celon.

"Sit down, Eaton, and bite your tongue or I'll free Rydor to finish what you started." Burlay glanced at Nuri. "Since this is an emotional time for our ruler, I, as First Council, shall take over." He glanced up and down the podium. "I see no one has an objection. Now, I believe Shayla has something to show us."

CHAPTER THIRTY ONE

Rydor strained against the guards' unyielding grasp. He wanted to rush to Shayla and hold her in his arms. She was deeply hurt, and it was all because he dared love a princess. It was undeniably cruel not to send her a message of love, but she had to believe the worst about him. This was the Shayla he needed to cement their plan. Any attempt to calm her would alert the council, but nothing could stop the guilt that ripped his heart in two.

"Shayla, please. Show us the rod." Burlay walked around the table to where Shayla stood and put his arm around her.

In all the excitement he'd forgotten the rod. Shayla's arm rose from the fold of her gown. This time even he gasped along with the crowd. The rod was dark crystal again, but it was one piece! When he held the Kiah over his head, he had never been so angry in his life. Every emotion from love to hate boiled through him. He truly wanted to kill Eaton and rush to Shayla. The joy that soared through him when he heard she carried his child had not only brought tears to his eyes, but it invoked his need to protect the woman he loved and his unborn child.

Nuri cleared his throat. "What is your point, Burlay?"

"Need you ask? Rydor stood before us the first time and claimed no tribe and no family name. He didn't lie. His tribe left him for dead and his father disowned him."

"That is a technicality."

"No. It's the truth. And you were all so busy watching Eaton's foolish display that you didn't notice when Rydor mended the rod. If he can mend the rod, he can win the battle for the Zareds." Burlay chuckled. "And as for being a coward? Eaton is lucky to be alive." He looked at Eaton. "You need to thank your guards."

Rydor could not look straight at Shayla, but out the corner of his eye he saw tears streaming down her face. She sucked in her bottom lip and hung her head. He had destroyed her spirit, he sensed it in his soul. Faith in their love was all that remained, and there was little faith left in her.

Burlay took the rod from Shayla and walked to Rydor. "Guards, release him." He extended his arms, the Kiah in his hands. "This belongs to you."

"Thank you." The moment he took the Kiah, a surge of energy bolted through him. Along with the boost came an increased sensitivity to Shayla's thoughts which were more than he could bear. Her trust was gone, and so was her faith. His past secret had torn them apart, and he prayed the secret he held could bring them together again.

"Now," Burlay said, returning to his seat. "I make a motion to support Rydor Celon as Kiah Master. Who better to fight for us than a man mistreated by the enemy?"

"As usual, Councilman Burlay, your words have earned you the position of First Council. However," Nuri hesitated. "What is to be done regarding Princess D'Par and Eaton Merrick's life-mating?"

"I believe," Burlay began, "the best interest of the Zared Tribe would best be served by keeping this meeting quiet and making no decision until after the battle. Surely they can wait three..." he checked his timepiece, "ah, make that two sun-cycles."

"So be it. My official decree is that no one in this room is to speak of this meeting. We will reconvene after the battle." The gavel slammed one last time. "Dismissed."

Rydor cringed when Jasmine sided up to him and slipped her hand under his arm. His distaste for the woman grew stronger with every advance she made. He longed for Shayla's touch, and if he could not have her, he wanted no woman.

"It's time to return to our quarters, Rydor."

The purr in Jasmine's voice made him want to barf. "My quarters. Feel free to return to yours." Rydor removed her hand and walked quickly toward the exit. He made his way through the crowd and hoped if he mingled well enough, Jasmine could not find him. He wanted nothing to do with Jasmine, but a warning went off in his mind. This was the test Olin had hinted about, and he knew if he did not act fast he would make the mistake of a lifetime. Several council members lingered, including Merrick. He quickly backtracked to find Jasmine.

Shayla was right behind Jasmine. Merrick and Eaton followed the two women closely. This opportunity was perfect, and only a fool would not use it to full advantage. Only the importance of the end result allowed him to bring such debilitating pain to Shayla. He already regretted what he had to do even if it were necessary.

"Jasmine, darling. I lost you in the crowd." Rydor slipped his arm around her shoulders, following orders from his logical mind which was in stark contrast to his heart's desire. "I wouldn't want anything to happen to my Focus."

"How thoughtful." Jasmine smiled.

Every bone in his body felt Shayla's anguish. His love for her had never been stronger or harder to control. It took every ounce of his strength to walk Jasmine to his room.

While he continued to escort Jasmine down the long hall, he could no longer ignore Shayla's heartbreak. Against his better judgment, he probed her thoughts. She was so devastated she did not notice his intrusion into her mind. His brief invasion verified what he suspected. She feared for his life and his child's, but it was her feelings of hate and betrayal that caused him to quickly withdraw. Guilt gripped his soul. She believed what he had done was unforgivable, and he would have to live with that the rest of his life.

Jasmine leaned her mouth to Rydor's ear."Don't look so glum, my sweet. I have plans to lift your mood."

"I'm sure you do." With every step Jasmine clung tighter and his heart pounded harder in his chest. Never had frustration or anger threatened him so deeply in his life. Even his father's betrayal was not as devastating as when Eaton slandered Shayla and his unborn child. If Burlay had not stopped him, he would have killed the man with his bare hands. At least the incident proved he was not the coward everyone believed him to be. He even surprised himself, but it was love that guided his actions and made him care. Love was a feeling he had never experienced until Shayla entered his life.

Shayla showed him the first honest love he had ever known. His mother tried, but Damek always found a way to stop her affections toward him. His father did his best to keep his mother from spoiling him, but if she had truly loved him as her child she would not have given up. True love could not separate anyone—ever. No one would keep him from the one person he loved—Shayla. He would move heaven and Zanthus to be with her.

Jasmine clung to him every inch of the way, but he barely noticed her. His mind was on Shayla from the glow of her beautiful hair to the tips of her perfect toes. She was his, and he would have her once again. He had faith—that was all he had at the moment.

The four guards that escorted them stopped abruptly at the door and opened it for them. They stepped inside and he heard the bolt slide into place. Would he ever be a free man again?

He walked to the bathing chamber, grabbed a damp cloth and wiped the blood from his arm. He knew Jasmine watched him even though his back was to her. He did not like the woman. There was something about her aura that felt wrong. Time would reveal all.

Jasmine took the cloth from Rydor's hand. "Let me do that for you."

Rydor pulled his arm from her hand. "It's fine." He walked back into the sleeping chamber to the gold inlaid wardrobe, opened the door and pulled out a shirt. When he tried to slip an arm in the sleeve, Jasmine grabbed the fabric from behind and pulled it from his grasp.

"You won't be needing that."

She ran her hands over his bare chest and traced his longest scar. "Don't." He pushed her hand away, then put some distance between them.

"You shouldn't be ashamed of your body. Your imperfections don't bother me." Jasmine smiled. "I can turn out the lights."

"Leave them on." He felt the tickle of her psychic probe, and immediately erected a wall. She was weak and he read her frustration through the uncomfortable vibration. Even if he found her attractive, she could never be his Focus. They were not compatible on any plane, and she did not fool him. She was working against him, not with him. He knew from the first time they practiced, and the only change he detected was in her duplicity.

Jasmine went to the refreshment center and poured two drinks. He turned his back to her, but watched her every move in the mirror over the dressing table. She pulled a vial from her sleeve and emptied it into one of the glasses of wine. He'd been waiting for her to use an aphrodisiac on him. It worked for Brina, but Jasmine was sixteen annual-cycles too late for that trick.

She strutted toward him and handed him the tainted drink. He smiled at her and pretended to take a sip. "Why don't you find something more appropriate to wear?"

"I thought you'd never ask." Jasmine started to take off her gown.

"Not here. Dress in the private room. I want to be surprised." He winked at her and she took the bait. She grabbed a nearly transparent sleeping garment and disappeared into the small room behind him. The moment the door closed he switched the glasses and sat on the chair by the table, grateful for a moment's reprieve.

The door opened all too soon and Jasmine posed provocatively. "You look lovely." He almost choked on the words, but she had to believe he was serious. She ran to him and kissed him on the lips in a way that forced him to return the favor. Her fingers threaded through his hair, and he responded with a sexy groan. He hoped she took the gesture as approval, even though it was a groan of distaste. She pulled back and he silently exhaled in relief.

"First we finish our wine." She picked up her glass and took a drink. "This will be a moon-cycle you'll never forget."

"I'm sure." He downed his wine in one long swig, not wanting to take the chance she would switch them back. Experience taught him a man could not fight the effects of the love drug, but he could easily control Jasmine. He watched her polish off her drink and lick her lips.

Jasmine blinked heavily. "Come to bed with me." She laid down and motioned for Rydor to join her.

He stared at her for a moment and wondered how her features could change so quickly. "You don't look well." In mere seconds her skin turned completely pallid and her seductive smile faded to a painful expression. Rydor felt her forehead. Whatever she had used in the drink caused her to feel cold and clammy. "Jasmine?"

She could not speak. He picked up her hand and found every muscle limp and unresponsive. Her eyes closed. This was no love potion. He lifted her lids and found her eyes had rolled back. She gasped for air. "Jasmine!" He shook her. She suddenly went rigid, her head tilted back on the pillow. It sounded as if she were choking. He grabbed her shoulders in an effort to help her sit, but her body went limp. With one last gasp for air, her heart stopped beating.

He immediately began every method he knew to save her life, but nothing worked. No heartbeat—nothing. If he had not switched the drinks he would be lying there—dead. Gently he brushed hair from her face and took a step back. He may not have cared for the woman, but he certainly had not wanted her dead! There was only one answer, Jasmine worked for the Voltrans. There could be no other explanation.

How on Zanthus was he going to explain this? Nuri would believe he killed her to serve his own needs. He believed the worst was over at the council meeting when the proof of his and Shayla's love was revealed. Now he had a dead woman in his bed and they were locked in together, guards at the door so there was no doubt he would be held for her murder. And since Burlay had ordered such an extensive physical of Jasmine, no one would believe she died of a heart attack at her young age.

Once Shayla heard this news it would cement his betrayal for all time. His plan dictated the necessity to get Jasmine out of the picture, but he and Rance had arranged for her to be kidnapped before the battle. Never had he intended to harm Jasmine. Sabotage had always been a real possibility, but he never considered that Jasmine would try to kill him.

He stared at her lifeless body, another of Damek and Turic's casualties. How many more would there be? The Voltrans had to be stopped, but he could not do it alone.

"This is not good. Not good at all."

Rydor glanced up in time to see Olin materialize on the other side of the bed. "I can't argue with that."

"Things have taken strange turns indeed."

"You know about the emergency council meeting?"

"I'm a wizard. I know all and see all."

"Yeah, you're everywhere and nowhere. A lot of good it's done." Olin walked to the soft, upholstered chair and made himself comfortable.

"Oh ye of little faith."

"Where has faith gotten me? Shayla has been disgraced, Nuri won't allow her to be my Focus, Jasmine is dead and I can't even count my enemies, they're everywhere."

"Did I not tell you there were lessons and tests you must face in Terita?"

"You did, but..."

"But nothing. I've trained and advised you all I can, however, I cannot give you faith, patience, or Shayla. Those things you must control within yourself. You know this, yet you question everything!"

"Shayla is hurt. She believes I've betrayed her; and, in a sense, I have. What we shared is gone. Maybe we never had it."

"Doubt will destroy you."

"What about Jasmine?"

Olin conjured a glass of wine and took a sip. "Jasmine destroyed herself."

"No one in Terita will believe that."

"Then it's up to you, my boy, to set them straight."

"Me? The Voltran traitor?" Rydor laughed. "All that wine you drink has dulled your mind."

"You're strong, Rydor, and I have not lost faith in you. Deep within your heart and soul you know what is required of you, and you will do no less. Go back to those moments you and Shayla shared in each other's arms. Remember the moment your son was conceived, and you will find the force within yourself that no one can destroy."

"My son?"

"Yes. A son. And it's your desire for him to live in a free society, without the evil of the Voltrans."

"I want that for Shayla as well." He couldn't deny a word of Olin's wisdom. The man had never failed him yet. "It will be as you ask."

"Not as I ask of you, as you ask of yourself." Olin smiled. "It's not easy to hold the future of Zanthus in your hands, but it is the destiny you were born to fulfill. Your mother knew this and paid the price."

"I've never understood why she had to die so young." Aria's face formed in his mind. She was the kindest Voltran he had ever known, and Damek had taken advantage of that weakness. As her son, he inherited her compassion, which had cost him as well. The only way to justify Aria's life, the pain he suffered, and save Shayla and his son, was to defeat the evil.

"I see a spark of recognition in your eyes, my boy. Good. Don't deny your hatred or your love—control those emotions, channel them to do the most good."

"You're right, as always." He watched the gleam in Olin's eyes light up the room. "You're the father I always wished I had. I can't bear to think of the evil that spawned me."

"Have you ever considered that your father isn't evil?"

"Never. Damek has destroyed everything good in life, including my mother. I could consider him nothing less than the demon he is."

"Do some soul searching."

The wizard gave him the strangest look. How could he possibly believe there was one good bone in Damek's body? Olin often went off the deep end. Then again, he had never proved the old magic man wrong in all the annual-cycles they had been together. But the idea of Damek having any redeeming qualities was a travesty.

Olin's form faded as usual after a thought provoking lecture. He knew what he had to do, but he could not get Shayla's words out of his head. She told him she only bonded with him out of duty. Was that the truth, or was she trying in vain to save him from the council's retribution?

She was convincing, yet he refused to believe she meant what she said. Her tears were real, and she was not a woman easily disposed to crying. This was all his fault. He had been stupid to think he could push her away with his half-hearted attempt to make love to her at Cindra's. He thought he could convince her he no longer loved her if he withheld the out of body mating in the fourth dimension, and by erecting a mental wall so strong she could not access his mind. His success at making her cry tore him apart then, as well as now.

Shayla told the council she did not love him, but he wanted to believe she was only doing her duty by telling the council what they wanted to hear. He wished it were possible to tell her how much he still loved her, but that had to wait. In two sun-cycles he planned to get his princess back in his bed. Until then he could only hold her in his heart. She belonged with him, and he would move mountains to have her.

CHAPTER THIRTY TWO

Shayla lay on the soft bed, her hands rubbing her abdomen. It would not stay flat for long, living proof she betrayed Eaton and the royal name of D'Par. She wanted to blame her pregnancy for the uncontrollable tears even though she knew it was Rydor's fault.

Rydor made no attempt speak to her, except to ask why she neglected to tell him she carried his child. He also told the council he cared nothing for her! Was that to save his hide, or had he finally admitted the way he truly felt? His lies were numerous and she no longer believed a word he said.

All of Olin's warnings flashed in her mind. Olin vehemently insisted she let no one come between her and Rydor, but it was Rydor himself who stood in the way of their happiness. Happiness. It was a dream she would never realize. How could she raise Rydor's child life-mated to a man she did not love? Eaton seemed a fate worse than death, but she would do anything to preserve the life within her, a life that was created out of love. Rydor did love her when this child was conceived, that she was sure of.

Even Olin's warning not to trust her father now seemed real and logical. She had been so sure he would willingly accept her choice of Kiah Master without question and allow her to act as Focus. The revelation that Rydor was the son of Damek Celon, a coward disowned by the entire Voltran Tribe only confirmed her suspicions...he did not trust her. What was love without trust?

Her body ached for his tender touch, but his arms would never be around her again. It was over, and there would be a high price to pay for them both for sharing that love. There was a part of her that would never believe he meant what he said. Their bond had been too special. How could two people mate and share everything including thoughts in another realm suddenly decide there was nothing between them?

She shook her head. She also told her father and Eaton that she had no feelings for Rydor. In her heart she knew that was a lie, so she was as guilty as he was, but that changed nothing. If neither of them admitted the truth again, the lies would become reality. She once heard someone say that a lie told long enough became truth. Now she knew what it meant. Rydor would always be the love of her heart, even if she were relegated to Eaton's bed.

She'd loved Rydor with every part of her body and soul, even though it was an impossible match. Rydor gave her no reason to believe in him. She had lost count of the opportunities she gave him to confide in her, and how many times she begged him to reveal his secret. Now that she knew his secret past, she knew what destroyed him.

As if the truth of his heritage was not enough, he had openly welcomed Jasmine to his bed right in front of her. He may not have said the words, but she knew that look in his eye, the one he used on her many times. Jasmine would bond with him this moon-cycle, and she would lose him forever.

The thought of Rydor sharing with Jasmine what she had believed was hers alone, destroyed what little hope she held for the future. She had been a fool to trust him with her heart believing he loved her. Although the biggest mistake could lie in trusting him to be Zared Kiah Master. He might only have agreed to ensure a Voltran victory.

They were both caught in circumstances beyond their control. She could not blame Rydor without accepting her part of the responsibility. She wanted him as badly as he wanted her. Rydor had told her there were things about him she would be better off not knowing. She was the one who assumed his secrets could not possibly be as bad as he claimed.

Her selfish needs no longer matter. Whether Rydor loved her or not meant nothing next to the survival of Zanthus. Neither should she question Rydor's loyalty. He had even more reasons to hate the Voltrans than any Zared citizen. She saw and touched his scars, she felt his inner goodness and shared his concerns over the future of the planet.

As princess, her people's needs came first, no matter how painful. As a woman, she would grieve her lost love until the sun-cycle she died. For the moment, her only hope was for Rydor to bond so completely with Jasmine that Turic and Brina stood no chance to win the battle.

The true victim in all this was Rydor. He never had lasting love in his life. She had seen how happy and content Rydor had been when they bonded and shut out the rest of the world. He was entitled to happiness, but she doubted he would find it anymore than she would. They had both lost something the moment they left the oasis, something very precious and fragile.

Had Rydor pushed her away because he knew he could never have her? She might never know the true answer. He would also lose his child as well, a child she knew he wanted. He had valiantly protected the life she carried and threatened anyone who touched her. No matter what he said or did, she knew a part of him would always love her. She would cherish the time they had together. She would give a fortune to hear him call her Sutae one more time. She never fully understood Rydor's words at the time, but the meaning was now abundantly clear, "Love always hurts."

***

Rydor paced the width of his room. He had stopped himself from contacting Shayla so many times he had lost count. The battle was so close he could feel it, yet his heart felt nothing but pain.

Damek had stolen his life yet again. As a child, Damek took his mother, of that he had no doubt. Then Damek had tried to take his physical life. Shayla and his child would be the final sacrifice to the Celon name.

Rydor Celon, the coward, lost again. No. Losing Shayla and his child were sacrifices he was absolutely not willing to make. There had to be a way. It was time to dissolve the black cloud of doom he lived under.

Could love conquer all? It was an idyllic thought, but there was little else to hope for. Olin preached patience and faith. He prayed the wizard was right, because he loved Shayla to the depths of his soul—now and forever.

The door opened. He turned to face Rance, but the Zared Warrior's gaze was fixed on Jasmine's body while the door slowly closed behind him.

"What in the name of the Gods happened here?"

"I thought she was putting an aphrodisiac in my drink so I switched them. I had no idea it was a fast acting poison. I never dreamed she would try to kill me. What is going on?" He looked at the serious expression on Rance's face, but his thoughts were a total mystery to him. All he could hope for was a friend and not an enemy.

Rance walked to the chair and fell into it. "I came to warn you. I was afraid I'd be too late." He shook his head. "This complicates matters, as if they weren't bad enough already."

"Have there been new developments?"

"Where do I start?

Rydor took the chair across from Rance. "Tell me everything. How can I fight anyone if I don't know what's going on?"

"I know, and you have every right to be upset. Things are really messy at the moment. I'll try to enlighten you, just calm down, Rydor. I know you're upset about Jasmine, and Shayla, but..."

"How is Shayla, and tell me the truth!"

"Calm down, my friend."

"Are we friends?"

"Yes, and you can trust me. My loyalty is with Shayla, which means you as well. I know you're skeptical, as you should be, but I will not let you down. I promise."

"I am glad to hear that." The sincerity in Rance's voice rang true. He had to trust someone. "Now, please, tell me about Shayla."

"When you left I escorted Shayla to her quarters. She said nothing to me, or anyone. I felt so bad for her. I've never seen her cry like that. She's always been so strong."

Rance did not have to tell him about Shayla's anguish, he knew it well since he felt it himself. "Go on."

"I placed guards at her door since I was off duty, then headed to the Warrior's Club."

"Warrior's Club?"

"It's where we congregate to socialize and drink. Anyway, when I got there, I found Arden. He had quite a head start. He was alone, so I sat with him. That's when he propositioned me."

"For what?"

"To join the Voltrans! He said he worked for them. He even showed me a Voltran communicator, and bragged how he'd told them of the emergency council meeting."

"I thought all communications were out."

"The Voltrans sabotaged the Zared and Quelan systems, theirs remains intact."

"Who did Arden speak to?"

"Damek and Turic Celon." Rance cleared his throat. "Your father and brother."

"Never refer to them as my family." Rydor gritted his teeth. "I don't claim them, and they don't claim me."

"Sorry."

It took effort to suppress his anger enough to listen to Rance. "What else?"

"Arden said the Voltrans were going to reward him beyond his greatest dreams when they rose to power, and that I should join them before it's too late. If I didn't, they'd destroy me after the battle."

"They're that sure they're going to win?"

"Of course. They planted Jasmine here to insure their success."

"How long have they been planning this?"

"Since before the challenge. Finding out you were alive was a total shock to the Voltrans—all the Voltrans. They planned to kill the Zared Kiah Master from the start, no matter who was chosen." Rance looked straight at Rydor. "They never planned on you!"

"I'm sure they were delighted to learn I was the Master."

"Arden did say...well, you don't need to hear more."

"I know what they think of me."

"Arden said Turic is already celebrating victory. He figures even if Jasmine fails to kill you, you'll lose with her as your Focus. All that matters is stopping them." Arden stared at Rydor. "Promise me you'll destroy them."

"Without Shayla as my Focus I can't win."

Rance glanced at the bed. "Well, Nuri certainly can't insist on Jasmine, and there isn't time for you to work with another Focus. He'll have no choice. " He scratched his chin. "What are we going to do with her?"

"I have a plan, but it's risky."

"Rydor, I must admit, I didn't like you when we met in the Badlands. In fact, I wanted to kill you and your cat. But you're a good man, and you make Shayla happy."

"How can you say that? I've disgraced her and caused her nothing but pain."

"I saw the love in her eyes the moment I found her. She'd do anything to protect you. No, my friend, I know true love when I see it." Rance laughed. "I'm afraid I might have been just a little jealous."

"There was something between you?"

"No. I just felt a special bond with her. We were very close, but once she found you, her eyes saw no one else."

"Let's pray you're right, because I need her like I've never needed anyone in my life."

"Tell me about your plan."

Rydor grinned. "If it works, we can dispose of Jasmine and Arden at the same time."

CHAPTER THIRTY THREE

Ruler Nuri tapped his pen on the desk. "Please, Shayla, be seated."

She stopped her pacing and did as he asked, but she had no idea why he called her to his office. If he thought he could convince her to abort her child he was dead wrong. She would fight him like she never fought before. No one would touch Rydor's child.

"I'm afraid there is more bad news, and it involves Arden."

"What has he done?" Arden would do nothing to hurt her, or Zanthus. He had been her personal guard for several annual-cycles. "Tell me."

"It seems that he drank too much last moon-cycle at the club. This morning he was found unconscious in his bed, but he wasn't alone. Jasmine was lying next to him, very naked...and dead."

Shayla gasped and her hand automatically moved to cover her wide-open mouth. "How could that be? I thought Jasmine was with Rydor. What was Arden doing with her?"

"I left strict orders for Jasmine to stay with Rydor until the battle." Nuri hung his head. "Rance informed me Arden bribed his friends who were guarding Rydor's door to let her out."

"Why would Arden go to all that trouble just to have an affair?"

"It goes deeper than that." Nuri looked his daughter in the eye. "They both worked for the Voltrans."

"More betrayal? When will it end?" She knew the answer as sure as she knew her name. "Where is he now?"

"In the holding cells with the two guards he bribed. They're all traitors, and will face charges after the battle."

"Along with me?" Her father glanced up, a frown on his face. So many things were going to happen after the battle. "What if there is no after the battle?" She watched him shake his head. "If you do not make me Rydor's Focus we are doomed to fail."

"I still cannot allow you to..."

"You have no choice. There's no time for Rydor to work with another Focus even if you *could* find one!"

"I can't risk your life—you're my daughter!"

Shayla took a long, deep breath then let it out slowly. "You weren't so happy to claim me last moon-cycle."

Nuri raked his fingers through his hair. "I had no choice, it's law."

"The rules are none, the rules are all." She noted recognition in his eyes. "You know what I have to do. Rydor and I can save our people, not separately, but together. You can punish me however you choose once we win. If we lose...it won't matter."

"I don't like this at all." Nuri tapped his fingers on the desk in front of him.

"You must make this decision as Supreme Ruler, not as a father." Her heart beat rapid against her chest. They both knew what the answer had to be, so what was taking him so long?

"You will life-mate Eaton after the battle. That is my condition."

"I'll take banishment before I abort my child."

"I could never banish you. Don't you know that?"

"If I don't life-mate, you have no choice. It's Zared law." Her father's face was pained and pale. He was in a difficult position. When she chose to love Rydor, she somehow knew their love would come to this impossible decision.

"You will life-mate Eaton immediately after the battle."

"What about my baby?"

"I'll assure your child's safety."

"Then I will perform my duty as you request." She would detest every sun-cycle she spent with Eaton, but relish every moment with her baby. If she refused there might be no baby, and she already felt like a mother. Mothers gave their lives for their children if necessary, and this was the epitome of necessary.

"So be it." Nuri stood. "You and Rydor may practice together in the garden with a chaperone. Nothing improper is to take place between you. Is that clear?" He watched her nod. "I will not have you disgrace the royal name, or Eaton any further."

Shayla's heart felt so heavy it took all her strength to stand and walk to the door. He said he would not banish her, which had given her hope, but his voice was cold and void of all emotion. She could only hope he still loved her, she was his daughter, his only child. Was this how it would end between them? She heard her father clear his throat. She turned and waited to hear a word of compassion.

"Prepare well, we leave for the Holy Temple of Caelum at sunrise."

Hope for a relationship with her father was as useless as hoping for a future with Rydor. All she had to hold on to now was her child. Everything seemed hopeless, but if her child were to stand a chance of survival, she and Rydor had to win the Ultimate Battle.

She left her father's office and walked to the garden, two guards in step behind her. Arden was under arrest, but where was Rance? She felt so alone. How could she work with Rydor? They had to share thoughts and feelings—they had to be honest. That was a laugh. He had never been honest with her, and she doubted he would start now.

The undisputable truth remained—she loved Rydor with every ounce of her being. She was angry with him for keeping his identity a secret. If he had told her the truth, she could have found a way to avoid the ugly scene in front of the council. Then again, she might not have insisted he become Kiah Master for the Zared Tribe.

Rydor had Damek's blood in his veins, and that was something she had trouble comprehending. Was Rydor the kind loving man she knew and loved? Or was it all a ruse to gain her trust and sabotage the Zareds' attempt to win? It was all so confusing. One troubling question remained, and she would ask Rydor the minute she saw him.

She exited the palace and walked across the perfectly landscaped courtyard to the fountain in the center. The low wall of the rippling pool invited her to trail her fingers through the cool water. Memories of the lagoon swam through her mind. She sat on the rock wall surrounding the pool. It was impossible to dismiss what she felt for Rydor when he invaded her every thought.

"Princess D'Par."

Rydor's voice vibrated through her. She did not have to turn to know how handsome he looked, but she did. He wore the black garments he was given, which made him appear even more dark and mysterious. This sun-cycle she noted one more obvious trait she never saw before—a dangerous and foreboding glint in his eyes.

"I was told you wanted to see me."

"Ruler Nuri has consented to allow me to be your Focus. We're to practice together before the battle. We leave at sunrise tomorrow."

Rydor glanced over his shoulder at the two guards behind him, then at the two men by Shayla. *Must we have so much company?*

Orders. Shayla stared at the stones beneath her feet. It was hard to look into the depths of his questioning blue eyes without crying. He may have betrayed her, but her body did not lie—she wanted him. Did that make her a traitor as well?

"Shall we begin?"

He sat on the lawn a few feet in front of her and assumed his meditative position. She stood and crossed the few steps to join him. It seemed strange to do this in a gown. She sat on the soft grass and adjusted her skirt. *Rydor, I have a question I must know the answer to, and please, be honest.*

Are you saying I lied before?

You didn't tell me everything. Isn't that the same thing? She watched him bristle, but she shoved all emotions aside because she had to know.

I told you I claimed no tribe and no family. That was the truth.

You should have told me you were a Celon, that Damek Celon is your father and Turic is your brother. She took a deep breath. *And your scars are because you're a coward.* The pain on his face bore through to her bones, the same as it had the last time she used that word. She wanted him to deny he was a coward and stand up for himself!

I was born a Celon. My father disowned me when I wouldn't complete the Voltran rite of passage. I was beaten and left for dead. Olin and Una found me and I've lived on my mountain ever since. You know the rest.

Shayla sighed. *I know only the first born male of a family is supposed to have the power of the Kiah. That explains you, but what about Turic? How did he become so powerful?* Rydor stared at her for the longest time, shoulders back, muscles flexed, lips pursed.

What's your point? He let out a deep breath. *Are you saying you don't want to work with me?*

I just...

Don't trust me? He grinned. *I understand. Tell me to leave and I will. Tell me to fight and I will. It's up to you. But if you don't trust me, I fear for both of our lives. Turic will use our weaknesses against us. You've seen what he can do.* Rydor took a deep breath. *And you have our child to consider, or will Eaton have his way and force you to abort?*

Our child is safe. Eaton and I will raise him well.

Rydor's hands fisted. *You're a fool if you believe Eaton will raise a bastard.*

She hung her head. The word bastard made her skin crawl, but that's exactly what their child would be in Eaton's eyes, her father's eyes and her people's eyes. Only she and Rydor understood the love that conceived the new life—a love that could never be. *I will life-mate Eaton.*

As you should. Anything for your people.

His words were a knife through her heart. He believed she had turned against him, had no faith in him. He could be right. It was all too easy to believe the worst about Rydor when everyone around her despised him for being a Voltran coward. Deep in her heart, she knew how wrong they were.

At least you've never lost your desire to win the Ultimate Battle, Princess.

That has never changed. There was a hatred in Rydor's eyes that terrified her. What was going through his mind? There was no need to use her special senses to know his hurt and anger. He had erected the locked door once again, but this time she knew she would never see inside.

CHAPTER THIRTY FOUR

Rydor clutched the leather case that held the Kiah while he stood next to Rance in the transport depot and waited for the High Priests, the council members, Ruler Nuri and Shayla. The sun hid behind the distant hills, the city of Terita shadowed in the early morning light.

Shayla was the only light in his life, and he had no desire to return to the lonely solitude of Spirit Mountain—alone. He refused to believe she wanted to remain in Terita, life-mated to a man she did not love. No more games, no more plans. He would fight to the death for the woman he loved.

"Rydor," Rance began, "I want to wish you luck."

"Luck will play no part in this."

"Be that as it may, you have my full support. I'm sure the others support you as well."

"No one trusts me, but they need me to fight for them."

"That will change. They'll accept you as I have. I'm sure of it."

"Rance," Rydor turned to face the warrior. "You have been a loyal friend, and I will not forget what you've done for me."

"Considering what lies ahead for you, I've done nothing."

"Will you do one more favor for me?"

"Anything."

"Protect Shayla and my child."

"You'll be able to do that yourself once this is over."

"Not if I'm dead." Rydor's hands fisted at his side. "Shayla will life-mate Eaton after the battle. I may not be able to stop it. Just promise you'll keep her safe. I don't trust Eaton." He took a deep breath. "If Turic should win, don't let him near Shayla."

"You have my word." Rance slapped Rydor on the back. "I don't like all these alternatives, my friend. Please, tell me you'll win the battle, as well as the fight for Shayla."

"That's my plan."

Footsteps echoed in the marble halls as the entourage approached. The priests in their long, glossy brown, hooded robes and the councilmen in their royal finery all walked toward them. He sensed Shayla's nervous depressed thoughts even though he could not see her. Ever since their last coupling she had changed. He hurt her, but he would never pull away or keep a secret from her again. He prayed there was still enough love between them to face the enemy and survive.

Rance bowed when Ruler Nuri stopped in front of him. "We're ready, Sir."

Nuri nodded once. "Lead on."

Rydor followed Rance to the large craft that would take them to the Holy Temple of Caelum. He stepped into the vehicle and moved to the seat in the back and carefully watched the others file in. All twenty rows filled before Nuri and Shayla took the last available place in front. He could barely see the top of her blond hair through the crowd, but he caught a glimpse of the elegant blue gown that covered her from neck to toes.

He remembered all too well what her skin looked like, how it felt, and the sweet fragrance he loved to deeply inhale. By the Gods, he wanted her still and always would. Everything he ever loved had been taken away, and Shayla was no different. The thought of her in Eaton's arms left a bad taste in his mouth.

"Don't look so glum, my friend. You'll be fine."

Rydor glanced at Rance. "I plan to win this battle, but nothing will be fine. Look," He nodded his head forward.

"You mean Shayla?"

"She's sitting between two men who have betrayed her, while I keep my distance. It isn't..." How could he say more when he was just as guilty?

"Fair?" Rance cleared his throat. "For what it's worth, I don't trust Eaton myself. You're a far better man than he could ever be. I'm sure Ruler Nuri will see that in time."

"Time? You speak as if we had some. Just swear to keep your promise." He watched Rance lower his head. Rance knew as well as he did that what happened to him would dictate Shayla's future. He could easily win the battle and lose the war.

Nuri had no reason to change his mind about the proposed life-mating. His child would be raised a bastard, and he knew all too well what that felt like. Damek may be his father, but he would always treat him as a bastard son rather than a firstborn heir. He had tried so hard to please the man, but every effort met with failure. Nothing he or his mother had done was ever good enough. Damek blamed his mother for giving birth to a cowardly son and had made her life a living hell. Somewhere in the pit of his stomach he knew Damek caused her death.

Shayla had asked him about Turic's powers if he wasn't a first-born male. It was a valid question, but one that left him asking even more. All he could do was dismiss the exception. No one knew what the Kiah could do, so how could they possibly know who had the power?

The transport hummed through the air at an incredible speed for such a large craft. Sixteen annual-cycles had brought leaps and bounds in technology, but he wished he was alone with Shayla on Spirit Mountain. There they shared of themselves with no outside intervention. Shayla had given him the one missing link in his life—love.

They would soon arrive at the temple grounds, and he would face his past for the last time. Would he be forced to bid farewell to the woman of his heart? His resolve to fight for her was stronger than ever, but he was only one man. He could not change Zared traditions, and he would never force Shayla to abandon her rightful position. But he prayed he could at least give her a choice.

Time dragged as the semi-arid landscape gave way to rolling green hills speckled with majestic trees and an occasional small lake. The further they traveled toward the center of the planet the more lush the scenery. He remembered well the beauty of the Voltran territory, an odd coincidence considering the evil that bred there.

He stared out the window and wondered what his dear, departed mother, Aria, would think if she knew her two sons were about to fight to their deaths? It was good she did not have to witness the event. No woman should be put through such torment, but Damek would revel in blood fighting blood.

"Rydor, look," Rance said, pointing to the other side of the vehicle. "The three temples of Caelum."

"One for each tribe."

"Only a few privileged priests have been here. It's magnificent. You can plainly see from the air how each temple is situated at different points of a perfect triangle."

The area within the triangle belonged to no tribe. Each side represented the boundary between the tribes. The planet had been divided into three equal territories long ago to settle disputes. It was then the priests and elders of each tribe conceived of the Ultimate Battle to prevent further war, and this sun-cycle it would again become one.

While the transport descended the magnificent architecture, three matching white temples were connected by double rows of white columns which supported a covered passageway around the perimeter. Long white benches ran the length of each side. The large center area consisted of a manicured green lawn, a stark contrast to the flawless white. Everyone on the craft stared out the windows in total admiration for the perfect setting.

They hovered low, then parked behind the massive domed circular building with tall columns all around. "Do you think the temples will crumble at our presence?"

"We're not that bad, Rydor, but I do expect nothing will be the same after this sun-cycle."

"So I've heard." He watched Eaton stand and offer his arm to Shayla. He gritted his teeth as the light-haired warrior escorted her out. Shayla did not belong on Eaton's arm. Rydor loved her like no man ever could. They shared a part of themselves no one would ever understand. They were joined, heart, body and soul. He prayed it would be enough.

Rydor stood, leather case in hand, and followed Rance into the bright sunlight. One of the priests motioned everyone into the pristine temple through large double doors. Everyone took a seat inside on the white, marble bench that jutted from the white walls and followed them around the entire circumference.

A strange sensation pulled at him. Thousands of voices whispered in his mind. He recognized them for what they were—the collective consciousness of everyone who went before, those now assembled, and those yet to come. The esoteric melded with reality, and the combination made his head feel light. This sun-cycle would be filled with strong emotions and bizarre happenings, something he and Shayla must overcome.

The priests closed the doors, and the eldest stepped into the center of the circle. He raised his arms and chanted a prayer that echoed in the sacred chamber.

"Will Master and Focus step forward." The priest waited, lowering his arms to his sides as Rydor and Shayla walked to him. "Kneel, chosen ones, and receive blessings from the Gods. For this sun-cycle you fulfill your destiny on behalf of the Zared Tribe, before the eyes of these witnesses."

The priest's words blurred. Rydor opened his mind to Shayla, visualizing her as she was at the oasis, naked and wanting him. She glanced at him, her familiar blush verifying she received his message.

What are you doing? We're in the temple!

I'm sorry, Sutae, it's what I want.

Don't do this, Rydor, please.

Others have come between us, but this sun-cycle you must trust only in me—in the love we share. If you don't, you risk not only your life, but the life inside you.

You tell me to trust in you when you betrayed me? I think not.

I never betrayed you.

You kept your secret, Rydor Celon, and that was the biggest betrayal of all. You've bonded with Jasmine, and you'd be standing here with her if she wasn't dead! So how can you ask me to trust you when you've never been honest with me!

Because I love you, Sutae. I always have.

And I'm supposed to believe that? Why are you here?

Shayla had every right to feel as she did. His plan had worked too well. He had to make her understand, for her and their child. *I'm here to serve you, because I love you. I have no interest in the Voltrans, except for keeping them out of power. I've never lied about that. Just because my name is Celon is no reason to assume I believe in what they're doing.*

The priest finished his lengthy prayer then took the leather case from Rydor and pulled the Kiah free. He blessed it, prayed over it, and held it for all to see. Ceremoniously he placed it in Rydor's hand.

"Wisdom of the ages will descend on the warrior who believes." The priest clasped his hands before him. "Knowledge and love are the tools against evil, the catalyst that binds. The rules are none, the rules are all. Only the purest heart will find victory." He looked into Rydor's eyes. "What do you say, chosen one?"

"I am Kiah Master. I am worthy."

"And what do you say?" He stared at Shayla.

"I am Focus. I am worthy."

"The Gods have spoken. They grant you their protection, and we, their humble servants, offer our support. Now rise and face the enemy. Fight for Zared freedom."

CHAPTER THIRTY FIVE

Rydor stood and offered Shayla his hand. When he pulled her to her feet, the warmth of her hand in his reminded him of what he had missed these past moon-cycles without her. The priest opened the doors behind them. They walked hand in hand through the doorway, down the steps and onto the soft grass to stand in their corner of the triangle.

He took her cheeks in his hands and tilted her head to look at him. *I never meant to hurt you. Everything I did was for you. How could you believe I could touch another woman as I have you? I'm sorry Jasmine is dead, but I swear by all that's holy, I never laid a hand on her.*

It doesn't matter. I'm to life-mate Eaton. What was between us is in the past where it belongs.

No! You belong to me, and I will have you again. We have a child to raise.

Eaton and I have a child to raise.

I don't know how, but I swear to you, we will be together. Eaton will not lay a hand on you or our son.

Son? How do you know it's a boy?

I feel his vibration. He's strong.

But I'm not.

You are, you'll see. His life had never belonged to him, and it was time to change that. A new resolve coursed through him. He refused to believe a cruel twist of fate united him with Shayla, only to rip her from him. He planned to protect her and fight to keep her. If he died in the process, so be it.

I can't do this, Rydor. I thought I was brave, but I'm not. My father...

Do not think of your father, the priests, Eaton, or the enemy. Focus on me. Follow my lead without question. I will win for the Zared Tribe.

Turic may be my brother by blood, but I will do what is necessary.

You'll kill him?

If I have to.

You're capable of murder now, after failing the Voltran rite of passage?

Her words cut deep, but he'd never been more sure of anything. Yes, Sutae. I can and will destroy him, but if you believe me a coward, we are doomed.

Rydor faced Shayla. Her hand shook, her body trembled. He wanted so badly to take her into his arms. He did not have to look along the sidelines to know every Zared in attendance studied their every movement, but this might be his last chance to embrace her and tell her what was in his heart.

She looked away from him, and he feared she was lost to him forever. He pulled her close and held her head to his chest. Her breasts pressed into him, and he wanted her more this moment than he ever had.

He found her lips and kissed her the way he'd dreamed of all those moon-cycles without her. Her tongue found his, and he tasted what was again forbidden to him.

But you said you cared nothing for me.

I love you, Sutae. Always remember that. You also said the same.

I told my father and the council what they wanted to hear.

Rydor pulled back and smiled. *As did I, my sweet princess. Everything I did was for you—for us. I had to pretend I didn't love you, and that was the hardest thing I've ever had to do. You had choices to make. You had to decide where your loyalty lay. I didn't want to force you into anything, or disgrace you, and in that I'm afraid I've failed you.*

Oh, Rydor, you could never fail me.

But I have. I had to make you hate me so you could be the princess the council needed you to be. And to flush out the traitors, everyone had to believe there was no love between us. I planted my seed that grows in you now, and that was something I had no right to do. Rydor cupped her cheek with his hand. I love you, Sutae, with all my heart and soul.

You mean...

I meant what I said. I love you, Shayla. You have my heart, mind, body, and soul. I will die protecting you...and our son. You are my love. There never was, nor will there ever be another. Tears welled in her eyes and one spilled down her cheek. He wiped the moisture from her face. *I thought that would make you happy.*

Rydor, you don't understand. I must life-mate Eaton. I promised my father. It's the only way I could save our child. I want to believe we can be together, but I know my father, and...

Believe him, child.

That's Olin's voice! Rydor, where is he?

Rydor pointed to a hill in the distance. He knew Olin would be here, and his presence was more than welcome. Olin, my friend. It's good to see you.

You didn't think I'd miss the grand finale did you? He chuckled. *Besides, I had to make a delivery. Olin gestured to a tree next to him.*

Rydor smiled when he saw Una lying in the shade, her mate standing guard over her, licking her neck. *Thank you, Olin.*

Before the battle begins, I have but one thing to say. Trust in your love.

We will, Olin. He glanced at Shayla. *We will.*

Across the arena, Turic and Brina confidently assumed their position. In the other corner, Akela and Mandel waited. A melodic horn sounded from each of the three temples. The haunting melody played while a priest from each tribe walked to the center, each carrying an ancient scroll. In unison they read the inscribed words aloud.

"This sun-cycle the three tribes of Zanthus will become one. One government, one people, to be ruled by the victor of the Ultimate Battle. All people of Zanthus will live by this rule. As foreseen, a few lives will be lost to insure the many. The rules are none, the rules are all, only the victor knows the true meaning of this statement. As foretold by our ancestors, let the battle begin."

Rydor? Do you really believe we can win?

Yes.

Tell me what to do. I'm scared.

He glanced at Shayla and her bottom lip quivered. *Trust me.* He stared into the depths of her dark brown eyes. *And you must not care if I live or die. Fear is your only enemy.*

How can you say that? Of course I care if you live or die. A tear rolled down her cheek.

Then concentrate on my living and do everything within your power to keep me that way. He kissed her cheek, the salt from her tears a reminder of the pain they both shared. *Sutae, don't cry. Don't show Turic and Brina weakness. Be stronger than you've ever been. Have more faith than you've ever had, and love me enough this sun-cycle to last a lifetime.*

Shayla tilted her chin up and took a deep breath. *You're right, as always.* She glanced at the ground then back up at Rydor. *I'll try.*

Don't try. Do it. There was nothing more he could say, no more he could do. He wanted for her to tell him she loved him, but he understood her reluctance. There was no more time to bond or cement their relationship, the moment of truth had arrived. In his left hand he held her hand, in the other he grasped the Kiah. No one knew exactly what its powers were, but after this sun-cycle it would be history for all to remember.

The acoustics in the outdoor arena were perfect and he heard Turic and Brina's laugh as if they were standing right in front of him; but this time their evil voices were aimed at the Quelan team. The four adversaries began to walk the path of their own tribe and met in the center, Mandel held his Kiah Rod like a sword with a very serious expression on his face. Turic mimicked him and held his rod in the same manner.

"Do you think it's a sword, Mandel?" Turic touched the tip of his rod against his opponent's.

Mandel pulled back. "It is a sword of honor, something *you* know nothing about."

Brina stepped to Turic's side. He pulled the rod back and she grasped the free end so they were joined by the straight crystal length. "Akela!" Brina laughed. "Have you nothing to say before you die?"

"You're disgusting, Brina. You even dress like a whore!"

Akela thrust her nose in the air and Rydor cringed at Akela's mistake. If she thought she could best Brina with insults, she was sorely mistaken. Brina was the Queen of Insults. He glanced at Shayla. She stared at the foursome, her bottom lip sucked in, her eyes squinted against the bright sun directly overhead.

"I may very well be a whore, Akela, but you'll never know what you're missing." Brina smiled at Turic, then looked Akela in the eye. "You obviously don't know what to do with a man, especially with that wimp next to you. He doesn't look like he could satisfy a girl, let alone a woman. But then, you wouldn't know, would you? You're too moral to couple with a man who isn't your life-mate."

"And I shall be rewarded for remaining pure, unlike *you*!"

The rod they jointly held turned red, and Rydor knew Turic and Brina were growing angry, not a good sign for the Quelans.

"I tire of your dribble, Akela. Make your move, Mandel. Or aren't you capable?"

When Turic sneered at the couple, Mandel rushed Turic and Akela reached for Brina's throat. Suddenly Mandel and Akela were thrust back by an invisible force, both landing on their backsides, sprawled on the lawn.

"Shall we, my dear?"

Turic and Brina's wicked laugh echoed up and down the crowded corridors as they lifted their Kiah Rod high above their heads, each holding one end. Red turned to blue, then blue to white. From the clear crystal, two bolts of lightning spewed forth and entered the prone bodies on the ground. Mandel and Akela lay dead. Turic pulled Brina to him and gave her a long, torrid victory kiss, making as big a spectacle as possible.

It's our turn, Sutae. Rydor took her hand while they waited for the Quelans to remove the bodies of their fallen Master and Focus.

I can't believe what I just saw! They killed them so quickly, so easily.

Shayla looked at him with fear in her eyes. *Learn from their mistakes. Do not play the verbal game with them. Turn your fear into anger. They will not win. We've faced them before, we can do it again.* With that said, he led her toward the center of the triangle where Turic waited with a satisfied grin.

"It's so good to see my cowardly brother and his illicit concubine. I've waited a long time to finish what should have been done sixteen annual-cycles ago. You didn't deserve to live then, and you don't now."

"Blood on your hands makes you overconfident, Turic, but make no mistake by calling me brother."

Turic laughed. "You don't know how true that statement is."

"Rydor, darling," Brina began, "you're looking quite capable. I just don't know why you brought *her* with you."

"Jealous, Brina?"

"We were good together."

"That depends on your definition of good, now doesn't it, Brina?" Rydor saw a flicker of anger in Brina's green eyes. Brina would lose control faster than Turic, and he wanted her distracted. "Of course, you can't hold a candle to Shayla. She's more woman than you could ever be."

Brina pulled the rod from Turic's hand and pointed it at Shayla. Just as a fiery bolt formed, Rydor stepped in front of Shayla and intercepted the current with his Kiah Rod absorbing the jolt. His hands burned from the heat, but he held fast. "I'm sorry, Brina, I didn't mean to insult you, I was only speaking the truth."

"It's time to deal with me, coward." Turic took a step closer. "And when I'm done, I'll judge for myself if Shayla is a better lover than Brina."

"So, you're going to kill me and let her live?" Rydor laughed. "When did you develop a heart?"

"Heart has nothing to do with my sexual appetite. When I tire of the bitch, I'll..."

Rydor pointed his rod at Turic and smiled when a blue beam struck him in the stomach and knocked him to the ground. He landed hard on his back and just lay there for a moment without moving. At least he now knew the rod could be manipulated the same as thoughts in the fourth dimension. Now he had a better idea of how to fight fire with fire.

Turic rose to his feet, rod in hand. "I will kill her the moment she no longer pleases me."

"*If* you live that long."

"I will *never* die by the hand of a *coward*." Turic gripped his rod tightly and fixed his gaze on it. In a flash it turned into a sharp, steel sword. "You remember our sword fights as children? I won because you were always the epitome of a coward."

Rydor took a deep breath and willed energy into the rod in his hand, turning it into a superior weapon to Turic's. In the blink of an eye he held a grand, jewel-handled sword. He had not meant to create a more expensive weapon, only one to best his brother's.

"You've developed a grand taste. However, you won't be any more successful than before." Turic touched Rydor's blade with his.

The clang of metal against metal rang loudly and echoed through the marble corridors behind them. They both twirled their swords while they circled each other. *Shayla, beware of Brina while I fight Turic.*

I'm fine. I will not let her get an upper hand on me. You concentrate on Turic, he is far more dangerous than Brina.

Turic had always been an excellent opponent, and he was obviously better now. He had neglected to mention that as a child, he consistently allowed Turic to win because he never wanted to hurt his younger brother. But that was the past. The playing field was now equal.

Rydor parried with Turic, whose every successive move became more violent. Childhood games were over. This was a fight for their lives, and the lives of every inhabitant on Zanthus.

"So, brother, you've become stronger, but you're still a coward. You can't kill me and you know it."

"Care to bet your life on it?" Rydor gritted his teeth and warded off blow after blow. Turic did not use his usual finesse, he was trying to hack off any body part he could reach. Rydor ducked and thrust his head into Turic's stomach. He managed to knock him backwards to the grass. They rolled on the ground, their swords lying where they fell.

Rydor, watch out! He's got a cutter! Shayla ran for the swords.

Rydor stopped Turic's deadly thrust toward his chest with his forearm. The cutter ripped through his skin, and he felt the familiar warm trickle of blood down his arm in about the same place that had barely healed from Eaton's attempt to kill him. He pushed Turic back with his feet and rolled away to regain his footing. Turic found his sword once again and ran toward him.

Out the corner of his eye he saw Shayla rush toward him, sword in hand. She tossed it to him. He caught the handle just in time to stop a lethal blow. Metal clanged, their grunts and groans the only other audible sound in the arena. Again and again they dueled as ancient warriors before them. No matter how advanced weapons became, warriors always chose the sword to prove their superiority.

Then he heard Shayla's and Brina's voices behind him, but he did not dare to take his eyes off Turic's weapon. *Are you all right, Shayla?*

She didn't answer. He fought his way around Turic so he could see the women. As he defended Turic's assaults, fear for Shayla cut through him. Seeing Brina trying to strangle Shayla gave him a surge of energy. With one upward thrust, Turic's sword flew into the air and he caught it, pointing both blades at his brother's throat. "Move back."

Rydor stepped toward Shayla, a sword in each hand. He moved one sharp tip to Brina's ribs. "Let go of her or die."

Without hesitation, Brina obeyed his command and ran to Turic, throwing her arms around his neck. *Are you all right, Sutae?* She nodded then hugged him around the waist.

You're bleeding. Shayla placed her hand over the cut on his left arm.

So is Turic. He watched Brina wrap a strip of cloth from her gown around Turic's thigh where a gash oozed red.

That's little consolation. Shayla laid her hand on Rydor's forearm.

"Come brother, let's move this battle to a higher level. I'm bored with the physical nonsense."

He watched Turic and Brina sit in a meditative position. He could kill them where they sat, but he would not take the coward's way out. He never condoned murder. If Turic died this sun-cycle, it would be a fair fight. *We'd better follow. But remember, if they leave the fourth dimension, we must immediately return to our bodies before...*

I understand. Shayla sat next to Rydor and closed her eyes.

Rydor floated out of his physical body, Shayla right by his side. Turic and Brina waited for them. The boundaries in the fourth dimension were limitless, which only added to the danger. They could die just as easily here as in the real world. Turic would never insist they meet on this level without a more diabolical plan in mind.

"Shayla, you poor misinformed princess. I have something to show you," Brina said.

Brina presented a bigger than life hologram of their affair all those annual-cycles ago. The shocked expression on Shayla's face was more than he could bear while she watched him take Brina over and over. Brina's voice cried out in passion. *She drugged me. It was the only way I ever would have touched her.*

But you're making love to her, Rydor!

Brina's laughter mixed with the vision's cries of passion. He had to make her understand. *She wants to agitate you. Don't let her. Yes, we had sex, but I never made love to her. No man can resist the power of that particular aphrodisiac. Believe me, Shayla.* He watched Shayla's eyes narrow and her chin tilt up the way it always did when she summoned strength from within.

"I'm not impressed, Brina," Shayla insisted. "You'll have to do better than that. Rydor is mine now, and there's *nothing* you can do about it!"

"Do you remember this, Princess?" Turic said, replacing one vision with another.

Rydor clenched his teeth when another hologram appeared. This time it was Turic who played the scene. He watched in disgust while Turic undressed Shayla and fondled her breast. His hands fisted at his side. "Do you think your intended rape will make an impression?"

"No, but her cowardly lover watching will."

He saw himself standing helpless while his brother's evil touched Shayla. Why had it taken him so long to free himself from Turic's invisible cage?

I don't understand, Rydor. What's he showing us? You'd never let him do that to me!

It happened. It was the first time we met in the fourth dimension. You thought it was all a dream. You were sleeping when...

I remember now! Shayla took a deep breath. "If Brina were the lover she claimed to be, you wouldn't have to look elsewhere for satisfaction."

"Bravo, Princess!" Turic stopped the vision. "So, the princess has fight in her. Good. She's going to need it."

When Rydor tried to step toward Turic, he found himself in a heavy, metal cage. He concentrated on how to melt the bars, but nothing happened. While he worked to free himself, he saw Turic restrain Shayla as he had before by tying her between two conjured trees. Free yourself, Shayla. Use your powers. Thoughts are things. Think of a cutter severing the ropes.

"Now, my dear. We must do something about your attire. You dress like an old scrub woman, when you should be wearing this!" Turic waved his arms.

Shayla's conservative gown was immediately replaced by the halter style Brina wore, where the neckline plunged to the waist with no undergarments. Rydor's mind was on Shayla, and he knew he had to block her out long enough to escape.

"Thank you, Turic. I never liked the way my father made me dress. This is much more appropriate, considering my attributes." She stared at Brina.

Brina stepped closer."You're nothing but a whore! You can't fool me!"

"You're right." Shayla laughed. "Guess I can't fool a fool."

Rydor struggled to free himself and cursed to himself when the same technique he had used before had zero effect on the cage. Turic had obviously learned how to strengthen his powers. Then he realized the cage meant nothing, and he willed himself outside of it.

"Brother, you are slow at this." Turic kissed Shayla's lips. "She is sweet, isn't she?"

Anger surged. He turned that emotion into the darkest creature his mind could imagine and willed the monster to attack Turic. He smiled when the tall, hairy beast grabbed Turic and walked off, Turic's pathetic screams turned faint as he disappeared from sight.

"Brina!" Rydor watched her turn and run toward him. It's a pity you're growing so old." He visualized Brina's beautiful face aged and wrinkled, her smooth skin dry and withered. Then he willed a tall mirror to face her and laughed when her tortured screams pierced his ears.

While Brina was occupied with her sudden bout with old age, he rushed to Shayla and freed her. "You did well, my love."

"I have an excellent teacher."

"Be prepared for the second round. Turic will be back with a vengeance."

Shayla looked Rydor in the eye. "Kiss me."

He pressed his lips to hers and held her tight. She tasted sweeter than he remembered, even her kiss felt different. Her body pressed against his, and he felt her firm breasts soften. He pulled back and found an old wrinkled woman in his arms. Even Shayla's hair had turned so white and thin it barely covered her scalp.

Rydor turned to face Brina. "I'll kill you!"

CHAPTER THIRTY SIX

Shayla's hands touched the leathery planes of her face. Brina turned the mirror toward her, and she knew it was Brina's revenge for what Rydor had done to her. She had to reverse it fast, even her energy had ebbed to that of an old woman. She pictured herself young again, her skin smooth, her hair golden blond and full. Relief spread through her when she caught a glimpse of herself in the mirror.

A hand clamped down on her shoulder and she felt an evil vibration course through her. She closed her eyes and willed Turic backward, wishing he had no arms to grab her with. When she turned, he was several feet behind, the sleeves of his shirt empty. She laughed.

"Think you're clever, huh?" Turic's arms reappeared and he walked toward her.

She envisioned a deep chasm between them. He immediately halted long enough to place a bridge over the gully, then continued toward her.

"Not bad, Shayla, but not good enough."

Brina's scream made her turn and run to Rydor's side. He'd placed Brina in a pit of snakes and she was losing her mind, clawing at the earthen walls that surrounded her. Snakes slithered around her legs, up to her waist, quickly making their way to her neck.

Turic stood on the other side of the large, round pit. "You know she's afraid of snakes."

Shayla watched snakes turn to cuddly, fuzzy Atews, every child's idea of a pet. Rydor's gaze remained on Turic. Both men had dangerous looks in their eyes.

"Why didn't you kill me when you had the chance?" Turic circled Rydor.

"I still don't believe in murder."

"Then you will lose this battle, brother. Only one of us can walk away."

"Nothing says I have to kill you to win." Rydor stared at Turic. "There are no rules."

"It doesn't matter what you believe. You won't live to see victory, or your child's birth."

"Your spies keep you well informed."

"Merrick will do anything for power. He believes he and Eaton will be rewarded once I win. Merrick never was too smart." Turic laughed. "And as for the pregnant princess, well, I can't let your child live."

Out the corner of her eye, she saw Brina emerge from the pit, a cutter in her right hand. Shayla turned and shoved Brina in the chest to stop the downward thrust of her arm before it connected with Rydor's back.

"You little bitch!" Brina yelled.

I'll take care of her. Stand back, Sutae.

When Rydor reached for Brina, she turned to look for Turic. She would have to stop him before he could make a move on Rydor while he was occupied with Brina. *Rydor, Turic is gone!* No sooner had she sent the message than he crumbled to the ground, grabbing his side. His eyes were closed and he didn't move. "Rydor, get up!"

"You see, he's a coward!" Brina laughed. "One more thrust from Turic's sword and your lover here will be finished."

Turic was a bigger threat to Rydor than Brina. If Turic attacked Rydor's body while he was out of it, he would die without the chance to defend himself. Shayla willed herself back, instantly feeling heavy. When she opened her eyes, Turic stood over Rydor's body holding a sword. "You're the coward, Turic Celon, if you kill a defenseless man!"

"You left him with Brina." Turic laughed. "Maybe I won't have to kill him after all."

She had to stall Turic long enough for Rydor to regain his composure. *Rydor, come back!* There was a deep wound in his side and blood seeped from the gash. She saw Rydor's sword by her feet and picked it up. It was so heavy she could barely move it with two hands.

"Aren't you the heroic one, Princess. And I suppose you're going to kill me with a sword you can't even lift?" Turic laughed long and deep. "You are a very amusing woman. I will enjoy you."

Shayla managed to point the blade at Turic, but he quickly disarmed her with one swipe of his sword, the weapon landing close to Rydor's lifeless form. Her heart nearly stopped when Turic touched his sword to Rydor's chest. "Do you want all these witnesses to see you claim victory like this?"

"It matters not how I win."

"What about Brina? Don't you want her by your side to see your act of cowardice?"

"I don't care about her."

"You care about no one but yourself." *Rydor, wake up! Come back!* Shayla prayed Turic did not see her desperation. This battle was not going like she planned, nor was it as simple as she hoped. She never dreamed she would have to face Turic. Now Brina was with Rydor doing who knows what. She glanced at Rydor, the sight of his blood a cruel reminder she might lose him.

She watched in horror while Turic slipped his blade inside the front of Rydor's shirt. Instead of one last lethal blow, he sliced off all the buttons so the shirt fell open. *Rydor, I love you. I've always loved you. Please come back to me, now before it's too late.*

"Calling your lover? I'm afraid it's too late. He's about to take his last breath." Turic turned toward his audience. "Here lies a coward. A man not fit to claim victory. He not only disgraces himself, but Princess D'Par as well. She carries his child, his bastard child."

For the first time, Shayla became acutely aware of gasps from the crowd. Brina stood. What had she done to Rydor in the fourth dimension while Turic abused him in the physical? She had never felt so alone or scared in her life. She refused to lose Rydor. *Get up, damn you! Fight! I love you. I trust you. I want you. Don't you dare leave me now!*

Oh Sutae, your words are music to my heart. I've waited a long time to hear you say that to me.

Where are you?

Right here with you. Where's my sword?

Not a foot from your right hand.

Good. Where's Turic and Brina?

About twenty paces away, their backs are to you.

Shayla's hand flew to cover her mouth when Rydor sprang to his feet, sword in hand. Then the sword transformed back into the Kiah Rod before her eyes. He ripped off what was left of his shirt, his powerful scared chest exposed for all to see.

"The Voltrans will rule Zanthus!" Turic yelled to the audience, holding his sword high above his head.

"The Zareds will rule Zanthus," Rydor retorted.

Turic turned. "You're only alive because of Shayla. She actually convinced me it would be cowardly to kill a defenseless man. But I'll not make that mistake again."

Rydor laughed. "The almighty Turic admits a mistake? I find that hard to believe. No, brother, you only wanted a spectacle to make you look important. A showcase for your evil."

"Listen, good people of Zanthus. The bastard coward speaks." Turic turned his sword back into a rod. "You shouldn't have called me brother."

"Why, because I'm a disgrace?"

"No, because you're a bastard and only a half-brother! Our slut of a mother carried you before she life-mated Damek. Your father is some lowly Zared, as was our mother. Damek only life-mated her because he liked her body, and using her pleased him."

"I don't believe you." Rydor glanced at the Voltran gallery. "Damek, come forward."

Rydor be careful. This could be a trick. Rydor's skin was pale. He was losing too much blood. She prayed his body would not betray him. He had to finish. *Be strong, my love.* She walked to his side. Her heart warmed when he looked at her with love and true admiration in his eyes.

You're my strength. He grabbed her hand and squeezed.

Damek stepped onto the lawn and walked toward Turic. He stopped next to his son and crossed his arms over his chest. "What do you want?"

"Is this true?"

"Of course it's true. My only regret is not killing you the moment you were born!"

His hand slipped from her grasp. Shayla saw him tremble with anger, but he maintained control and gripped the Kiah so tight it turned clear, then gold. She had seen the Kiah turn many colors, but never gold. What did it mean?

"You should have done it at birth, then you could have saved yourself the disgrace of my cowardice. Then again, you did enjoy the drama of my beating. All that blood and pain really pumped you up, didn't it? Enjoy the moment, Damek, because your reign of terror is finished."

"You don't have the guts. You were a coward then, and you're a coward now!"

"I'm relieved to know you're not my father. Who is?"

"That's why I killed the bitch, she wouldn't tell me."

"Get off the field, you make me sick."

"I think I'll stay and watch Turic finish you off, you miserable excuse for a man. Even the word coward isn't strong enough to describe you."

Rydor pointed the Kiah at Damek. Shayla opened her mind to him and sent strength. She was not sure of what he was up to, but she would support him. The Celon's deserved whatever punishment he wanted to give, including death.

Yellow sparks flew from the tip of the rod and sent Damek reeling backwards as if some invisible force pushed him through the air. He landed hard against one of the tall, white columns, the only fatal injury was to his pride.

"Relieved to only be my half-brother, Rydor?"

"How long have you known?"

"Father told me just before the battle. He thought I might be able to put the information to good use, and the priceless look on your face says I succeeded."

"You've succeeded in nothing but destroying lives. Consider this battle your last act."

"Talk is cheap!" Turic leveled his rod toward Rydor. Shayla watched in horror when a blinding bolt of energy flew toward Rydor. He held his rod, a hand on each end and moved it to intercept the ball of fire. The impact was so fierce he stumbled back a step. She glanced up at Brina's shocked face.

The bright ball danced on top of Rydor's rod. He molded it somehow, as if he were playing with it. He raised the Kiah chest level then thrust it forward as far as his arms allowed. The glowing fireball flew back to Turic and knocked him to the ground. Then she heard something she never thought she would when Turic let out a most childish, agonizing scream.

Join me, Sutae. I know the secret of the Kiah.

She hurried to his side. *Tell me.*

Love. Pure, honest love.

But you turned the rod gold when you were angry, maybe it's pure anger.

No. I only held my love for you, our child, and love for my mother in my heart.

Shayla touched the rod, heat searing her palm. She faced Rydor and laid her hot palm against his chest. *You've never been a coward. Your only crime is honor, which only a man with a good heart can possess.* She looked into his eyes. *I'm so proud of you, and I've never loved you more.*

He glanced at her. *I love you more than life itself.*

Her heart was so full of joy she could not even answer him, Rydor was the man she always knew him to be. She had been a fool to let anyone convince her otherwise. *No matter what happens, we will be together. Our child will be raised by both of his parents. I'll follow you back to Spirit Mountain where no one can ever come between us again.*

Brina helped Turic to his feet. "How touching, It's good you have your last private communications. And while you're at it, say good-bye to your woman, because from this moment on she belongs to me."

Shayla moved to Rydor's side and saw Turic's eyes widen as he studied Rydor's chest. She too looked at his chest and her own eyes widened in shock. *Rydor, your scars—they're gone!*

He glanced at his bared flesh. *Your love healed me, Sutae.*

No, it was you. It was always you who had the power.

Our power is together. And it is very strong. Stronger than I imagined it could be.

"I don't know what kind of tricks you're playing, but nothing has changed! Scars or not, we all know what you are." Turic took several steps back and held his Kiah Rod across his chest. When he reached Brina he gestured for her to hold the other end. "Let's finish this. I tire of the game."

Brina hesitated. "I tire of your lust for Princess D'Par. I heard what you said about me."

Shayla listened to the pair argue like children. *Rydor, now is our chance. They're not paying attention and we could...*

We will not commit murder.

I can't believe you're so kindhearted after all the Celons have done to you.

He smiled at Shayla. *I've faced the demons of my past that have tried to destroy me. I nearly died once for my moral convictions, and I'm prepared to face death again if necessary to uphold my beliefs.*

That's why I love you so much. She sent him a mental picture of them making love in the lagoon and laughed when he gave her a slow, sensual grin.

He glanced at the arguing couple, then at Shayla. *You're bad, and that's the way I like you.*

Shayla's heart swelled so full of love there was room for nothing else. Not only was he the most handsome man on the planet, but he loved her, the woman. Rydor had never been impressed with her royal title. He wanted and loved the woman she was, and through him, she had found her true self.

She pulled her eyes from his handsome face to see what the enemy was up to. Turic appeared angrier than she had ever seen him, and Brina was pushing her luck insulting his virility the way she was. Just then Turic backhanded her and knocked her flat on the ground. He raised his rod and sent another ball of fire straight for Rydor, yelling, "Die!"

Sparks flew when Rydor's rod absorbed the attack. This time he did not play with it, instead he created a second one of his own and returned it with a speed so fast no one could dodge the impact.

Turic sank to his knees and cursed so loud everyone in attendance could hear his every profanity. It was good to see him receive some of his own medicine. The man was evil and should be destroyed, but she would leave that up to Rydor.

Turic grabbed Brina's arm. "Get up bitch. Help me!" Brina grabbed one end of the rod while Turic held the other.

Shayla accepted the end of the golden rod Rydor offered. She knew without question, she trusted Rydor with her life. His mind touched hers, and he sent her every emotion he was feeling. Pride, confidence, peace and love flowed through her with an invigorating surge. She felt the vibration from the top of her head down to her toes.

I fixed the rod so it will not burn you. Rydor slipped one arm around her waist, his other hand tightly grasped the Kiah Rod. *Together, Sutae, always.*

Before she could answer, a powerful blue bolt flew at them. Rydor guided the rod to intercept and held her steady against the impact. The destructive blast ricocheted off their rod and returned to the enemy double force. She watched, horrified when Turic and Brina sank to the ground, their bodies twitching. They each took a long, gasp of breath, but it was their last.

It's over. Rydor pulled Shayla into his arms and kissed her.

Passion replaced reason. All she could think about was making love to the honorable warrior who held her in his arms so tenderly she wanted to cry. He opened his mind to her and she saw the locked door disappear, his deepest thoughts finally wide open for her inspection. He was as full of love and happiness as she was, and she never wanted this moment to end.

Familiar voices drew nearer to them, but it did not deter her from tasting and enjoying her man. Even Turic and Brina's death did not deter her pleasure. Both of those Voltrans were evil to the bone and deserved their punishment. Of that she was more certain than ever. At least now the entire planet could finally live in peace. It would be sweet, and long overdue. They could no longer ignore the shouting people that finally broke them apart. All good things seemed to come to an end.

"Are you all right, daughter?"

She smiled at her father. "I'm fine. And so is Rydor."

"Yes, of course, Rydor." Nuri bowed his head. "I owe you a sincere apology, along with my thanks."

"Apology accepted. Your people are now safe."

"Since you harbor no hard feelings, I invite you to attend Shayla's life-mating ceremony this moon-cycle."

The grassy field no longer belonged to them. All the priests gathered around Rydor, babbling about the Kiah, asking what he had done, how it worked, amazed the rod was still gold. The councilmen joined the jubilant crowd and everyone tried to congratulate them at the same time.

Shayla's stomach felt queasy, her head began to spin and her legs would no longer hold her. The bright sunlight turned dark and she felt herself fall.

Rydor caught Shayla in his arms and cradled her to his chest when she fainted. A hush fell over the crowd and they all stared at him holding Shayla. "I fear this ordeal has taxed the princess."

Councilman Burlay cleared a path for Rydor. "Make way, make way,".

Under the shade of the canopy, Rydor laid Shayla on the empty bench. He knelt by her side and held her hand. He desperately searched her mind but found nothing. Nothing was actually a good sign. He'd know if she, or the baby, were in distress.

"Step away from my betrothed."

"Afraid she won't have you, Eaton?"

Eaton pulled his arm back and took a swing at Rydor. Fortunately, he caught Eaton's wrist before his fist connected with his chin. "I've fought all the battles I intend to fight this sun-cycle. Now, if you want to live, get out of my face." He released Eaton and stood.

"You can't talk to me like that!" Eaton rubbed his wrist. "I'll have you..."

"You don't listen well, do you?" He was sorely tempted to beat the man to a pulp, but this sun-cycle had provided enough fighting for a lifetime.

"Get out of here," Merrick said to his son.

"Ruler Nuri," Rydor began. "Arrest this man. He is a traitor."

Nuri stepped forward. "You can't be serious."

"He's dead serious." Burlay moved closer to Rydor. "I can verify what he says. I've had Merrick under investigation. He has indeed supplied the Voltrans with secret information. In exchange he was promised a position of power with the victorious Voltran Tribe for himself and Eaton."

"This changes matters." Nuri rubbed his chin. "Lock Merrick and Eaton in the temple secure-room until we're ready to leave."

Burlay bowed. "It will be my pleasure."

Rydor watched Burlay and three priests escort the two whining men to the Zared temple. He turned his attention back to Ruler Nuri. "I assume this means Shayla's life-mating to Eaton will be cancelled?"

"It does. I will not give my daughter's hand to a power mongering traitor!"

Rydor sighed in relief. At least one obstacle had been removed, but Nuri did not appear in any condition to make further decisions concerning Shayla. Nuri stepped past him and picked up Shayla's limp hand.

"My precious daughter, please, forgive the foolishness of an old man."

It was time to give them a few moments alone, so he walked back onto the lawn and glared at the Voltran delegation. He never wanted to kill Turic and Brina, but the power of the Kiah had been too strong to stop. It was as if the decision had been taken from him.

He glanced back at Shayla. She was in good hands with Nuri. It was time they became closer. This ordeal had taken its toll on everyone. The Quelans remained seated, watching the commotion quietly. He knew how hard it was to swallow one's pride.

This was a monumental moment that would never be forgotten. One sun-cycle he hoped he could tell his son about the bravery of his mother. Shayla had been his light in the darkness of the storm. She did love him, but he had always known.

Rydor glanced up and saw Damek kick Turic's lifeless body and he screamed, "You failed me!" The man lacked a heart. Learning Damek killed his mother came as no surprise. Deep in his soul he always knew the evil man was responsible. But now he could let it go since nothing could or would change the past.

He returned to where Shayla lay peaceful in the shade. She deserved a rest. He was so proud of her. She fought like a warrior and loved with all the passion of a woman. He leaned down and kissed her forehead, all too aware of Nuri's gaze.

Nuri looked at Rydor. "You care about her."

"I love her." Rydor stepped back. "I love her very much." He was not sure what to make of the expression on the ruler's face. Nuri had much to adjust to, as did everyone. Everything on Zanthus from this moment on would be different, and no one was sure of all the changes that would occur. It was time to walk away.

Angry voices in the arena pulled him back toward to the lawn. Councilman Zane Burlay and Damek were arguing, their voices clear and concise, the conversation extremely angry. What was the man up to now? Surely he knew it was over for him. He should be locked in prison for life, although that was still a possibility. He listened intently while he moved closer.

Zane punched Damek in the face. "It's time you paid for killing Aria."

Damek wiped blood from his nose with the back of his hand and laughed. "Why should you care about the whore?"

"She was a lady you didn't deserve. I loved her. You destroyed her!"

"It was you! You're the bastard's father!" Damek pulled a cutter from his boot. "If the whore had told me who you were, I would have killed you instead!"

"Put the weapon down," Zane prodded.

"So, you're a coward. Now I know where Rydor got it from. You can't kill me anymore than that coward son of yours." Damek rushed Zane, thrusting the cutter toward his chest. "You're the bastard's father, you deserve to die!"

"And you killed Aria, the only woman I ever loved!"

The two men fell to the ground and rolled over and over and both of them struggled for control of the cutter. Rydor desperately reached for Damek, but it was too late. He shoved Damek off of Burlay who lay on his back, eyes closed. He rolled Damek over and saw the dagger lodged deep in his chest, blood pulsing from the wound that pierced his heart.

Rydor held his breath. Finally Burlay moved and he exhaled deeply. He offered his hand and helped Burlay to his feet, years of regret reflected in the deep blue of his eyes. Zane held fast to Rydor's arm. "Thank you, Rydor."

"I believe you've earned the right to call me son."

"I would be honored, Son." Zane hugged Rydor then stepped back to look at him. "I loved your mother as you love Shayla, but I never meant to kill Damek. We struggled and..."

"I understand. No need to explain." For the first time he felt a father's love, and he admired the man who looked at him with respect. Maybe there was a God after all.

"Rydor?"

He turned at the sound of Shayla's voice. "Sutae! Feeling better?" She buried her head in his chest when she saw Damek's bloody body. "It's all right." He stroked her soft hair, inhaling her sweet scent.

"It's good to see you together...Son."

Shayla straightened her head. "What did he say?"

"Princess Shayla D'Par, I'd like you to meet my father, Councilman Zane Burlay."

Ruler Nuri walked up behind Shayla. "Is that true?"

Councilman Burlay pulled his shoulders back. "I'm proud to say it is."

"You never told me her name." Nuri shook his head. "In all those annual-cycles, you never told me her name."

"I tried to keep her alive by giving her up, but..." Zane looked at Rydor. "If I'd have known I had a son, I would have come for you. I never would have let that evil man raise you."

"I believe you."

Nuri cleared his throat. "Let us return to Terita immediately. We have much to settle."

CHAPTER THIRTY SEVEN

"I don't know what's taking them so long." Shayla pressed her ear to Rydor's chest and enjoyed every beat of his heart. "I'm so afraid they're going to send you away." She lifted her head. "If they do, I'll go with you. Cave living wasn't so bad."

"You want our child reared in a cave?"

She laughed. "It was good enough for his father, wasn't it?" Rydor laid a hand on her cheek and she heard a growl. "Look, Una's mate doesn't like you touching me."

"I never should have insisted they return to the city with us. He's nothing but trouble, that one."

Shayla laughed. "Those two Semitas have everyone scared out of their wits."

"I know."

"Why, you devil. You enjoy intimidating everyone with your cats." She kissed the back of his hand. "He needs a name. We can't keep calling him Una's mate."

"Dima."

"Why Dima?"

"It means protector, which it seems he's quite good at. He growls every time I touch you."

"Dima it is." She kissed Rydor on the cheek and blushed when Rance winked at her. She had actually forgotten that Rance was waiting for the council with them. Outside she could hear the jubilant partying in the streets. Her father had wasted no time in announcing the Zared victory, but she could not understand what the council wanted of her and Rydor, and why it was taking forever for them to be called inside.

"Rance," Rydor said. "I've told Shayla what a help you've been, and we both want to thank you again."

"I've always been your faithful servant," Rance said, bowing to the couple. "And I shall continue to serve you."

Before he could reply, the tall double doors swung open and the page made his announcement.

Shayla accepted Rydor's arm and proudly walked by his side to stand before the High Council. Everyone looked so serious it sent a chill down her spine. All she could do was plead her case when they tried to send Rydor away. She refused to be separated from him. As much as she loved her father, she would defy him and leave with Rydor. Her mind was set and nothing would stop her.

Ruler Nuri stood. "Princess D'Par, Rydor Celon," he greeted. "The council and I have pondered the future of Zanthus. We have reached no decisions lightly. What transpires here between us will alter forever the lives of everyone on the planet."

She thought she saw a hint of a smile on Councilman Burlay's face, but he immediately sobered. The priests watched from the galley seats along the sides, quiet as usual. At least her father appeared stronger and more in control than he had for quite some time, more like the man she left before her quest for a Kiah Master.

"I, with the agreement of my council, have decided to relinquish my rule."

"Father! You can't do this, what..." Her father held up his hand, and she knew immediately she just overstepped her bounds with her outburst. Women had no say in government, and that would never change.

"Since we will be the ruling body for all three tribes, as prescribed by the Ultimate Battle decree, it is time for a more powerful ruler. We need a man who can rule with honor and isn't afraid to keep the peace, no matter the cost to himself or his people."

Shayla studied the faces of the council as they all nodded in agreement. She glanced at Rydor. He stood tall next to her, his long, dark hair gracing his shoulders, his piercing blue eyes fixed straight ahead. *Do you have any idea what is going on here?*

I wish I did. Just know I love you and will fight to life-mate you. I will not let you go again, Sutae.

She held back a smile and squeezed Rydor's arm tighter. He was her strength against all odds, and she would defy her father and her people to be with him. True love came but once in a lifetime, and it was worth any sacrifice.

"Rydor Celon," Nuri continued, "you proved your worthiness as a Zared even before you knew there was Zared blood in your veins. You have accomplished what no other man could. You have freed the people of Zanthus from the most destructive evil force we have ever known. And for that, we are eternally grateful. And because of this gallantry in the face of adversity, we hereby grant you full citizenship as a Zared Warrior. Do you accept this unprecedented honor?"

"I accept your generosity and thank the High Council. However, I have one request that must be met." Rydor glanced at Shayla.

Nuri raised his hand. "Please, wait until we've finished, then your request will be heard."

Shayla's heart beat so fast she could barely catch her breath. She knew Rydor referred to their life-mating, and she was as anxious as he was to hear the answer. Why had her father insisted he wait. They had already waited far too long.

"Councilman Burlay." Nuri motioned to the man on his right. "Will you please read the Council's decree."

Zane Burlay stood and unrolled the parchment in his hand. "The new world government of Zanthus will begin this sun-cycle as prescribed by the elders two-hundred annual-cycles before us. The victorious tribe of the Ultimate Battle is to choose a new leader, and we hereby decree that Rydor Celon is the new, Supreme Ruler of Zanthus."

Rydor's surprised gaze met hers. She was as speechless as he was, but there was a vibrant spark in his eyes and she knew he was pleased. Burlay's voice pulled their attention back to the council.

"Rydor Celon is granted full authority to commence his duties. The second duty our ruler is to perform, will be to select a twelve man council. The third duty is to address the people of Zanthus on the restored communications system. After the first three duties have been completed, Rydor Celon is free to rule as he sees fit." Burlay glanced up at the couple. "Are there any questions?"

"Only the obvious. What is my first duty?" Rydor questioned.

Zane Burlay smiled broadly. "To life-mate Princess Shayla D'Par this moon-cycle. Have you an objection to your first duty?"

"I would object if it were not my first duty."

Nuri stood. "Have you any objections, daughter?"

Shayla struggled to find her voice. She had never been so stunned in her life. She cleared her throat. "I will do my duty and life-mate the new ruler, Rydor Celon." She could not stop the smile on her face any more than she could stop her heart from beating.

The council cheered, the priests clapped loudly. Rydor's lips found hers in the most passionate kiss she had ever received. It was a dream, a dream she never wanted to wake from. *I love you, Rydor.*

You could never love me as much as I love you, Sutae. I will never let you go.

I'll never let you go.

"Excuse me, Ruler Celon, but I'm ready to hear your request now."

Shayla listened to her father laugh, a sound she missed dearly. Rydor ended the kiss, but his passionate gaze remained fixed on her. *You'd better answer him, Rydor.*

How can I when I only want to be alone with you?

As Olin would say, patience, Rydor. The sound of his deep, warm laughter filled the room, and she knew she was the luckiest woman on the planet.

"I'm not sure he has a request," Burlay added.

"Only one," Rydor answered. "I want my father, Zane Burlay to stand with me when I life-mate this intelligent, precious...beautiful woman."

"I would be honored to stand by your side, Son."

CHAPTER THIRTY EIGHT

Rydor waited at the altar in the ornate temple, Zane by his side. They had spent the afternoon talking as father and son. He had admired and respected the man since they first met, but now he was proud to call him father. Zane told him how much he had wanted to life-mate his mother, and how devastated he was when he learned of her untimely death.

It was because of Zane's love for Aria that he fought so hard to unite him with Shayla. He only learned he had a son when Damek confronted him. The turn of events was ironic, but he could not be more pleased. At last he knew the truth behind his mother's death, and he took comfort in the knowledge that his mother had been truly loved by Zane, even if she paid for that love with her life.

His mother's death was not Zane's fault. The blame belonged to Damek who killed her. As he was learning with Shayla, love was a powerful force that could take on a life of its own, no matter what forces worked against it. He leaned his mouth close to Zane's ear. "Where is the priest?"

"Be patient. He's very old."

"Couldn't you find a younger priest?"

Zane smiled. "He's not exactly a priest. He's the priest's mentor. A kind of spiritual advisor who has been given special authority to perform the ceremony. He said he knows you and is very fond of you."

"I know of no such man."

"I think you do." Zane looked behind the alter. "Here he is now."

Rydor turned and his jaw dropped. A gray-haired man wearing a deep purple robe and a floppy purple hat climbed the podium steps. "Olin!"

"Rydor, my boy." He smiled. "You didn't think I'd miss this happy sun-cycle, did you?"

"No, but..."

"You asked me once what I did when I wasn't with you. Well, now you know."

"I don't know what to say."

"You could thank me. It took a lot of work to get you and Shayla together. You weren't exactly receptive to the idea in the beginning. Remember?"

"I loved her from the moment I laid eyes on her."

"I know you did. But you certainly were stubborn."

Rydor laughed. Olin was right, but he would never admit it any more than he would be stubborn where Shayla was concerned. The processional music began and he turned to face the entrance. Shayla stepped into view holding her father's arm. She was the picture of loveliness in the traditional pale pink colored gown. Her blond hair spilled freely over her shoulders, just the way he liked it.

Her smile lit up the entire temple. She was beautiful, and she belonged to him. From behind her flowing skirts, Una and Dima bounded forward, a huge pink bow tied around each of their necks. Why on Zanthus had she brought the cats with her?

They wouldn't be left behind.

How did you know what I was thinking?

It's written on your face.

Una sauntered to his side and sat next to him. Then he saw the ring attached to her bow. He smiled. Not only had Shayla learned to love him, she had become attached to his most faithful companion. He swelled with pride when Shayla took her place next to him with her father. Dima squeezed between her and Nuri, a ring attached to his bow as well.

Rydor took her hand in his the moment Olin began to speak.

"Never has there been a greater love, and there may never be one again. These two lovers wish to break from tradition and pledge themselves to each other in their own words. Shayla has requested to be first. Shayla."

"To my beloved warrior I give my body, my mind and my soul. I vow to love you for eternity, to bear your children, and care for you as no other. I will allow no one to separate us again. My life belongs to you."

"Rydor," Olin coaxed.

"Sutae, my precious love. I too give my body, my mind and my soul. If it were not for you I would have no life. You have given me the will to live, you have taught me how to forgive, but most of all, you have shown me how to love. Your precious gifts I hold in my heart. I will love you beyond eternity and cherish every moment with you." *And you will rule by my side as an equal.*

Do you mean that?

I've never meant anything more. You are my partner for life in every way. He grinned. *You're so beautiful when you smile like that.* He loved the way she blushed.

Rydor followed her lead and removed the ring from the Semita's bow. She slipped the crystal band on his finger with a kiss, and he slipped hers on her finger. Once the ring was in place he kissed her finger.

"Rydor and Shayla are the first two to be united under the new government. May all future unions be so blessed." Olin smiled at Rydor. "You may kiss your mate and seal your bond."

Rydor pressed his lips to hers and pulled her close. This was the moment he never thought would happen, yet she was in his arms, returning his kiss with all the passion he had come to adore. He wanted her now, it had been too long. He ended the kiss and turned toward the audience. "Honored guests. Please celebrate our union with us in the great hall. We will join you later." He scooped Shayla into his arms, ignoring Dima's growl and Una's glare.

What are you doing?

Taking you to bed.

Rydor! We can't. It's not proper. It's rude to leave our guests like this.

No, Sutae, it's rude of our guests to keep us apart. I've waited as long as I intend to. It's past time we bonded once again. I've missed you so.

And you're bad, Rydor Celon. Just the way I like you.

But you love me.

Always.

ABOUT THE AUTHOR

Born in Michigan and raised in California, Kathleen is now a twenty-nine year resident of Missouri, living in the beautiful Ozarks. She lives with her husband of forty-nine years and her dog, a Boxer named Ginger. Her son, daughter-in-law, and three fantastic grandchildren live close and keep her life busy.

Writing is Kathleen's passion, which she became serious about when she first moved to Missouri in 1987. Always a fan of sci-fi and romance, she loves combining the two elements into stories of *love and adventure in another time and place*.

OTHER PUBLICATIONS BY KATHLEEN GARNSEY

Available at amazon.com, barnesandnoble.com, booksamillion.com and other online retailers.

Warrior's Link
The Alluring Traveler
Hawk's Redemption

www.ingramcontent.com/pod-product-compliance
Lightning Source LLC
Chambersburg PA
CBHW061558170626
46811CB00001B/243